Lee Carroll is a pseudonym for the writing partnership of award–winning novelist Carol Goodman and her poet husband, Lee Slonimsky. Their first novel together was the acclaimed *Black Swan Rising* (available in Bantam paperback and ebook). They live in Red Hook, New York.

Acclaim for *Black Swan Rising* and *The Watchtower*:

'A unique, imaginative and above all enjoyable tale of vampires, alchemists and fairies in New York'
LOVEVAMPIRES.COM

'Engaging writing . . . wonderful descriptions . . . well-drawn characters . . . there's going to be a sequel and we can't wait!' *SFX magazine*

'Lee Carroll creates an unsuspected Manhattan touched by magic, and reinvents the epic quest in a startling contemporary way. It's Pandora's Box turned cybernetic!' ERIC ORMSBY

'Engaging writing keeps you savouring each page'
Imagine FX

'Fey mythology with alchemy, demons and vampires . . . a winning combination'
LOVEVAMPIRES.COM

'Will enthral and enchant the reader'
FALCATATIMES.COM

'I now can't wait for the third book in this trilogy!'
NOTESOFLIFE.CO.UK

Also by Lee Carroll

BLACK SWAN RISING

and published by Bantam Books

THE WATCHTOWER

Lee Carroll

BANTAM BOOKS

LONDON • TORONTO • SYDNEY • AUCKLAND • JOHANNESBURG

TRANSWORLD PUBLISHERS
61–63 Uxbridge Road, London W5 5SA
A Random House Group Company
www.transworldbooks.co.uk

THE WATCHTOWER
A BANTAM BOOK: 9780553825688
9780553825695

First published in Great Britain
in 2011 by Bantam Press
an imprint of Transworld Publishers
Bantam edition published 2012

Copyright © Carol Goodman and Lee Slonimsky 2011

Lee Carroll has asserted his right under the Copyright, Designs and
Patents Act 1988 to be identified as the author of this work.

This book is a work of fiction and, except in the case of historical fact, any
resemblance to actual persons, living or dead, is purely coincidental.

Addresses for Random House Group Ltd companies outside the UK
can be found at: www.randomhouse.co.uk
The Random House Group Ltd Reg. No. 954009

The Random House Group Limited supports The Forest Stewardship Council
(FSC®), the leading international forest-certification organisation. Our books
carrying the FSC label are printed on FSC®-certified paper. FSC is the only
forest-certification scheme endorsed by the leading environmental
organisations, including Greenpeace. Our paper-procurement
policy can be found at www.randomhouse.co.uk/environment

Typeset in 11/14.5pt New Caledonia by Falcon Oast Graphic Art Ltd.
Printed and bound by CPI Group (UK) Ltd, Croydon, CR0 4YY.

2 4 6 8 10 9 7 5 3 1

MIX
Paper from
responsible sources
FSC
www.fsc.org   FSC® C016897

To our daughters, Nora and Maggie

Contents

Acknowledgments

We thank once more our most perceptive and helpful US editor, Paul Stevens, our publicity person at Tor Books, Aisha Cloud, and the fine agents who sold the trilogy, Loretta Barrett and Nick Mullendore. First-time thanks go to our astute new agent, Robin Rue, the most energetic and enthusiastic Simon Taylor and Lynsey Dalladay at our British publisher, Transworld, and our editor, Sebastian Pirling, at our German publisher, Heyne/Random House, who have all been fabulously supportive.

We would like to thank the brilliant poet and critic Eric Ormsby for his public and private support for Lee Carroll. As *The Watchtower* is part of a trilogy, we renew our gratitude for all those mentioned in *Black Swan Rising*: Harry Steven Lazerus, Wendy Gold Rossi, Scott Silverman, Nora Slonimsky, Maggie Vicknair, Ed Bernstein, and Sharon Kazzam. We'd also like to thank Amy Avnet for her advice on jewelry making. Deborah Harkness's outstanding scholarly work on Elizabethan science, *The Jewel House*, has provided invaluable background information.

Wonderful poets and writers Katherine Hastings (*Updraft* and *Sidhe*), Elizabeth Coleman (*The Saint of Lost Things* and *Let's*), Marcia Golub (*Secret Correspondence and Tale of the Forgotten Woman*), and

Lauren Lipton (*It's About Your Husband* and *Mating Rituals of the North American Wasp*) have rendered superb feedback to Lee Carroll as both novelist and poet.

The Will Hughes poem 'Her Ship's Dark Shape Drifts Slowly toward the Sun' was published in slightly different form and under the title 'Farewell' in *Pythagoras in Love* by Lee Slonimsky, and appears by kind permission of Orchises Press.

Nothing would be possible without our loving and supportive families.

The
Watchtower

1

The Pigeon

The park outside the church smelled like pigeon droppings and cat pee. At least I hoped it was cat pee. After my first week in Paris, I realized that I hadn't seen any cats. Pigeons, yes. Each morning I sat with the pigeons and the still sleeping homeless people, waiting for my chance to sit inside the smallest, and surely the dimmest, little church in Paris in order to wait some more . . . for what I wasn't sure. A sign. But I didn't even know what form that sign would take.

It had all started with a silver box I found in an antiques shop in Manhattan, which I had unwittingly opened for the evil Dr John Dee – yes, John Dee, Queen Elizabeth's alchemist, who should have been dead almost four hundred years, but wasn't – unleashing the demons of discord and despair onto New York City. With the help of some fairies – Oberon, Puck, Ariel . . . the whole Shakespearean crew plus a diminutive fire sprite named Lol – I had gotten the box back and closed it, only to have it stolen by Will Hughes, a rather charming four-hundred-year-old vampire whom I'd fallen in love with. Will had taken it to open a door to the Summer Country and release a creature who could make him mortal again so we could be together, so I suppose I could forgive him for that. But why hadn't he taken me with him? I would have followed Will on the path that led to the Summer Country. Will had told me on the first night we met wandering through the gardens outside the Cloisters that he had taken the path once before, following signs left behind by his beloved Marguerite, who turned out to be my ancestor. The first sign had appeared outside an old church in Paris. The path always changed, Will had told me, but it always started in that church. You just had to wait there for a sign that would tell you where to go next.

So when, months after Will disappeared, just when I thought I'd gotten over him, an anonymous art buyer sent to my father's gallery a painting of an old church in Paris, which my father identified as Saint-Julien-le-Pauvre in the Latin Quarter, I knew the painting must have come from Will and that he was asking me to join him on the path to the Summer Country.

I made my plane reservation right away and booked my room at the Hôtel des Grandes Écoles, the little Latin Quarter pension where my parents had spent their honeymoon. I told my father and friends Jay and Becky that I was going to Paris to research new jewelry designs at the Louvre and in the Museum of Decorative Arts. I read in their eyes how thin the pretext was, but they hadn't questioned me too deeply. After the events of last fall – a burglary, my father getting shot, me ending up burned and battered in Van Cortlandt Park in the Bronx – they didn't need to know more to think I could use a couple of weeks away. And what more diverting place to go than Paris?

If they had known I planned to spend my mornings

sitting in a dim, musty church waiting for a sign from my vampire lover, perhaps they would have suggested a month in the Hamptons instead.

On my seventh morning in the church I had to admit that the old women with their string bags and the old men with their copies of *Le Monde* were all more likely to receive a sign from the doe-eyed saints on the walls than I was. I slipped out of the quiet church, avoiding the eyes of the black-robed priest, who, after seeing me here for seven mornings in a row, must have wondered, too, what I was looking for, and escaped into the only slightly more salubrious air of the Square Viviani.

Like the church, the Square Viviani needed something to boast of besides its homeless inhabitants and free Wi-Fi access. For Viviani, it was the oldest tree in Paris, a *Robinia pseudoacacia fabacées* planted in 1602 by the botanist Jean Robin, now leaning so perilously toward the walls of Saint-Julien that I found myself worrying that one of these mornings, on which I would no doubt still be sitting here waiting for my sign, the oldest tree in Paris would fall onto the oldest church in Paris and collapse with it, like the two old drunks curled up like nesting spoons on the next bench.

To keep such an event from happening, the city of Paris has propped the twenty-or-so-foot-tall tree up with a cement girder ingeniously sculpted to look like a tree itself, and the actual tree has been fortified against some blight with an unsightly patch of gray cement, one large enough that I could probably have squeezed into the hole it filled. It made me feel sorry for the tree ... or perhaps it's just that I was feeling sorry for myself.

To make my self-pity complete, a pigeon landed on my head. I was so startled I let out a yelp and the pigeon flapped indignantly to my feet and squawked at me. It was an unusual one, brown and long-necked, perhaps some indigenous European variety. I looked closer . . . and the bird winked at me.

I laughed so loud that I woke up one of the sleeping drunks. She clutched her ancient mackintosh around her scrawny frame, pointed her bent fingers at me, and gummed a slurry of words that I interpreted to mean *He fooled you, didn't he?* Then she put her fingers to her mouth and I realized she was asking for a cigarette.

I didn't have a cigarette so I offered her a euro, and she slipped it into an interior pocket of her mac, which I noticed was a Burberry and her only garment. She pointed again to the brown pigeon, who had taken up a commanding pose atop the *Robinia pseudoacacia*, from which it regarded me dolefully.

'Amélie,' the woman said.

I pointed to the pigeon and repeated the name, but she laughed and pointed to herself.

'Oh, you're Amélie,' I said, wondering if it was her real name or one she'd taken because of the popular movie with Audrey Tautou.

'Garet,' I told her, then gave her another euro and got up to go. If I needed a sign to show me that I was spending too much time in the Square Viviani, it was being on a first-name basis with the homeless there.

I decided to go to the other place I'd frequented this week – a little watch shop in the Marais. The owner, ninety-year-old Horatio Durant, was an old friend of my parents'. On the first day I had visited him, he took me on what he called a horological tour of Paris.

'They should call Paris the City of Time,' he declared, striding down the rue de Rivoli, his cloud of white hair bobbing like a wind-borne cloud, 'instead of the City of Light.' He showed me the enormous train-station clock in the Musée d'Orsay and the modernist clock in the Quartier de l'Horloge composed of a brass-plated knight battling the elements in the shape of savage beasts. He took me to a watch exhibit at the Louvre, then to the Musée des Arts et Métiers to see the astrolabes and sundials, where I fell in love with a timepiece that had belonged to a sixteenth-century astrologer named Cosimo Ruggieri. It had the workings of a watch revealed through a transparent crystal, but its face was divided into years instead of hours. Stars and moons revolved around the perimeter, and inset into a small window, a tree lost its leaves, gained a snowy mantle, sprouted new leaves, and turned to blazing red. I sketched it again and again, making small changes, until I found I had an unbearable itch to cast it into metal. Monsieur Durant told me I was welcome to use his workshop. He lent me not only his tools, but also his expertise with watchmaking. A week later I had almost finished it.

After I left the park and took the metro to the Marais, I spent a few hours happily etching the last details on the timepiece. I had modified the design by adding a tower topped by an eye with rays coming out of it.

'That's an interesting motif,' Monsieur Durant remarked when I showed him the finished piece. 'Did you copy it from someplace?'

'It was on a signet ring I saw once,' I replied, without mentioning that it had been on Will Hughes's ring. Will had explained that the ring had belonged to my ancestor Marguerite D'Arques. The symbol represented the Watchtower, an ancient order of women pledged to protect the world from evil. Four hundred years ago Will had stolen the ring from Marguerite and left in its place his own swan signet ring, which had subsequently been handed down from mother to daughter until my mother had given it to me when I was sixteen just months before she died.

'A watchtower for a watch,' Monsieur Durant remarked, squinting at it through his jeweler's loupe. When he looked up at me, his eye was freakishly magnified and I felt exposed. Did Monsieur Durant know about the Watchtower? But he only smiled and said, 'How apropos!'

After I left Monsieur Durant's I stopped on the Pont de la Tournelle. As I watched the sun set behind the turrets of Notre Dame, I realized I hadn't made my evening vigil at Saint-Julien-le-Pauvre. Checking my new watch, which now hung around my neck, I saw that it was almost ten o'clock. The long days of the Paris summer had fooled me. I felt a twinge of guilt then, followed by a pang of grief. I wasn't going to get a message. If Will had really sent the painting of the church – and even that certitude was fading fast in the limpid evening light – perhaps he had only sent it as a farewell. An apology for betraying my trust and stealing the box. A reminder that he'd needed it to embark on his own quest for mortality. Perhaps it served no more purpose than a postcard sent from a foreign land with the message *Wish you were here.* It hadn't been an invitation at all.

With another pang I recalled another moment by a river. That very first night I had spent with Will we had sat on a parapet above the Hudson and he had told me his history. 'When I was a young man,' he had begun, 'I was, I am sorry to say, exceedingly vain of my good looks, and exceedingly shallow. So vain and shallow that although many beautiful young women fell in love with me and my father begged me to marry and produce an heir, I would not tie myself to one lest I lose the adulation of the many.'

I remembered looking at his profile against the night sky and thinking that he might be forgiven a little vanity, but that he had surely gained depth over the centuries.

But had he? Might I not be just another of those young women who had adored him and whom he had spurned?

The sun-struck water blurred into a haze of gold light in front of my eyes. I thought it might be one of my ocular migraines, but then I realized it was only my tears blurring my vision.

He isn't coming, he isn't coming. I heard the words chiming inside my head as the bells of Notre Dame began to toll the hour.

How many disappointed lovers had stood on this bridge and thought those words? How many had leaned a little farther over the stone parapet and given themselves to the river rather than face another day without their beloved?

Well, not me, I thought, straightening myself up. As I did, I felt the timepiece ticking against my chest like a second heart. I looked at it again, pleased with the work I'd done. The week hadn't been a total waste. The timepiece would be the basis of a new line of jewelry when I got back to New York. I'd found exactly the inspiration I'd told my friends I'd come here looking for. Could I hate Will for calling me to Paris if this was the result?

No. The answer was that I couldn't hate him. But that didn't mean I had to spend the rest of my vacation sitting in a dark, musty church waiting for him.

I walked slowly back toward the Square Viviani. I had never tried to go to the church after dark, mostly because of the concerts that were held there at night. Tonight was no exception, but I thought if I waited until after the concertgoers left, I might be able to sneak in. I felt I had to go tonight while my mind was made up. I had to go one last time to say good-bye.

The concert was still going on when I got there, so I waited in the square for it to finish. At first the square was crowded enough with tourists that I didn't worry about being safe here at night. This area by the Seine, across the river from Notre Dame, was especially popular with the students who filled the schools on the Left Bank during the summer. I listened to a group of American girls laughing about a man who had approached them outside Notre Dame that day.

'Was it crazy pigeon man again?' a girl with wavy, brown hair and a dimple in her left cheek asked.

'No,' a red-headed girl answered. 'It was crazy pigeon man's friend Charlemagne man!'

'Oh, yeah!' a third girl with black bangs low over her forehead replied. 'The one who went on about how Charlemagne was a great man and he founded the schools so we could come here to study art. Don't you think he's got Charlemagne mixed up with Napoléon?'

'I think he's got more than that mixed up!' the dimpled girl responded.

I listened to them dissect the crazy ranting of the two street characters – I'd seen them myself in the square in front of Notre Dame – and then go on to talk of the paintings they'd seen at the d'Orsay that day, the eccentricities of their art teacher ('What do you think he means when he says my lines need more *voce*?'), and the accordion players on the metro ('I like the one at the Cluny stop whose accordion sounds like an organ'), and I thought, how wonderful to be a student in Paris! Why shouldn't I enjoy myself the way they were, reveling in the whole scene instead of waiting for a sign that wasn't going to come?

The girls talked until the one with the brown, wavy hair looked down at her watch and gasped. 'We're going to miss the midnight curfew if we don't run!' she said. I was as startled, looking at my watch, as she was by how much time had passed. As they hurriedly left the park, I noticed that all the tourists were evaporating into the night. The last of the concertgoers were hurrying away – all except one tall man in a long overcoat and wide-brimmed hat who'd paused at the gate staring in my direction. Perhaps he was just waiting for someone – or maybe he was a thief waiting for the park to clear out so he could rob me – or worse. Certainly the homeless people wouldn't be of any help. The ones who were left in the park – Amélie curled up in her raincoat with her companion – were already asleep or passed out.

I got up to go, my movement startling a pigeon roosting

on a Gothic turret. It was the long-necked, brown pigeon. He landed a few feet from me and fixed me with his strangely intelligent eye. Then he fluttered up to the leaning tree, landing on the scarred bark just above the cement gash. His claws skittered for purchase there for a moment. His glossy brown wings gleamed in the streetlight, revealing a layer of iridescent colors – indigo, mauve, and violet – beneath the brown. Across the Seine the bells of Notre Dame began to chime midnight. The pigeon steadied himself and began to peck at the cement. Startled, I noticed he pecked once for each toll of the bells.

Okay, I thought, someone has trained this bird and is having a laugh at my expense. Could it be that man in the long coat and hat waiting at the gate? But when I glanced over, I couldn't see the man at the gate anymore. I couldn't even see the gate. A ring of darkness circled the square that was made up of the shadows of trees, but also something else ... some murky substance that wasn't black but an opalescent blend of indigo, mauve, and violet – the same colors in the pigeon's wings – a color that seemed to be the essence of the Parisian night.

As Notre Dame chimed its last note, I looked back at the tree. The gray cement was gone, peeled away like a discarded shell. In its place was a gaping hole, pointed at the top like a high Gothic arch. The brown pigeon stood at the center of the arch staring at me. With a flick of its wing – for all the world like a hand waving me in – he turned and waddled into the vaulted space inside the tree as if going through his own front door. Clearly that's what the gap in the tree was – a door. But to what?

Perhaps I had misread my invitation to come to Paris,

but surely this was an invitation. Maybe even a sign. I might not get another. I got up and followed the pigeon into the oldest tree in Paris.

2

Shattered Glass

'The poet is coming!' Will Hughes said.

'What?' Bess, his companion of the moment, asked.

'Christ, I completely forgot!' Will declared. A slender, pale-skinned youth in his late teens, he propped himself up on one elbow in the luxuriant grass. He and Bess had been lying in the shade of his favorite secluded grove on his father's estate, Swan Hall, and now when he reached into his pocket and extended his pocket sundial into a sliver of sunlight, the shadow indicated it was already past two. The sonneteer must be waiting for him in the great hall. The servants wouldn't admit him to the study where they usually worked together unless Will was actually in the house.

He pictured his tutor sitting on one of the huge wooden benches just inside the front door, legs crossed, his features with a superficial air of patience that didn't quite conceal his irritation at being kept waiting. Which, since his tutor and the poet were the same person, could be a displeased moment that would soon find its way into a sonnet, complaining again about 'the young man,' whose father, Lord Hughes, knew to be him, Will. Will thought he'd better hurry, especially as he had to first usher Bess covertly off the grounds of Swan Hall via a winding, secretive route. Neither of them were exactly . . . dressed yet. Will would pay a price with Bess for rushing her off, yes. But he took a deep breath and clambered to his feet.

'I'm really late,' he mumbled.

'You care about that poet so much,' Bess complained as Will hoisted her to her feet. She put up her coils of glimmering black hair and then adjusted her bodice without her usual pretense of modesty. 'I have so little confidence in us having a life together! Perhaps you would be happier with that weird man, even if he is old enough to be your father.'

Will grinned at her ingratiatingly, then pulled her to him for a kiss that lingered. Lingering kisses were known to soothe Bess – and not just Bess. The last point being, after all, the heart of the problem the poet had been hired to address. Bess – who in any event had been deemed unsuitable by his father – had her competitors. But none of them, including Bess, persisted in Will's thoughts the way the poet or his words did. A few of the poet's lines were running through Will's thoughts now, as he and Bess hurried down the footpath that exited the estate at a location where large bales of hay were stored:

The truth in love inebriates like wine,
until time turns it false as mountain snow
white clouds will conjure, giving us a sign
we never know the truths we think we know.

Will didn't fancy himself a poet yet, but these lines by his tutor ran in his mind right now so compellingly that he suspected he might want to someday try spinning a poem of his own. Or maybe it was just the charismatic influence of the poet that made these lines surge within him. The poet's eyes twinkled, and his pale lips curved into a quick smile, but it was the sense of almost immeasurable depth about him that Will found irresistible.

Maybe the man's depth also made him write and speak so convincingly about immortality, about how begetting children could make a father live forever.

Of course, that was the message the poet had been hired to deliver, as Will knew his father was anxious to have him give up dalliances and focus on a special someone, in the interests of both procreation and probably also some lucrative interfamily business arrangement Lord Hughes could finagle from his only son's nuptials.

Though lately the poet had been flirting with another theme – how poems themselves could provide immortality – and for some reason that had seemed to draw Will even more forcefully to him.

Then *we never know the truths we think we know* was interrupted in his head as he realized he'd lost track of time standing at the boundary of the estate, Bess glaring at him.

'Will!' This exclamation, uttered as she stomped her foot, cut off his reverie. She held out her arms and stood poised, waiting for the expected kiss. He obliged her, and with a caress beyond that, and finally they parted. Will watched Bess continue on her way with a hopefully sufficient pretense of concern, until she vanished behind the hill.

Bess had recently been getting more insistent on their

future together, yet there was, even his father's wishes aside, to be no future. She was quite the satisfying lover, with her ample curves and bright blue eyes, but he needed to at least feel for her what he could for a poem: *The truth in love inebriates like wine.* He needed to be in love like that if he was going to love at all. Bess's perfumed curves and sensuous lips weren't getting him there. He sounded out the line now as he headed back toward Swan Hall, in an emphatic iambic beat that was all the rage of England, sweeping over the countryside alongside the popularity of the sonnet.

The lines would sound even better in a few minutes, coming at Will's request from the beautiful lips of the poet.

When Will came into the great hall, the poet was sitting exactly where he had expected him to be sitting. But his expression radiated despair, not impatience.

'I am sorry for the delay,' Will said stiffly, uncomfortable at the man's expression. 'I was . . . detained.' Then he winked to suggest the risqué nature of his detention. 'Lost track of time.' No point in lying. When it came to love and its lesser cousins, the poet could see through flesh and bone.

There was no response in the poet's features to Will's words or presence. He continued to look agitated; his high, round brow was furrowed, one of his cheeks was damp as if he'd just wiped away a tear, and his eyes darted nervously as if on the lookout for a rabid bat. But after a while he reached out his hands to take Will's.

'I came here with exciting news today,' the poet said, 'and also anticipating as always another of our beautiful hours. But who did I find waiting in the hall but your father. Fine enough. But my conversation with him did not go well.'

'My father! He's not due back until after sundown. He's here?' Will would never have risked his dalliance with Bess had he known his father to be at the estate. The gruff, old autocrat's obsession with the marriage issue – and his capacity for disinheriting Will – made being caught with Bess too outrageous a chance to take. Suspicions among the servants about his activities were tolerable. But not a chance encounter with the lord while Will was with so inappropriate a lady.

'He's gone off again but will be back soon. He'd come back early on some pretext from business in London. It sounded like the real reason for his sudden return was you.'

'Me!'

Edgar, his father's footservant, emerged from the passageway that opened onto the great hall near the front door and began to officiously polish the handle of a sword hanging on the wall to his left. Will and the poet were lingering longer than usual in the hallway before entering the study, and even their subdued voices could probably be heard elsewhere in the cavernous, drafty house. This moment wasn't propitious to do anything unusual. Will rose in silence, letting go of the poet's hands, and walked toward the study, the poet following him. Edgar allowed himself a glance behind him before returning to his polishing. It was just as well that Edgar hadn't seemed to catch a glimpse of their hand clasp.

Entering the study, Will sat in a chair at an oak desk

where his favorite onyx writing pen gleamed on its marble stand, and the poet sat in a plain maple chair facing him, from where he had a clear view of Will's features though his own were in shadow. 'Lord Hughes said that you and I should remain here until he returns, even if it is several hours. The good lord has a special person he wants you to meet.'

Will groaned.

'He also said to convey his caution to you that you are to be punctual for all future meetings between us. If there are any.'

'But why are you so agitated? I'm the one he's bringing someone to meet! Or, some*thing*, more likely.'

'Because I came here today, in addition to the usual instruction, to tell you remarkable news. Unfortunately I blurted it out to him. He took to my news like a sledge-hammer to glass. So I'm sitting here now plucking the glass slivers out of my soul.'

Will winced. He'd never known the poet to use such dramatic language in conversation before. And he was baffled as to the facts. 'What is shattered?'

'My life circumstances, since your father will not pay me what I am owed for tutoring you.'

'But why would you ask for payment now? Our studies continue through the end of the year.' It was May.

The poet stood up for emphasis. He extended his hands in front of him, palms up, in a gesture of beseechment.

'Anne and I have not had the happiest of unions, Will. You must have gleaned this a hundred times, a thousand, from things I have said. Indeed the heart of my message to you has been for you to select your own mate and not let circumstances do it as I unfortunately have, though I understand your father's oversight is a burden I did not have to cope with. But I have made my mistake and paid my price in suffering, though I cannot swear that all my moments with Anne have been miserable – we've had some happiness, too . . .

'But now, in the past year in London, I have met the woman of my dreams, my soul mate, the infinitely lovely and tender Lady Marguerite D'Arques, whom both my blood and my mind summon me to be with. And if I do not go to be with her now, she will be returning to France in a fortnight, because of a family crisis. Her sister – an evil woman – is plotting to take over the family estate in Brittany. I have beseeched Marguerite to put aside all thought of her ancestral riches and throw in her lot with me. But I must at least be able to provide her with a roof over her head. I cannot go to her penniless!' At this thought the poet gasped, and his palms closed to fists. He trained his gaze more directly on Will, though his eyes were filling with tears.

Will was speechless. The crisis sounded dire, but some good news was in what the poet was saying, for the poet. But no good news for Will. After a pause he offered modest congratulations and best hopes for the crisis. Then he added, anger welling at the apparent end of his own relationship with the poet, which had meant so much to him, 'What of all your speeches to me of the sanctity of marriage? On offspring as immortality? Are you having children with Lady Marguerite?'

Will wished he'd replied more sympathetically. But he did not want his tutoring by the poet to end. And he knew that his father, on the subject of contracts, including marital, would be implacable. Lord Hughes's worldview had no shades of gray. And no sympathy for romantic love.

'That's the view your father hired me to promote. But I'm tired of deceiving for pay. Children do bring a kind of immortality, yes. One subject to the whims of fate, but one that can go on a while with good fortune. But a greater immortality is the love that should precede them, and that can inspire great art as well. My sonnets for example, which are not subject to war, or accident, or illness. I hold no hope for the salvation of Sundays, so love and art are my beliefs, and their immortality is greatest when they combine to create great love and art. This is the truth I have discovered in life, not the clichés your father hired me to spout.

'Even the actor who recites great lines onstage achieves immortality, for lines can live on in the minds of his audience. It's a crime that I've been speaking to you of rank begetting, which a mongrel or rabbit is capable of.

'But I rant too long. I must leave Stratford for London because if I don't, Marguerite, the only woman I have ever loved, will go. That is the heart of it.'

'Your family?'

'Susanna and Judith will be provided for. Unlike Anne, I love them, but I cannot live a lie with them any longer. If your father cuts me off from the ten thousand pounds I am due, I am offered employment in London as an actor and writer. I had hoped to go to her better provisioned, but she cares so little for material things that I believe we can get by. Still we must have something . . .'

Then the poet, his eyes glistening, approached Will. He stretched his hands out and took Will's hands. Will let him do it with reluctance; he understood the force of his tutor's emotion, but was appalled at the sudden end to their tutorial friendship, and the indifference toward him it suggested. True love notwithstanding.

But the poet went on, 'Don't think I am neglecting our bond. I will approach the subject of your future with a new sonnet, composed feverishly this very morning and already recorded in my memory.' He recited it while gazing into Will's eyes. The tremor in his voice told Will that every word of it was genuine:

When London sags with mediocrity,
your presence on the stage will thrill, astound,
and save next winter from despondency:
you will be King of Thespians. So crowned!
Late winter streets are dark there, teem with cold,
but even shadows will have learned your name,
a prominence to warm you when you're old,
such acting and such writing granting fame
to outwit death. Will Hughes you are the sun
to shine on all of England! – greater than
mere birthchanced heir, The Hughes's only son:
the legacy of such a gifted man
should be his fire within, that's never ash,
his blood that flows immortally. My wish!

The poet dropped Will's hands as if overcome by emotion and retreated a few steps from him. Will was dumbstruck at the enormity of the poet's belief, and at the prospect of the upward cataclysm that would occur for him were he to take this message literally.

The poet went on, 'So I urge you, with every fiber of my being, to accompany me to London and join the much esteemed acting company at which I have been offered employment. My assessment of your talents is as objective as Pythagoras's the area of a triangle. Leave this crass estate, this money-monastery. Your gift for poetry and your sheer presence can make you an immortal and allow you to escape from the clutches of whatever creature Lord Hughes is bringing to you this very hour.'

Will thrilled to the poet's confidence in him. The poem's rousing conclusion, its references to immortal blood and fire, set off some tingling, suppressed sense of destiny. He had the intuition that this destiny could be buried in his family's primordial past, an awareness with a quite tenuous basis – some whispers he'd heard among the servants when he was much, much younger; ambiguous words his long-departed mother had once said to him – regardless, the word *blood* seemed to revive this consciousness. Perhaps among his remote ancestors one had once achieved great glory. And he should – must! – do the same. *Blood* – possibly something about the kind running in his veins was special.

Will then tried to dismiss his reaction, as it seemed ridiculously self-important, and he had practical concerns to weigh. But it wouldn't go away even as he voiced his concerns to the poet.

'Swan Hall may be a money-monastery as you put it, but it has been home all my life. I am flattered that you would even consider asking me to accompany you to London, but my father would disown me if he knew I considered the notion.' The exchange of the lands and wealth of his inheritance for the trumpeting of a sonnet seemed more reckless to him with each word he uttered.

'You can be employed as an actor with none other than the King's Players themselves at a considerable stipend,' the poet countered. 'For they are my new troupe. We can continue our private lessons. You will become the great poet and actor destiny wants you to be.' The poet clapped Will enthusiastically on the shoulder. 'You can be my protégé, Will Hughes. My offspring in the realm of beauty. As my own son, Hamnet, would have been had he survived. Think about it, man! An immortal. Living forever on the page and in the hearts of the English nation. The world!'

Will was moved by the soaring enthusiasm of the poet. But though he admired the poet's willingness to risk the small fortune Will's father owed him, his bravery concerning Will's far greater personal legacy seemed a trifle facile, like the brave noble fighting in the rear to the last yeoman. It hurt him to hurt the poet, but he stepped pronouncedly away, retreating into an alcove above which hung the family coat of arms – a black swan rising on a silver field – and a pair of crossed swords. Responding to the wounded look in the poet's eyes, he murmured, 'I need time to take this in. It would be such a different world. I feel like I'm standing now with both feet planted on either side of a chasm while the earth is shaking, the chasm widening.'

'I do understand, Will.' Slowly, a bit sadly, the poet returned to his chair and sat down.

Then came a fierce knock on the door. They knew from

the imperiousness of the sound that Lord Hughes had returned. Will walked unenthusiastically to the door and opened it. He offered his father a distant but respectful bow, then stared appraisingly and for a painful length of time at the bashful young woman his father escorted, whom Will recognized as Lady Celia, the future Duchess of Exeter. She was attired in a billowing floor-length dress so modest it were as if the spirit of a nun massacred by King Henry VIII inhabited her. Her face was broad at the temples and narrow at the chin, giving the superficial effect of some strange drinking cup. Her shadowy gray eyes – at first cast down and then raised slowly to meet Will's – glowed only like the faintest embers of dying coals. The scar across her lower left cheek did not help her loveliness, nor the faintness of her eyebrows. Will looked away with a cruel abruptness as her eyes met his, a mocking half smile playing at the corners of his lips. It was dangerous to behave this way in front of his overly dignified and occasionally bellicose father. But he couldn't help himself. This woman could be the death of him!

Lord Hughes was tall and retained both the lean muscles of his youth and the severe expression of his time as a military commander. Though long out of the king's service, he wore a uniform this afternoon. His features had so many angles to them they might have been a geometry lesson; they were dominated by two piercing eyes that would have done any raptor proud. The angles sharpened and his eyes glared as he observed his son's rudeness. But Lord Hughes was not going to stand down from the appropriate polite formalities with a sudden expression of wrath, at least not if he could help it.

'Son, this is Lady Celia, the future Duchess of Exeter, whom you have once before met at court in London. Your ladyship, this is Will Hughes, my only son and heir.'

The bow and the curtsy that followed were as feeble as if those performing them were no longer living. The lady had noted Will's cold arrogance and might well have been said to be mortally offended already. Nonetheless, she began to steal furtive glances at his sleek and luminous features even amid her wounded irritation, showing a sudden spirit that Will had a history of evoking even among the most sheltered of females. For him, her presence was so heavy it seemed to have caused all air to be drawn out of the room, leaving him no options for breathing. But he tried not to direct further exasperation at her. The source of his repression was his father, not her.

Will's loyalty to Swan Hall swung on one side of an alchemist's balance right now, while the other weighed a possible new life in London. Avoiding Celia was on the same iron tray as the poet, the poet's sonnet, and the Globe Theatre. On the opposite tray a grand pile of gold bars lingered powerfully, gleaming.

'May we enter?' the lord asked sarcastically, as Will continued to stand in the doorway. Will whipped away from him with an obedience so quick it also flirted with sarcasm and went back to his desk. Lord Hughes strode heavily into the center of the room, Celia a few paces behind him. The poet stepped forward to face Lord Hughes; from the rear it looked to Will as if he might have been trembling slightly. He bowed and mumbled, 'My lord,' in a voice so tentative Will had to strain to hear it. Lord Hughes nodded impassively, then presented Lady Celia with a small gesture.

'My lady graces this afternoon and lights up the room as if a second sun has suddenly arisen,' the poet said.

Will marveled at the man's ability to let images flow even in the most adversarial of settings. His father addressed his next words to the poet.

'You must pardon this interruption. An urgent matter has arisen which the three of us must resolve.' A wave of the lord's right hand seemed to include the window behind the desk as a fourth party to the negotiations. There, a heavy curtain embroidered with a biblical scene of Jesus turning water into wine was drawn against the afternoon sun, obscuring the stained-glass window itself. 'I am mindful of our discussion a short time ago and have reached a decision which should enable you to go on with your life.'

Will was struck by how much his father's beneficent tone toward the poet contrasted with the tension in his physical bearing. Perhaps his father was directing his internal wrath right now more at his son than his son's tutor. Perhaps Will should have been a little more cautious in his dismissal of Lady Celia.

The poet bowed again and said, 'Yes, my lord?'

'You have served well as my son's tutor and have been an admirable model for him with your brilliance. I am sure he has absorbed a lifelong benefit from knowing you. However your outrageous demand as to ending instruction early, and, even more shocking, your intention to break your marital bonds, have convinced me that these lessons must cease immediately. I have found a better method for persuading Will of his obligations. The Lady Celia will be the perfect bride for him. Let us waste no more time. I will more than generously pay you for all your lessons through today, and you can go on your merry way. As for you,' the lord added, gazing with some ferocity at Will, 'your trifling with my wishes is over. You must ask the Lady Celia's hand in marriage.'

'When, my lord?'

'Now.'

'Now? I have only been in her company a few minutes.'

'You have known her long enough. Too long, in fact. You should have proposed at the very sight of her. But from what I know of this young woman's kind and forgiving nature, I suspect she may not hold your slight against you forever. Isn't that right, my lady?'

The lady nodded the most demure of nods, but looked unhappy.

'Well, I'd sooner lie with a rotting horse,' Will said. 'And if I knew her fifty years, I wouldn't ask for her hand in marriage.'

Then Will took a deep breath. He'd astonished even himself with such provocative language. But he had felt a deep sense of relief uttering these obnoxious words. As if he no longer had to live the lie of obedience to his father.

Lady Celia stamped her feet furiously and said to Lord Hughes, 'Sir, I cannot stay in the presence of such a lout. He speaks filth to me! Your son has a beautiful face but his soul is revolting.'

She began an exit but found her way impeded by the grip of the lord on her elbow. A dowry of fifty thousand pounds plus a partnership in the prosperous import business that her family owned wasn't a matter to be flamed away in the heat of the moment. Nor was the lord going to give up so easily regarding his son's recalcitrance. Admittedly these nuptials weren't off to a promising start. But he'd see what could be done about that.

He drew his sword, to suggest to Will and the poet his passion to protect the lady and her dignity. 'Further insults, men, will be cut off.'

The sight of the sword was cautionary. Both Will and the poet knew the lord kept in good shape and did not have the most prudent judgment.

'Do stay with us here, my gallant lady,' Lord Hughes went on. 'My son will be on his knees before you in a minute, weeping his apology and requesting your hand as I have so ordered.' He tentatively let loose of her wrist. She shuddered, then cowered in place.

Sword in left hand, Lord Hughes approached Will, leaned forward, and slapped his cheek with his right hand, reaching across the desktop with enough force to knock Will out of his chair and send him sprawling. The lord was big, but it was still a startling feat of strength. Will uttered a cry of pain threaded with embarrassment. Then he recovered enough to get back up and glare at his father, muttering threats, before sending a glance at Celia so savage she recoiled from it. He was rubbing his cheek with a solicitude reserved only for himself and those of fairer visage than the lady.

The poet, appalled at Lord Hughes's brutishness (not that his pupil was being gallant), strode toward him and waved an impassioned hand. 'I must protest,' he proclaimed. 'This lad has done nothing to deserve your contempt for him. He has tried to heed your message. It's only that he has a fine soul and needs time to discover himself and find exactly the right companion. I would have you refrain from further violence.'

Lord Hughes laughed despite his bitter mood at the thought of taking direction from a wife-betrayer. He slapped the poet across his cheek using the flat side of his sword blade. Only the faintest line of blood was drawn, nothing significant; the litheness and accuracy of his sword's upswing were impressive to behold. The poet fell back down hard and barely managed to keep his head from knocking against the slate floor. He struggled upright as Will gasped and Lady Celia fled.

As he rose, his features crimsoning, he reached behind himself for the maple chair and whirled and hurled it at the lord with a strength not obvious in his slender frame. The chair struck Lord Hughes a full blow in his mid-section, knocking his sword away and the wind out of him. Will's father crumpled, then stretched full out on the floor moaning.

The poet quickly picked up the sword. He backed away to the window, then ripped the curtain down with one motion. Will had to cover his eyes against the dazzle of sunlight flooding the room. The poet's gesture had revealed a stained-glass scene of a beautiful youth playing his lyre to a black swan that glided over a blue pond. The poet pointed wildly at the window.

'See here the swan, symbol of your family, harkens to Orpheus, god of poetry and music. This is the heritage Will should be loyal to. This is a worthy god for Will to follow,' the poet shouted at the prostrate Lord Hughes. 'Not the mammon of your idea of matrimony.'

Will, observing all this, might have been expected to feel

some filial loyalty at his father's moans and the poet's condescension. But the only loyalty he felt was to the poet.

'He has sonnets and theater in him, not obedience,' the poet went on. 'But you don't want those things in him, you soulless creature.'

In his fury the poet gripped the sword handle with both hands and shattered the window with a spinning blow. 'You will not so shatter Will, whose beauty has been wasted on you!' he exclaimed. He dropped the sword, climbed through the window, and set off down the hill toward the closest exit from the estate.

Will watched him depart. Shards of glass, strewn from the sword blow across the stone pavement bordering the house, glittered as if they noted the extinction of art. Indeed, it gave him pause that a man with such a sense of art as the poet could have destroyed such beauty. But it must have been the actor, the dramatist in him that felt the need to add such an exclamation point to his assertions, Will reassured himself. If his own wicked father hadn't foolishly slapped him, none of this would have happened.

He knew, without even needing to think about it, that his father's violent intimidations had made his decision for him. An inchoate force seemed to summon itself up from deep within him and coalesce into a single message. Through a trick of fate the one image preserved in the wreckage of the window was the black swan. Outlined now against the blue sky, it seemed to hover, as if ready to take flight. A sign, surely, that the time had arrived for Will to take flight as well.

As his father climbed to his feet, still glaring at him and

then shaking a fist impotently in the air as if that gesture might restore his dignity, Will said, 'You cannot rule over me. I am going away to London, with the poet.'

His father's fist-shaking ceased with a shudder that always made Will think afterward, reflecting back, of someone cowering before eternity.

Will went over the window ledge, careful not to disturb the glass swan, and down the hill, following the poet, carrying his father's sword. Everything else at Swan Hall he left behind. There might have been a final faint cry behind him, a beseeching, cut-off wail – but whether it came from his father or issued miraculously from the glass swan as a clarion cry to adventure – Will wasn't sure. He would not pause to listen more.

3

Jean Robin

I followed the pigeon through the arched opening in the tree, leaving the streetlights of the Square Viviani behind me. Their light was replaced by an incandescent glow from deep within the tree . . . too deep. The tree shouldn't have gone back that far. It was as if I were looking through the tree and the stone walls of Saint-Julien-le-Pauvre into the church itself, where a thousand panes of stained glass glittered in the dark. Only Saint-Julien-le-Pauvre didn't have stained glass. Not like this anyway. The only place I had seen stained glass like this was at Sainte-Chapelle, that perfect jewel box created by Louis IX in 1248. But that was across the Seine on the Île de la Cité, and that chapel was reached by narrow stone steps that climbed *up*. This stained-glass sanctuary was below me at the bottom of a flight of spiral stairs that dropped into the earth like a well. The brown pigeon waited on the top step. When I moved forward, he cooed and hopped down to the next one. I followed, pulled as much by the glittering, multicolored light as by the steady chortling that came from the bird like the patter of a tour guide.

'Watch your step, please, come this way, this is one of the most remarkable sights in all of Paris . . .,' I imagined him saying as we made our way down into the underground hall of stained glass. I recalled the first time I'd gone to Sainte-Chapelle with my mother; I'd been grouchy and tired from waiting on line, complaining to her that I didn't need to see yet another church. They all looked alike after a while, I'd said, as I followed her up the tightly twisting stone steps. Then we emerged into the upper chapel and I was silenced. It was like popping your head out of a rabbit hole and finding yourself in the Emerald Palace of Oz. A blaze of light, distilled through innumerable panes of brightly colored glass, enveloped us. The room seemed to be floating like a hot-air balloon. I remember feeling as if we had come untethered from the earth.

I had that same feeling now even though I was descending *into* the earth. At the bottom of the stairs I stepped into a high-ceilinged room, its arched roof supported by twisting columns and covered with an intricate pattern of stained glass in every color of the rainbow. One moment it seemed as if the predominant color was blue, then violet, and then crimson. The colors *were* changing, shifting as I watched them. It was like standing in a planetarium watching the dome of the heavens move above me. Then something else occurred to me: if I was below the ground, and it was night, where was the light coming from?

As if in answer to my unvoiced question, a shard of colored glass fell from the ceiling, spinning through the air like a maple seedling. Others joined the crimson, blue, and emerald rain. I ducked, sure that the whole ceiling was about to crash down on my head, but when the first shard of glass hit me, it had all the force of a dandelion puff. I held out my hand to catch another. An amber droplet landed in my palm and looked up at me with the face of a Botticelli angel. I looked up again, gasping. The entire ceiling – of a room as large as Sainte-Chapelle – was made up of live fairies, each one glowing like a Christmas bulb.

'Light sylphs!' I exclaimed, recalling the creatures I'd glimpsed the night I'd spent with Will Hughes in Fort Tryon Park.

The little creature hissed and threw up its hands. A torrent of unintelligible speech, accompanied by expansive hand gestures, shrugs, and much expressive rolling of the eyes, issued forth. I had the distinct impression that it was not pleased.

'The light sylphs . . . are their . . . American cousins,' a gruff voice from the far end of the hall laboriously croaked. 'These creatures prefer to be known as the lumignon.'

I turned in the direction of the voice. At the far end of the hall I saw a throne elaborately carved out of the same dark wood as the twisted columns. An empty throne. Was the voice coming from behind it?

'The word . . . has an inter . . . esting derivation,' the voice rasped. 'From the Latin *lux*, of course . . . meaning "light" and the Old French *mignon* . . . meaning a "favorite" or "darling," perhaps . . . originally from the Celtic *min*, meaning "tender, soft." So, "tender lights." They aren't always so . . . tender, though.'

A deep rumbling noise came from the throne. The wood creaked and groaned. The twisted columns on either side of me shivered and writhed like live snakes, and the black tracery between the panes of light trembled. I saw now that the hall was all of a piece – a giant root system. The black lines between the lights – what would be lead joinery in stained-glass windows – were tiny roots, the columns were thicker roots twisted together, and the throne was the thickest root of all: the taproot. But where was the voice coming from?

I took another step forward. 'But then you would know that, Garet James.' The voice came more fluidly now, as if it had only needed a little exercise to get it working. 'You've already had some experience of our friends the fairies, haven't you?'

I stopped, midway down the nave, frozen to the spot. 'How do you know my name?'

The rumbling sound began again, this time louder. It shook the tiny lumignon from their perches in the high roots so that they fell in a colored rain all around me. He – it? – was laughing.

'Ah, the name of Garet James, Watchtower, travels far. It's true I can't exactly go abroad any longer, but I have my . . . informants. You could say my roots in this world and yours *run deep.*' Again the creature's laughter shook the hall.

'And what do they say about me?' I asked, approaching the throne while stealthily trying to get a look around it to see where the speaker was hiding.

'They say you come to the church of Saint-Julien-le-Pauvre every day, sometimes twice a day. We've seen your kind before, waiting for a sign to set off on your quest for the Summer Country. Indeed, we saw another one – one who could only come after dark – quite recently.'

'A man?' I asked, hating the eager hope in my voice. Hadn't I decided earlier today to give up on Will Hughes once and for all?

'Not exactly. A man once . . . but now a creature of the night . . . a . . .'

'Vampire, yes, I get it,' I said irritably despite my relief at the news. I was beginning to find my interlocutor's speaking style annoying. And his game of hide and seek. I made a quick feint to my right and then dashed left around the wooden throne. There was nothing there.

Peals of gruff laughter shook the hall – and they were coming unmistakably from the throne. I came around and stood in front of the huge mass of carved wood – only it wasn't carved, I saw now. The root had grown into the shape of a chair, twisting itself into arms and legs, swelling into rococo curves that suggested some anthropomorphic design. A bulbous area looked like a head, tapering roots suggested fingers at the end of the curved arms and feet at the end of the legs . . . I peered closer at one of the feet . . . and then recoiled in astonishment. There, at the end of the roots, was a sliver of toenail.

I looked back up at the bulbous area at the head of the chair into two dark knotholes sunk deep into the fibrous wood.

'What are you?' I asked in a whisper.

The wood slenderly twisted into what I realized with mounting amazement was a smile.

'I am Jean Robin,' the root answered, 'once *arboriste* to kings and now' – he chuckled – 'just *arbor. Enchanté*, Mademoiselle James.'

I recollected my manners enough to reply, 'I'm pleased to meet you, too, Monsieur Robin. I've heard of you. You planted the tree in the Square Viviani.'

'Yes, little knowing I'd spend eternity below it . . . or

rather, as part of it.' He chuckled again. Now that I was closer, I could make out his features better. He had a high-domed forehead adorned with delicate swirls that I guessed were the remainder of what hair he'd had in life, small, round eyes surrounded by laugh lines, and a dimpled chin that disappeared into rings of rough-skinned root. The face of a small, jolly man whose life as a tree root these last four hundred years had not robbed of his sense of humor.

'If you don't mind me asking, how . . . ?'

'How did I get into my present ligneous state? No, I don't mind at all. It's rare I get any visitors, you know. Please sit down.' He slid his eyes toward a low spot before the throne where one of the tree's roots broke the surface, forming a little stool. I lowered myself down on it carefully, surprised to find it rather comfortable.

'Yes, well . . . ahem.' Jean Robin cleared his throat, which sounded as if it had been coated with sawdust. I noticed that a number of lumignon had come to sit on his shoulders and his knees as he began his story, their little, pointy faces cupped in their diminutive hands as they listened. 'As you may know, I devoted my life to trees and rare plants.' I didn't have the heart to tell him that all I knew about him came from the plaque in the park above us, so I nodded, which seemed to please him. 'I was rewarded for my endeavors by being made *arboriste* to King Henry III in 1585. I created the first botanical garden in Paris in 1597. My nephew, Vespasien, and I traveled far and wide – to Spain and Africa and even to your native Western Hemisphere – for my collection. Indeed, it was from those shores that I brought this specimen that has been named for me: *Robinia pseudoacacia fabacées.*' As he pronounced the name of the tree named for him, I thought I detected a change in his sooty brown complexion, a flush of green chlorophyll, which I imagined was a root's version of blushing.

'It was my garden that inspired the Messieurs de la Brosse and Hérouard to found the Jardin des Plantes. They moved many of my specimens there, but not this one. My nephew, Vespasien, insisted they leave it here because he knew what had become of me. I hate to think what would have happened had they tried to dig me up!' He shuddered so hard that a few of the lumignon perched on his shoulders and knees flew up in a flurry of multicolored wings and then settled down again. I noticed that when they brushed their wings along Jean Robin's 'skin,' the wood gleamed more brightly. They were, I saw with wonder, polishing him.

'But how . . . ?' I began.

'Ah, it happened when I was seventy-nine. I knew I had very little time left on earth . . . heh, heh, I didn't know yet how much time I'd have under it! . . . and I'd come to visit my dear pseudoacacia, which I'd planted twenty-seven years earlier. I just wanted to make sure it was doing well . . . growing straight, you know, with enough room to spread its roots. The pseudoacacia likes to spread its roots. It was a warm summer day and the tree was in full bloom, its lovely white blossoms scenting the air. When I'd pruned a few branches and cleared away some saplings, which threatened to encroach on its space, I sat down in its shade and leaned my head on its trunk. I could feel the lifeblood in me fading as I listened to the sap flowing strong in her veins. I remember I had the distinct idea that as long as the sap ran in the tree I'd planted, I wouldn't really be dead.' Jean Robin's voice, which had grown from gruff to wistful, lapsed into silence. I thought I could hear in that silence the rustle of a summer wind through leafy boughs and the sultry drone of bees in the heavy-hanging blossoms. I waited for him to finish his story.

'When I woke up, I was here in the lair of the lumignon below my beloved pseudoacacia. They had lain me among the roots – to die, I imagine, but then the tree itself wrapped its roots around me and took me into itself. It fed me its own sap as a mother would feed its young, sharing its own lifeblood with me. Over time its cells replaced my own, much as quartz crystals may grow in wood, turning it into petrified wood, and I became as you see me now. A wooden man or, as I prefer to think of myself . . . a manly root!' His chuckle was more constrained than before. I had the feeling that reliving his past had made him a bit melancholy.

'That's amazing,' I said. 'And you've remained so . . . alert. How did you learn to speak English so well?'

'Ah, my friends the lumignon, recognizing my hunger for knowledge, have brought me books and information over the years. That's how I learned about you. The fey community has been all abuzz about the arrival of the Watchtower in Paris.'

'The fey community? You mean there are more of them?' Although I'd met half a dozen fairies in New York, I hadn't thought of them as a community exactly. They had seemed more like a handful of scattered exiles who had all managed to disappear without a trace once they were done with me. It hadn't occurred to me that there might be a larger population here in Paris.

'Oh my, yes! The Parisian fey community is one of the largest and oldest in the world. It is composed of three main classes . . .'

The minute he began, I knew I'd made a mistake. He was a botanist, after all, trained to classify and catalog. I could be here all night listening to a disquisition on fairy phyla while what I really wanted to know was when Will had been sighted in Paris and how long ago he had left. I felt bad interrupting him, though. As he had said, he didn't get many visitors, and I figured it wouldn't hurt to know a little more about the local fairy population. They might be able to lead me to Will. So I settled onto my stool to listen.

'The arboreal fey, or *les fées des bois*, are considered by most experts to be the original indigenous species,' he was saying. 'They are so old that they don't remember themselves when they first came into existence, although one I've spoken to remembers sabertooth tigers . . .' Jean Robin spent the next ten minutes discussing the difficulty of dating the arboreal fey, their habitats – parks, mostly – and demeanor. 'They are very shy and reclusive. They often attach themselves to a particular tree, like this one. My informants tell me that there are still substantial nests in the Jardin des Plantes, the Luxembourg Gardens, the Bois de Boulogne, and the Parc Monceau. The largest population in the Île-de-France is in Fontainebleau. They are, in general, a merry and simple people, fond of French home cooking – they adore crêpes! – singing and dancing – they invented the cancan.

'Then there are the light fairies – or *les fées des lumières* . . .' He went on to describe various types of light fairy, including the lumignon, who derived substance from the light and color in the stained-glass windows of the great cathedrals: Notre Dame, Sainte-Chapelle, Saint-Eustache, Sacré-Coeur, Saint-Séverin . . .' I lost track of all the churches where the light fairies roosted. 'Most experts agree,' Jean Robin concluded, 'that the lumignon evolved from a species of flower fairy and that they first appeared in Paris with the advent of the great Gothic cathedrals, but whether they were attracted to the area *because* of the windows or if they originally inspired the creation of the first stained-glass windows, there continues to be dispute—'

Jean Robin was interrupted by a violet-colored fairy loudly chattering in his ear.

'Yes, yes,' he said, his gnarled features creasing with merriment, 'I'll tell her that. My friend has reminded me that there's a long tradition amongst the lumignon that Abbot Suger was introduced by Eleanor of Aquitaine to a lumignon who inspired him to create the windows of Saint-Denis.'

I recalled what Oberon, the King of Fairies, had told me about the relationship between mortals and fey: 'The humans we touch bloom in our company. They do their best work while we drink of their dreams.' Thinking of the great flowering of Gothic stained-glass windows under the direction of Abbot Suger, it wasn't hard to imagine that he'd been touched by the fey.

'And then there are the *fées de la mer*,' Jean Robin said in a graver tone. The violet lumignon on his shoulder startled at the name and flew into the air. All the light fairies that had been roosting on top of Jean Robin took wing, like a flock of finches at the passing of a hawk's shadow.

'Sea fairies? What would they be doing in Paris?' I asked.

'They aren't native to the region. In fact, the tree and light fairies refer to them, somewhat disparagingly, as "the boat people." They came down from the sea on the Seine, exiles from a great cataclysm. Some say it was the drowning of the island of Ys.'

The name Ys stirred an old memory. My mother had told me a story once of a fabled kingdom off the coast of Brittany ruled by nine priestesses and one king. The king's daughter Dahut gave the keys of the sea gate to a traitor, who opened the gates and drowned the city.

'The boat people were the founders of the Seine's boatmen's guild, which gave Paris its coat of arms and motto: *fluctuat nec mergitur* – "she is tossed by the waves, but does not sink." They tend to be a bit haughty, as exiled royalty often are, but there's no denying that they have been responsible for the greatest scientific and aesthetic achievements—'

A crimson light fairy dive-bombing into Jean Robin's face put a stop to his speech. He chuckled good-naturedly. 'Well, enough of that. I imagine you are more interested in learning the whereabouts of your friend the vampire.'

'I'm not entirely sure he *is* my friend,' I answered, 'but, yes. Of course, I appreciate all you've told me about the different kinds of fairies . . . it's fascinating . . .'

'Tut, tut,' he said, blushing green, 'no need to flatter an

old man, although it is nice to have a visitor with a brain larger than a nit.' I would have expected another dive-bomb attack from the lumignon at this remark, but instead I felt the brush of wings against my skin, and looking down, I saw that several of the multi-colored fairies had settled on my arms and in my lap. 'Your voice is so much more soothing than their eternal whine. You must visit again.'

'I'd love to, only I do have to find Will Hughes first. Have you . . . I mean, have any of your informants seen him at Saint-Julien's?'

'Yes, he showed up in Paris during the winter and began to frequent the church every day. At first we paid no mind to him. Over the centuries he's come many times to Saint-Julien's. In fact, the park outside the church was where I first met him.'

'Wait, you met Will? Before you became . . . were turned into . . .' My agitation caused the lumignon on my arm to stir, but then they stroked my arm to calm me down, which, oddly, worked.

'Before I entered my arboreal state? Yes. We both were mortal then, and we both had foolish notions of what might gain us immortality. I had just planted this tree. I remember I bragged to him that I looked to trees for my immortality, and he said to me that he looked to love. Little did we each know what form our ambitions would make of us.'

He paused and I thought I saw a sadness come over his wooden features, but then his lips quirked up into a crooked smile. 'Funny how we've both ended up in the dark, eh? And yet when I met him I thought to myself, "Ah, there's a young man who loves the light and is loved by the light." The sunlight, you see, had turned his hair to gold. Has he grown darker over the years he's spent out of the light?'

'His hair is darker than it looks in his portrait,' I answered, trying hard to keep my voice even. The image of Will standing in the sunlight had caused something to contract in my chest. Only the soft murmuring of the lumignon, who were in my hair and about my face now, kept me from openly crying.

'Interesting,' Jean Robin replied, his woody brows furrowing. 'So much is not known about the vampire. If he were truly *undead*, then there would be no change over the centuries, but I have wondered if the vampire's state is not somewhat akin to mine, and if, just as the tree cells and sap replaced my human cells and blood, so some other substance has replaced the vampire's cells and blood.'

'Do you think, then, that the process can be reversed? Will thinks that if he can summon a creature in a lake who was able to make a fey mortal, he can be turned back into a human.'

'Ah, so that's why he's so anxious to find his way back to the Summer Country.' The knotted roots growing over Jean Robin's shoulders rippled, and I realized he was trying to shrug. 'I don't know, but I'd be curious to find out! You must follow him.'

'Yes, that's what I'd like to do. I've gone to Saint-Julien's every day for a week, but there's been no sign. How long was Will here before he got a sign?'

'Let's see . . . he arrived in January and then he disappeared in May . . .'

'Four months! I could have to wait four months?'

'We've watched seekers wait years. But then, for some a sign appears after only a few days.'

'And there's nothing I can do to hurry it along? There's no other way to find the path to the Summer Country?'

'No. At least I think not. Probably not.' The roots that made up Jean Robin's body writhed with discomfort. 'The stories of another way are most certainly rumors.'

'What rumors?' I asked, plucking a fairy out from the inside of my T-shirt. The little creatures were becoming quite intrusive.

'Well, as I mentioned before, the boat people . . . er . . . the *fées de la mer*, that is . . . reportedly come from the lost kingdom of Ys, and some believe that Ys was part of the Summer Country. So it makes sense that the door to the Summer Country might have been created by the sea fairies—'

'Ouch! I think one of your little friends just bit me!'

'Oh, no, they don't have teeth – thank God! – but they do like to sew, and they're sometimes rather clumsy with their needles. Anyway, as I was saying, if anyone could tell you a shortcut to the Summer Country, it might be one of the boat people.'

'And how do I get in touch with them?'

'Well, that's the problem. They're not exactly . . . welcoming. Especially to foreigners. Ironic, since they themselves are immigrants, but that is often the way, don't you think? The more established immigrants are mistrustful of the more recent arrivals.'

'Yes, I'm sure,' I said, trying to cut off another lecture,

'but isn't there any way to talk to one? Surely there must be some sort of go-between.'

'Why, yes! How astute of you to think of it! There are channels of communication between the more en-lightened of each nation of fairies – an academic community, so to speak. I suggest you speak to my old friend Monsieur Lutin at the Jardin des Plantes. He can usually be found at the Labyrinth. Tell him that Jean Robin sent you. He might be able to get you an introduc-tion to one of the boat people.'

'Monsieur Lutin at the Labyrinth. Okay. Just one more question—'

'Um, far be it from me to stifle anyone's intellectual curiosity, but I'm afraid you'd better be going. If you intend to ever go at all.'

Jean Robin slanted his eyes meaningfully toward my feet. Following his gaze, I was shocked to see that a fine network of roots had been sewn over them. Light fairies were darting back and forth, knitting the roots into a pair of tight stockings. When I tried to extend my hands to shoo them away, I found they were bound together in my lap. It took all my strength to break the finely stitched bonds. I kicked off the roots from my feet and stood up, scattering an infuriated flock of lumignon.

'I apologize for my friends. They saw how much I was enjoying your company and thought you'd make a nice companion for me.'

I was about to reply angrily, but then I saw that the gleam in his eyes had grown and spilled down his cheeks in long, resinous streaks. 'No harm done,' I said, shaking the last of the root threads from my hands. 'I'll send your regards to Monsieur Lutin, then?'

'Yes, please!' Jean Robin said, brightening. The lumignon had already swept away his sap-filled tears with their wings. 'Ask him to send me some samples from the Alpine Garden. I would love to see some edelweiss again as a reminder of my journeys through the Alps.'

I told him I would deliver his message.

'Good luck to you, Garet James. It has been a great pleasure making your acquaintance. Please don't hold it against the lumignon that they tried to detain you. They did it for love of me.' His rooty lips twisted into a rueful smile.

'Yes,' I said, smiling back. 'I can see they do love you very much.' I said au revoir then and turned away, thinking as I climbed back up the stairs that if this was what came of being loved by the fey, then I'd rather do without their love.

4

The Party

Will Hughes was too concerned about his father's troops possibly waylaying him on the road to London to immediately follow the poet there. Instead he fled west to Cornwall, to the tiny Roman fishing village of Marazion. There he concealed himself for a week, mostly in the cellar of Stephen Fawkes, whose son Charles, a year Will's junior, he had once befriended at a fencing competition and corresponded with occasionally.

His cellar days were gloomy and tedious, mostly spent reading by the light of a dripping candle, and he had to constantly remind himself how awful it would be to be brought back to Swan Hall in shackles as an alternative, mistreatment he knew his father to be capable of. He lived that week only for the brief time when dusk was under way, making him difficult to recognize when he went outside, but leaving enough light to get about in.

Cornish twilight had a rustic beauty to it, the moon silvering shallow waves of the Irish Sea, while sea winds softly rustled tall grasses bordering a sandy beach. Will didn't stroll the beach itself, but he'd walk along paths cut through dense underbrush inland, enchanted by the sound of waves and the sight of gulls gliding downward in final dives as the world blackened around them. On a few occasions, as the sky came within an inch of darkness and he knew he had to turn back, Will froze in his stride, beset by a sort of premonition. He'd feel for an instant as if he'd materially blended into the night, become a part of it, and that this was in some way going to be his future, no longer a part of the everyday world of flesh and light. Will shook off these unsettling sensations, for they had no rational basis. But he was disturbed enough by them each time to consider whether it might be more prudent to return to his father. The answer to that question, however, optimistic lad of nineteen that he was, was always a resounding 'No!'

After a week he'd had enough of these moments of being a shadow among greater shadows, alongside the dreary dankness of the Fawkes cellar. He purchased a two-year-old silver horse, Owlsword, from Stephen Fawkes and rode to London, three nights galloping and three days restlessly sleeping in the most secluded woods he could find. In a brief meeting before their mutual departure from Somerset, the poet had given him a note to obtain lodgings under the name Sam Andrews at the Hungry Steer, a tavern with rooms above at 10 Harp Lane. The location was in a fast-growing slum to the west of the Tower. The proprietress of the Steer was Ophelia Garvey, a woman of rough demeanor and advanced years whose response to most attempts at conversation was a glare. She was, however, helpful enough to direct him to a nearby inexpensive stable to board Owlsword, Will having gotten attached to the frisky but amiable young horse during their ride to London.

His first few days in London were barely an

improvement on his time in Cornwall. There was some obscurity in the crowds that bustled about, but not enough to let him comfortably linger in public, or dine out, or look for the poet at the Globe Theatre or at the building owned by the King's Players nearby. And he had no idea where the poet's lodgings were. Nor could he try to rekindle the handful of other acquaintanceships he had in the city. There had been no public disclosure or legal restraint by his father in regard to his flight, but that could just be his cagey stealth at work. Clarification – some communication if not a definite truce (reconciliation seemed out of the question) – was required before Will could feel safe in public. He would simply have to wait to be contacted by the poet.

He spent his days in his room reading poetry by Thomas Wyatt, Philip Sidney, and Christopher Marlowe, or in random walks, the collar of his doublet pushed up and pinned together to hide his face as much as fashion allowed. His signet ring he took off and looped onto a chain he wore around his neck and under his shirt, lest someone see it and recognize the family crest. Nights he dined mostly on bread and beer in his tiny, barely furnished room, waiting, wondering if the poet's possible abandonment of him might not be worse than his father's scorn.

Six days after his arrival, Mrs Garvey knocked on Will's door just at sunset in an unusually talkative mood and gave him a gilt-edged envelope.

'Ay, some fancy-pants rode up just now with three black feathers in his cap, on a horse what looked like it had been polished like a statue. For Samuel Andrews, Esquire.' Mrs

Garvey paused to look quizically at Will, not for the first time, as if he might be Samuel Andrews and he might not be. No doubt many years of being a landlady for the transient had nourished some instincts in this area. 'And look at the gold on it,' she went on. 'Had I known you keep this kind of company, I'd be charging you twice as much. Three times.'

Will laughed to humor her. 'I am grateful for the consideration you have shown with your modest charge,' he said somewhat formally, wondering how best to flatter her. It wouldn't have mattered, as Mrs Garvey shut the door to his room before his sentence was fully out of his mouth and stormed away. Perhaps his language had been too upper-class for her taste.

Will opened the note. It was from the poet. Will recognized his elegant script immediately from drafts of sonnets the poet had shown him:

Dearest Will,

Your becoming a member of our troupe has been mildly delayed by some Machiavellian shenanigans among the patrons but I nonetheless expect to have Lord Grosvenor's signature on the necessary documents within a fortnight. In the meantime it is a great pleasure for Marguerite and I to cordially invite you to a celebratory gathering we will be hosting this coming Sunday evening at 6, at 22 Lyme Street. The point of the celebration you can guess!

Yours in deep comradeship
and with even deeper admiration

Three evenings later, Will walked to 22 Lyme Street for the poet's Sunday gathering. He wore the fine gray doublet, crimson-tinted black silk cape, and ruffled white shirt he had purchased the day before at Gresham's Royal Exchange. The buckles on his new belt and boots gleamed as though polished with a cloth made from light.

It had rained hard until the middle of the afternoon, but the sun had been out for hours now, giving the soaked streets a gloss and gleam to match his apparel; the very air had a radiance to it as if its usual smoke and odor-stained texture had received a scrubbing. With little more to go on than the aristocratic stationery of the invitation, Will was anticipating as he walked an elegant dinner for a select few. It would be thrilling to see the poet again and meet some of his theatrical friends, not to mention the beautiful Marguerite. He felt as if he were strolling into his future.

As he approached Lyme Street he could see, a mile away at the merge of Cornhill and Threadneedle Streets, the golden grasshopper suspended above Gresham's Market, one of the latest additions to the still sparse London skyline. It shone like a second sun, just above the horizon. *You are the sun to shine on all of England*, a line from the poet's sonnet celebrating him, ran unbidden through his thoughts. He hoped the evening would be like a coronation, for more than one great public life to come.

But as he approached 22 Lyme, he suspected that his concept of a refined occasion might not have been accurate. A raucous din seemed to be coming from the new, well-timbered house of three stories at that address, which had ceremonial pennants in an array of colors flying from all its eaves and windows. The din became more distinct the closer he approached, one percolating with chattering voices, loud guffaws, boisterous boasts, and even the occasional inebriated shriek. Will allowed himself the preposterous hope that another party was taking place in nearly the same location, but his final few strides forward educated him that this was not so.

His mood sank in anticipation of a tiresome evening dodging drunks and feigning vulgar merriment, though he could not imagine how a sensibility as refined as the poet's could have attracted the vulgar babble he was listening to. But he moved bravely onward. He wasn't shy, and he could get through the evening – no doubt, if all else failed, by charming whatever circle of youthful females gathered around him.

Will plowed through the throng congregating at the doorway and, once inside, began to methodically seek out the poet. But the crowd on the first floor was so dense that moving through it was like trying to navigate swamp grass. And the first few people he queried seemed ignorant of the gathering's purpose, gazing back at him drunkenly, so asking for the poet's location seemed futile. He found it convenient to fall in with a trio sitting at a cramped table playing ruff and honors in need of a fourth. After a round of introductions to Tom, Pete, and Finn, he managed to angle his rickety chair so that at least he could catch glimpses of the first floor's entrance and main staircase and, in the meantime, pass the time tolerably well. Sooner or later the poet and Marguerite would no doubt be moved to introduce themselves to the crowd.

Will gave an imitation of following the game's fluctuating fortunes but primarily observed the first-floor hubbub.

The swath of sound included everything from giggles to arguments; the quality and cost of attire male and female varied widely; an endlessly abundant supply of liquor was evident, though he couldn't tell where the serving table might be; all in all the chaotic party looked as if it had been planned by pulling in random passersby from a busy London street, no more. It wasn't a theater crowd or a rough crowd, an intellectual or a degenerate crowd, a devout or an anarchical crowd, though here and there individuals of all these stripes and many others could be distinguished. Even the footman, a dark-skinned Moor liveried in royal purple, defied easy characterization. In fact, he seemed the most regal of all the occupants. It was a flotsam-of-London, top-to-bottom crowd. Will grew more agitated as he perceived that the nature of this party contradicted the picture the poet had drawn for him, of personally welcoming him to London – surely a more intimate setting could have been found for their reunion!

Then on some mysterious signal the crowd fell silent throughout the house. Will put his cards down on the table, got up without even a nod to his fellow players, and followed the direction of staring eyes into a large central room dominated by a wide staircase. The going was still tangled and impeded, but he was able to employ the stealth and steel of muscle that had stood him in deft stead as a fencer to maneuver all the way to the staircase railing. A roar of acclaim went up as, Will observed, the poet and his radiant-eyed, dark-haired lover strode out on the second-floor landing, basking with smiles in the applause. Will managed to catch the eye of the poet, who responded with a warm wave and a twinkle in his eye. The poet whispered to his lover, who glanced down at him with a welcoming smile as well.

Meeting Marguerite's gaze, Will experienced a transformative shock. He felt at once as if he had known her all his life *and* that he had never before beheld such beauty. Love for her surged through him, a love so complete it were as if he had physically merged with her. Not the simple merge of lovemaking, but a consummate merge as if their atoms and electricity had intertwined, their veins and brain cells, muscles and bones. For a dizzying instant, he felt as if a second person were within him, filling him with an unspeakable elation that nearly caused him to faint. Then for an even more fleeting instant he was actually inside her mind, gazing down at himself from the second-floor landing and seeing a young man whose face had been transported by ecstasy.

In that moment of twin vision he noticed something else. The Moorish footman was also looking up at Marguerite with a similar expression on his face, only *his* passion was mixed with something else. Envy and hatred. Yet, Will wasn't sure of whom.

Then he retreated back inside a shaky self. But the upheaval inside him was transcendent. They were each other's destiny. Not only had he encountered the great love of his life but he had learned something crucial about himself, Will realized. He could fly – not literally, but spiritually. His soul was not bound to his own flesh the way a living person's should be. It could escape his flesh, as the souls of the dead did. But he wasn't dead. He was very much alive.

Will fought with himself to suppress this wild reaction. The poet was important to him, and his bonding in such a way with the poet's love was worse than backstabbing, it was a sort of treason. Observed in another, it would have disgusted him. But he was in the grip of some unnatural force and could not suppress his emotions.

The sound of two cymbals clashing came from Will's left. The timing must have been choreographed: the poet and Marguerite began to address the crowd from the top of the stairs.

'Heartfelt greetings, friends, without further ado . . . my beloved Marguerite and I have jointly composed a marriage sonnet by way of thanking you all for coming. Let us recite it now.'

'Marriage sonnet!' an old man in a shabby black robe standing near Will muttered, with the faintest trace of an Italian accent. 'Let the man be free of the wife he already has! Or is bigamy not a crime in sinful London?'

Several people standing near him hushed him impatiently. Will caught a glimpse of a gleaming crucifix around the man's neck as he turned his head to glare in turn at his critics with piercing brown eyes, then returned his sharp gaze to the podium. The man's hostility disturbed Will, despite the deep inconvenience for his new emotions of any nuptials between the poet and Marguerite. Will resolved to keep an eye on him.

The poet began:

The sweetest words I've ever heard are those
with which my Marguerite professes love
for me eternally; this great crowd shows
how much you too are moved and so I'll wave
in gratitude that you've come here today.

The poet had fastened his gaze on Marguerite while reciting, but now he faced the throng and waved in a grand manner, to which there was an enthusiastic response with a few exceptions, such as that of the footman, who whispered to a man dressed in rainbow hues, 'Such a union never will last!' *What impertinence!* Will thought, focusing instead on the familiar sound of the poet's voice. Even though he himself had been struck with desire for Marguerite, he would never dare to interrupt the poet's recitation. His voice had a ringing clarity, indeed majesty, to it Will had not heard in private, and he did not wonder at it given what depth of inspiration he now knew Marguerite could inspire.

Marguerite continued:

Our love's a brighter sun than summer noon's,
and yet as soft as a slow breeze in May,
and will survive in rhymes amidst the ruins
of fortunes, mansions, nations. Let us cheer
you all for your great warmth – that you've come
    here—

Will swam in the flow of Marguerite's voice as in the gentlest of rivers, near oblivious to the joy she showed in this proclamation of her and the poet's love for each other. Somehow, he was managing to disregard that formidable obstacle for the moment.

Marguerite went on:

—to celebrate our union. Love has won!

The poet stepped forward to conclude, smiling at Marguerite:

Our marriage bed awaits, if not tonight
then soon: our flesh and blood will be as one;
enough of this world's darkness. Love is light!

To renewed applause, the poet and Marguerite then began a ceremonial descent down the stairs, greeting the partygoers, especially those they recognized, with a regal yet congenial air. Will leaned forward over the stair railing so that he could greet the poet and be introduced to Marguerite, but the couple went in different directions midway down the stairs, as if carried off by conflicting currents, so that in another minute Will found himself nervously bowing to Marguerite alone, taking and gently kissing her small, finely gloved hand.

'Wondrous lady, I am Will Hughes, tutored by your beloved and now come to London to join the King's Players.' He gazed into Marguerite's eyes as he rose from his bow. Meeting Marguerite's gaze was like diving into two deep pools of blue-green light. He felt himself again swooning with ecstasy. As he regained his composure, he saw a flash of recognition in Marguerite's eyes and waited hopefully for something more – a profound look, expressive words, some other reassurance – but she just nodded with an amiable smile and appeared about to move on to her next congratulator. Was it possible she did not feel what he was feeling? Had the flash of recognition simply been her recalling his name? Or maybe, he tried to reassure himself, she was more adept at masking elation than he was?

Perhaps in response to his perturbed expression, she did add, 'Yes, Will, I have heard wonderful things about you. I am very pleased to meet you.' But she moved on.

'Wait, please!' he called, catching awkwardly at her sleeve. 'I must see you—'

She glanced sharply back at him.

'I mean, the two of you . . . in a less hectic setting and as soon as possible? May I pay a call on you tomorrow? Or Tuesday?'

'I am sure there will be an occasion for it,' Marguerite said distantly. She seemed to reflect for a moment, then glanced more directly into his eyes again. Will thought he saw a tremor pass over her features. But if it had, she retreated from it.

'I must go,' she said with formal coldness. 'We will send you a note.'

'I know you have something to tell me,' Will said with an uncomfortable smile.

Marguerite's expression grew pained, and she moved on to a large woman in a flowery dress, who held out both hands to her in a warm greeting. Will turned away then in despair, finding the front door with much more ease than he had found the stairs, and leaving the party without bothering to seek out the poet. His elation had turned to ashes with Marguerite's final chill words.

Darkness had fallen outside, broken only by inter-mittent torchlight along Lyme Street, as if Will had plunged into a pool of gloom emanating from his mood. He could not believe that Marguerite had not felt what he'd felt, but it appeared to be true! Why had she rushed away like that? And what did her pained look mean? Of course, things might be awkward among the three of them for a while if his and Marguerite's feelings were truly aligned, but the poet's plays were filled with more entangled circumstances than theirs that were nonetheless overcome by the parties to them. This woman wasn't one of the inane flirtations at Swan Hall! She was his love and his destiny. He would suffer unbearably over her if she couldn't be his.

So engrossed in this view of possible heartbreak was he that he didn't feel the intrusion of a hand in his satchel until it had begun to withdraw. Whirling, he caught the pickpocket by the arm. It was a young boy – one who had been at the party whom the others had called Finn. Round eyes blinked in a round face beneath a tattered cap.

'I wasn't stealin' nothin', sir, I was putting something in.' The falsetto voice made Will look twice at his captive. He might be a boy . . . or might be a girl, he couldn't say. He snatched the cap from the pickpocket's head . . . and was startled to discover pointed ears.

'If you look, you'll see I've given you the address where they stay. Go there tomorrow morning; the poet will be out. And do not delay. She is smitten by his words but she will be drawn to your blood.'

'But how do you—'

The pointed-ears waif twisted out of Will's grip and vanished into the shadows. Swearing, Will dug in his satchel, expecting that his money would be gone, but found that everything was intact. In addition was a scrap of paper with an address written on it: 39 Rood Lane, written in a flowing script that Will was instantly sure must belong to his beloved Marguerite. It was far too fine and feminine a hand for the androgynous waif. Will kissed the paper, imagining that he kissed the fingertips of she who had written it.

His steps were much lighter all the way back to the inebriated din of Mrs Garvey's tavern. The occasional torch was more than a match for the blackened gloom of London's night. He was in love, so swept up in his passion that he did not notice the old Italian priest, who had eavesdropped on his encounter with Finn, following him back to his lodgings.

5

The Labyrinth

I slept late the next morning – past nine – for the first time since I'd arrived. I awoke to the sounds of guests eating their breakfasts in the courtyard garden. When my father had called the Hôtel des Grandes Écoles to get me a room on such short notice, Madame Weiss, the owner, said she would of course find a way to fit in the daughter of their dear old friend Margot James. On arrival I found that 'fitting me in' meant giving me a ground-floor room the size of a largish walk-in closet. But, though I imagined that the ground floor wouldn't be everybody's choice, I found I rather liked it. It was just around the corner from the kitchen, where I could get hot water for tea at all hours of the night, and I was close to the pretty garden. So close that I had to keep the shutters of one window closed because it looked out over the little tables where breakfast was served. The other window faced the side garden, which was gated off from the other guests. A black iron grating (but no window screen) was over the window to keep out intruders, and a tall, leafy sycamore blocked the view from the neighboring buildings. The huge tree took up the entire view, filling the room with dappled green light and birdsong. Lying in the double bed that took up most of the room, I felt as though I were floating in a rustic gazebo, an effect reinforced by the room's blue toile wallpaper featuring frolicking shepherds and shepherdesses, grazing deer, nymphs, and fauns.

This morning the room was also filled with the smell of coffee and buttery croissants, and the voices of two small American children discussing what they wanted to do that day.

'The puppet show!' the little girl shouted.

'The sailboats!' her brother insisted.

'Another day at the Luxembourg,' the mother sighed.

'I'll take them,' the father said. 'You go shopping in the Marais and we'll meet you for falafels on the rue Rosiers.'

Give the man the Father of the Year award, I thought as I got dressed in navy capris, a crisp white, buttoned shirt, and slip-on canvas shoes. The puppet show and the boat basin at the Luxembourg sounded fun, but I was headed in the opposite direction to find someone called Monsieur Lutin at the Jardin des Plantes. I checked my outfit in the mirror, wondering if it was chic enough to meet a Frenchman in, and decided to add an Indian print scarf around my neck.

By the time I got out to the courtyard the American family had gone and a German couple had taken their place. I nodded to them because I'd exchanged a few words about the weather with them yesterday in stilted English – which made us old comrades in the world of the Hôtel des Grandes Écoles. The hotel had the air of an old pension out of an E. M. Forster novel where English spinsters and clerics go year after year and all get to know each other. Only my getting up before breakfast hours and spending my days in a musty, old church had kept me from becoming better acquainted with my fellow guests. I didn't know the mother and the daughter whose table I sat across from – Canadians, I soon guessed from their conversation – or the man sitting by himself in a shady corner writing in a leatherbound journal. He did raise his eyes from his notebook when I sat down, though, and inclined his head to me in a courtly, old-world bow. I smiled back, pleasantly struck by his eyes. They were deep chocolate brown – the same color as his longish, silky hair – with a touch of creamy gold at the center like a dollop of foam resting on a cup of dark coffee. He smiled at me, too, and realizing I'd been staring at him way too long, I ducked my head to retrieve my Paris guide from my bag.

When I looked up again, he was bent over his journal. A writer? I wondered. Perhaps gathering material for a book set in Paris? An academic or a journalist? His rumpled linen suit, worn leather attaché case, and straw hat looked curiously antiquated for someone in his early thirties. Since he hadn't spoken, I didn't know what nationality he was, but from his coloring I would guess Italian. A newspaper was folded on the table beside him, but I couldn't see what language it was written in.

Madame Weiss interrupted my speculations by coming herself to say good morning and take my order. 'Mademoiselle James,' she cooed in the same tone as the pigeons in the garden, 'we have seen so little of you! You are very busy doing your research, eh? Just like your mother when she stayed here, always busy!'

I smiled at Madame Weiss. She must have been at least eighty, but she was slim as a girl of twenty in a black pencil skirt, loose cream silk blouse, and high-heeled sandals. Her gray hair was impeccably cut in a soft, chin-length bob. A silk scarf patterned with seashells was deftly knotted on her shoulder. 'Really?' I asked. 'Do you know what she was so busy doing?'

She shrugged and pursed her lips. 'There is so much to do in Paris. Who can say? Would you like a café au lait? Croissant? *Jus d'orange?*'

I said yes to everything and Madame Weiss patted me on my shoulder, covertly rearranging my scarf as she did so. I was sure it looked ten times better. I turned my attention back to my guidebook, determined not to stare back at the Italian journalist (as I'd decided to think of him). I was here to find Will, I told myself sternly.

But it's not as though you're married to him, another voice intruded into my head. I recognized this voice as belonging to my friend Becky Jones. She would probably point out that Will had betrayed me and that only yesterday I'd been about to give up on finding him. But then my encounter with Jean Robin had changed all that. I had been waiting for a sign, and although I hadn't gotten one that told me how to find the Summer Country, I'd gotten a referral to someone who could help me.

I looked up the Jardin des Plantes in my guidebook and read that it had been founded in 1626 by Jean Hérouard and Guy de la Brosse. I recalled that Jean Robin had mentioned them last night as the two men who'd been inspired by his work to create the botanical garden. The garden featured a natural-history museum, a botanical school, a zoo, an alpine garden, and a labyrinth, which contained the first wrought-iron structure – a gazebo built in

1788 – and a 'majestic' cedar of Lebanon that had been planted in 1734.

I wondered if the cedar of Lebanon housed a bevy of tree fey. Perhaps that was where I'd find Monsieur Lutin. Jean Robin hadn't given me any more specific instructions than to go to the Labyrinth. I didn't even know what kind of creature Monsieur Lutin was.

I flipped to the map section at the back of the book and plotted out a route to the park, which looked to be a ten-to-fifteen-minute walk away. I closed the book just as a waitress appeared with my breakfast tray. I looked up, hoping to get another glance at the handsome Italian journalist, but he was gone. He'd left his paper, though, and I decided to swipe it to get a clue to his nationality. When I'd retrieved the paper – an *International Herald Tribune* – I forgot all about trying to find out more about my fellow hotel guest. Staring out from the page was a picture of Amélie, the homeless woman from the Square Viviani. The caption below said that she'd been found dead at dawn, drowned in the Seine.

I walked to the Jardin des Plantes thinking about poor Amélie. According to the newspaper she'd been a great beauty once, an artists' model and mistress of several well-known artists, but she'd fallen on hard times. The reporter implied that her death was most likely a suicide. Pausing above a flight of stairs, I recalled Amélie's yellow, nicotine-stained fingers, scabby knees, and toothless gums. How sad to go from being a vaunted beauty to a scrawny creature sleeping on park benches. As I passed the Arènes de Lutèce, the remains of a Roman arena, I noticed a few more homeless people gathered on the benches in the adjacent park. I stopped and looked at the scene. There was the man in the Renaissance beret – Amélie's friend. Did he know that Amélie was gone? Should I speak to him? I took a step into the park, but then I looked across the sandy circle and noticed that someone else was watching the group of homeless people – a tall man in a long coat and wide-brimmed hat. Could it be the same man whom I'd glimpsed last night standing outside the Square Viviani? I took another step forward and the man suddenly retreated into the trees. When I looked back at the area where the homeless people had been gathered, they were all gone. I looked all around the arena for any sign of Amélie's friend, but finally gave up and continued on my way to the Jardin des Plantes. All along the rue Linné, though, I had the feeling that I was being followed. At the corner of rue Cuvier, next to a fountain featuring snakes, crocodiles, lions, and other exotic beasts, I turned sharply around, half-expecting to surprise the man in the long coat and wide-brimmed hat, but all I found were the scaly snakeheads on the fountain spewing water – and they were creepy enough. Still I couldn't shake the sensation that something bad was at my heels – or maybe up ahead. After all, I was on my way to a labyrinth – which, I reflected uneasily, was the legendary home of the Minotaur. I wasn't going to meet a Minotaur, was I?

I'd met a dragon in New York and survived it, I reflected as I followed a sign pointing to LE LABYRINTHE up a steep path. I passed a tall, feathery tree labeled CÈDRE DU LIBAN and scanned its roots for any portals, but found none. I continued on the hedge-bordered path, which circled around a small but steep hillock. Less a labyrinth than a spiral. Good, I thought, no minotaurs lived in spirals as far as I knew.

At the top of the path was the cast-iron gazebo, a pretty, whimsical 'folly' capped with two interlocking rings that looked like one of the astronomical devices I had been sketching in the Musée des Arts et Métiers recently. When I got to the foot of the stairs leading up into the gazebo, I stood panting slightly from the climb, staring up at the gazebo. On top of it was a bronze arrow pointing northwest. I knew because back in New York an earth elemental named Noam Erdmann, mild-mannered diamond dealer by day, had implanted a compass stone into the palm of my hand. I wondered if the direction meant something. Was it pointing toward where I had to go to meet Monsieur Lutin? How *was* I supposed to find Monsieur Lutin? Should I stand in the gazebo and shout his name?

I was about to give it a try when a man in a blue jumpsuit appeared around the last curve of the spiral path waving his arms and shouting something in French. From the official-looking patch on his jumpsuit I guessed he was a gardener, but I couldn't figure out what he was yelling about.

But he wasn't yelling at me; he appeared to be yelling at the hedge. He bent down, thrust his arm into the branches, and pulled out a small, squirming child – a little boy wearing red shorts and a Tintin T-shirt. The gardener deposited the boy on the path and, waving his finger in the boy's face, delivered an impassioned tirade, the gist of which was that the boy was going to get his eyes poked out if he kept climbing in the hedges. The boy listened, his eyes wide as saucers, then ran away. About five feet from the irate gardener he plunged back into the hedge.

I had to stifle a chuckle. I saw now that low, narrow tunnels snaked throughout the hedges. It *was* a maze. I knelt down to look through one of the tunnels . . . and met two large, yellow eyes. They belonged to an extremely small and wrinkled old man who sat cross-legged under the hedge. His skin was the color of old paper, his beard snow-white. He wore blue trousers, a white shirt, red suspenders, and a red cap. He was the spitting image of a garden gnome.

'Garet James?' he asked in a surprisingly deep voice for such a little person.

'Monsieur Lutin?'

'*C'est moi.*' He patted his chest. Then he crooked one gnarled finger and gestured for me to follow him into the tunnel.

I looked behind me to see if the angry gardener was still patrolling the hedges. I couldn't even begin to imagine how pissed off he'd be by an *adult* crawling into the hedges, but then, I reflected as I started crawling, that was probably the least of my problems.

I saw immediately that the gardener had been right about the threat to corneas. I was so busy fending off stray shrubbery branches that I lost sight of Monsieur Lutin's blue-clad derrière . . . and when I looked up, it was gone. But where could he have gone? I hadn't passed any intersecting tunnels.

I got my answer two minutes later when I fell into a hole. I dropped about four feet onto a stone ledge next to

Monsieur Lutin, who was sitting cross-legged and chuckling.

'Thanks for the heads-up,' I said in English.

'*De rien.*' He tipped his red cap at me, then, switching to English (as most Parisians did when they heard my French), he pointed to something behind me. 'You will be more comfortable walking the rest of the way, Mademoiselle.'

I got up, brushing the dirt from my capris, and looked behind me. The inside of the hill was hollow. A narrow pathway, hewn into the stone-paved walls, circled down into darkness. It was impossible to tell how far down it went, and the outer edge had no railing.

'It's better if you take the inside,' Monsieur Lutin said, touching my elbow. 'I know the path. You might want to have your own light, though.'

He snapped his fingers and a small flame leaped from his thumb. Oberon had taught me this trick back in New York, but after the High Bridge Tower fire, my hands had been bandaged for weeks and then . . . well, I'd been afraid to try it again. The scars still on my hands reminded me too painfully of what it felt like to be burned.

'Go ahead,' he urged. 'Best to get back on the pony, as you Americans say.'

Embarrassed to look like a coward in front of a three-foot-tall man, I touched my fingers together, recalling Oberon's instructions: *Concentrate on the heat your aura produces . . . When you can feel a spark, snap your fingers together. . . .* I could almost hear Oberon's voice in my head, which was not an altogether welcome sensation. After all, in his quest to get the box first, Oberon had paralyzed me and left me to die – well, Will said he thought Oberon probably knew that Will would get to me first. Still, I hadn't thought kindly of the King of Fairies since. The fire trick *was* useful though. When I could see a pale blue glow limning the tips of my fingers, I snapped them together. A small flame leaped from my hand and I held my thumb up to keep it steady.

'Good,' Monsieur Lutin said succinctly. 'Let's go!'

'Where are we going?' I asked as we started down the curving path, which was the mirror image of the spiral path I'd climbed outside the hill. I noticed that the walls were roughly paved with broken stones that looked as if they'd been salvaged from Roman and medieval ruins. There were fragments of inscriptions in Latin, shards of stained glass, bits of broken crockery, and stone gargoyle heads – a hodgepodge mosaic.

'My colleague tells me you wish to contact the boat people. Well, you can't go to them empty-handed – they're quite formal about such things – so we are going to the gardens to collect a little bouquet for you to bring with you. They love flowers, but you have to be careful not to bring them just *any* sort of flower.'

'They sound sort of snobbish.'

Monsieur Lutin shrugged, which made his trousers hitch up. 'Ah, well, they *were* the lords and ladies of the Summer Country.' He sighed wistfully when he mentioned the Summer Country.

'Are you from the Summer Country, too?'

He laughed. 'All our kind were originally from the Summer Country. At the dawn of time the Summer Country and this world coexisted, like two streams that ran parallel to each other, but as humans gained more power and began altering the earth – building roads, damming rivers, draining swamps – the Summer Country became like a mist that lay upon the land, thick in places, thin in others. The humble people of the Summer Country – the fairies and goblins, gnomes and sylphs, elves and brownies – came and went between the worlds freely. In places where humans paid homage to us – a grove they wouldn't cut, a spring they consecrated with a little statue, a cave they painted with their images – we settled down. Like this place.'

He held up his thumb-flame to cast a bigger light. We'd come to the bottom of the stairs. The floor was paved with wide, rectangular stones, which were engraved with the shapes of men in armor and ladies in long medieval gowns. Monsieur Lutin touched his thumb to a candle in a wall sconce and lit it. The light filled a tiny niche that held a statue of a diminutive man with a beard and pointed cap.

'Is that . . . ?'

Monsieur Lutin struck a pose in front of the statue, one hand on his hip, the other stroking his beard. 'A good likeness, don't you think? Mind you, I only had a little following in the days before the Romans came. And a few Romans were happy to pay tribute to me, too. But then times changed and no one came anymore to keep my shrine. In the Middle Ages the people began to use this as a garbage dump! Well, I couldn't have that, could I? So I've kept it clean inside, used the pieces of things that were worth saving to decorate – what do you Americans call that?'

'Recycling,' I said, looking up at the crazy-mosaic walls. 'You did all this?'

'Oh, yes, all the interior decorating to be sure. *And* I gave Edmé Verniquet the idea for the gazebo on top.'

'It's beautiful,' I said truthfully.

Monsieur Lutin shuffled his feet and fiddled with his suspenders. 'I'm so glad you like it. . . . I don't have many visitors . . . but we mustn't waste time.' He took off down a long, low tunnel and I had to scurry to keep up. 'What was I saying? Oh, yes, I was telling you the history of how the Summer Country became closed to us. Many of us settled where humans made shrines to us, but the sea fairies wanted their own kingdom from which to rule the humans. They built the city of Ys on an island in the sea, which floated between the worlds, where humans could come pay homage to them. Many-towered Ys with its great seawall that kept the tides between the worlds at bay. More than any of us the sea fairies thrived off their contact with humans, so much so that the nine priestesses of Ys brought a human king to rule over them . . . or at least they let him think he ruled over them. He was more like a sacrificial goat. The human king of Ys was obliged to go each month to a sacred grove where any human might come and challenge his sovereignty in a fight to the death. Then the new victor would become king.'

'That sounds pretty barbaric,' I said when Monsieur Lutin paused at a low, arched door to fumble in his pocket.

'The lords and ladies of Ys came to thrive on such displays of . . . loyalty. Some say it was decadence that destroyed the city.' Retrieving a large ring of keys, he counted off keys until he produced a big brass skeleton key, which he held up, gripped in his fist. 'The king's daughter gave the key to the sea gate to an evil sorcerer who promised to take her away, but who opened the gates instead. The city was drowned, most perished, but some survived. They fled to the mainland seeking refuge. Along the way they created doors to the Summer Country so they'd be able to go back.'

As he mentioned the doors, he fitted the key into the lock and opened the door in front of us. I followed him through, out into the open air, and was startled to find myself in a densely landscaped garden. Narrow paths twisted through groves of pine and fir and rocky out-croppings planted with a myriad of flowers and shrubs. The garden was sunken below ground level, secluding it from the rest of the Jardin, and was empty except for one gardener, who was wearing the same type of blue jumpsuit as the gardener from the labyrinth. *'Bon jour, Solange! Ça va?'* Monsieur Lutin called to the gardener. 'I just need to pick a few samples for a friend. *D'accord?'* The gardener smiled and waved back at Monsieur Lutin as if he was used to seeing three-feet-tall gnomes wandering around the Alpine Garden.

'So what happened then?' I asked as Monsieur Lutin stooped to pick a long-stemmed, blue flower.

'As the boat people created their doors, they shut others. The fabric of mist, which had flowed freely over this world, evaporated. Creatures like myself could no longer slip from world to world. Some were trapped in the Summer Country, others like myself were trapped in this world.'

'Kind of like the Berlin Wall.'

'Yes, and the boat people became the gatekeepers, deciding who could and couldn't travel to the Summer Country. As you can imagine, that made them unpopular with some, but then it also made it very important to keep on their good side if you wanted to ever be able to visit your relatives. . . . Ah, blue gentian, she'll like those. . . . But then even the boat people began to lose their ability to move from world to world. If they became too attached to a human, for instance . . .'

Monsieur Lutin interrupted his narrative to scramble up a rock outcropping to pick a white, woolly flower that I thought might be edelweiss. I was standing by a small ornamental pool into which a miniature waterfall flowed. The scene reminded me of the brief glimpse I'd had of the Summer Country, when I'd had to step in front of the silver box to close it. I'd seen the enchanted pool with a black swan floating on it. Transported back in time, I'd seen an ancient story reenacted before me: a youth who'd followed his true love to the swan pool at sunset even though he'd been forbidden to do so, watching the woman he loved turn into a black swan. The swan maiden, seeing that she'd been betrayed, had begun to fly away, back to the Summer Country, and the young man, unable to bear losing her, had lifted his bow and shot her.

'Like the first Marguerite,' I said to Monsieur Lutin, who'd climbed back down and was standing by my side looking into the little pool. 'She made her beloved promise not to come to the swan pool when she turned back into a swan, but he did and then shot her with an arrow.'

'Only to keep her from leaving him,' Monsieur Lutin said, taking my hand and leading me to a little bench in a patch of sunshine in a secluded spot. 'She wasn't killed, but she could never go back to the Summer Country again. For love of the young man she pledged herself to protect humankind forever. She became one of the four Watchtowers.'

'But why? A human had betrayed her. Shouldn't that have made her hate human beings?'

'You'd think so, wouldn't you? Most of the fey who are betrayed by humans do hate them. They become vengeful.' He motioned for me to bend down so he could whisper in my ear even though we were alone in this part of the garden. 'Some say that the fey who were captured and tortured by humans because the humans *believed* they were demons *became* demons. Imagine being tortured by the creatures you loved, whom you thought of as your children.'

Although we were sitting in the warm sun, I shivered. If what Monsieur Lutin said was true, then human beings had created demons. 'It would drive you mad.'

'Yes. But your ancestor Marguerite became all the more attached to humans. Marguerite knew that her human lover betrayed her because he wanted to keep her with him. She never forgot the intensity of his love for her. Now the boat people, they both love and hate humans. They've tasted the human's ability to love and they've become addicted to it. They seek out human lovers who will sing their praises, sculpt them in marble, paint their faces, and write love poems to them. In exchange the humans they touch taste immortality. The world's greatest art comes from these unions, but they're fragile. They never last long.'

I nodded. 'I know. My father is an art dealer so I grew up among artists. I've seen what happens to them when their inspiration deserts them.' I remembered my father's protégé, Santé Leon, who killed himself just before his first big show at the Whitney. And my father's best friend, Zach Reese, who had turned to drink when he couldn't paint anymore. At least Zach had started painting again, but so many others had been damaged by their brush with the muses. It was why I had decided to become a jeweler instead of an artist. 'You make it sound very dangerous to go near the boat people.'

'Oh, it is! Of course you have a touch of them in you and that's very powerful. I wouldn't dream of sending you to them otherwise. But don't forget, you're also part human. You've already succumbed to the attraction of the vampire. There are other creatures who are far more potent and seductive than him whom you will meet.' He held up the bouquet of delicate alpine flowers he had gathered for me. My mother had loved wildflowers and had taught me the names of many. I recognized blue gentian, white edelweiss, yellow cinquefoil, and purple thistle, but a half a dozen of the flowers I didn't know. He plucked one of these out of the bouquet, a sprig of small, purple orchids. Inside each flower's throat was a purple heart ringed with white. He tore off one of the green leaves, rubbed it between his fingers, and held it up for me to smell.

'Mint.'

'Alpine calamint,' he said. 'Keep this one for yourself. If you find yourself falling under the spell of any of the sea fey, take it out and smell it. It might bring you to your senses.'

'Might?'

'It's the best I can do. I could tell you to go home now and forget Will Hughes, the silver box, and the

Summer Country, but I don't suppose you would listen.'

He looked at me inquisitively. *Could* I just go home? I wondered. I'd been on the verge of giving up last night, but now . . . knowing that there was a chance I could find Will . . .? True, he had taken the box from me, but he had done it so that he could become human again. He had done it so he could sit in the sunshine as I was now. How could I begrudge him that when all *I* wanted to do was sit in the sun with him just as I was sitting on the bench beside Monsieur Lutin right now? Besides, since I'd gotten to Paris, I had this feeling that Will was heading toward me. I knew it was silly. I knew he was probably far away on the path to the Summer Country, but I also had this strange conviction that we were on parallel paths, like the two paths that spiraled up the Labyrinth, one outside the hill and one inside, with only a thin wall between us. Sooner or later, our paths would have to merge. 'No, I don't think I can,' I said finally.

'I didn't think so. Here.' He handed me the bouquet. 'Take these to Madame La Pieuvre at the Bibliothèque Océanographique. She's one of the most civil of the sea fey and acts as a sort of liaison between them and us lesser fairies. If anyone can help you, she can.'

'Thank you. You've been very kind. Earlier when I was walking up the Labyrinth, I was afraid you'd turn out to be a Minotaur!'

'What an idea!' He chuckled and slapped his hands against his knees. A cloud of greenish yellow dust – pollen from all the flowers he'd collected – rose around him like a halo. 'Everyone knows that the Minotaur lives under the Gare de l'Est!'

6

Alchemy of Blood

The morning after the party dawned with a radiant light, a shimmer of summer. The rays that balmed Will's cheeks through an open window also awoke him with a pleasant start. He sprang out of bed with a sense of energy and purpose this entire desultory period had lacked: Marguerite. He whispered her name to himself as if it were an incantation, an alchemical caress of his tongue. The thought of her seemed to flow through his veins with flaming resonance.

Will dressed with whatever peacock tilt his wardrobe allowed: white-plumed, ruby-red hat, ruffled white shirt and silver vest, dark blue trousers, and gleaming-buckled boots, all of it a compromise between exuberant nobility and being a dandy. His attire served no purpose as to approaching Marguerite successfully, but it reflected his mood.

He lingered longer than usual over Mrs Garvey's simple breakfast, as he knew the difference between paying an early call and paying a too early, rude one. After eating endless buttered rolls and drinking several glasses of ale, Will at last saw the sun lift a few inches over the horizon and knew he could go on his way.

As he started out on this most reckless errand, Will did not conceal from himself the possible lunacy of what he was doing. For one thing, propriety, given the poet's marital status, required that Marguerite not be at the poet's lodgings this early in the day. And if she was there anyway, given Will's new status as the poet's rival (at least in his own mind), calling on Marguerite with the poet around was the last thing he should do. He was acting as if Marguerite were the poet's daughter and he was coming to court her!

Patience should have been his priority with this most dangerous attraction. He should have waited weeks, or months if necessary, to approach Marguerite alone. But he could not control his new emotion, and therefore patience wasn't a choice.

Will couldn't stop recalling for even a minute the moment he'd first looked into Marguerite's eyes from the bottom of the stairs, a transformative experience that was like a gaze into a second universe much grander than this one; that was why he had set off on this walk. He felt as though a new kind of blood were flowing through his veins this morning. The energy in him was so deep it might have come from primal elements of the physical world, fire in particular. The sun seemed to confirm this. As it rose higher – he could already feel that this was going to be an exceptionally hot day – he could feel its rays as if they were a wind at his back, pushing him on, a coconspirator in his improbable love.

When he glanced down at the pavement for a moment and observed his right hand swinging through a swath of sunlight, he stopped still in his tracks with a sensation somewhere between terror and awe. For an instant, his hand seemed to have become transparent. Sunlight pulsed right through it as if shining through flesh-tinted air. At the same time he thought he could detect, faintly, with sight so ethereal it was almost not physical, tiny, whirring particles in the space his hand occupied. Particles so tiny, and colorless. As if the idea of small particles making up matter and flesh were quite real. Such a scientific fancy had been the talk of the London cafés lately after a broadsheet by the renowned scientific thinker Sutherland Hopkins. *Atoms*, he had called them, the word used by the ancient Democritus.

Yes, London right now was aflame with scientific fire, Will had been there long enough to know, pioneers and innovators working away in its nooks and crannies, then bringing their thinking to the cafés and meeting halls where much of the city's robust intellectual life took place.

The solar effect went away and his hand became fleshly dull again. When he tried to repeat the effect by stopping suddenly and glancing down, he couldn't. But he continued to reflect on this odd moment. Perhaps his approaching Marguerite had so concentrated his physical being that he was now in a different relationship even with sunlight, he thought feverishly. Perhaps his atoms had lives of their own! Or else he was so much a lover now that his very flesh had fallen in love with sunlight, and that was why he had observed flesh and light in such an intimate merge, if only for an instant.

Will knew these to be the thoughts of a poet more than a rational thinker, let alone a scientist, but he was convinced his atomsight had been real. Then he turned onto

Rood Lane and felt the sudden palpitations of a wild heart, driving all other thoughts and sensations away. He could almost not bear the surge of anticipation. He approached the poet's very doorstep, where Marguerite might likely be! As to considering her not being there, he didn't; he had thrown all emotional caution to the winds.

The quality of the streets had increased during his walk, Will had noticed, but he was still startled by the grandeur of 39 Rood Lane, the poet's address and the finest building on the block. The poet had been working as a tutor, so Will wondered over the affluence of 39's appearance, though he knew tutoring wasn't the poet's only income.

Thirty-nine Rood was a five-story town house of polished rose brick, with two expensive Florentine glass windows on each floor like the square, polished eyes of a geometer. Glass windows were the latest trend, and Will had only seen them in elegant neighborhoods. As to polish, the brass knocker on the front door, four steps up from the street, was so brilliant Will could not look at it for long.

The gleam that penetrated next was not from an architectural embellishment but from the jacket buttons, belt and boot buckles, and sword hilt of a footman with an unusually regal bearing, who stood at the top of the steps as if waiting to greet him. Will recognized the dark-skinned Moor he'd seen at the party and suspected the footman could be out there as a warning to a love-crazed interloper such as himself. Even the ability to reduce himself to atoms would not suffice to slip past this puffed-up warlord. Will reached in his pocket for the note he had brought for such an eventuality, and as he did so, the sentry extended a note to him as well. Will ignored it.

'Would you be Mr Will Hughes, *sir*?' There was no mistaking the dismissive tone of his *sir*. He moved the note closer to Will's chin.

'*Lord* Hughes,' Will said, his heart sinking at this confirmation that the sentry posting was for him. Marguerite must have told the poet *everything* for this footman to be there. Reflecting on that horrible fact, he took the note. It could be the only communication he'd ever receive from the poet or Marguerite again.

'Thank you for this kindness,' Will said, referring to the note, though he doubted its contents were kind. He went two steps up and said, 'Now I must formally request admission to call on the most gracious Lady Marguerite.' He bowed, alertly, keeping in mind the possibility of being shoved down the stairs.

The footman laughed. 'Is milady expecting you?'

'Not precisely. But there is an urgency.'

'Well, be off with you then! I've not heard good things about you.' The Moor cocked his fist and circled it in a vague way not far from Will's jaw.

Swordsman that he was – though without sword – Will could scarcely suppress challenging this over-metaled oaf to a duel. But he did not know what Marguerite's relationship with the creature was, and clearly the man was following someone's orders.

Just as clearly, he might well have miscalculated Marguerite's reaction to meeting him. Will needed to retreat and reflect. Marguerite had certainly shown loyalty to the poet over him, a display that cut him like a scythe. Better now to just hand over his own note, be gone, and hope for the best in the end.

The footman took his proffered note with a grimace, ripped it into several pieces, and then, by some sleight of hand that Will was not able to follow, lit the pieces on fire! His note fragments blazed bright in the morning air – as bright as his hopes had been mere moments ago – and then were extinguished in a rain of ash.

At least he'd memorized the love sonnet included in the note, Will thought with remarkable patience. This was severe provocation, but the need for restraint still applied. He went back down the steps, turned, and said, 'You've elicited extraordinary self-control from me, man. That's your great fortune. It's my duty as the noble person you're not and never will be to warn you that my pacifism is not infinite.' Will cocked the feather of his hat at him, as if mockingly suggesting a duel, then went on his way. He heard the footman laughing softly at him as he walked on.

A couple of blocks away, where the footman could not have seen him any longer, Will opened the note he'd been given. The envelope was white, but the parchment inside was black, written on in a hand Will recognized as the poet's in an ink of bright red. Eight lines of iambic pentameter:

For Will
'Betrayer' is too kind a word for you:
I treated you just like a son and now
you try to steal my love! The night sky's blue
and dung bright gold when I ever allow
you near my love or me, ever again.
You blacken words like 'mentor,' 'ally,' 'friend.'
Go slither off, foul snake, your hole awaits,
midhell, red hot. Beware my love that hates.

Will walked for a while with the rapidity of a madman, as if physical exertion might sweat the now even-further-sharpened pain out of him. He zigged and zagged the teeming streets, walking a rough rectangle among Fylpot Lane, Thames Street, Petit Walas, and Tower Street, finally beginning a roundabout semicircle back toward Harp Lane and Mrs Garvey's. The day was as hot as his early sense of it had predicted, as if Hades were paying a visit by air as well as incident. By the time Will had caught his first glimpse of the sun-splashed Thames, the river filled with a variety of vessels flying multicolored nautical and national flags with an array of symbols on them, his gaudy attire was soaked through with sweat to a near uniform gray.

The hope that kept him half sane while on this most despondent walk was that the frontstep encounter had been the poet's doing alone, as the note seemed to be. Though Marguerite must have been trusting enough of – and sufficiently allied with – the poet to have mentioned Will's approach to her, perhaps she hadn't anticipated such jealous anger. Perhaps her ensuing protest against the poet's instructions to the footman had been so fervent that she was bound and gagged this very moment on one of the upper floors, weeping and moaning. Such a mental picture enraged Will so at a couple of points that he actually turned and headed back toward 39 Rood, but recollecting his lack of a sword and the miserable fact that Marguerite must have told the poet about him, he caught hold of himself and resumed his melancholy meander.

Another possibility, of course, was that the poet and Marguerite were of one mind concerning his brazenness, in which case he might as well pitch forward into the sizzling, fetid street now and lie there until he expired.

All his conjecture, whether of the more or less hopeful kind, was excruciating in another way. Despite his attraction to Marguerite, Will still felt a deep, near-filial bond with the poet, and the notion of the poet's hating him now added a deep lugubriousness to all his moods and thoughts. He'd neither considered nor expected that the poet would learn of Marguerite's effect on him so quickly, and that he had was a crushing reality.

Finally Will grew tired to the point of collapse from his fevered meanderings and developed a blazing thirst to go along with his bleak ruminations. He slumped down into a chair at an empty table at Baker & Thread's, a large, early-opening saloon in the Seething Lane section about two miles northeast of Mrs Garvey's.

Drying his face with a napkin, he ordered two foaming glasses of ale from a serving woman whose aging features were as wind-creased as a ship's prow.

'What size, sir?' she asked him.

'The largest size you've got. And a pudding to go with them.'

'What kind?'

'Any kind!' He was exasperated, but she was, after all, simply trying to take his order. 'Sweet,' he relented. 'Please make it sweet.'

And there Will was sitting nearly two hours later, in the same slouched-back posture as when he had given his order. His chair, barely in the shade when he'd first sat there, now took the full blaze of the sun, but he was too lost in despair to move. Will was halfway through his sixth drink now, all paid for in advance as he was not previously known to the establishment. The remains of a largely uneaten luncheon order of beef stew lay pushed aside on a plate to his left.

Just then a lumbering bear of a man approached him, tipped a rakishly perched ship captain's hat at him, and asked if he could join him. Will had observed the man gazing at him for a time from a table in the inner recesses of the tavern.

'Who would you be, sir?' he asked, glancing at him.

The man had a heavy, black beard, sunken, dark eyes, and deep jowls and was wearing a many-buttoned coat the dark gray wool of which was too thick for the weather. In the blurring effect of a blinding sun, Will thought he could indeed have been taken for the offspring of a bear and a human. Taking Will's question as an invitation, the man sat down with a force that jarred table, plates, and glasses. The serving woman cast a glance in their direction. Will pushed his own chair back from the table to contradict any sense of hospitality.

'Guy Liverpool's the name,' the man said heartily, passing a finely engraved calling card – it looked as if it had been sprinkled with gold dust – to Will, who didn't immediately take it. Liverpool then put the card faceup in the middle of the table and extended his beefy right hand toward Will instead. Will was tempted not to take the hand either, finding this man somehow repulsive, but after an insulting pause he did give a light grasp in return, calculating that the man would grow insistent if he refused. He glanced down at the card:

GUY LIVERPOOL
ALCHEMIST IN THE EMPLOY OF SIR JOHN DEE

No address, or other information of any sort.

Will gazed wonderingly up into the man's black eyes, shadowy and impossible to read with any acuteness in their hollows. He'd heard of Dee, of course, if not of this gargantuan employee; John Dee was the best-known alchemist in England, though a table visit from the king himself was not going to impress him much in his love-crushed state. Dee was a learned man of letters as well as an alchemist, and his personal library was reputed to hold tens of thousands of volumes and rival the Crown's. Dee was so celebrated – a sometime adviser to kings – that Will, upon reflection, could not readily accept that this man had a connection to him. Anyone could print a card!

Dee was also rumored to have flirted with practicing black arts. On at least one legendary occasion, the so-called Wormwood Convention, he and some associates had tried to summon supernatural beings. It had been written about in 'the press' (pamphlets at that time) and also been the subject of posted broadsheets. Some anonymous witnesses stated afterward that Dee had not cared about the nature of the beings summoned so much as that a being from another world appeared. Will, who'd heard about these notorious endeavors even in the countryside, was not attracted to a mind-set in which no difference was detected between angel and devil. He picked up the card and moved it back across the table to Liverpool. If the man was offended, his hirsute features did not show it. But his next words to Will were quite bold:

'What exactly would your occupation or education be, m'lad?' he asked, eyeing Will's attire, which, even with the grayish cast his perspiration had given it, was of aristocratic quality. 'This is an odd hour of the day not to be gainfully employed!'

Liverpool glanced up at the sun as if it were a moral censor. Then he took from a gaudy pocketbook that contrasted with his bleak coat two small lumps of metal, one gold and the other lead. He put them on the table, but then covered them with a handkerchief as the serving woman approached them; he sent her off with an order of Spanish wine for both of them, one that Will, tired of ale, did not protest.

After a pause, Will said, 'My situation would be none of your business.'

Now Liverpool's features did look hurt: his jaw dropped, his lips formed a compressed oval that resembled a pout, and his eyes narrowed to slits. He moved his chair back from the table as if recoiling from Will's comment, rattling the table and the dishes on it. Will noticed that nothing connected the chair to the table or the dishes, casting doubt as to how this ripple effect occurred. As he pondered this question, a chill crept up his spine.

He'd been attacked by the devil once today already, in the form of that miserable footman. Was it happening a second time? He was not going to sit here idly and suffer black wizardry, in the wake of a severed love. Yet, he was not quite ready to get up and leave.

'It's just that you look an unusually bright and energetic sort,' Liverpool said plaintively. 'Not meaning to offend. You look that even with all the liquor you have in you, at this ungodly-early hour. So, here I am, your humble servant Guy Liverpool, with a remarkable opportunity to present to you, and you're discouraging me. It beats the damnation out of me, I tell you.' Liverpool looked around as if he were desperate to escape this social encounter, so profound was the pain that Will had inflicted on him.

'Opportunity?' Will asked. He suspected Liverpool was at best just putting on some silly wizard's show for him.

But, he'd almost certainly blown up his acting job this morning, he reminded himself, which was the rationale for even being in London. And he wasn't returning to his father's house, he reminded himself more adamantly. Maybe he should hear the oaf out – to a point. 'If it's alchemy, my good Mr Liverpool, I have to caution you against bothering to speak. I am of noble lineage. A metal trade is, put bluntly, beneath me!'

Liverpool drew in a long, whistling breath, as if his patience were sorely tried, before replying, 'It is a sort of alchemy, lad, but not of the base-metal kind, you may relieve yourself on that point. I must rebuke you none-theless, though. Sir Dee, one of the great minds of this or any other time, is an alchemist. That's no mere craft, no sport for gutter guilds. Its source is a heightened spirit, same as any preacher's is. But please, let me not digress . . .'

Will yawned.

'Along the streets surrounding this tavern, in this very Seething Lane neighborhood sometimes referrred to as Exchange Alley, a new sort of alchemy is coming into our fair land. Slinking in and out of the darkest corners for now, but make no mistake that this is the port of entry and it is coming. From the Low Countries, the exalted spirit of which contradicts their names; note that *Holland*, for example, is but one added letter from spelling *Holy Land*.

'The public isn't aware of this tide yet, just a select few. Which I am inviting you to join. Visionaries who ride this tide using their energies, intellects, spirits, and – if I may be so presumptuous – fortunes, though only to what extent prudence dictates, will be richer and more venerated than the greatest of alchemists. The new alchemy requires no tools, no chemicals, no base metals. No fire or air. Only the vision to ride the tide and, if I may add this, a facility with numbers.'

'Numbers?' Will was not a mathematician, but he did enjoy working with the numbers involved in writing formal poetry.

'Yes, numbers.'

'What exactly is it you speak of, then?' Will asked in a more energetic voice than before.

'The stock market, my boy, the alchemy of which can perform miracles no metal ever forged can dream of.' Liverpool propelled his chair back to the table's edge. 'A place where a mere piece of paper is worth a pound one day and a hundred pounds the next. Certain streets are starting to seethe with it, on the sly, of course, as the king's agents are all about. It won't be lawful until the chancellor of the exchequer figures out a way for the king to get his fair share! Or more.

'This is the true alchemy, son! I'd like to introduce you to it. The alchemy of "all that glitters *is* gold." Where those in the know reap all that glows.'

Will allowed himself a minute to ponder the man's ravings.

Wealth could make a crucial difference to him, for whatever of his hopes remained with Marguerite after the morning's calamity, and for continued independence from his potentially vengeful father. And he *was* attracted to the number logic of poetry, the math of its rhythms, even if the crassness of commerce had never appealed to him. But he suppressed this reaction. He'd received no tangible evidence to support anything Liverpool had said, and John Dee was someone who had summoned demons with aplomb.

Liverpool, observing Will's hesitation, grew more expansive. 'If riches are not enough, son, ponder immortality. Eternal glory will come your way for being part of such a grand innovation as the stock market, which will reveal all preceding economies for the crudities they are. But then there's also the physical immortality this wealth can be used to find. Because, in the end, life's all in the blood, my boy. In the blood.'

'What?'

'If we can transform the nature of human blood in the same way the stock market is changing money, in the same way the ancient alchemists changed lead, we can live forever, man. Simple as that!'

Will's thoughts went to that sunlight, passing through his hand as if it weren't there, hours ago. Delineating the very atoms of his hand! Was a new sort of blood possible?

But he could not linger on such wild hopes, not with this bearish man still directing a heavy, burdensome stare at him, not on a day when the deepest romantic hope of his life had been dashed. He'd had enough dreams for one day.

Even as Liverpool removed his handkerchief to show that both metal lumps were gold now, something Will dismissed as magic, he got up without a further word and stalked away from the table, onto the crowded pavements. Ten feet away, he turned back toward Liverpool to say, 'I'm at Mrs. Garvey's in Harp Lane if you care to bring me actual evidence of this alchemy, more than rhetoric and scheming. Documents, for one. I am neither fool nor waif to be trifled with so. Good day, sir!'

'Expect me soon,' Liverpool replied in a booming voice. 'As lead turning to gold before your eyes has not been enough!' His eyes were already scanning the tavern's shadowy interior, as if for other prospects.

Will strolled briskly back now to Mrs Garvey's. He remained exhausted from walking, drinking, exasperating conversation, and heartache, but the prospect of deep rest in his bed overcame all his fatigue.

Though, one thing he couldn't bear much anymore was heat. He crossed abruptly over to the shady side of the street, diving for the shadows as though diving into an ocean of coolness . . . and collided with a man so muffled in black robes that he'd been indistinguishable from the surrounding shade.

'Excuse me,' Will said.

'*Prego*,' the dark-robed figure muttered under his breath, darting quickly into the even deeper black of an alley like an eel slithering into the shelter of a shoal. A flash of gold accompanied his retreat – a cross at his neck that Will recognized. It was the censorious priest from the party. Will shuddered at the coincidence as if a black cat had crossed his path, but then dismissed his reaction as an aftereffect of his earlier disappointment and his meeting with Guy Liverpool. It was little wonder that an Italian priest would lurk in the shadows. Catholicism was a serious offense here in England. The priest was the one who should be afraid. Not him.

7

The Octopus

Early the next morning I took the bouquet Monsieur Lutin had given me (kept fresh in a water glass during the night, then wrapped in wet paper towels and secured in my messenger bag) and started off for the Institut Océanographique. I took the rue l'Estrapade past the walled garden of the Lycée Henri IV, just one of the many buildings in Paris named for that monarch. Pausing to read the plaque on the school, I realized that Henri IV had ruled France when Will Hughes first came to Paris looking for Marguerite. As I continued down the street, I wondered what Paris had looked like then. Had Will walked on this very street, searching the crowded Latin Quarter for signs of his beloved Marguerite? Certainly now there were 'signs' everywhere – a tin cutout of a man cranking some kind of steaming cookpot, an enormous bronze key hanging from a locksmith's shop, the seal of Paris carved into the cornerstone of a building . . .

I stopped in front of that one to look closer at a ship riding the waves. Ships were all over Paris – even on the lampposts outside the Opera House – because of the crest. I had never thought it strange, but now that I knew about the *mer* fey I wondered if the symbol was a sign of their dominion over the city. I looked again at the card Monsieur Lutin had given me. *Madame La Pieuvre, Conservateur de Bibliothèque, Institut Océanographique.* My experience with librarians was limited to the draconian doyennes at the main branch of the New York Public Library, where I often went to research images for jewelry designs. I could only imagine how severe the head librarian at a prestigious Parisian institution might be.

So when I arrived at the building on the rue Saint-Jacques and found the cast-iron gates of the institute locked, I felt a guilty sense of relief enhanced by the forbidding appearance of the building. Twin gold seahorses stood sentinel on either side of the gate. Above them hovered an enormous gold octopus, its tentacles spread out as if to catch the unwary visitor. I quickly checked the library hours on the sign, saw I had an hour to kill, and decided to spend it walking in the nearby Luxembourg Gardens.

I sighed with relief as soon as I walked through the park gates and into the deep greenery of an allée of pollarded plane trees. Could there be anything more French than a double line of old trees evenly spaced? The proportions felt just right, as if the world were ordered. I felt my pace – and my heartbeat – slow. You couldn't rush through an allée; you had to stroll.

The shady allée opened onto a broad, green circular lawn, embraced by a double, curving balustrade topped with marble urns overflowing with purple, yellow, and white flowers. Flowers in the same palette bordered the lawn. I sighed aloud. It was like walking into an impressionist painting – specifically John Singer Sargent's *In the Luxembourg Gardens*. As a child I'd often fantasized about being able to walk into a favorite painting . . .

I came to an abrupt stop. On the other side of the lawn, in the shadows of the trees, stood a tall man in a long coat and a wide-brimmed hat. I caught my breath at the sight of him not *only* because he was clearly the same man I'd seen the night before last in the Square Viviani and yesterday in the Arènes de Lutèce, but also because seeing him here, while I'd been thinking about stepping into a painting, had jarred another memory. When I'd studied the painting of Saint-Julien-le-Pauvre, the one I believed Will had sent me, I had experienced a momentary vision of the painting as a live scene – and into that scene had walked a man in a long coat and a wide-brimmed hat. *This* man. Could it be that he was an emissary sent to lead me to the Summer Country? If so, he was a rather coy emissary. He'd already turned and was striding away from me.

I ran after him, into the paths that meandered around the playground and the beehives, bumping into old men playing *boules* and stylish women on their way to work. I caught a glimpse of him exiting the park through the south gates, but then I got held up by traffic crossing the rue Auguste Comte. By the time I got to the other side, I thought I'd lost him. The avenue de l'Observatoire was divided in the middle by a park punctuated by statues and bordered by rows of chestnut trees. I couldn't tell what side of the street he'd gone to, and he could be lurking behind any of the trees or statues . . . then I saw him – or his hat, actually – over a statue of a naked woman halfway down the block. He was walking south.

I followed, feeling almost as if he wanted me to, as if he

were leading me somewhere. But when I got to the end of the avenue de l'Observatoire, the man was gone. I looked all around and circled the Fontaine des Quatre Parties du Monde twice, even looking hard at the fountain to make sure he wasn't lurking behind a dolphin or rearing horse, and scanned the street. But no one was in sight but a uniformed guard standing at the locked gates of the Observatory.

I approached the guard smiling, trying to formulate the French to ask after a mysterious man in long coat and hat without seeming like a crazy American. Five minutes later the guard wore the same blank, slightly bored, and disdainful expression as when I'd approached him.

'Could I be of some assistance?' a man's voice from behind me asked in British-accented English.

I turned, relieved to hear my mother tongue, and found myself staring into a pair of deep-chocolate-brown eyes.

'Oh,' I said. 'You're at my hotel, aren't you?'

'Yes, I recognized you from breakfast. Roger Elden.' He held out a hand and I took it. His skin was warm and slightly damp.

'Garet James,' I replied.

'Are you attending the colloquium, too?'

'Colloquium?'

He pointed to a poster affixed to the gate. *Dark Matter: Theory and Observation*, it read in English and in French.

'Oh, no!' I assured him, thinking I'd had plenty of dealings with another sort of dark matter this past year. 'I thought I saw someone I knew heading this way and then he disappeared. I was trying to ask the guard if he'd seen him, but I'm afraid my French isn't very good.'

Briskly, Roger Elden asked me what my friend looked like ('He always wears a wide-brimmed hat to keep the sun off his face because he's . . . sensitive to the sun,' I improvised), then asked the guard in fluent French whether he had seen a man fitting that description. The guard became pleasant and voluble under Elden's interrogation, but the end result was that he hadn't seen any such man and had not let anyone into the Observatory all morning.

'I am the first one here, you see,' Elden explained to me. 'I am using the Observatory's library for some research. I am, how do you Americans say it, quite the nerd!'

I grinned. 'Hey, I'm a card-carrying nerd myself. I was on my way to the library at the Institut Océanographique.'

'Really? Are you a marine biologist?'

Too late I realized I now needed to come up with a lie. It had been fun for a minute to chat with a cute guy and not think about otherworldly assignations. Trying to stick to as much truth as I could, I told Roger Elden that I was researching aquatic shapes for a new line of jewelry. I showed him the watch I'd made. 'It's based on one I saw at the Musée des Arts et Métiers. I put a tower on the back of this one, but I might put an octopus on another.'

Realizing I was going on a bit and that the British astronomer (even cooler than Italian journalist!) was staring, I shut up.

'You know,' he said, looking up from the watch, 'if you like old gadgets, you'd love to see what they've got inside the Observatory. They've got fabulous antique equipment. If you like, I could show you one night *and* show you the night sky over Paris. I have permission to use the Observatory after hours.'

'Wow, that would be cool . . . can I get back to you on that? I'm not sure what my plans are.' *I might be embarking for the Land of Fairy anytime now*, I thought, but luckily didn't say. I *would* meet a guy with potential just when I was making some progress on my quest.

'Sure. I'm in Paris for the rest of the week. Call me if you have a night free.'

We exchanged cell phone numbers and went our separate ways – he into the Observatory, me back up the avenue de l'Observatoire to the Institut Océanographique. I approached the building a bit more cheerily this time. I had made a friend in Paris – a regular human friend – and a good-looking one at that. Even if this Madame La Pieuvre tossed me out on my ear, it wouldn't be the end of the world. When I stood in front of the black iron gates, though, I had another attack of nerves. The octopus seemed to be regarding me suspiciously as I opened the gate, as did the orange and white clown fish in the aquarium in the center of the high-ceilinged atrium. I checked in at an office in the lobby and was told that I'd find Madame La Pieuvre in the library on the third floor. The clerk seemed to be an ordinary human with only the average snootiness of a Parisian bureaucrat. Perhaps this wouldn't be so bad, I thought, walking three flights up the curving marble staircase. On the third-floor landing was a glass case displaying a huge nautilus shell and a small card that read SONNEZ ET ENTREZ. I rang the bell to the single door and, without waiting to be asked, turned the knob.

A long corridor lined with glass-fronted bookcases stretched in front of me. At the end an arch framed a small, sunlit alcove where a slender, silver-haired woman sat before a wooden card file. I waited a moment for her to turn and notice me, but she was apparently too absorbed in sorting through a stack of index cards. I started down the hall slowly to give her time to notice me, pausing to glance in the cases, which were full of the hollow shells of strange sea creatures – giant spiny sea urchins, spiraling pink conch shells, pale prickly starfish – none of which were more striking or exotic-looking than the woman who sat in the alcove. She was at least in her mid to late sixties if the polished silver of her hair was an indicator, but her oval face and high forehead were perfectly smooth and unlined even in the strong sunlight filling the nook where she sat. As I got closer I did notice a faint mottling on her skin that might have been freckles or liver spots, but which gave her the look of a rare spotted animal rather than an old woman. Her silver hair was swept back in an elegant twist fastened at the back with a mother-of-pearl clip in the shape of a nautilus shell. Her pearl-gray dress was cut from a heavy silk that shimmered in the sunlight like sharkskin. A matching cardigan was tied smartly over her narrow, sloping shoulders, her slim, bare arms tapering to long, narrow hands that plucked deftly at the stack of cards in front of her. When I was only a few feet away, she turned and, lowering a pair of half-moon reading glasses down her snub nose, smiled.

'May I help you?' she asked in English. I was used to Parisians figuring out I was American after a sampling of my spoken French, but I hadn't realized that the very sound of my footsteps was enough to announce my nationality.

'Are you Madame La Pieuvre?' I asked.

'*Oui*,' she answered with a sharp inhalation and a coquettish tilt of her wide, oval head.

'I have something for you.' I dug in my bag and retrieved Monsieur Lutin's bouquet – a bit worse for wear from its travel in my bag, but still fragrant.

Madame La Pieuvre closed her heavily lidded eyes and inhaled, producing two little dimples on either side of her nose. 'Ah, *Helianthemum ledifolium*! It reminds me of walking on Mt Olympus. And edelweiss!' She opened her eyes and, touching the white flower with the tip of a pink-polished nail, said, 'How kind of Monsieur Lutin to remember that it is the favorite of *ma chère amie*. How is the little man? I haven't seen him in ages. I am afraid he has become quite the recluse. You must be someone special for him to have given you an audience.' She pushed her glasses up the shallow ridge of her nose and peered at me. Magnified by the lenses, her dark eyes glistened like surf-polished pebbles.

'Jean Robin sent me to him . . . first I hung around Saint-Julien-le-Pauvre for a week before I got to see Jean Robin.' Too late I realized how petulant my voice sounded – like the impatient American of stereotypes – but Madame La Pieuvre only laughed and adjusted the sleeves of her sweater over her shoulders.

'Some sit their whole lives in Saint-Julien without a sign. The path to the Summer Country is harder and harder to find . . . some say it has vanished altogether.'

'But Jean Robin said that Will Hughes found it and left Paris in May.'

'Ah, so it's Will Hughes you're following,' she said, her black eyes glittering. 'He is a very charming man . . . when he was a *man* at least.'

'You knew him before?' I asked, wondering how old Madame La Pieuvre really was. And *what* she really was. Something about the way her hands moved restlessly across the surface of her desk was unnerving, and the sweater draped over her shoulders bunched oddly as she shrugged off my question.

'*Bien sûr*. I met him on his first trip to Paris when he was pursuing your ancestress Marguerite. He fancied himself desperately in love, although at the time I wondered which he was more in love with – Marguerite or the idea of immortality. I tried to tell him then how very dull eternity could be, but of course he wouldn't listen. I suppose you won't listen either if I tell you to give up your quest to find Will and the road to the Summer Country.'

'*Can* you tell me how to find the Summer Country?' I asked instead of answering her question. Or maybe that *was* my answer.

'I can put you in touch with those who can,' she said with a sad smile. 'Have a seat and I'll take a look through my files for the best contacts.'

She brushed the tips of her long, tapered fingers across the brass-plated cabinet drawers like a blind person reading braille. The gesture was somehow so private and sensual that I looked away, examining the alcove more closely. The coffered ceiling was painted in blue and gold, the wall painted pale turquoise, giving the light a faint subaqueous quality. In addition to the sea creatures behind glass, shells and pieces of coral were strewn across the surface of Madame La Pieuvre's desk. We might have been sitting at the bottom of the sea. Even the way the librarian languidly plucked at the file cabinet suggested a swimmer stroking through water. Mesmerized, I watched as she plucked one card, then another, then another . . .

I blinked. She was holding three cards in three separate hands. A fourth hand idly tucked a stray hair back into her chignon. She looked up and noticed me staring.

'I thought since you're practically family you wouldn't mind. I can work so much more quickly like this.'

'No, not at all. I didn't mean to stare.'

She trilled a long musical laugh. 'I'm a hybrid. In the old days the sea fairies intermarried with the sea creatures. My mother was a princess of Ys and my father was an octopus,' she told me as if explaining that she was half Irish and half Italian. 'The younger generation is ashamed of the offspring of these unions – the mermaids, selkies, undines, and other hybrids such as myself – but we serve a purpose. We're not too proud to mingle with what they call the lesser fey – the lumignon and the tree spirits . . . ah, like this one.'

She held up a card in one of her hands. It was covered in a series of stray pencil marks that looked like a child's scribbles. I moved closer and saw that the marks were moving, spreading across the page like tree branches.

'Sylvianne, queen of the tree spirits. She sent a traveler to the Summer Country a few years ago. She might be able to help you. The trick will be convincing *her* to do it. I will introduce you, but I can't guarantee anything.'

'Does she live far away?' I asked, wanting also to ask why I was being sent to a *tree* fairy when I'd been told to seek out a *sea* fairy, but then that seemed rude, as if I were criticizing Madame La Pieuvre for her race's failings.

'Oh, no, only a few blocks away, in the Luxembourg Gardens. In fact, why don't you come to my apartment this evening? It's right outside the garden and I could walk you over.'

She wrote down her address – 1 avenue de l'Observatoire – on a card while simultaneously reshelving two books and rearranging her hair.

'It's hardly a place for a young woman to walk alone after hours. We've had some . . . incidents lately . . . I'm afraid your vampire friend is not the only dangerous being to stalk the streets and parks of Paris after dark.'

8

A Cloaked Figure

Several hours later, just before midnight, Will found himself sitting at the same curbside table at Baker & Thread's where he'd spent the midday hours. As if it were his new home. Wandering late-night streets after a long daytime sleep, as despairing and morbid as dreamless sleep can be, he'd gone there almost out of a sense of routine, a sense that if this was where his mourning over Marguerite had begun, it might as well continue there.

He reflected back on his long sleep, as a rehearsal for the much longer sleep awaiting him if Marguerite did not somehow still save him with her love, for he had little doubt that he would do away with himself otherwise. His very atoms seemed to have slowed down in sleep with despair, for he'd felt an extraordinary numbness upon awakening. It seemed hours before he'd shaken his limbs enough to sit up in bed, and when he sat up, he was not certain if it was as a living being or as a ghost. But, eventually, he did resume a facsimile of wakefulness, and then he felt the need to soothe the blistering solitude of his hovel by leaving it.

Though B&T's was famed throughout London for the singular lateness of its hours, this was a Monday, and as

Will looked around, he saw it was nearly deserted. The pronounced shadow of a four-story stone building across the street enveloped his table in deep gray even amid the silver radiance of a full moon. Will could barely discern his own hands, resting atop the table.

Only one other patron seemed to be on the premises, a figure in a thick black cloak and shawl heavy for the season. He sat in a chair tilted back against a brick wall, well into the interior, his chair pitched so far back it looked as if he were trying to press his body into the brick. What need for protection motivated this posture? Will wondered. He tried to peer more closely at him but his back was turned and all Will could make out was his cloak . . . which suddenly reminded him of another cloaked figure – the Italian priest whom he'd run into on the street yesterday. Could the knave be following him?

The server, a graying matron who might have been the sister of his midday waitress, came to take his order, a tankard of ale with some bread and cheese. 'Say, do you know who that fellow is?' Will asked as she started to walk off. He gestured toward the cloaked figure.

'No, never saw him in here before.'

As she retreated, Will, angry at the thought he was being followed, stood and slowly approached the cloaked figure. Halfway across the room he considered retreating. He didn't have his sword with him. What if it was the Italian priest? What if he was a spy sent by his father to monitor his behavior and report back on his activities? Or worse – force him bodily to return to Swan Hall? Or even worse – what if he'd been hired by the poet to kill him for daring to court Marguerite? Will hesitated, nearly turned back. But his youthful aggressiveness got the best of him.

'Reveal yourself, knave,' he proclaimed in a voice that was loud enough to disguise the slight tremor he felt in his throat. 'I would know who my tormentor is!' He flicked the cloak away from the man's face . . . and nearly fell over with shock. His tongue didn't work and neither did his ears, for she – it was most definitely and gloriously a she! – had started to speak and he couldn't hear her. Only his eyes remained steady, eyes that had received an impression that rocked him, which would be the impression come to his mind whenever he thought of this moment afterward, which would be often.

A cloud in the night sky must have moved, for the water in her glass, perfectly clear a moment earlier, suddenly seethed with moonlight, with a silver brilliance so intense he had to look away. Alchemy again, he couldn't help but think, though by whom or what he had no idea.

Maybe love was alchemy, too, it occurred to him. Transmuting matter into spirit.

'Lord, it's you,' Marguerite was saying. 'The source of my troubles.'

Hearing this backwardly encouraging comment, Will felt almost invited to sit down at her table and did. He gazed at Marguerite, beside himself with hopefulness. Her blue-green eyes were perfect, so much so that they appeared otherworldly; so were all her oval features. Her expression was grim, befitting some reversal she'd apparently suffered, but there was hope for him, he couldn't stop thinking. Even to be the source of her troubles, he needed to have *some* significance.

She leaned toward him slightly. 'Did you follow

me here? Why? Didn't you get our note this morning?'

The harshness of her words, her tone, lashed his hopefulness with mockery. Especially painful was the word *our*. But he noted also her tears, her quivering lips, and decided not to fall into the trap of offended repartee; solicitude was a much better choice. There was some tangle of emotions and events here, and he needed to untangle it.

'As the heavens are my witness, I did not follow you here, beautiful lady,' Will said. 'I did receive the poet's message earlier, but it did not banish me from the streets or the taverns. Had it, and had I known it came from your heart as well as his, which I don't, I'd be at the bottom of the Thames right now, of my own free will. Draw your own conclusions as to why destiny has flung us together here tonight. I do!'

Marguerite stared into Will's fervent eyes. Once or twice her lips began moving as though she were going to speak again, but then she would lapse back into silence. Then, with no warning, she put her face in her hands and began to sob. Will moved in a gingerly way to console her, wondering if he might be so bold as to put an arm around her shoulders; which he did. He had only one, wildly exalting thought: *If I'm in her tears, I could be in her heart!*

She sobbed so long that the serving woman, having brought Will's ale to his table first, eventually brought the tankard over to him at his new table. When the sobs ceased, Marguerite looked back up at Will, took a deep breath, and said, 'The poet has lost his mind! When I was fool enough to tell him of our encounter at the party, he flew into a jealous rage. He said you would never have behaved so disloyally without encouragement from me, which of course is untrue. Then he insisted that he and I marry immediately, to ward off further transgressions from "evildoers," as he termed you. This though he is already married and famously so. When I cited the law and Christian decency to him, he said we were beyond the "iron rule" of both. As he put it, "Man's loving heart is the greatest savior this earth has seen, and poetry is that heart's scripture." Fancy words he has a gift for, and I was moved by them. But not enough to enter into a blasphemous marriage, for which refusal he then cast me out of what was suddenly "his" house.

'As I thought about all our circumstances during the very long afternoon, however, I forgave him his acrimony and cruel expulsion and decided to try to reconcile. After all, it was the depth of his passion that had incited his crazed proposal – alongside his deep sense of betrayal by you, if I may be so bold – and I *could* forgive him such passion, especially as he'd never laid a hand on me nor threatened to.

'But when I came back in the early evening, just a few hours ago, with an open heart and even a tiny regret for *not* marrying him, I was treated on the doorstep to the sound of a woman giggling from an open third-floor window, *our* bedroom window, followed by loud, raucous laughter from two. I hesitated but continued to the top step, from where I heard the poet shout mockingly, "*Marry me, marry me,*" in an affected high-pitched titter. Then he lowered his voice to an unnatural boom: "But I'm already married, you whore." The ensuing peal of laughter from whomever he was with was enough to frighten a crow from its senses, and indeed the sky then turned black with fleeing, cackling crows.

'I saw no need to go upstairs and surprise him and whatever creature he consorted with. The picture was clear. Who knows what the poet told the poor wretch? Certainly, he couldn't neglect his own loins for even a day.

'I have chosen to move on. The poet is morally worthless. His words may be beautiful, but they grow like fetid orchids in rank soil.'

Marguerite began to sob again, heaving sobs that would have made other heads in the tavern turn had anyone else been there. This time she was less alone in her sobs. She had collapsed as if unthinkingly into Will's arms; Will picked her up and put her in his lap, and there she stayed.

While holding Marguerite so, and the facts of her story, put Will infinitely ahead of where he had been just a few minutes earlier, he now began to lament his lack of prominence in her narrative. He seemed to have been a mere catalyst for tumult. After Marguerite regained her composure and returned to her chair, Will asked, 'What possessed you to tell the poet about me in the first place? You might have suspected he would see my approach as a betrayal.' Her answer might not be kind, but after his suffering he had a preference for truth over fantasy.

Marguerite wiped away tears with the delicate heel of her hand, then fastened her gaze upon him once more. Despite his trepidation, Will thrilled to this gaze, his blood tingling.

'We share everything, the poet and I,' she said. 'We are one. Or were until this evening.'

The first of these words were as well received as an

executioner's ax, but Will kept his composure. And waited. Hoped, in silence. For more words.

'Still, there is . . . maybe . . . another reason.'

'What?'

'There's no point denying that I did feel . . . something . . . when you approached me last evening. Nothing romantic, mind you,' she said sharply, eyeing his hand, being lifted as if to grasp hers. He withdrew it at once. 'Something, indeed, I've never felt before, and which I did puzzle over afterwards. It had nothing to do with heart or body, or even mind, but maybe it did have something to do with my soul – until I cut it off. Yet, I haven't quite suppressed it. I even felt it a bit this evening when I first saw you, to be honest. It's like a spiritual elevation, but so very fleeting.

'The poet by the way is not only a man of phenomenal eloquence, he also does have a spiritual awareness in him despite his lack of religion. Perhaps I thought I might find understanding for my sensation in speaking to him about it. But all I got was rage. And I can't *believe* the poet went so swiftly to another's arms when he was supposed to be so delirious with love for me as to be willing to defy law and tradition! Cannot!'

Marguerite began to weep again, but her tears were more shallow this time. That emboldened Will to grip her hand now. 'A spiritual bond is the deepest bond two people can have,' he whispered. 'We need not be church believers to recognize that our immortal souls are more important than anything else.'

Despite her grief, Marguerite's lips curled into the faintest of smiles. 'On whose authority do *you* speak so of souls?'

'"Man's loving heart is the savior,"' Will echoed the poet. He leaned toward Marguerite and brushed his lips against hers. She did not recoil.

The silver light in her glass seemed to have turned red suddenly, as if the love pulsing through Will's veins surged outside his body now, into the tavern's dense air, red atoms dancing amid colorless ones in joyous excitement, water reflecting his atomic dance the way a pond would sunlight.

Marguerite returned his kiss.

9

Edelweiss

Madame La Pieuvre had told me to arrive at her apartment at ten thirty that night, so I decided I'd better take an afternoon nap to be alert for my foray into the nighttime world of the Parisian fey. A wind had come up on my walk back along the rue l'Estrapade, rattling on their hinges the giant key and the man cranking his cookpot. It smelled like the sea and promised rain. The tree outside my window was thrashing when I lay down; the rain when it came sounded like a volley of gunfire. Instead of keeping me awake, though, the sound pulled me into a deep sleep and followed me into my dreams.

It was the swan dream again, the one I'd had dozens of times before, only it had never rained in this dream before. Now I stood at the edge of a pool watching a white swan gliding across rain-spattered water. Above the steady beat of the rain rose another sound – hoarse, bleating cries that rent the air as regularly and painfully as the lightning split the darkness. One of the flashes of lightning revealed a figure on the other side of the pool – a woman in a white nightgown that clung to her like a second skin, revealing each curve and swell of her lithe figure. Another flash of lightning bleached her figure to marble white and revealed her face . . . *my face*. I might have been staring at my own reflection *in* the water rather than looking across the water, only while I stood on the edge of the pool this doppelgänger was wading *into* it, the white cloth of her nightgown billowing up to the surface like a bank of clouds bearing the moon aloft through a dark storm-riven sky. She was making her way toward the white swan, who was swimming in circles, craning its neck to the sky and uttering those piteous, wild cries. It seemed to be circling some darker mass within the water, but it wasn't until the woman (Marguerite, I suddenly knew) reached out her arms and gathered up that darkness that I saw it take the shape of a black swan. As Marguerite cradled the limp creature in her arms, I smelled the acrid tang of sulfur and singed feathers on the air. The lightning flashed again, this time not just illuminating Marguerite and the swans, but striking them, making them glow incandescent. I expected Marguerite and the living white swan to burst into flame – or at least collapse and drown – but neither took any more notice of the lightning flashing through them than of the steady stream of rain falling over them. Suddenly I knew what I was watching. The white swan was one of Marguerite's sisters, but the black swan, its lover, was a mortal creature subject to the vicissitudes of flesh. Marguerite had come to comfort her sister because she knew the pain of seeing her mortal lover die. How many mortal lovers must she have seen grow old and die – or be struck down – in the long centuries of her existence? I felt her weariness – her grief – as she held the dead swan in her arms and lay its long neck against her breast. The white swan twined its own long neck around its lover's, then both it and Marguerite keened their sorrow into the rain. Their voices sluiced through my breastbone so sharply I awoke, shivering in my darkened bedroom at the Hôtel des Grandes Écoles. The rain had come into the room through the open window, soaking the sheets twisted around my legs. For a moment I thought it was the dead swan wrapped around my limbs, dragging me down into the dark water.

The rain had stopped by the time I reached the avenue de l'Observatoire, but flashes of lightning still lit up the Paris skyline, and I could hear the steady drip of water falling from the trees in the park as I walked along the boulevard Saint-Michel. The garden gates, I saw as I rounded the corner of the rue Auguste Comte, were locked. How did Madame La Pieuvre plan to 'walk me over'? Was the Luxembourg like New York's Gramercy Park in that the surrounding apartment tenants had a key to the park? No. 1 avenue de l'Observatoire, a lovely beaux arts building with marble caryatids and columns framing the windows, was right across the street. Looking up, I saw that it was topped by an octagonal tower that stood out against the night sky like an echo of the Observatory dome at the end of the street. I wondered if Roger Elden was there now, watching the sky. I felt for my cell phone in my pocket. I was half tempted to call him and ask for that after-hours tour he'd offered. Gazing at the night sky seemed a lot safer right now than going to meet the queen of the forest in a locked park.

But, no, Madame La Pieuvre was expecting me; I couldn't disappoint her. As I started to cross the street, a movement on my right in the shadow of the park's iron gates caught my eye. I glanced in its direction and a shadow detached itself from the gloom – a shadow shaped like a man in a long coat and a wide-brimmed hat.

'Hey!' I called, throwing all caution to the wind. This was the fourth time I'd seen this guy. Clearly he was following me. At the sound of my voice the shape rippled, bunched, and then shot upward. I froze, watching the man vault straight up and over the high spiked gates. The only person I'd ever seen move like that was Will Hughes, but it couldn't be Will, could it? I'd seen him in the daylight. And why would Will flee from me? Unable to answer that question – or any of my questions – I gave up staring at the locked gates and crossed the street. Maybe Madame La Pieuvre would have answers. At least she might have a key.

I rang the bell beside Madame La Pieuvre's name and was rung into an elegant courtyard full of potted camellias. Gas lamps added to the air of nineteenth-century Paris. I might have been paying a visit to Dumas's famous courtesan instead of a librarian. An octopus-librarian, I reminded myself as the ornate cast-iron elevator carried me up to the sixth floor.

The elevator let me out on a marble landing also full of potted plants. In addition to the camellias there were azaleas, miniature roses, orchids, plumeria, bougainvillea, and other, exotic flowers I couldn't identify. They were all in shades of coral, shell pink, and bone white so that I felt as though I might be under the sea. The splash of water added to that impression. I followed the sound through wide-open doors into a foyer with a marble fountain of a naked nymph held aloft by a fish-tailed triton. The statue was so old that the fingers of the triton grasping the nymph's hip had all but merged with her flesh. The nymph's face was worn down to the smoothness of a mask. Still, the panic in her eyes was as immediate as if she had only this moment been seized. I had an urge to intervene . . . to save her . . . only in the few seconds I had looked into her eyes I was already unsure if what I saw there was panic or excitement. While one of her hands pushed the lustful triton's face away, the other gripped his muscular thigh, her fingers taut against his scaly flesh.

'My dear friend Gianni had a trick for capturing the moment of *capture,* did he not?' a voice behind me inquired.

I turned and found Madame La Pieuvre in a floor-length, sea-green caftan embroidered with white tentacles. She held a glass of champagne in one hand, a bottle in another, and an empty glass in a third. A fourth arm snaked out from behind her back and gently caressed the nymph's marble face. 'I recall the young girl who posed for this. She was half in love with Gian Lorenzo and half frightened of him. I used to say that he seduced his models and then abandoned them just to give them this conflicted look on their faces.'

'Gian Lorenzo?' I asked. 'Do you mean Gian Lorenzo Ber—'

'Please don't get Octavia started on all the famous artists she's known,' a woman's voice called from another room. 'You'll never make your appointment in the Luxembourg.'

Madame La Pieuvre smiled and, leaning closer to me, whispered, 'She's jealous of the ones who painted me nude. But Adele is right. You have a rendezvous in the park at midnight and I have a few particulars to share with you. Come . . .' She draped one arm around my shoulders and steered me in the direction from which the second voice had come. We entered an elegant salon furnished in gilt and silk-upholstered Louis Quatorze furniture and thick Persian rugs, all in shades of blue and green that recalled the sea. Floor-to-ceiling windows were open to a terrace affording a view of the Luxembourg and, in the distance, the Eiffel Tower lit up like a Roman candle. I was so taken by the view that I didn't immediately notice the petite woman seated in a deep, silk-upholstered bergère armchair. When I did look at her, I gave a little start of surprise. It was Madame Weiss, the proprietor of the Hôtel des Grandes Écoles.

'I believe you've met Adele before, *oui*?' Madame La Pieuvre asked, pushing me gently forward with one arm while pouring champagne into a glass with another.

'I didn't realize' – I faltered awkwardly as Madame La Pieuvre handed a glass to me while refilling Madame Weiss's glass and casually draping an arm over her friend's shoulder – 'that you were acquainted with the fey, Madame Weiss. Did my mother know when she stayed with you?'

'Please call me Adele . . . and, yes, your mother knew of my . . . *liaisons*. Our families were long acquainted. During the war your grandmother and my mother worked in the Resistance together. And it was your mother who introduced me to Octavia.' Adele smiled lovingly at Madame La Pieuvre – a look that suddenly recalled to me the conflicted longing in the marble nymph's eyes. But why conflicted? Octavia La Pieuvre looked gentle and refined –

no rapacious triton. It wasn't fear that was mixed with Adele's love, though; it was sadness. When I looked back at Madame La Pieuvre, I saw that same sadness reflected in her dark obsidian eyes. But when she trained her eyes back on me, the sadness vanished.

'Adele's family has long been friends to the Watchtower – as have my people despite the occasional differences of opinion. The more snobbish of the *mer* fey looked down on Marguerite for choosing to become mortal, but I have always respected her choice. She did it out of love—'

'And look what she got for it!' Adele interrupted angrily. 'That silly boy became a vampire just as she became mortal. So after all that they still couldn't be together.'

'Yes, it was regrettable that Marguerite sacrificed her immortality for a lover who was clearly not worthy of her love *at the time*. But I have noticed as the years have gone by that Will Hughes shows signs of maturing into the kind of man who might someday be worthy of the Watchtower.'

As Madame La Pieuvre spoke, her eyes remained on me, but one of her hands slipped into Adele's lap to grasp her hand. I reflected that their version of the Will and Marguerite story was not *exactly* as Will had related it to me, but I didn't think it prudent to get in the middle of their argument.

'If he were worthy, would he have taken the box from Garet and abandoned her?' Adele demanded.

'How—?' I began, appalled that the details of my love life were public knowledge. But the two women ignored me.

'Clearly he loves her. Why else would he send her a sign

to join him on the road to the Summer Country? Perhaps he only wished to spare her the difficulty of the initial stages of the journey.'

Madame Weiss made an exasperated sound. 'Typical of you immortals – always thinking you know what's best for us poor weak humans . . .'

As Adele continued, complaining about the high-handed approach of supernatural beings to mortals, I realized that the women weren't really talking about me and Will anymore – they were enacting some old conflict in their own relationship. I could see the women's love for each other beneath the anger in the way Madame Weiss looked into Madame La Pieuvre's eyes and in the way Madame La Pieuvre's hands roved restlessly over her lover's hair and arms, trying to soothe her. Clearly, that one of them had two arms and the other had eight was not the problem. The problem was that one of them, Adele Weiss, would age and die and the other, Octavia La Pieuvre, would live forever. At first I thought that perhaps Madame Weiss had begged Octavia to make her immortal – as Will had told me he had begged Marguerite – but as I listened I realized it was the opposite. Madame La Pieuvre was offering to end her life with her Adele.

'I could go with Garet to the Summer Country and ask *her* to make me mortal. Then we could age and die to-gether. It's what I've always wanted,' Madame La Pieuvre said, turning to me, her black eyes glistening with unshed tears, 'to end my long life with the person I love the most.'

Adele opened her mouth to say something but Octavia placed a long finger on her lips. 'It might be our only chance, darling. I'm sure that Garet is meant to make the

journey. I could go with her . . . *let* me go with her, *please!*'
Then, turning to me: 'That is, if you don't mind, my dear.
I promise that I can be of help to you along the way as
guide and interpreter.'

'I suppose . . .,' I began, but stopped when I saw Adele's
tear-streaked face. She shook her head, the droop of her
shoulders expressing a resignation that seemed habitual.

'I see there's nothing I can say to stop you,' Adele said
to Octavia. 'And you . . .' Adele turned to me. 'I just hope
that the creature you find at the end of the road is worth
it.'

Then Adele got up, smoothed her skirt, and walked out
of the room.

'*Mon petit Edelweiss!*' Octavia murmured. Several of
her arms drifted in Adele's direction as she left, but didn't
touch her. One drifted to her own hair and patted her
already immaculate chignon, another plucked a white
blossom from the bouquet that I'd brought her from
Monsieur Lutin earlier today. She brought it to her snub
nose, closed her eyes, inhaled the sweet scent, then put the
blossom back into the bouquet.

'Please don't mind Adele. It pains her to think of me
giving up a second of my life for her sake, but she simply
doesn't know how very wearing immortality is. It isn't for
her sake alone that I seek a release from it, but it *would*
give me great pleasure to end my life with hers.'

'Can't you just . . .' I faltered, unsure how to delicately
suggest suicide.

'Even if I destroyed this fleshly body, the bit of myself
that is fey would linger in bodiless form for all eternity.'
Octavia leaned closer to me, her black eyes glittering and

all her arms floating in the air around her like the ethereal spirits she spoke of. 'I once encountered a bodiless fey spirit in the forest of Brocéliande – a poor tortured creature who had killed herself for love of a mortal. Her cries were enough to tear your heart in two. No, what I crave is the release of mortal death while holding the hand of my beloved.'

Octavia held out the hand that had held the white edelweiss blossom, her fingers cupped as if she still held the flower, then held out another, and another, until eight empty hands were before me, each one begging for one thing.

'Of course,' I said, unable to resist such an entreaty. 'I'd be honored to have your company on the journey.'

10

Lightning

The next few weeks were the most glorious of Will's life. He saw Marguerite nearly every day, and her insistence that their relationship was to be viewed as 'spiritual,' not 'romantic,' seemed to be honored more in the breach than the observance. Or, as Marguerite would occasionally concede, amorousness could have spirituality at its core, and so could Eros.

On a few difficult occasions he was a mere confidant, supporting her in her not-yet-completely-concluded separation from the poet. Those days had their bitterness, but he managed the bravest face possible while with her. And he managed to restore his own spirits afterward, though with a difficulty he compared to ascending the slick, mossy walls of a well.

Their love had moments of ecstasy that he'd never experienced before and hadn't imagined possible. Such moments did not flow only from lovemaking; they could arise from the most innocent of gestures, such as smiling deeply at one another upon first meeting, or holding hands on a London street shadowy enough to make that safe. Or from a few inspired words.

One thread of uncertainty did, however, run through

and occasionally threaten to tear this tapestry of love. Will was never quite sure to what degree Marguerite was leaving the poet for him, or to what degree she'd been *tossed* by the poet to him. Not as a favor to him, of course, but in the sense that Marguerite may simply have been taking shelter from their terrible fight. She spoke now of the depth of her spiritual feeling for Will – how even the poet conceded the depth of Will's soul – but both poet *and* Marguerite had signed off on the foul sentry's greeting and that glacially cold note . . . where were Will's spiritual qualities then?

Subtly but discernibly, Will could feel himself once or twice holding back from complete immersion in love for Marguerite. No doubt this was a transitional sensation – difficult nuances were to be expected – but he did hold back in moments, if anything because of fear. The ecstasy had been real, but so had been the initial pain, the suddenness of coming together, the change in his life so sharp that it was naturally coupled with insecurity. In rare moments, he even looked for solace at other women. But those moments were few and far between.

This intense love affair lasted for about three weeks. Then came an event so powerful that it changed everything between them. Will was to remember the event as if it were part of his mind since the womb.

They had spent an idyllic afternoon in a meadow by a pond, about twenty miles north of London, where they had ridden on horseback with picnic lunches. The whole afternoon was as serene as any since Eden, Will fancied. The moment he recollected best was when he glanced at the pond after one prolonged and melting embrace and saw two swans swimming side by side, their necks amorously intertwined as if inspired by Will and Marguerite's example. The swans were under an overhang of foliage that shadowed the sun-ribboned water, but Will was sure of what he saw. The male swan was black and the female white, despite the rarity of the former. When he pointed out the near miraculous coupling to Marguerite, suspecting she'd respond to it, as he had, as an omen of their improbable love, instead her forehead creased with worry, her eyes darkened, and she looked away from him without a word.

'What's the matter?' he asked, taking her hand.

She looked back at him, her countenance still cloudy. 'These swans remind me of an old family . . . tradition. A story of our founding.'

'Really? Another coincidence that convinces me we were indeed meant for each other. There is a story about a swan in my family as well.'

Instead of receiving this news with joy, Marguerite turned pale. 'What is the story?'

'Oh, it's a child's fairy tale, to be sure, about a mysterious and beautiful maiden who fell in love with one of my ancestors and married him on the condition that he never follow her to the water at sunset. Of course he does – what man wouldn't suspect some adulterous dalliance? – and he surprised her in the moment of turning into a swan. At the sight of him she began to rise from the pool, but rather than lose her forever, he shot her down with an arrow.'

'How cruel!' Marguerite exclaimed through trembling lips.

'He only meant to keep her from fleeing,' Will explained – although in truth this part of the story had always bothered him as well. 'She didn't die, but she did leave him. She promised, though, that she and her kind would always look over him and his descendants, see?' Will pulled out the signet ring he still wore on a chain around his neck and showed Marguerite his family crest. She touched the carved insignia gingerly with her fingertips as if the metal were hot.

'Hughes . . . it's so common a name,' she murmured. 'I didn't realize . . .'

'Realize what, darling?'

But she only shook her head. 'You were right. This . . . *coincidence* explains so much. We were meant to meet . . . why fight it?' She was trembling so hard that Will took her in his arms to warm her, but it took a long time to dispel the chill from her flesh.

They did not return to the city that night. It was the first time, Will realized with no small excitement and pleasure, that Marguerite had been willing to stay with him overnight. Will could not help but attribute her willingness to the 'coincidence of the swans,' as he put it to himself. For the first time since he'd fled his ancestral home, he blessed his lineage.

Marguerite led them to a tavern with rooms to let not far from the pond, a place she denied any previous experience with (except having heard of it), though in that regard Will suspected otherwise. But her past was her business. He still preferred not to ask too many questions. Their glorious future together was what mattered.

They dined surprisingly well, given the rural setting, and then, tired from the heat and love of the afternoon, retired early. The sky was now a perfect pitch of lavender outside their room's window, which looked out from the rear of the tavern onto a straggly yard, then a dense stand of maple trees amid tangled underbrush. The unusual light revealed heavy clouds moving in, the air growing damp and close with impending storm. Will and Marguerite embraced as they stretched out on the narrow bed, as if sheltering from the weather. They'd managed to doze off lightly when a thunderclap severe enough to shake the tavern's timbers brought them to sitting up straight. Then a few lightning-to-thunder sequences erupted in quick succession, followed by a fusillade of rain against the bark-shingled roof, volleylike, with a sort of military precision. It sounded to Will as if water might be warring on the earth, an audacious attempt at overthrowing one element by another. Then came another bolt of lightning, not followed by thunder but instead by a piercing cry from the woods outside, perhaps from an animal injured by the lightning bolt, or claw, or teeth, or knife.

Their room was nearly pitch-black now. Marguerite got up clutching her nightgown, then lit the candle on their night table and brought it over to the window, though its glow was not going to penetrate the darkness very far. Beyond the yard, the window looked out on impenetrable obscurity. Will got up as well but more lethargically, not particularly moved by the mayhem of the storm or its possible victim, and came to stand by Marguerite's shoulder. The next bolt, shimmering silver as if a large diamond in the sky had exploded into splinters, illumined nothing below but the yard's high grass.

A second cry pierced the air. Marguerite turned to Will and said, 'I've got to go see what that is.'

In the flash following next, her face struck him as incomparably beautiful. The thunder that exploded was so loud Will had to repeat his response. 'I'll go, too,' he told her, though he was still naked. 'It's too dangerous out there.'

'Silly boy. One of us must stay up here and keep a lookout for the other. Stay by the window. Just in case I wind up screaming, too.'

Will put a restraining hand on Marguerite's arm, but she spun away from him and was out the door and down the stairs before he could even find the chair over which he'd draped his clothes. When he heard her open the yard door, he decided he'd better stay at the window to watch her. Marguerite strode out into the center of the yard, her nightdress billowing about her in a warm wind, like the wild wings of an uncertain angel. She glanced around closely in the thick grass; then, apparently having seen nothing in the yard, peered into the woods.

'Be careful, please!' Will called down to her, with little confidence she could hear him. The wind was blowing the leaves in the woods at an upward angle now, as if it originated in some vent in the earth, and likely it had cast his words away from her.

A third cry tortured the air. Marguerite must have had a sense of where it came from for she grew more focused in her gaze, looking at the woods to her left. She took three steps in that direction, and then Will saw, to his horror, a bolt flash only about twenty feet over her head and plunge toward the ground. The bolt had three vertical lines of sizzle within it that showered sparks everywhere. One of the lines struck Marguerite in the head and made her entire body luminescent.

Will screamed at the top of his lungs, no heed to propriety or anything else, expecting Marguerite to become a statue of char, to disintegrate. But she didn't; she barely broke stride, her only reaction a brief nod as if she'd shaken off an unpleasant sensation. She continued into the woods.

Modesty never entered Will's mind as he ran out of the room, down the stairs, and across the yard into the woods. At first he was relieved *not* to find her, as that proved she hadn't died right on the spot, but as he flailed deeper into the woods without coming upon her, he feared that the lightning had struck her senseless and that she was now wandering in the woods out of her mind. Anything might happen to her . . . she might wander down to the pond and drown!

At that thought he increased his speed, running in the direction of the pond, but before he could reach the water, he collided with the object of his search . . . and was repelled by a cataclysmic shock some ten feet backward through the air and hard into a tree, knocking him down.

'Will!' Marguerite cried, running to him.

He looked up and thought he must have died and gone to heaven. Surely the creature crouched above him was an angel. Her body was luminescent, her veins glowing with liquid fire, her face as radiant as a full moon.

'What are you?' he asked when he'd regained the breath to speak and realized he wasn't dead. 'What in the world – or outside of it – *are* you?'

11

Queen of the Woods

'There are a few things you should know about Sylvianne before you meet her,' Madame La Pieuvre told me as we crossed the street to the Luxembourg. Although the night was warm, she had thrown a dark cloak over her shoulders that she clutched at with one of her long, thin hands. She lifted her head to the sky and a spatter of raindrops fell onto her face. It was quite dry where I walked a few feet beside her. 'Sylvianne is a very old spirit. She was here when the *mer* fey arrived from Ys. At first there was fighting. I'm afraid that the *mer* fey are not the most tolerant of creatures. They took control of the islands in the Seine and tried to evict the tree spirits from their homes. But the tree folk can be quite *tenacious*. They become attached to places and the trees that grow there. Since the *mer* fey couldn't kill the tree folk themselves, they cut down the trees that were their homes. In retaliation the tree folk kidnapped and tortured the humans who were dear to the *mer* fey.'

'That's awful,' I said, recalling the man I'd seen leap the fence into the park. Was he one of the tree fey – or one of their human companions? Either possibility was not reassuring. I shivered. The night felt suddenly cold to me and I wished I had Madame La Pieuvre's cloak even though hers was now soaked with the rain that fell only on her – as if she were drawing water from the sky. Perhaps this was her personal hydration system. When we reached the tall iron gates to the park, Madame La Pieuvre produced a large, heavy key and fit it into the lock. I touched my hand to hers – it felt like old velvet worn down to the nap and was slightly moist. 'Do they still do that?' I asked. 'Do they still torture humans?'

Madame La Pieuvre shook her head, scattering raindrops, without meeting my eye. 'They agreed not to as part of the Trêve de Gui – the Mistletoe Truce, so called for the sprig of mistletoe held over the heads of the rulers of each people – that was signed between the *mer* fey and the tree folk. But by then the tree folk had acquired a taste for human company. They like to *play* with them . . .' She looked up, suddenly apologetic. I think she had forgotten for a moment that I was human. 'Their play is really quite harmless . . . usually. I believe most of their human companions *enjoy* it. But they can be a little . . . rough. I will tell them that you're under my protection and that should keep them in line . . . only . . .'

'Only what?'

'Well, they sometimes take a perverse pleasure in appropriating the favorites of the *mer* fey.'

'Oh,' I said, laughing. 'That shouldn't be a problem. I'm no one's favorite.'

'Oh, my dear,' Madame La Pieuvre said, stroking my cheek with her velvet hand, 'you're Will Hughes's favorite, and that will particularly annoy Sylvianne as I believe she had *une petite* crush on him when he first came to Paris and is still angry at losing him to Marguerite. Let's just hope that she's gotten over him.'

As she turned the key, I said I hoped so, too. After all, I added to myself, it had been over four hundred years. Even Will's charms couldn't linger that long. Could they?

As we stepped into the park, I noticed that we passed through a shimmering curtain of violet mist, much like the haze I'd seen in the Square Viviani when Jean Robin's tree had opened up for me.

'Fairy shroud,' Madame La Pieuvre informed me when she saw me looking back. 'To keep unauthorized mortals from witnessing fey activity. From outside, the park appears empty.'

So far it appeared empty from the inside. We were walking along the allée of pollarded plane trees, the only sound the rustle of the heavy leaves. With the light of the city blocked by the fairy shroud, the park was as dark as the middle of a primeval forest. I looked up toward the sky, but the leaf canopy was so dense it would have blocked any moonlight or starlight even if the park hadn't been covered by fairy shroud. I couldn't see the leaves overhead, but I could hear them, layers upon layers of damp leaves rustling in the breeze, making a sound like running water. The sound stirred something in me, a feeling that made my heart race, but whether with fear or excitement I wasn't sure.

It's just the Jardin du Luxembourg, I told myself. *You walked in this allée earlier today and admired how ordered the trees were . . .*

A leaf brushed my face and I brushed it away. My hand grazed rough bark . . . but we were walking down the center of the allée, weren't we? How had this slim sapling broken through the neatly ordered line of pollarded trees? Had we strayed from the allée?

I turned to look back toward the park gates, and a thick vine dropped over my shoulder.

A vine? In the meticulously manicured and landscaped Luxembourg Gardens?

Then I felt the soft velvet of Madame La Pieuvre's hand gently but firmly unwrapping the vine from around my arm. To my relief I could see her even in the dark. Her round face glowed softly against the backdrop of tangled forest.

'The trees—,' I began, but she silenced me by placing a damp velvety finger on my lips.

'They're listening,' she whispered. Placing one of her fingers to her own lips, she simultaneously untangled three more vines that had insinuated themselves around my arms and neck. She wrapped one of her arms firmly around my waist and propelled me down the allée – or at least down what used to be the allée. By the faint phosphorescent glow of Madame La Pieuvre's skin, I could see now that the ordered line of trees had grown – in hours – into a dense and wild forest. The tree trunks here were twisted and gnarled, like coastal trees that had grown in a steady wind, and they were festooned with heavy vines looping down into the path. If not for Madame La Pieuvre's many hands fending them off, I would have gotten tangled in them. Even the ground was no longer the level, dusty path I'd walked on earlier today. Roots buckled the earth and twisted beneath my feet. I tripped over one and would have fallen, but for Madame La Pieuvre's firm, many-handed grip. She scooped me up and carried me over the last few yards of woods into an open clearing where she dumped me onto the soft lawn.

'That patch becomes more unruly every year,' she said, smoothing her hair and straightening her cloak while helping me to my feet. 'The *mer* fey used to believe that pollarding the trees would keep them from breaking free at night, but it only makes them angry and more fractious. Many of the old allées have become impassable at night.'

I looked back at the dense stand of trees and wondered how we were going to get out of the park, but I didn't have time to ponder that question because Madame La Pieuvre was purposefully striding across the lawn toward the statue of Diana, which glowed with the same phosphorescent light as Madame La Pieuvre emitted. The open sky above the park, although still veiled by the iridescent fairy shroud, also let in some light – a flickering, multicolored spangle that I guessed came from the Eiffel Tower in the north, and two yellow beacons from the south, like twin cat eyes, which came from the direction of the avenue de l'Observatoire. I was going to ask Madame La Pieuvre about the lights, but when I reached her, I was distracted by the display in front of the statue.

A dozen candles had been lit at the statue's base, explaining why it glowed, as well as heaps of flowers, fruit, and small glasses of bitter-smelling, green liquid that cast an emerald glow on the base of the statue.

'Who left these?' I asked.

'Worshippers of the tree spirits,' she said, kneeling

before the statue and lifting a rose to her nose. 'There have been cults dedicated to the tree spirits here since before the Romans came. They simply changed their names to Diana and Faunus and Silenus so that the Romans would let them be. When the Christians gained power, they laid their offerings and lit their candles to the Virgin Mary and the saints. During the Terror they hid their relics in the catacombs. In this day and age they call themselves Wiccans and neo-pagans and come to places where the tree spirits still hold rule.'

Madame La Pieuvre stood and looked around her. Other lights were flickering at the edges of the shrubbery. I stared at one candle shrine before a statue of a dancing faun. The face of the faun in the flickering candlelight seemed to be laughing. As if in response to my thought, I heard a scrap of laughter rise in the air from the trees behind me – *Had there been trees there when I walked in the park earlier?* – and then an answering peal of hilarity from deep within the gardens near the carousel. Something white flashed in the onyx-green woods and someone – or *something* – shrieked.

'So it's just people,' I said, picturing young girls in the white, embroidered camisoles and slips sold in flea markets and young, goateed boys in skinny jeans and vintage vests – the type of students and tourists that filled the cafés and streets of the Latin Quarter – wandering the dark park in search of an authentic Parisian adventure.

'People,' Madame La Pieuvre replied. 'And those that feed off them. Come . . .' She wrapped two of her arms around me tightly and pulled me toward the Grand Basin.

'Sylvianne holds court at the Medici Fountain. Stay close to me.'

We skirted the Grand Basin, which lay eerily calm in the center of all the moving foliage, and the Luxembourg Palace – or at least I assumed the palace still stood where I had seen it this morning. Drapes of violet and mauve fog fell over it now.

'To shield the guards from what's happening in the park,' Madame La Pieuvre answered my unasked question. We followed a narrow path – narrower than I recalled these paths being – past a statue of Silenus cavorting with a bevy of naked nymphs. More candles, flowers, and glasses of green liquid stood around this statue. The green-tinged candlelight gave the satyr's face an even more salacious leer than usual.

'These statues,' I asked as we approached a long, rectangular basin of lily-pad-covered water, 'are they here because this is a favorite place of the tree folk – or do the tree folk frequent the park because of the statues?'

'A little of both,' Madame La Pieuvre replied. 'Humans often erect shrines and statues of pagan gods in places where they've glimpsed . . . well, something they didn't understand. And then the fey are drawn to these places. They like nothing more than to be flattered in marble and bronze.' She gestured toward the group of statues at the end of the long basin. Candles flickering in a shallow grotto illuminated a tarnished bronze giant hovering over two slim white figures carved from marble.

'The Cyclops Polyphemus surprising the lovers Galatea and Acis,' Madame La Pieuvre informed in a tour guide's voice. 'Do you know the story?'

'A little . . . from art history class. Polyphemus loved Galatea, but Galatea loved Acis, right? It doesn't look good for poor little Acis.'

'Polyphemus killed him,' Madame La Pieuvre said, the tour guide's smooth voice replaced by an anguished rasp. 'Tore him limb from limb in front of poor Galatea's eyes. She poured her tears into his blood and begged the gods to prolong his life in one form or another. You see, she knew she would live forever and she couldn't bear to live an eternity without him.'

I glanced at Madame La Pieuvre. Her face glistened with moisture, but whether from tears or the rain she drew to herself, I couldn't tell.

'The gods took pity and turned Acis into a river. It flows past Mt Aetna in Sicily, where Galatea still resides.'

I wanted to ask which gods these were she spoke of – were they another species of fey or some higher power? – but we were interrupted by a trilling voice that seemed to come from the trees above us.

'What a lovely story, Octavia. And told with such *emotion*! To think some say the *mer* fey are cold-blooded! But then you're only half fey, aren't you, *ma chère*. Your molluscan father must have been quite passionate.'

I turned to find the source of the voice – and to turn away from Madame La Pieuvre's inky blush – but nothing was behind us but a stand of slender poplars swaying in the breeze. But one, I noticed, was swaying in a different direction from the others. I stepped closer and stared at the slender, silver-barked form until a silver-skinned face emerged from the bark and slim arms twined out of the branches. The tree woman stepped forward gingerly – I would almost say *woodenly* if she hadn't had such an air of refinement about her – on long, bark-sheathed legs. Her feet were covered in roots, and leaves sprouted from her fingertips. Instead of hair, long branches swayed from her scalp, polished green leaves quaking as she laughed at the expression on my face.

'Have you never seen a dryad, human?' the tree woman asked in a tinkling voice that sounded like wind rustling through leaves.

'I've met a number of fairies, but never one like you,' I admitted. 'And one man who's been turned into a tree.'

'Ah, you must mean Jean Robin. He's a different sort of thing altogether. He was once human. I, I assure you, have *never* been human.' She pronounced the word *human* with a distinct curl of her full, resin-slick lips, making sure to distinguish herself from a race she clearly thought little of. She needn't have bothered. Although she shared the same barky skin as Jean Robin, no trace of humanity was in this creature – not in her willowy movements or almondshaped eyes, which glistened with sap. As she walked past me, the leaves in her hair and on her fingertips trembled like castanets. I smelled the sharp tang of resin and chlorophyll in the air. She seated herself in the grotto on top of the statues of Acis and Galatea, nestling herself snugly into Acis's lap (and rather smothering Galatea).

'No one would ever accuse you of *that*, Sylvianne,' Madame La Pieuvre said smoothly. 'Although I see you still keep human companions.'

Madame La Pieuvre looked pointedly toward the trees. Following her gaze, I realized someone was there. I hadn't seen him at first because he wore a dark-colored sweatshirt, the hood pulled low over his forehead. His skinny, jean-clad legs were pulled up to his chest. Without looking at the boy, Sylvianne extended her long, silver-barked arm and crooked a leaf-tipped finger. As if pulled by a string, the boy unfolded his long legs, rose unsteadily to his feet, and stumbled jerkily toward the dryad. As he passed by me, I smelled the same bitter smell I'd detected in the glasses of green liquid set before the statues. *Absinthe*, I realized. The boy reeked of absinthe. He was so unsteady on his feet that he would have fallen headlong into the fountain if Sylvianne hadn't grasped him roughly by the arm and pulled him into her lap. He collapsed spinelessly into her embrace and looked up into her face with the devoted eyes of a poodle. I noticed that his sweatshirt had the words BARD COLLEGE written across the front and he had exactly the type of hipster goatee I'd imagined earlier for the pagan worshippers.

'He's sweet, isn't he?' Sylvianne said, stroking the boy's silky hair. 'I found him sketching Polyphemus late one evening and invited him to stay with me for the summer.'

'And then you'll let him go?' Madame La Pieuvre asked. 'He must have a family—'

'*I'll give him back when I'm done with him!*' Sylvianne roared, the leaves in her hair thrashing. 'You are not one to speak, Octavia. You have kept your own human pet for over fifty years.'

'She's not a pet and she's not bewitched like this boy is,' Madame La Pieuvre spat back, her own appendages bristling. Her skin appeared mottled and darker than before.

'Far worse for her then! When I am done with this boy,

he will go back to his pathetic little life with only the vaguest memories of a misspent adventure abroad. *Your* concubine must spend every moment of her life knowing that you will survive her by thousands of years . . . and thousands of lovers.'

'Not everyone is so voracious in her appetites,' Madame La Pieuvre hissed. Her face was puffed up. Recalling what I'd learned about octopus behavior from a *NOVA* television special, I decided I'd better step in before someone got inked.

'Ladies,' I said loudly enough to be heard over the swish of leaves and tentacles in the air, 'I'm sure we've all made some choices in our lives that we regret. I, for one, got myself involved with a vampire last year.'

The effect of my announcement on Sylvianne was instantaneous. She stood up so quickly that Bard Boy nearly rolled into the fountain. He managed to catch himself into a ball at Sylvianne's feet with reflexes that made me suspect he wasn't as out of it as he appeared. Every leaf on her head bristled and her silver skin turned ashen.

'Which vampire?' she spat.

I wiped a sticky drop of resin from my face. Too late I recalled Madame La Pieuvre's warning. Well, too bad. If this creature could poach college boys from my country, I could give her a little competition.

'Will Hughes,' I said with more confidence than I felt. 'He's the reason I'm here. He sent me a message to join him on the path to the Summer Country.'

'Then why aren't you on it?' Sylvianne replied, folding her arms across her chest. 'Didn't he leave you a clear sign? Maybe he changed his mind. As I recall, he was quite fickle as a young man – although also quite delightful.' She reached down and distractedly stroked Bard Boy's hair.

I shrugged. 'Maybe he did, but that doesn't mean I'm going to give up. He took something of mine and I want it back.'

'Oooh.' Sylvianne pursed her lips and made a sound like doves cooing. 'A woman scorned, is it? He took something from me, too!' She unfolded her arms and beckoned with a leafy finger, just as she'd summoned the boy before. I looked at Madame La Pieuvre for guidance, but she was still puffed up with anger, inky blotches staining her face. Maybe she was angry with me for not taking her advice about not mentioning Will's name. Well, at least I'd gotten the dryad's attention.

I walked toward the grotto, carefully stepping over Bard Boy's legs – and over the other figures that had quietly crept around the fountain's base while we talked. Looking down I spied humans and *others* – a satyr with cloven hooves, a girl with a long tail, a deer with wide, sentient eyes – but I didn't see the man in the long coat and wide-brimmed hat. Where did he fit into all this? I wondered. When I was a few feet away, Sylvianne beckoned me to come closer and then wrapped a leafy arm around me and pulled me into her lap, just as she'd held Bard Boy a moment ago. For a moment I worried I could become her next pet, but then all worries passed away. I was sitting on a branch in a tree listening to the wind in the boughs, nestled in the crook of two branches as securely as a baby bird in a nest. The bark felt warm with the day's sun. Resting my head against it, I could hear sap flowing, strong as the pulse of the earth. I wanted to do nothing more but close my eyes and nap for a hundred years. This must have been how Rip Van Winkle felt when he rested his head against an old oak for a little after-lunch nap. Or how Jean Robin felt just before he metamorphosed into a tree.

Then I heard her voice inside my head.

I loved him, too, for a little while, and I thought he loved me. He told me he wanted to go to the Summer Country to become immortal so we could be together for all time. I gave him a branch from my hair to give him entrance to the Summer Country. But it wasn't for me, it was for Marguerite! He betrayed me. Me! Sylvianne, Queen of the Forest.

He betrayed me, too, as a matter of fact, I told her without moving my lips.

Is that why you want to go to the Summer Country? To make him apologize?

Was it? I wondered. Was that why I was so determined to follow Will Hughes – to hear him say he was sorry that he'd left me behind in New York? Well, maybe that was *part* of the reason. Enough so that it wouldn't be a complete lie to agree with Sylvianne.

'Yes,' I said, 'and when I find him, I'll make him apologize to you, too. After all, we girls have to stick together.'

Sylvianne leaned back and held me at arm's length to look at my face. This close I could see that her skin was paper-thin and peeling, her lips flaking and chapped. Resin pooled in her eyes, and when she spoke, her voice was as dry as bare twigs scraping against one another.

'That would be . . . nice. All I've ever wanted was an apology.'

'Then you'll get one,' I promised.

Then she whispered in my ear what I needed to do to find the path to the Summer Country.

doomsight

Back in their room, back in their bed, Marguerite turned toward Will, took his face in her cupped hands, and told him the truth about herself. She told him even as the last flashes of lightning from a now diminishing storm illumined her face and its uncanny, ethereal beauty.

Marguerite told Will that she was of the fey and immortal, and that was why she'd been able to shrug off the lightning bolt as if it were a moonbeam. She could be physically killed, nowhere near as easily as a mortal but in a few specific ways, but not by lightning because it came from the light as she did. The bolt's effect on her had been that of pouring a few drops of water into a half-full glass. None. They were of the same element. He had been accurate in his observation.

'The fey,' Will reflected wonderingly, even as he thought to ask if the poet had known this. But Marguerite was so exhausted now that the instant they fell into each other's arms in a relieved embrace, she fell into the deepest sleep.

Will was fatigued as well, but he lingered awake a few minutes experiencing the most unbounded sort of joy any lover could experience. His beloved, the most precious person in the world to him, could live forever! As long as she took precautions against the small list of dangers she'd alluded to. Her own flesh and blood would not betray her with age as his would, with this symptom and then that, and then some crushing new weakness or annihilatory event, the sad way of mortal flesh.

No greater revelation than this was possible for a lover!

Will joined Marguerite in her deep, tender sleep, the rest of the blessed: a serene glow seeping into the cells of his brain and blood, the atoms of his flesh, even into his poetic and mathematical soul.

Second to sleep, he was first to awake, before the sun had poked above the horizon. Though nothing regarding immortality had changed overnight, or could have, Will awoke with a vague dread suffusing his mind and blood, the same mind and blood so gifted with serenity in sleep. Unable to remain still, he got up quietly so as not to wake Marguerite and went out into the still morning. He walked in the direction of the pond where they'd been the previous day, as if the black and white swans they'd seen there made it a reassuring place, despite her dismayed reaction to the story of betrayal and wounding with an arrow.

The storm had passed, leaving a rose and gold dawn promising a beautiful clear day. Why, then, did he feel this apprehension? After a few inchoate moments, he identified the source of his dark sensation. If Marguerite was going to live forever and he was going to die, he could never be to her what she was to him . . .

Yes, as mortals they might be separated by death but not for long, and each could still be the central love of the other's life. But with Marguerite immortal, no matter how much she loved him or came to love him, time would fade all their memories for her, stretching them out like ocean crests vanishing at the horizon, and she would *always* find another 'great love of her life.' That was natural, not immoral. She'd always be young. He could ask her to wait for him while he was in prison, or away in war, or while captaining a ship, but not *forever*. No lover could ask another to wait *forever*. That was a true life sentence for the heart.

Will saw himself, grimly, as one love of multitudes stretching out toward infinity, eventually a pathetic point coming when Marguerite could not recall him or his name. The image cut him searingly, to the bone, in a way no other thought in his life ever had. This was jealousy akin to terror!

Will could not help but cry out, as if echoing the wailing creature the night before, and as he did, he saw where those cries had come from. There at the shore of the pond lay the black swan they'd seen earlier – dead, its beautiful long neck lying limp in the tall reeds. Will let out a moan, only this one was answered by a soft hand on his arm and an even softer voice speaking close to his ear.

'Poor thing. I tried to save him last night, but it was too late. Listen. His mate is pining for him still.'

Will became aware then of a plaintive mewling coming from the reeds. The white swan was hidden in them, hiding her face from the sun as she lamented the loss of her mate.

'Is that how you'll cry for me when I am dead?' Will asked.

Stung by the bitterness in his voice, Marguerite withdrew her hand. 'God willing, that day is a long way off. Let us not think of that now.'

'But I must think of it, Marguerite. I have so much less time than you. Please don't get me wrong. I think it's wonderful that you can never die, and I will never have the pain of seeing your death, or watching you grow old. I would die a million times rather than subject you to either! But the cruelty of our situation, Marguerite, is that in time I will pass from your sight, then from your memory, in the blurring of other loves you may have. . . . I will die with you fierce within me, but for you I will be a mere spark of sunlight; a spark on the sea amidst millions of sparks.' He flung his hand at the pond, which had come alive with the rising of the sun. 'And I don't know that I can bear this.'

'It's not like that, Will. Not at all. You mustn't think of us that way.' She took his hand in hers and kissed it gently.

But this wasn't the response he was looking for. Will needed her invitation to join her in the immortal world. 'How is it not like that, my love? Tell me! Why will you not have infinite lovers if you live infinitely?' He withdrew his hand as if she were threatening to have an affair.

'I do not experience time the way mortals do. My lives go on, but they are boundaried, and different from each other, in a way a mortal could not understand. Multiple, infinite – whatever you want to call them. But different from one another. Do not lose yourself in silly numbers and the strangeness of time. I am here for you now, fully, and forever. That is all any man can ever expect of a woman. I will *never* leave you!'

Marguerite took a deep breath, more like a stifled sob.

Words, he reflected, with some bitterness. She was giving him words, and near-incomprehensible ones. They might make sense to another immortal, but not to him.

As the rays from the rising sun reached the side of the pond where they stood, Will held out his hand in the light. Once again he saw his flesh turn transparent. The blood flowing inside seemed to run gold. What if there was an alchemy that could turn not lead to gold, but mortal flesh to immortal? Inspired, Will turned and pulled Marguerite toward him. He whispered, 'Make me an immortal, my love. That is the answer. The sadness of mortality will *never* enter our lives.'

She broke away and replied in a trembling voice, 'I cannot do that, Will.' And she began to weep.

He embraced her and tried to wipe away her tears. 'Why?' he stammered. 'I still do not understand.'

'Being immortal is *worse* than being mortal,' she finally answered, pulling away. 'You watch everyone you know grow old and die. *Everyone!* Can't you understand? The desolation far outweighs this splendor that you and I have found. Believe me, it does. Immortality isn't a blessing. It's a curse!'

He knelt before her. 'But we would always have each other.'

Silence.

'I'm not even sure I *can* do it,' Marguerite said after several more painful moments had passed. 'That crossing is the most dangerous of all. There is always a price to be paid, whether the journey is successful or not. And success can't be known in advance.'

'We would always have each other,' Will repeated. It was his only solace, and she tortured him now by not having any interest in it.

'*I*'d rather die than have *you* suffer the pain of being immortal,' Marguerite insisted. 'That very pain which I have suffered.'

She burst into more sobs and collapsed onto the grass. Will lay next to her to comfort her, but as he did so, he saw his new world going up in flames. As if the gulf between them had caught fire. That gulf, between mortal and immortal, burned as if empty space were as treacherous and flammable as love.

They rode back to London together a few minutes later, silent all the way. They went their separate ways at their usual place of parting, also without another word. And neither turned around to watch the other ride away.

Until this point, Will and Marguerite had had regular daily meetings. They met at the southwest corner of Prince Street and Orange Lane at 11:45 a.m., a crowded and anonymous spot where their daily time together could begin, or, if some obstacle to such time had appeared, where they could arrange a second rendezvous for later. Will had not yet come to Marguerite's lodgings – the ones she had obtained after her flight from the poet – because of the danger of the poet spying on her there. Nor had she come to his, for similar reasons. In the rare instance when Marguerite had not been able to come to their rendezvous, she had sent him a note before he left to meet her.

But for three days after returning from the trip to the north, Marguerite did not appear for their rendezvous, and

Will had not heard from her otherwise. He'd waited more than an hour for her each appointed time, gazing into the flow of pedestrians in all directions like a sea captain's wife peering into distant waves for a familiar ship. But crowds remained coldly alien, people mere whitecaps lifted by an inhospitable wind. And the hours after these disappointments had been barren and broken, except for an occasional firestorm of rage or regret. He raged at such an oppressive fate in love, regretted that he had not made clearer (or known sooner) to Marguerite his desire to go on with her no matter what the barriers between them.

Of course he preferred that they go forward as immortals, and *of course* it seared him to think that he would lose her so quickly to a multitude of future lovers. But just a few moments that first midday without her convinced him that having Marguerite around in the present was much more crucial than morose speculation about some abstract future. In any event, if they could only spend time together again now, he would gradually become so much a part of her that she would be overwhelmed by his pain; then she would feel compelled to make him immortal.

When he doubted such a benign outcome was possible anymore, he found bleak inspiration for the writing of new sonnets in his torment, scribbling in iambic pentameter on scraps of paper he kept in his back pocket while endlessly wandering London streets:

> *Her ship's dark shape drifts slowly toward the sun,*
> *whose flaming sphere floats briefly on the sea;*
> *and Marguerite, whom I'll no longer see*

invades my thoughts: my suffering's begun!
Impossible, that she and I are done!
Yet as the ship turns dot there's no more 'we,'
and once it vanishes our history
is boundaried in the past, like time undone,
as hard to cling to as the pink twilight
or salt-veined breezes winging past the shore.
The sun descends; eternal victor night
engulfs the presence that I so adore.
Nor will new love console me; it's my fate
to understand my heart an hour too late.

He'd made up a seaside narrative in this poem, to fit a wholly uncertain set of facts. Tragic poems were an outlet, and he often recited 'Farewell' and others like it on the long walks he took to distract himself from his sorrow.

On the fourth day of Marguerite's absence, Will gave in to desperation and started to wander toward her lodgings, which were in Mynchen Lane. He did this against fierce internal resistance that had stalemated this impulse on the first three days. His resistance was made up of fear of further rejection, of not wanting to take any chances of running into the poet, and of pride resisting the implied surrender of going to her lodgings. But in the end nothing could suppress his overwhelming need to be with Marguerite. He felt a need to embrace her that was deeper than his need to breathe.

But Marguerite wasn't at her lodgings. Not on the first knock and not on the hundredth. He had refrained from pounding too loudly in deference to the neighbors, but there was no way she could have been inside and not heard him.

He'd glanced furtively about for some other means of entrance besides the front door, but even if he'd discovered one, there was no sense to attempting such entry in daylight. Dense curtains rendered all windows inscrutable. Peering down the alleys lining each side of the house, he made out a walled garden well to the rear, belonging to either the house where Marguerite lodged or to a neighbor. Its eight-foot walls topped with thick and sharply pointed black iron spikes did not invite casual entrance, night or day. But he could try coming back with a small ladder, since he was athletic enough to take the wall on from a lesser height. No other possibility came to eye or mind.

Will finally got himself to leave, but only with a promise to himself to return after dark.

He wandered nearby streets, further dejected by her absence at home, for a long time. Finally, he felt a thirst that made him seek shelter in the familiar shadows of Baker & Thread's, where the hour, well past midday dinner, made privacy likely and prices more modest. (He couldn't go too long without reflecting on his only other deep concern besides Marguerite, which was how his acting possibilities had vanished and his money would not last forever.)

He sat down at an awning-solaced table. Then almost immediately he caught a glimpse, within the tavern's interior, of a seemingly familiar set of broad shoulders under a red, collarless Spanish cloak. When the man shifted his shoulders and threw back his rough mane of shiny black hair, Will realized who it was, surprised that recognition was possible through such slivers of appearance. But maybe the man had made more of an impression on him in their first encounter than he'd previously realized.

Indeed, this man *had* occurred to him as someone to consult with in the terrible days since his breach with Marguerite, due to his employer's reputation. Any solution this individual could offer would be at best unwholesome, perhaps sinister, not remotely comparable to walking into immortality in a loving way with Marguerite. But Will felt no harm could come from approaching the man and having a small discussion. Marguerite's absence was destroying him. Only a fool thought salvation needed to be perfect. It just needed to be.

Will walked over to face him, bowed deferentially, and murmured in a low voice, 'Lord Liverpool.'

He didn't recall the man's having a title and doubted he did, but this was a moment for deference. Liverpool, who was contemplating his glass of ale as if its foam mapped a route to the Orient, did not initially glance up at him. But when Will circled closer, bowed, and called him 'Lord' a second time, Liverpool did look up with beer blurred eyes and seemed to think he recognized Will, though his words indicated he had mistaken him for another.

'Trader boy!' he exclaimed. 'One of my finest hires. How goes it in the offices of Dr Dee? Just this very morning his lordship happened to compliment me on how skillful you are in pricing certificates. You must be a lad of great wealth already!'

Then Liverpool glanced more closely at Will's attire and recognized that that probably wasn't the case. 'Or,' he retreated, 'you may be luxuriating in possession of an even greater wealth than gold; that would be time well and happily spent! Are you so employed?' he inquired, observing the blank expression on Will's features. 'But why do I ask?! Who could not be happy in proximity to the greatest intellect of our time, as you spend your days?! Sit down, lad, and let me offer you a drink! What brings you to these dank shadows at a time of day when most traders are closing their books and planning their evenings?'

Will lowered himself into an empty chair at the table. He knew he was being taken for someone else. He sat anyway, as a line of inquiry, concerning the happiness Liverpool had made flippant reference to, had occurred to him.

'My good man, I am not currently in the employ of Sir John Dee.' Will spoke slowly, not entirely trusting Liverpool's rationality, as a dark-haired serving woman came over to their table. He ordered a glass of ale. 'You and I have had a discussion on Sir Dee's commercial theories recently, but I have not entered his employ. I have been distracted by a much more pressing matter. One that requires a different sort of alchemy than the stock market can offer, or even the traditional lead-based kind.'

His ale arrived, and a gulp soothed Will's parched mouth and seething throat. He dried his sweaty brow with the thick paper the server had put under his drink.

Liverpool gave him an appraising gaze. 'What situation could compare to the alchemy of stock certificates, if you don't mind my asking? To an entire nation about to convert all its paper to gold?'

'You touched on it a moment ago, mentioning happy moments in the same breath as riches. I am in a crisis of the heart, sir, where happy moments are the rarest currency of all. I beg for a loving moment like a starving man might for a loaf of bread. Indeed my condition is a perfect despondency of love. With no apparent cure.'

'Alchemists of our day, Sir Dee first among them, can concoct a potion for a trauma such as yours,' Liverpool replied. 'A not uncommon trauma, in a world that has not been forged to perfection, in affairs of the heart least of all. The only drawback being, such potions usually need to be made to order and are not inexpensive.' Liverpool ran a surveying gaze again over Will's attire, wondering, Will conjectured, how much of a love-blind spendthrift he might turn out to be if he was so miserly regarding his attire.

'This is not a matter of unrequited love,' Will told Liverpool. 'This is a question of one lover needing transformation so two lovers can be together. An insurmountable challenge for any alchemist, I fear.'

'Transformation,' Liverpool repeated, twisting his hands as if, by their becoming better acquainted with each other, they might help with a solution. Rather than admit his ignorance of Will's meaning, he then tried a little humor. 'You are in love with your hunting falcon, perhaps? Or a deer? And you want to cross that natural boundary between them and you? Yes, I'm not sure the alchemist's craft is advanced enough for that.'

Disappointment and exasperation merged in Will's expression. He sat in sullen silence and listened to Liverpool's continued rant.

'There is indeed a transformation impending in currency that can grow like a gargantuan, in coins that will jangle louder than an avalanche, and in certificates that will glitter with an aura brighter than the sun's.

'Transformed commerce lies at England's feet now, carried here by secular angels of markets and math. Dee himself spoke of our nation's mathematical future in his brilliant introduction to Henry Billingsley's *Euclid*, recently reprinted. You can be a leader of this new world, son. All it will take is a small investment and the larger portion of your rational mind!'

'Lord Liverpool, what I mean by *transformation* has nothing to do with the crassness of commerce. I have found a love so exalted I could not find the smallest trace of the material world in her if I looked with the finest magnifying glass. I am referring to the plight of a mortal like myself who falls in love with an immortal and cannot cross that boundary to be with her forever. And who therefore requires help in crossing that line, whether from sorcerer or preacher, alchemist or poet, wizard or astronomer, or the devil himself matters not! Your employer, Sir Dee, is rumored to have the most extraordinary powers. Can he help me? Can you? Can anyone in England? In the world?' Will stifled a sob. The solitude of his dilemma, the inability of anyone else to comprehend it – not that he had tried to communicate it before now – seemed one of the most hurtful things about it.

Then he observed out of the corner of his eye a sudden darkening in the street. A corresponding shadow came over Guy Liverpool's features, as if Will's emotional outburst had unnerved him. Sudden clouds must be smearing the sun, but they had arrived with incredible speed, since Will had entered the tavern under a sheer blue sky.

Looking about nervously, as if the change in weather showed the moral darkness of even discussing such a topic as Will brought up, Liverpool then retrieved an engraved card from a purse tied around the peasecod belly of his doublet and proferred it to Will. When Will glanced at it, he saw this card's design was different from the one Liverpool had previously given him. The first card had tiny gold bars superimposed on lead ones, but this one's was simpler: white lettering on a black background, with a few stars here and there. It read, *Sir John Dee, Master of Night. 22 Rufus Lane, Mortlake. By Appointment Only.*

'You may approach Sir Dee, any time after sunset, on this matter of which you speak. I will let him know you are coming. But best to be subtle, even obscure, at first. As you have been with me.'

'I did nothing of the kind,' Will protested. 'You wouldn't let me get a word in edgewise.'

Liverpool waved off Will's protest as if it were a buzzing fly. 'Yes, strike a misleading chord with Sir Dee, so he may think you've come to him on the topic of commerce. He may let his defenses down. Perhaps you will gain his sympathies. And don't think that I'm not sympathetic; I have no doubt your worry is real, but it is a bit beyond my own area of expertise, so that I cannot help you personally. Indeed I wish you well and will only expect suitable compensation, which can be paid me right in this very tavern, if you succeed in your quest through the services of Sir Dee. But if you do embark on this most awesome of journeys, keep in mind that crossing over – "transformation" as you call it – can annihilate the voyager, even dislodge the earth that birthed him. Your beloved best be worth these sorts of risks, son. And you'd better be prepared, from what I've heard rumored over the many years, to die during the journey.'

Now there was a second darkening in the street, then a brilliant flash of lightning followed by thunder. Hailstones began to drop with a sound like bullets fired from the clouds striking the pavements, followed by large raindrops falling with a sound like blood spattering.

Will, weary of Guy Liverpool's portentous perspective, said a hasty farewell, slapped two shillings down on the tabletop for his drink, and sped off into the deluge. With a new chance at immortality, he felt as if he could walk between the hailstones and raindrops. And walk between them he nearly did.

haRlequin

The next day I caught a train for Fontainebleau.

'I have to go alone,' I'd told Madame La Pieuvre after we'd left the Luxembourg. 'Sylvianne told me so.'

'What else did Sylvianne tell you?' She still looked puffed up, but the inky blotches on her face were fading.

'She told me that tomorrow night the Wild Hunt rides through the Forest of Fontainebleau, and that if I stopped in front of the head rider and demanded passage to the Summer Country, he would have to give it to me.'

'Oh, is that all?' Madame La Pieuvre asked, arching one eyebrow. 'Why not tell you to stand in front of a speeding train while she's at it?'

I recollected her words as I hurried toward my track at the Gare de Lyon. Surely Madame La Pieuvre had been exaggerating. She'd been angered by Sylvianne, but she herself had said that the tree folk's treatment of humans was harmless. *Mostly*. And sure, *Wild Hunt* sounded scary, but when I'd looked it up last night on the Internet, I'd found out it was merely the name for a gathering of fairies. It was also sometimes called the Wild Host, Woden's Ride, or, in Old North French, la Mesnée d'Hellequin, none of which sounded quite as ominous as *Hunt*. *Hellequin* turned out to be an ancestor of *Harlequin*, the masked and diamond-suited jester of commedia dell'arte. What could be more harmless than that?

Besides, I was going with a personal calling card from the Queen of the Forest. Sylvianne had given me a small twig from her 'hair' to hold up in front of the riders and assured me that it would keep me safe. So I had nothing to worry about . . . unless the twig was a secret message like the death sentence borne by Rosencrantz and Guildenstern in *Hamlet* indicating that the bearer should be killed on the spot.

I shook my head free of these thoughts as I boarded the train, took a seat on the upper level, and tried to focus instead on the excitement of the trip. After all, what could be more evocative of adventure and romantic travel than these big, old European train stations? From the top level of the double-decker train I had a wonderful view of the great vaulted ceiling and the enormous clock hanging from it. Shields with the insignia of French provinces lined the walls. At the top of a great staircase was one of the last of the grand railway restaurants: Le Train Bleu. My mother had taken me there for ice cream during the summer I was sixteen, and she'd told me that she had gone there as a girl, first when she and her mother took the train from her little village in the south up to Paris. She'd told me it had been the last place she'd ever seen her mother, who had later sent her back into the country just weeks before the Germans marched into Paris.

Suddenly the bustling train station transformed before me. Instead of tourists rushing to catch their trains for their holidays in the Midi, I saw hordes of frightened families pushed by black-booted soldiers onto freight cars. I heard the cries of mothers calling to their children and the shrill commands in German. And standing in the center of it all was the man in the long coat and the broad-brimmed hat I'd seen five times now. And he was looking right at me . . .

I startled out of my vision to find myself surrounded by three loud and boisterous teenagers crowding into the seat across from me. One of the girls was opening a window and shouting in English to hurry up, *for fuck's sake*. She collapsed into her seat in a fit of giggles, hiding her face in her friend's lap. Still half dazed by my vision – I'd been having quite a few of them lately, hadn't I? – I stared at the girls wondering why they looked familiar. Then I realized they were the same girls I'd seen a few nights ago in the Square Viviani – the art students who'd rushed off to make their midnight curfew.

'Don't mind Sarah,' one of the girls, a redhead, said when she noticed me staring. 'She's got Tourette's.'

Sarah punched her friend in the arm and collapsed in another fit of giggles.

'I've heard worse,' I assured them. 'Are you girls going to Fontainebleau to sketch?' I pointed at the portfolios they all carried.

'Yeah,' the redhead, apparently the designated speaker, answered. 'Our art teacher says that Fontainebleau has been an inspiration to artists for centuries and we ought to "take our line for a walk" there.'

Sarah dissolved into another fit of laughter. 'We were going to spend the weekend in Nice, but Becca's parents pitched a fit.'

The third girl, a gamine with black bangs and dark eyes, blushed. 'They didn't think it was safe. They're freaked out by reports of missing students.'

'They think she's going to end up like that boy they found this morning in the Seine,' Sarah said, her voice suddenly sober.

'What boy?' I asked.

'Do you still have the paper, Carrie?' Sarah asked the redhead.

Carrie handed me this morning's *Herald Tribune*. On the front page was a photograph of nineteen-year-old Sam Smollett, a sophomore at Bard College, who had gone missing from his dormitory a week ago. He'd been found drowned in the Seine this morning.

Bard Boy, I thought, recognizing the boy I'd seen with Sylvianne last night. Had he broken away from her dominion last night and thrown himself into the river? Or had someone decided to deprive the Queen of the Forest of her special pet? I recalled the man in the overcoat and hat I'd seen vaulting into the park last night. That made twice that I'd seen him at the scene of a crime. And I'd just seen him standing in the station. Had he boarded our train?

I glanced around the car nervously, but there was no sign of the man in the long coat and hat – although, if he took them off, would I recognize him? What if his next target was one of these three girls?

I tried to focus on the girls' conversation again, if only to slip in some warning to them about staying out of dark, deserted parks at night. They were discussing the history of Fontainebleau.

'Our teacher says it's the birthplace of plain air, or something,' Carrie was saying.

'*En plein air*,' I gently corrected. 'And he's right. Before the impressionists, painters came out to the woods of Fontainebleau to paint outdoors instead of in their studios. They were called the Barbizon school for one of the villages.' I gave a little lecture on the Barbizon school to the three girls, supplemented by details I'd learned on the Internet last night. They listened patiently and politely, like the three nice American high schoolers they were. I ended by stressing that the painters worked during the daylight. The woods could be dangerous at night.

'Are you an artist?' Carrie asked, ignoring my warning.

'A jeweler.' I showed them the watch I'd recently made and the swan ring and pendant I always wore and they immediately became more animated. Sarah had seen some of my pendants at Barneys, which instantly gave me more 'cred' than all the art history knowledge in the world. We talked about different art schools in New York City and where the girls were thinking of going to college. Becca, who was from Texas, said her parents were against her going to art school in Manhattan; Sarah said her grandparents refused to let her use her college fund for anything less than an Ivy; while Carrie said her mom wanted her to go to art school but that she wanted a more general liberal arts college.

'I don't think I can take four years of emo art kids,' she said.

The girls' chatter made the trip fly by and distracted me briefly from my worries over the two drownings. We were heading away from Paris, where they'd occurred. Still, I was happy to learn we were all staying at the same hotel – the Aigle Noir – right across from the entrance to the château and park. I could keep an eye on the girls tonight.

I resisted the urge to follow when they ran off toward the park with their sketchbooks right away. It was full daylight, after all. And I'd be better off resting now so I could be more alert tonight.

I checked in and was shown to a pretty toile-papered room overlooking the town square and the high walls of the château. The square was full of outdoor cafés, a carousel, and a stage being set up for some kind of evening theatrics. The bright, colorful scene full of tourists and day-trippers from Paris belied any dark activity behind the high walls. I'd imagined coming to Fontainebleau that I'd be plunged into a dark, trackless wilderness, not this bucolic scene as peaceful and harmless as the shepherds and shepherdesses frolicking across the tame toile land-scape on the wall. I fell asleep lulled by the music of the carousel and the plump, smiling faces on the wallpaper.

My dreams started peaceful enough as well. I was in a green meadow. I could hear the bleat of sheep in the distance and the sound of bells. I walked to the top of a hill and looked down on a valley dotted with quaint stone cottages and hedgerows. A giggling girl ran past me, her frilled petticoats frothing around her plump legs. A boy in striped trousers and loose shirt pursued her. A couple of sheep frolicked nearby. I walked a little farther on and *another* girl ran past me, also in frilly dress and low-cut bodice, and yet again a boy in peasant attire followed her, along with the same retinue of sheep. I had an uncomfort-able feeling of déjà vu. When the scene repeated a third time, I spun around, annoyed that I seemed to be stuck in a repeating loop . . . and then I saw that the same scene – running shepherdess, following shepherd, bleating sheep – was repeated over and over again across the valley. I was stuck in the toile wallpaper; no matter how far I wandered, I kept encountering the same banal scene. I trudged on, looking desperately for a way out, but somehow knowing that I'd be stuck there forever.

I awoke in my room at the Aigle Noir, my heart pounding. The now maddening drone of the carousel and the voices of people in the square filled the room. In my confused half-asleep state I imagined the voices came from the figures in the wallpaper. The raucous laughter was from the leering shepherds – had they looked quite so lecherous before my nap? – the high-pitched squeals from the fleeing shepherdesses – had they looked quite so fearful before? But what was making those bleating sounds? They weren't just in my dream – they were here in Fontainebleau.

I got up and went to the window. My first surprise was that it was full dark. The clock on the night table read 22:33 – ten thirty-three, my sleep-addled brain deduced after a sluggish moment. I'd slept for over ten hours.

Ten hours stuck in that maddening wallpaper. No wonder I felt tired!

My second surprise was that I had apparently been transported to seventeenth-century France. Specifically a seventeenth-century performance of the Comédie-Italienne. The square was full of masked people dressed in elaborate costumes. I recognized the whitened face and loose white blouse and pantaloons of Pierrot, the tattered dress, heavy eye makeup and tambourine of Columbine, and the diamond-patterned costume and black-and-red mask of Harlequin. The actors were circulating among the crowd, drumming up enthusiasm for the coming performance, no doubt.

There was nothing sinister in that, I assured myself as I got dressed and went downstairs. I had time for a quick bite in a café before heading off for my meeting. I picked an outside table so I could watch the theatrics. There were jugglers and flame-eaters and a man in an owl mask doing magic tricks, but the main narrative thread consisted of the love triangle between Harlequin, Pierrot, and Columbine. Pierrot was forever mooning, his white face a perfect doleful moon, for his beloved, but whenever he seemed about to realize his dream of winning her, Harlequin would devise some way of keeping them apart. Then he would sweep in himself and whisk Columbine away in his arms.

'Poor Pierrot,' I heard someone say in English. 'He never wins.'

I turned around and saw Sarah with her friends Carrie and Becca at a table behind me. They waved for me to join them and I went over to their table for a coffee and to see the sketches they'd done of the château and gardens. Their happy, sunburned faces and full sketchbooks left me feeling like a mole rat for sleeping the day away, but I enjoyed looking at each girl's work – and I was relieved to see that no harm had come to them during the day. Carrie was clearly the most technically skilled of the three, but Becca had a nice lyrical touch for landscapes, and Sarah had a real flair for capturing gesture and expression – and she was the one who had drawn the most. Even as we spoke, she was sketching the figures in the crowd on her paper place mat. She was working on a portrait of Harlequin.

'You've really captured his devilish air,' I told her, admiring her sketch.

'He *is* a little devil, isn't he?' Sarah said, furrowing her brows together. 'But also . . . kind of handsome, don't you think?'

I looked at the figure in his diamond-patterned tights and fitted jacket hewing closely to a slim but muscular form. A black-and-red mask concealed the top part of his face, but his eyes seemed to glitter behind it and his mouth seemed very red beneath it.

'Yes,' I agreed with a little shiver. 'He's both – devilish *and* handsome. I read somewhere that Harlequin originated in a figure from the French passion plays called Hellequin, and he's supposed to be an emissary of the devil . . .' I trailed off, recalling something else I'd read last night when I'd googled the *Wild Hunt.* Hellequin had been identified as one of the traditional leaders of the hunt, and the pack of evil spirits he led were called la Mesnée d'Hellequin. Was it a coincidence that a Harlequin performed in the square on the same night the Wild Hunt rode through the Forest of Fontainebleau?

A strangled cry – like the ones I'd heard earlier during my nap – startled me out of my speculations.

'What *is* that?' I asked the girls.

Carrie and Becca laughed, but Sarah was intent on her sketch.

'Peacocks,' Carrie told me. 'They're in the Garden of Diana right through that gate. You can still go see them.

They're keeping the park open late tonight for the fête.'

'Oh, let's go!' Sarah said suddenly, looking up from her sketch. 'I bet the gardens are beautiful at night!'

Becca and Carrie said they were too tired and wanted to go to bed. Sarah looked as if she was about to argue, but she was distracted by the sudden appearance of Harlequin at the table. He'd popped up as quickly as a jack-in-the-box and grabbed the picture Sarah had done of him off the table. He looked at it, and then, holding it to his lips, bowed at Sarah. As he righted himself, I caught a glimpse of his eyes behind the mask . . . green eyes with glints of gold in them . . . definitely devilish and somehow familiar. Sarah blushed bright pink. I decided to use the moment to steal away for a quick turn around the garden. I didn't want Sarah getting the idea to come along with me. I couldn't bring anyone where I was going, and I didn't want her wandering away from me in the dark forest by herself.

I passed through the gate into the Garden of Diana and saw with dismay that it wasn't empty. Aside from the tourists there were a number of street performers of the sort that one saw all over Europe these days – mimes dressed in costumes mimicking famous sculptures right down to the marble veins or bronze patina painted on their skin. I spotted a winged Nike, head cloaked in black to approximate the headlessness of the original, and a rather risqué Venus de Milo, who wore long black gloves to give the impression of armlessness. There were lesser-known figures as well – a prancing faun whose original I had seen last night in the Luxembourg, and a host of gargoyles running in and out of the shrubbery. Cute, but I was supposed to meet my escort at the Diana Fountain at midnight, and Sylvianne had been adamant that I be there alone. It was a quarter to.

I approached the fountain at the center of the garden wondering how I could make everyone leave. A small group of tourists were gathered around the fountain taking pictures. As I got closer, I saw of what. A young woman, skin painted verdigris green and dressed in a belted stola of the same color, posed in front of the circular fountain. She was identical to the statue of Diana standing on top right down to the four hound dogs that surrounded her. The live dogs had also been painted verdigris green, hopefully with no damage to their skin, and sat as still as their bronze counterparts.

'*Magnifique!*' a woman in a stylish Breton fisherman's shirt and capris murmured as she clicked her camera. It *was* impressive that the street performer had trained her dogs to remain so still; they even managed to mimic the doleful expressions of the hounds on the fountain, and they didn't even flinch when a white peacock strolled by within an inch of their noses. I was so caught up in admiring them that I didn't notice the time passing until the clock in the town hall began chiming midnight.

Damn, I thought, *how will my escort appear with all these witnesses?*

I needn't have worried. As the bells tolled, the tourists and performers began to file out of the garden as if called away by the sound of the bells. They moved robotically, their eyes strangely glazed. It reminded me creepily of a scene from *The Time Machine*, in which the gentle Eloi responded to a summons to sacrifice themselves to the cannibal Morlocks. I had an uneasy feeling, though, that they were being led to safety while I was being left alone like the goat tied up for T. rex's snack in *Jurassic Park*.

When the clock had chimed twelve times, the only other living beings left in the garden were the Diana impersonator, her dogs, the peacocks, and myself. Perhaps the performer *was* my escort.

'Pardon moi,' I began. 'Êtes-vous mon guide?'

She didn't even blink. She was frozen in the perfect guise of a statue. I thought this was taking her act a bit too far and was going to tell her so when I felt something tug at my hand. I looked down into the amber eyes of a verdigris hound. It held my hand in its mouth gently, but when I tried to pull away, his jaws clamped down. There was a hound on either side of me, hemming me in, and one behind me. I could feel its hot breath on the small of my back.

'Okay,' I said, 'you don't have to ask twice. I'm ready to go.'

14

Euclid

Will's unease began the moment he dismounted from the carriage in front of the crumbling ruins of what the Mortlake watchman had called the Cottage. Perhaps it had been a mistake to come. The cottage looked like a ruined miniature castle, heaps of stones along its flat, timbered roof resembling the remnants of turrets; slits instead of windows in the stone first-floor walls; and a huge pile of rubbled masonry to the side that exceeded the scale of the standing building. A gleaming scimitar moon floated over the roof to the east. The place looked like the frontier out-post of a medieval army for which the battle had gone badly, and Will even felt an empathetic twinge for how these soldiers might have fared. For a fleeting second he even thought he could smell the hint of still-burning, tortured flesh in the damp and darkening air. But the remaining timbers looked sturdy enough, so at least the roof was unlikely to collapse on his head during the hoped-for interview.

Will watched the driver, whom he was paying a hefty fee to wait for him, tie up his horses and carriage to a wind-weathered timber pinned upright between two paving stones. Then the man returned to his elevated seat and put his chin in his hands, as if preparing to rest in that posture. Will knocked on the front door.

After a few moments, it was opened by a slender man with a gray, triangular beard and auburn mustache. His long face, with deep-set amber eyes and a prominent nose, resembled the sketch of Dee in the pamphlet Guy Liverpool had given him. But there was something penetrating, and condescending, about his gaze that no sketch could communicate. Dee stared at him with interest, but did not extend a hand. As Will continued to return his gaze, the man's appearance unnerved him. His eyes were intelligent and deep, but also cold, and, in a shadow cast by moonlight, they began to look more yellowish than amber, certainly a pigment he'd never seen in human eyes before. The catlike pupils were so narrow they were almost slits. Will observed that Dee's skin, despite his age, was relatively free of wrinkles, as if Dee, too, had immortality on his mind and had been making alchemical progress in that direction. *Despite his age* . . . but what was his age, anyway? It was hard to tell in this blade-angled moonlight. In any event, Dee was about to close the door and retreat without another word when Will forced himself to break the silence.

'Good evening, Sir Dee,' he said in a quiet voice. 'I'm—'

'Here to quiz me about Euclid, are you son? I don't mind the attention, but it's not fair that Henry Billingsley doesn't do his share of tending to the public nowadays,' Dee said in a low, meticulous voice. 'Oh, well, come in.' Dee stepped back and then ushered Will through a narrow hall into a small, square room, well lit by dozens of candles.

The room contained several high-backed, velvet-cushioned chairs, arranged around a long oak table that was unadorned. Perhaps this was a place for an entire group to summon spirits, Will thought, not entirely sarcastically. Dee took a seat at one end of the table and gestured Will to the chair opposite. Will was mulling over what Dee's Euclid reference could have meant, and weighing the relative risks of confessing ignorance and sitting in lost silence. He chose the latter.

Dee grew impatient again. 'You're quite the incurious interviewer, aren't you, boy? Have you at least got a name?'

'W-W-Will Hughes, sir. My apologies, I'm no expert in Euclid. I've heard of him of course and studied a bit of Greek for that matter, but my logical bent is centered on the math of music, as in poetry, and not that of measurement. Except when measuring out sonnets.'

Dee stared at Will as if he'd claimed to be an octopus. His eyes blazed briefly, as though they were made of the finest alchemist's gold. 'So you have not even *heard* of the new edition of Billingsley's 1570 translation of Euclid's *Elements* with my preface in it?'

The boom in Dee's voice now could have been the reason some of the stones had fallen off the cottage, Will thought.

'My preface which explains how math can transform England into the center of the world? How it can fill the void left by falsified faith and all manner of superstition, replace it with its own miracles but of logic and reason? How our very faculty of math *itself* is a miracle worthy of a new scripture?! Speak up, boy! Surely you know of this work that all London speaks of right now, thanks to the great grace of John Day, printer extraordinaire? Countless youth have been coming here recently to question me about my insights, my wisdom. They have become a nuisance in their numbers, but nonetheless I have continued to admit such youth, marking it the cost of my genius. But apparently that's not the attraction for the great' – Dee seemed to be searching for Will's name – 'Houghton, as you are. And if it's not, then what is?' Dee glared at Will.

Will vacillated as to the degree of flattery with which to respond, deciding not to claim to have heard of the Billingsley *Euclid*, let alone this new edition, let alone to have read it. Too much risk of Dee following up with questions. 'I come, in all my ignorance, on a different matter, Your Excellency. But surely it takes my breath away that you are so glorious an expert on this geometer as you remind me you are, and yet one of comparable stature in the, pardon the expression, dark arts. It is amazing that one mind can encompass two such areas of genius! And that is the Lord's truth.'

'"Dark arts"? What "dark arts"? There are none, I assure you,' Dee answered hotly. 'There's only the darkness of the population's ignorance regarding certain matters, a shameful state I have spent my adult life trying to correct. I shine the light of logic in the darkest of corners. For only by math's laws of probability can we witness something truly miraculous. If everyone walked on water, would Jesus doing it have been a miracle? Of course not! Singularity makes the miracle! That's what I do, with sacred math. Prove miracles. What do you do with your gifts – lad?'

'. . . I am a poet,' Will finally said, uncomfortably, since he lacked a book. Then his expression brightened. 'And a prospective trader in stock certificates, for which I have been having a discussion with Sir Guy Liverpool.' Why not say this? 'As you know, it was Liverpool who directed me here this evening. But the urgent matter for me on this errand, Your Brilliance, is immortality.' Will hoped that Dee would not be offended by such an inventive form of address. 'You have a great reputation in this sort of dark affair, as I mentioned, and I thought—'

As if it had taken several seconds for *immortality* and *dark* to register, Dee now stood and leaned dramatically toward Will across the table, seeming to elongate an elastic torso halfway along the table length as if he had serpentine powers. '*Silence!*' Dee shouted, pointing an adamant finger at Will. Will obeyed.

'It's no dark affair as you blasphemously put it,' Dee said in a tense voice, as though trying to restrain himself from violence. 'Immortality is like an alp in perpetual sunshine, a summit to which all of us alchemists aspire. Unfortunately I have not been able to personally reach it, no matter the numbers, incantations, geometries, séances, and charms I have tried, and you will note the mix of methods I cite. But I have not failed for lack of trying.' The force of Dee's personality was such, Will noted, that he seemed to brag when speaking about failure as much as when referring to success. Then Dee's expression turned wistful.

'Alas,' he went on, in barely more than a whisper, 'in such immortal research, I have recently happened to learn by accident the year of my physical death. Sixteen oh eight, a year even a novice like you can count to meaningfully. So

I don't have forever to work on this intractable problem. Sadly, as you've no doubt inferred, I have little to offer you, lad. But innate kindness compels me to query *you*. How have you wandered into such an interest, which usually arises in the aging, not in reckless youth?'

Will had not planned to convey this information unless absolutely necessary, but he reflected now on how unrealistic a hope anonymity had been.

'Sir, I have had the strange fortune to fall in love with a woman who is of the fey and immortal. Tragically, she can't or won't give me the means to transform myself so we can be together forever. I have decided to seek my remedy elsewhere. Without a solution I will go mad!'

Dee retracted slowly to his previous posture, somewhat like a serpent uncoiling back to being at rest. Or a new striking position. Will shook his head, trying to clear the webwork of unnatural impressions from his eyes.

'Who is the woman?' Dee asked sharply.

'I'd prefer not to say.' Will rose from his chair, nerves on guard against a sudden lunge by Dee. 'Now that I've learned my quest is futile, I'll—'

'Halt!' Dee commanded. Once again, something in his voice made Will do so. 'I said *I* have sought it in vain, young man. I said nothing of someone else's quest being futile. All lives and all circumstances are different. I have no way dismissed your entreaty. But we are helpless without a name. The fey are rare now in England, at this late day. I know of only a couple of possible candidates, and they merely rumored. And I cannot make a mundane person immortal, any more than a pigeon, or the wind. I need context, circumstance. Provide that, Will Hughes, and perhaps there's a glimmer of hope. We'll see . . .' Dee made an attempt at a smile, one so suffused with calculation that it made Will shrink back.

But he asked himself what choice he had except to go along with this conniver. Still, he had a dread of mentioning Marguerite by name that he neither understood nor seemed able to conquer. So he started to turn away again, trembling.

'I must go, sir. I—' But glancing back just once, Will froze, as the look the sorcerer (irrespective of his claims to logic) speared him with was as terrible yet magnetic a look as he'd ever beheld.

Dee screamed, in a way that filled Will's mind and veins until he couldn't breathe, *What is her name, foul maggot?*'

Will gasped for breath and thought he felt his body beginning to decay as if he'd just been murdered, maybe by the knife-edge of the scimitar moon above, he thought feverishly. He felt his body start to turn liquid, then ashen, then foul as a sewer. This sensation forced him to his knees, and he lay full out on the floor as if in imitation of a rancid corpse. He couldn't help it. *Capitulation*. The word popped into his thoughts as if a hot sword point inserted there. Only capitulation could bring relief, stop the death spiral. Whatever was left of his reason knew it was all a spell. But this conjurer's horror, writhed of worm and stench, was too much.

'Marguerite D'Arques,' he whispered, still lying stretched out on the cold and grimy floor.

Then he managed his body back up and into the chair, quivering with a suppressed sob he would not let escape his lips, lest Dee obtain such satisfaction. Will sat in the chair with the self-esteem of a worm. Maybe the king of worms, he thought despondently, maybe the Charlemagne of worms. But still a worm.

'Oh, *that's* the name,' Dee said simply, with a calm that infuriated Will. 'In that case, all is not lost. No. A simple plan may do. But before I reveal it, let me confess my surprise. I'm not up on the latest news. Isn't she still entangled with that lout of a poet from Stratford-on-Avon? Which makes you a victim, even one more time over, it would appear? Heh heh. Though your taste in loose women is, of course, no business of mine.'

Will tried not to take too much offense at Dee's leering tone. After all, he was offering a sliver of hope now.

'That's over, with the poet,' Will replied calmly enough. 'Destiny has brought Marguerite and me together. And I'll make sure it's for her entire lifetime, not just mine, if it's the last thing I do.'

'Yes, of course you will, my boy,' Dee clucked sympathetically. 'And I'm going to do my utmost to help. I cannot provide any guarantees, but these are more promising circumstances than I initially perceived. Promising!'

Will allowed himself to wonder why, but then he was suddenly beside himself with elation. His emotions were those of a man first told he had a month to live and then told he wasn't ill. 'How soon?'

'Soon enough,' Dee said soothingly. 'First there are a couple of practical tasks you must accomplish for me.'

'Such as?'

'I will need a couple of the good lady's possessions. Her silver box and her gold ring. With them worlds will open.

Without them, I'm afraid, all is lost. Do you know them?'

'Just the ring. It has a tower emblem on it. I have seen her wear it, though not often. I don't know any box.'

'The box will be unmistakable once it's brought into your presence. It's silver, with a swirling design, but I don't need to describe it. You'll *feel* it. It opens onto other worlds; it surges with an energy most people never get anywhere near experiencing in their lifetimes. Once you've felt the box, you'll never regret having been in its presence, nor coming to see me tonight either. And possibly your immortality will be just one more meeting with me away!'

'But how will I get these things? Are you asking me to steal them?'

'Well, that's your challenge. If Marguerite wanted you to be immortal, she'd have already given them to you. Perhaps – I don't know the woman or what's inside her psyche – perhaps you're all the more delectable to her for being fleeting. That would be typical, from a fey point of view.'

Will bristled, but endured the innuendo. What was crucial for him was to get these things and live on forever with his beloved – not to respond to taunts.

'It strikes me, Mr Will Hughes – and by no means am I asking you to steal or commit any other crime – that if you've had the singular fate to be this close to an immortal, and if you've made such an impression on me, the great John Dee, that I am willing to try the door to immortality on your behalf, that you'll have the intrepidness to bring me these items. Otherwise I will be disappointed in you, promising youth that you otherwise seem to be.'

'What will I owe you,' Will asked curtly, put off by such flattery while not being certain of its motive, 'for this profound service of yours, if it happens?'

'Owe?' Dee raised his eyebrows. 'The joy of immortal love is more than enough coinage for me, I assure you. I would not dream of something so crass as charging for your transformation!'

Will was not clear as to motive here either, but when he saw the opportunity to seal such a bargain, he took it. He walked to Dee's end of the long table and shook his hand. Dee's grip felt feeble, but the expression in his eyes crackled with intensity, as if he were flush with a lightning-like excitement. Will waited for Dee to escort him back to the front door, but then Dee indicated that Will should exit alone. 'I'm feeling a bit old tonight,' he told Will. 'Mentally, your visit has been a tonic for me, but physically I'm afraid it has been no help. But I look forward to your return with those items.' Dee turned away and vanished into the dark interior of the house.

Will, feeling a vague dread despite his new hope, perhaps at the idea that he had uplifted the likes of John Dee even for a moment, walked back out into a night in which the chill sharpness of moonlight was making the carriage horses shiver. Or maybe they were feeling the same dread he was. But after waking the driver with a firm clasp of his shoulder, and climbing back in the carriage, renewed hope bloomed again and distracted Will from dread. The hope was a dark flower, petals of black, but it seemed to be irrigated by his blood and to grow straight toward the moon. And toward all the immortal days to come.

15

The Wild Hunt

The hounds herded me down onto a long, wide path bordered on the right by a canal and on the left by a straight line of trees, and then they left me, bounding down the avenue as if they'd sensed prey. I could hear their baying long after they vanished in a cloud of dust at the end of the long path. Then I was alone in the moonlit woods.

At least it wasn't as dark as it had been in the Luxembourg. No fairy shroud lay over the forest. Instead, bright moonlight illumined everything, turning the dusty footpath into a long, broad silver ribbon. Nor had the trees broken rank like the ones in the Luxembourg had. They stood like sentinels alongside the allée, straight and dis- passionate as palace guards. The wind that now came bowling down the path barely rustled their leaves.

That was strange, I thought, stopping to listen. I could hear the wind, but the sound it made wasn't the thrashing of leaves; it was hoofbeats approaching fast, coming straight toward me even though I couldn't see anything ahead but a flurry of dust . . .

I scrabbled to the side just as the dust rushed past me, the sound of hoofbeats hammering in my ears. Then they were gone. I followed the path to the end and crossed to another path that ran parallel. The whole woodland was cut into long, straight avenues – not a trackless wilderness at all. When I was halfway down the next path, I heard the hoofbeats again, welling up behind me. I turned and tried to stand my ground, but at the last minute I ducked to the side again, my heart racing to the staccato beat of the pounding hooves. Instead of retreating this time the sound stayed with me, as if it had lodged in my brain, a maddening tattoo.

I took off into the trees, trying to stay off the paths, which I saw now were just great big runways for the hunt to barrel down. But I wasn't alone under the trees. Something – or *some things* – were moving along the ground, stirring the dry leaves with soft, padded paws and hot breath. *Hounds*. And their prey. People were in the woods, stragglers from the square who hadn't returned to their hotels when the bells tolled midnight, but who had instead been lured into the woods . . . and into the hunting grounds. The woman in Breton shirt and capris ran past me, leaves and twigs clinging to her disarrayed hair and a wild, unseeing look in her eyes. She was pursued by the invisible hounds out onto the broad path where she took off running on bare feet. A cloud of dust pursued her. I stared at it, trying to make out what was inside it . . . and then wished I hadn't.

Amid the horses and hounds were creatures with cloven feet and horns that were not quite human and not quite beast. Hair covered their haunches and long tails, but their chests and faces were bronzed bare. Most awful were the expressions on their faces. They grinned and grimaced and salivated, leering after the woman in capris in a way that combined hunger and lust in a queasy mix. Their pupils were vertical, oblong slits – like goats' eyes. *Satyrs*. I recognized them from pictures and statues, but these obscene creatures were nothing like the prancing goatmen of classical art. These were monsters.

When the dust ball caught up with the woman, I lost sight of the individual creatures inside it. Cries came from the mêlée that sounded like a mix of the peacock calls I'd heard earlier that night and snarling dogs. When the dust cleared, nothing was left. Not the horrible creatures of the hunt or the innocent woman who had fallen victim to it.

Okay, I thought, trying to keep panic at bay, *don't run*. They like it when you run. I had Sylvianne's branch. I'd come to *stop* the hunt and ask its leader for passage to the Summer Country, not *become* the hunt's prey. All I had to do was step out onto the path when I heard the hunt approaching again. I crouched beside the path and listened . . . and heard someone weeping.

Was it another trick of the hunt? A sound to frighten me into breaking cover? But, no – this sound was only too real. I followed it to its source and found, crouched behind a boulder, Sarah. Her pretty yellow sundress was torn, her bare feet were dirty and bleeding, her hair tangled into knots. In the hour or so since I'd seen her sketching in the square she'd been transformed from a plucky teenager to . . . helpless prey.

'Sarah, honey,' I cooed, coaxing her balled fists away from her face. 'You have to walk straight back to your hotel. *Walk*, don't run. Do you understand?'

She shook her head. 'It wants me to run,' she gibbered.

'Yes, it does,' I answered, feeling a chill at the truth of what she said. 'But you have to walk. I'll stop it and you keep walking. Okay?'

She shook her head again. Maybe I could make her stay hidden ... but then I heard the hoofbeats approaching and felt Sarah tense. She was getting ready to spring. I knew because every muscle in my body longed to do the same thing. The hoofbeats were in my veins, nudging my muscles to action. Every fiber of my being longed to spring from cover and race down the long, straight paths.

'Listen,' I said. 'Remember what your art teacher said about taking your line for a walk?'

A little furrow appeared between Sarah's carefully plucked and waxed eyebrows. I had a vision of who she was: a pampered daughter and good student despite her raucous laughter and bad language. She wanted hard to please. I just had to get her to please me and not the hunt.

'That's what you're here to do, remember? You're going to take your line for a walk. When I tell you to, you're going to walk *very slowly* back up this path like it's a line you're drawing with your pencil. A long straight line. You're going to make it perfect.'

'Perfect?'

'Yes, and you're going to follow it.'

'Like *Harold and the Purple Crayon*? I love that book!'

'Me, too.' I gave Sarah a hug. 'Just think about Harold and his purple crayon and walk the line. Slowly. Okay?'

She nodded. I had no idea if I'd gotten through to her. I didn't even know if I was going to be able to keep myself from running, but we were out of time. The hoofbeats were growing louder. The hunt was on the road, almost upon us, and my feet were itching to hit the ground running.

I stepped out into the middle of the path, holding Sarah behind me. Then I turned to her, looked hard into her eyes, and told her, 'Walk,' uttering the command as I would to a recalcitrant dachshund. I was ordering myself as well as her.

She turned around but I didn't have time to see if she walked or ran. The hunt was upon me. I turned to face it, drawing Sylvianne's branch from my pocket and brandishing it in front of me. Blooming out of the dust cloud I saw it. A team of horses lathered wet, flakes of froth like sea foam cresting the air. The lead horse reared, his hooves inches from my nose. A swarm of hounds surrounded me, their breath rising hot and sour around me, choking me, their noses nudging me, teeth clicking against my skin, urging me, *Run! Why didn't I run?* They whimpered and scratched at my legs. I smelled my own blood and felt how wild the smell made the hounds. A satyr crept up on all fours into the throng of hounds and sniffed at my crotch. I pretended I was a statue – like Diana in the garden – and stared straight into the malevolent yellow eyes of the head steed, and then, when his rider mastered his horse's head level to mine, I looked up at the rider.

He rose off the back of his mount like a wave cresting a rocky shore, poised to crash over my head. He wore a tight-fitting, black suit stitched with red diamonds and a mask that divided his face into red and black. The eye staring out of the red half was black; the one staring out of the black half was bloodred. A multicolored, tattered cloak billowed around him, moving in a wind that stirred nothing else. The whole forest had gone still as glass.

He licked his red lips with a blackened tongue. '*Run!*' he hissed. 'Why don't you run?'

I held the branch up in front of me. It quaked like an aspen. 'I'm not here to play your hunting game,' I said, my voice trembling like the leaves on the branch. 'I'm here for passage to the Summer Country.'

A great booming rocked the forest. For a moment I thought it was thunder, then I realized the rider was laughing.

'Passage to the Summer Country? And who told you I could give you that?' Then, crouching lower over his horse's neck; 'Do you know who I am?'

'I think you must be Hellequin, going by your outfit.' I paused, staring harder at that outfit. It wasn't a harlequin's suit he was wearing; it was his own skin, blackened by fire and tattooed in red ink . . . or blood, by the smell of it. And his mask was no mask. It was his face, half-blackened flesh and half . . .

I reared back. There was no flesh over the right side of his face, only bloody sinew.

He chuckled. 'My outfit, you say? This is what a thousand years of riding to the hounds does to a man . . . oh, yes, I was a man once. A fine man, a ruler, with palaces and châteaus and hunting grounds of my own. I liked nothing more than to ride to the hounds whenever I could. I liked it so well I tired of chasing fox and pheasant and boar and instead began to chase more interesting . . . game.'

His blackened tongue swished over his bloodied lips. 'Only one day I made the mistake of pursuing a creature who wasn't human. A woodland nymph who in the moment of capture cried out to her sisters to punish me. It was Sylvianne and her kind who cursed me to this . . . life, if you want to call it that. An eternity of riding to the hounds. If I ever dismount, they'll devour me. See, even now they lap at my blood.'

I looked down and saw that indeed the creatures swarming on the ground were licking the blood-flecked dust with their long black tongues. Even the satyrs. I felt bile rise in my throat.

'So, you can't give me passage to the Summer Country?' I asked, anxious to terminate this interview.

'Sure,' he said, extending a blackened hand out to me. 'Ride with me for a bit and we'll look for it together.'

'Um, no thank you. I think I'll go by foot. I'm sorry to have troubled you. I guess this was Sylvianne's idea of a joke.' I saw that now. She probably liked taunting Hellequin by sending hapless women such as myself to ask him for favors he couldn't grant.

'Yes, she's probably laughing about it now with her latest pet . . . unless . . .' His bloody lips pulled back over blackened gums and I realized he was smiling.

'Unless what?' I asked, adding a hopeful (hopeful that I didn't look as nauseated as I felt) smile.

'I do have an idea of who to send you to. A fey who once took pity on me and gave me a cool drink of water from her spring as I rode through the Forest of Coulombiers – Melusine. She'd know the way to the Summer Country. You'll find her at the Château of Lusignan.'

I didn't have the heart to tell him that the Château of Lusignan was rubble and that Melusine wasn't anywhere near there. The last time I'd seen her *in the flesh* had been at Governors Island in New York, and she'd been dissolving into a puddle of goo.

'Thank you,' I said, feeling oddly reluctant to disappoint him. Why? I wondered. He'd been a rapist in life and he was still abducting innocent young women. What happened to them anyway . . . ?

A gust of wind gave me the answer. Hidden in the folds of his cloak was the woman in the capris and fisherman's shirt. She was clinging to Hellequin's back, her eyes squeezed shut. She looked thinner than she had earlier . . . and as I watched, she grew even thinner. She was evaporating, leaving only a husk of skin behind her that clung to the shreds of cloth that made up Hellequin's cloak . . . which weren't shreds of cloth at all, but the husks of Hellequin's previous victims. Okay. I didn't feel bad for him anymore, just anxious to get away. Besides, I'd just recalled where to find Melusine.

'I'll be going now,' I said, taking a tentative step backward. The hounds and satyrs parted to let me go.

Hellequin gave me another grotesque smile. 'Good luck on your travels, Garet James, and remember, if you ever get tired of walking, just call my name and I'd be happy to give you a ride. I'll keep an eye out for you.' He flicked his cloak over his shoulder and I saw the faces of his victims distend with pain. Then he was gone in a whoosh of hoofbeats that made me want to take to my heels. It took every nerve in my body to make myself walk out of that forest without breaking into a run.

16

The Black Bird

'On the way back, I've got to stop for a wee time to pick up a passenger,' the driver said to Will as his horses and carriage trotted out of Dee's front yard. 'Hope you don't mind, Sir Hughes.'

Will was startled. This was the same driver who had brought him up from London; he hadn't observed any change in his appearance or attire when awakening him just now. But he was almost certain that his voice had changed to a deeper, gruffer one, with more of a brogue.

'Sir?'

'I don't mind,' Will said. 'I'm quite tired, but I assume your passenger will be punctual?'

'That he will be, sir! Yes!' the driver responded, with what seemed like excessive enthusiasm.

Will pressed himself into the corner of his plush seat, virtually into the carriage frame, as if to be as close to exiting as possible. Then he gazed out the window at the woods lining the road while they drove on. Uncertain as *it* was, the natural world seemed for the moment all he had to hold on to. Moonlight silvered the crowns of close-grown oaks and maples, casting dappled shadows on the road. Here and there Will thought he could see a larger, more furtive shadow moving amid the tanglement of the woods, with no idea what it could be from. A boar? A large dog or an apprentice escaped from an oppressive domicile? He didn't know. He wasn't sure he wanted to know. He clasped his hands together in his lap for comfort. They were still a ways from the city. But, for the first time since his flight from Swan Hall, Will had the sense that London was home, the place where returning meant comfort. A ways away.

They traveled on in silence, the pounding of hooves the only constant. Every once in a while the screech of an owl slit the air like a razorstroke lathered by moonlight, but otherwise Will had his conflicting thoughts to himself. Maybe the farther he got away physically from Dee, the better, he considered. But maybe he was being too hard on his somewhat peculiar host. Likely Will couldn't have made things worse by seeing him. And maybe he'd made them better. Will scented that black flower of hope again. It wasn't a sweet scent, yet it wasn't half unpleasant either.

But another jolt came when the driver pulled over in the middle of nowhere. Will, skittish about an additional passenger in light of his tense mood, and the alteration in the driver's voice, had at least hoped for a signpost, or a house with a lit window. Where the driver had stopped had no marker at all, just the shadow-dappled woods on one side and an open field on the other, tall grasses stirring there in the caress of a soft breeze.

'How will he find us?' Will asked. 'With nothing to guide him?'

'Who?'

'The new passenger – your friend.'

'Calm down, Hughes,' the driver said, chuckling. 'He knows the road well.'

Will glanced around at the blankness. 'I'm going to stretch my legs,' he told the driver, stepping down from the carriage onto the hard dirt road before the man could reply. Will began to pace up and down at the edge of the woods, observing brilliant pinpoint stars above him, listening to the wind rustle through leaves so brightly green they shimmered in moonlight, and to louder and not easily explained rustles coming from only a few yards into the woods.

Oh, to be back in my meager bed, Will thought. But better to shudder out here than return to the carriage and its creepy driver.

He heard an enormous rustling from farther into the woods, one that made him pause in his strolling to listen keenly, and even as he paused, he observed, from the corner of his right eye, a gigantic black bird rising over the open field opposite, flapping huge wings slowly. The woods immediately fell silent, or at least back to their murmur of crown sway, branch creak, and twig crack. Those moving shadows still seemed to move.

Will's gaze was fixed on the black bird, in growing astonishment. He began to realize that the bird was of truly spectacular size. Indeed he was afraid to estimate the wingspan, but when it hovered in line with the moon, it blotted out that white curve entirely. And when it soared higher, the wind seemed to pick up, as if its flight contributed materially to the wind's force.

Will was startled again by a man's voice coming at him from the open window of the carriage, the same window that he had moments earlier been staring out of.

'*Pardon moi, monsieur.* It is a beautiful night, yes, admittedly, but I am on an urgent errand toward the city. If you'd be so kind . . . ?'

Will squinted into the darkness to make out the man's face, but he was wearing a cloak with a hood pulled low over his forehead, making it impossible to see his features. The man must have come from the other side of the road and clambered aboard without Will's hearing him. So many sounds were abroad at the moment that they thwarted any logic to hearing. Perhaps the grass had been high enough to conceal the man's presence when they first pulled over. Will didn't want to consider any other explanations until he was safely home in bed.

Rather than ask the newcomer to give him his seat back, Will got in the carriage on the road side, shooting the black bird another glance as he did so. Fifty feet across, he guessed, though if so, that made it likelier apparition than bird. He felt the unnerving sense, as he ascended the steps, that the bird's moon shadow was concentrated on him. As if a living being could concentrate its shadow by will, the way a magnifying glass could concentrate the sun's rays to set a twig aflame. To what purpose, he couldn't fathom. But he hurried the final few steps into the carriage's shelter, bothered by the image of fire. He could only imagine what sort of fire the bird's shadow might set: maybe dark silver in color, and with flames that felt like ice!

Upon reentering the carriage, Will was struck by an odor that hadn't been in it before. At first it was not unpleasant, a smell of singed roses as if a garden had caught on fire, a domesticated scent with a flavor of the savage. But a hint of ash threaded through the scent soon became sulfurous, and this mix of the fragrant with the foul was oppressive. Will began to breathe through his mouth, then became aware of a proferred hand above his lap. He turned to the newcomer, who was smiling affably enough, and took the man's hand, but in that instant, strange things started to happen to the hand he took. The flesh seemed to peel away to a shimmer of delicate bones, the spaces between them glowing, and in the moments before Will fearfully withdrew his hand, he thought he was grasping whirls of tiny motion, not even bones left, spinning orbits colliding with his own with little zings of electric shock. That gave his own hand a buzzing, painful sensation, even as it then recoiled away from the newcomer's.

As if his atomsight had now become atomtouch! But then the sensation trailed away and the newcomer's hand, to appearances, returned to flesh.

All of it had happened so swiftly . . . but he had looked down and seen his hand holding virtually nothing, he was sure of it – not even the veneer of a hand, just its atoms – before he pulled away with a shudder.

'Charles Roget,' the newcomer identified himself.

'Will Hughes,' Will said softly. The man's name was French, but the accent was peculiar – more Italian than French – and contained a trace of mockery. Mockery, perhaps, of Will's fear. Only a fiend would mock so, Will reflected. That didn't mean he wasn't sitting next to one.

They rode on, the occasional lit dwelling becoming more frequent, indicating London's dawning proximity.

Then Roget snapped his fingers as if he'd forgotten something, leaned forward in his seat, and said casually to Will, 'Charles Roget's my Christian name, but in the street they call me Lightning Hands.'

Will was in no mood for repartee. But, fearing that even no response might incite the man to chatter, he turned toward him and murmured listlessly, 'Is that so?'

'If it weren't so, why would I say it?' Roget answered sharply. He leaned forward farther, flapped his arms forward, and his hands over his knees, then splayed the fingers on both hands downward toward the carriage floor. The finger splaying was done with profound slowness, as if it carried some hidden meaning. Will gazed at him wonderingly, then Roget snapped his fingers and tiny, iridescent lightning bolts flamed downward from his fingertips and scorched a small area of the carriage's lavender-carpeted floor, turning it a pink-tinted ash black that the subsequent bolts further illumined, reminding Will of the ash-tainted rose smell earlier.

Will felt a strong urge to fling open the door and hurl himself out of the carriage while it was in motion. He'd hit the ground rolling, he imagined, and—

Roget put a lank left arm around Will's shoulders in a comradely way that was the faintest bit improper and brought Will closer to him. 'I've spent decades studying the ways of lightning,' he said confidentially – as if Will were his oldest friend. 'In them lie the secrets to many of the world's ills, I believe. Disease, pestilence, decay – why perhaps even to that final ill – death. I believe that in the power of lightning might lie the secret of immortality. Would that be of interest to you, young sir?

Immortality? Now that would be a true miracle, wouldn't it?'

'*Miracle* is a word I associate with heaven. And our Savior. I'm not sure you're using it correctly. What you speak of sounds like the work of demons.'

'Ah,' Roget said, laughing with a crackling sound. 'There are no demons but the enemies who torment us on this earth.' He flicked his right wrist upward and sent off a bolt at an angle that caused it to nearly slit Will's right ear, then to pool harmlessly in brittle luminescence against the side window of the cab. The driver might have heard the sparking conclusion not too far from his perch, but gave no sign of it. Roget's crackle deepened with apparent amusement and Will felt even more afraid. His veins chilled with the darkness. But he had the courage to speak.

'Has John Dee sent you?' he blurted. 'As a messenger of his powers? Or, to threaten me in this vile way? It won't work, Monsieur Roget,' he added importantly. 'My miracle is stronger than yours. My miracle is love.'

Roget's crackle nearly became a shriek, then died away suddenly like a torch plunged into water. 'If you think love is stronger than lightning, you've got a lot to learn about life, boy. Lightning is a condensation of the universe itself. "Love" is mostly illusion, the mutant offspring of self-interest and moon shadows. As to Dee, that is but a worm to my dragon. I would no more carry a message for him than a hawk would for a goat!' By way of additional exclamation point, Roget fired off yet another bolt, brighter than the others, as if he had added fire and *urge* to it. It found the tiniest scrap of Will's chin before glancing off into a blur of brightness against the window.

Will grimaced with a fiery pain that, though tiny in diameter, carried the force of a too fierce pinch. Almost unthinkingly, he coiled and unleashed a savage left hook against Roget's jaw. The miracle worker seemed dazed for a moment, blinking heavily and doubling over, his skinny torso riding his bony lap. But when he came back upright, he held a gleaming Spanish buccaneer's knife in his right hand, one he'd evidently kept concealed in a scabbard affixed to his leg. He drew the knife overhead for a downward blow, grinning with wicked slyness at Will, though all of it a bit sluggishly as if he were shrugging off the effect of Will's punch.

The window to their right shattered with a metallic sound and both men glanced over to see what had happened, but the window was draped in black as though by funeral crêpe. Will took advantage of his opponent's distraction to leap from the carriage, rolling onto the ground as he'd reflected on doing moments earlier, hitting the ground with a jarring lurch and in a tangle of limbs despite his effort to remain bodily organized. Before he was able to get to his feet he saw Roget spring from the carriage, his black robe flapping behind him like the wings of the giant black bird Will had spied earlier. Something gold glinted at the man's throat and, as he leaped toward Will, Will felt the first prickling of recognition. He'd met this man before – at the party in London at which the poet and Marguerite had announced their engagement. He was none other than the Italian priest who had denounced their union as bigamous! Was he some avenging Savonarola whose mission was to punish adulterous fornicators? But why attack Will? Neither he nor Marguerite were married. And, perhaps more to the point, where had a priest learned to wield lightning?

All these questions were but the work of a moment, and then the man – priest or no – was above him, sword drawn, and Will saw that he would be run through if he didn't move quickly.

But before he could take evasive action, his assailant was jerked back as though on a string. He seemed to hover for a moment midair, his eyes growing wide, then he dropped to the ground, crumpling into a ball like a piece of scrap paper tossed impatiently away by a frustrated writer. Will looked up into the sky to see what force had so cavalierly disposed of Roget – and saw, hovering above him, the huge black bird. It was beating the air with its enormous wings, its beady, bloodred eyes focused on the inert, face-down figure of Roget. When Roget turned over, the bird dove at him, snapping at his face with its long yellow beak.

Roget screamed and, shielding his face with his arms, scrambled to his feet. Will saw that he was trying to snap his fingers again to generate one of his lightning bolts, but the bird wouldn't let him. It kept pecking at his fingers, drawing spouts of blood where before lightning bolts had sprung. At last Roget was forced to run for the woods to seek cover from the bird's attack. Will watched his halting, bird-pecked progress, grateful that the bird had chosen Roget to attack and not him.

'Oi!' The driver's exclamation brought Will's attention back to the coach. 'That there gentleman didn't pay me the last half of his fare.'

'That man was no gentleman,' Will replied, shaking his head. 'How did he engage your services in the first place?'

'I were drinking at the White Horse and he overheard me to say I was taking a young gentleman to the estate of the great John Dee. He told me he'd pay me handsomely if I'd pick him up on the way back, but he only paid half up front.'

'That will teach you to trust scoundrels such as he,' Will said, getting back into the coach. 'But if you promise to get us back to London without stopping for any new passengers – man nor bird – I'll make up what you lost.'

The driver was agreeable to Will's suggestion and whipped the horses into a fast gallop. Above the hoofbeats Will thought he could still hear the flap of a large bird's wings, but instead of making him feel threatened, the sound comforted Will, with the notion that he was being watched over from above.

17

The Astrologer's Tower

When I had confirmed with the night clerk at the Aigle Noir that Sarah had come back, I went up to my room to pack and wait for dawn and the first train back to Paris. I was too keyed up to sleep, so I sat at the window watching the stone walls around the château take shape in the gray light of dawn and thought about Melusine.

Oberon had introduced me to her in New York last winter. I'd recognized the name from the fairy tales my mother had told me, but the old, wrinkled homeless woman I'd first met in Central Park hadn't resembled the legendary fairy of folklore. Melusine was supposed to have been so beautiful that the moment Raymond of Poitou came upon her in the Forest of Coulombiers he had immediately fallen in love with her. She agreed to marry him on the condition that he never look upon her on Saturdays, but as in all such arrangements the mortal spouse eventually gave in to doubt. Spying on her in her bath, he'd seen her long serpent tail and blamed her for the aberrations in their children. When he rebuked her, she sprouted wings and fled, although she haunted the castle for generations. When I met her in New York City, she hung out by sewer manholes and park fountains. She took me on a tour, while in molecular form, through the city's waterways and tracked down John Dee to his lair beneath the East River. At least we had thought it was John Dee. The apparition turned out to be a trap and we'd both been flushed out into the bay. Because Melusine was a freshwater creature, she'd begun dissolving instantly. I'd just managed to get her to Governors Island before she dissolved entirely and then decanted her into an empty Poland Spring bottle.

The bottle was locked in my suitcase back in Paris. Her last request had been to bring her home, and I'd been meaning to take the trip to Lusignan as soon as I got my sign. Now it looked as if I might have received that sign. Maybe if I'd taken Melusine back to Lusignan right away, I wouldn't have had to wait at Saint-Julien's for so long or come here to Fontainebleau to meet Hellequin. I shuddered thinking of the ghoulish rider and his cloak stitched out of abducted women. *I'll keep an eye out for you*, he'd said. Even now I could hear the echo of hoofbeats. I had a feeling I'd never really be free of them.

Although it was still too early for the train, I got up to go, unable to stand the quiet of my room any longer. Even the repeating pattern in the wallpaper had become maddening . . . all those fleeing shepherdesses glancing coyly over their bare shoulders, so many leering shepherds . . . I looked closer at a patch of paper near the door and saw that one of the shepherds had sprouted horns, cloven feet, and an erection. Worse, the frothy bit of shrubbery behind him now disclosed the hunt in all its horrors – the flayed face of Hellequin, the faces of his victims fluttering in his cloak. I spun around to see if all the vignettes in the wallpaper now held this scene, but suddenly I didn't want to know. I could hear the hoofbeats in my head. I turned and left my room, closing the door behind me and making myself walk down the long, straight hall without glancing left or right at the wallpaper.

On the train back to Paris I picked up a discarded *Le Monde* and read about the fourth Seine murder. They were no longer being called suicides. All the bodies had been drained of blood. The Vampire Murders, they were being called.

It couldn't be Will, I told myself, wiping the newsprint off my sweat-slick hands. He never killed innocents and he had left Paris in May. A year ago I would have dismissed the appellation as a media affectation, but now that I knew vampires existed, I wondered not *whether* there were vampires in Paris, but *how many*. I'd never asked Will about others of his kind. The only other vampire he'd mentioned was the one whom John Dee had summoned to make Will immortal . . .

My sweat turned icy cold. Will had the box. He'd taken it to summon a creature to make him mortal. Had something gone wrong and he'd let out the vampire who had made him instead? Was that vampire now ravaging Paris for victims?

When we pulled into the Gare de Lyon, I experienced once again a moment of double vision – only now instead of seeing Holocaust victims being herded into freight cars by Nazi soldiers, I saw the crowds as so many beating hearts circulating blood for a centuries-old monster. I could hear the pulse of the crowd along with the hoofbeats that had lodged in my brain.

I hurried out of the station, urged on by that incessant beat, and walked across the Seine to the Left Bank. I found myself glancing toward the roiling water flowing under the Pont d'Austerlitz. Had it been only a handful of nights ago that I had looked into that water and wondered how despairing a person would have to be to throw themselves in? Had some monster of the night preyed on lost souls – such as Amélie and Sam Smollett – as they paused on the bridge's ramparts? Even though it was full daylight, I hurried on, barely able to keep myself from breaking into a run. Perhaps Madame Weiss would know something about the murders.

When I arrived at the hotel, though, I found that Madame Weiss was not there.

'She's gone to the country,' the manager told me, tight-lipped, her eyes slanting sideways. Then she quickly busied herself tidying up some sightseeing brochures that were already perfectly tidy.

'Madame Weiss looked upset when she left,' a man's voice informed me as I was opening my door. I turned and found Roger Elden leaning against the hall bookcase holding a cup of coffee. In my overtired state I wasn't sure which smelled better – the coffee or the clean tang of Roger Elden's cologne.

'Did she?' I asked. 'Do you know what was the matter?'

Roger shook his head, a soft brown lock falling over his eyes. I noticed lines around his eyes and some silver threaded through his hair that I hadn't noticed before, little signs of age that only made him better looking. Why was that the case with men? I'd never worried before about growing old, but I wondered now if Will wasn't able to become mortal again, what it would be like to grow old while he didn't. Especially with a man who might have cared so much about his looks that he'd traded daylight for eternal youth.

'. . . so if you wanted to come, tonight is perfect.'

'I'm sorry,' I apologized, realizing I'd missed half of what Roger Elden had been saying while I worried about my vampire ex (the one who'd abandoned me) noticing gray hairs and wrinkles. Talk about shallow! 'Come to what?'

'The conference is sponsoring a series of midnight tours of famous astronomical landmarks. I know it sounds eccentric, but what can you expect from a bunch of science geeks?'

I smiled. 'Hey, some of my best friends are science geeks. My friend Jay once dragged me to Nicolas Tesla's abandoned laboratory on Long Island.'

'Cool. Nick was a genius, but a bit of a nut,' Roger said, as if speaking of an old colleague instead of a scientist who had been dead for over fifty years.

'Where's the tour tonight?'

'The Medici Column. It's over by the Bourse on the rue du Louvre. There's a spiral staircase inside it that leads up to the top of the tower. It's normally closed to tourists, but it will be opened tonight for members of the conference.'

'And what's on top of the tower?'

He grinned sheepishly. 'A weird metal contraption built by a sixteenth-century astrologer.'

'Gosh, who could say no to that?'

'Really? You'd go?' He beamed at me so hopefully that

I felt myself dangerously close to tears. I had a sudden urge to unburden all my troubles to this complete stranger, but when I recalled how bizarre those troubles were, I told him I'd meet him at eleven thirty in the lobby and let myself into my room before I could make a complete fool of myself.

I dropped my overnight bag on the floor and collapsed onto the freshly made bed. The maids had left the window open, letting in a cool breeze that ruffled the lace curtains. Beyond them the green leaves made a soothing murmur. I felt as if I'd come home. I closed my eyes and fell into a deep sleep and a strange dream.

I was on a road – or perhaps *above* a road. I could see a carriage speeding along it as if I floated in the air. It was my job, I somehow knew, to keep whoever rode in it safe, but safe from what I didn't know. The countryside on either side of the road appeared peaceful – rolling hills, cultivated fields marked off by hedgerows – *England*, I found myself thinking with a pang that felt like homesickness. I followed the coach through twilight and into night until I felt so tired my limbs – *wings?* – began to feel as heavy as lead. I looked longingly at ponds surrounded by tall grass on either side of the road. *Good nesting ground*, my dream self thought. But just as I began to drift from the sky, I woke in the dark room with a start, feeling as if I'd not only slept the day away, but somehow slept years . . . even *centuries* away. And that I'd forgotten something.

Melusine.

I went to the closet and dragged my suitcase off the top shelf. The Poland Spring bottle was still inside. I jiggled it and held it up to the light, trying to see anything remarkable about it, but it just looked like water. Then I opened my laptop and looked up train schedules to Lusignan. After a half hour on the SNCF site, which kept crashing on me, I realized I had to catch a 6:10 a.m. train for Poitiers, then I'd have nine minutes to transfer to a train to Lusignan. If I missed it, I'd have to stay overnight in Poitiers because there was only one train a day to Lusignan. How remote was this place anyway?

When I googled Lusignan, I found out. Other than a Wikipedia entry on the Lusignan dynasty, I could find nothing about the town. When I tried to find a hotel, I got results for Poitiers. Apparently the town had no hotel. If I missed the one train back to Poitiers, I'd have to . . . well, I'd better not miss it.

By the time I finished plotting my itinerary it was 11:25. Roger Elden would be waiting in the garden. I put on a sweatshirt over my T-shirt and jeans and tossed the Poland Spring bottle into my backpack – just in case I didn't have time to get back here before the train. As I went out into the garden, I reflected that by the time I caught up with Will Hughes I would be nearly as nocturnal as he was.

Roger Elden was sitting at one of the little metal tables in the garden, a bottle of champagne and two glasses set up before him.

'I knew you'd make it!' he said, popping the champagne cork and filling the two glasses. 'You look like a woman who couldn't resist an otherworldly experience.'

'You have no idea,' I said, taking a glass. 'What are we drinking to?'

'To exploring dark matter and bringing the universe's mysteries into the light.' He held up his glass.

I held up my glass and clinked it against Roger's. The clear chime (where had he found two crystal champagne flutes?) reminded me uneasily for a moment of the bells tolling in the Garden of Diana last night, but I shook off the connection. 'To the light,' I said, echoing the last words of Roger's toast.

His glass paused halfway to his lips and he tilted his head at me. 'Exactly!' he said, breaking into a grin. 'To the light!'

The champagne was ice-cold and tasted mysteriously of orange blossoms and cloves. We finished our glasses, then Roger stoppered the bottle and put it into a padded carryall, which he put over his shoulder.

'I thought we'd walk. It's such a beautiful night. I love Paris after dark, don't you?'

I agreed and we started out, walking briskly down the rue Monge toward the Seine, then crossing the river over the Île de la Cité past Notre Dame, lit up like a great ship sailing along. I asked Roger how he became interested in astronomy, and he chattered happily about a boyhood fascination with the stars, an influential academic mentor, and an enduring quest to plumb the secrets of the universe. His favorite quote was Hamlet's: 'There are more things in heaven and earth, Horatio, than are dreamt of in your philosophy.' His favorite Crayola crayon was Midnight Blue (the same as mine), and his favorite song was Van Morrison's 'Moondance.'

Talking about musical tastes led me to tell him about Jay and Becky's band. He loved that they called it London

Dispersion Force and made me sing two of their songs after promising not to laugh at my voice. He failed dismally and we walked through Les Halles laughing like two drunks coming home late from the bars and cafés that filled the neighborhood. We were still laughing when we reached the Medici Column at the end of a long park. The conversation had made the walk go so fast I was surprised to reach it so soon – and a bit dismayed to find that no one was there at the column waiting for us.

'You said your geeky colleagues loved this sort of thing.'

Roger shrugged. 'They probably all went out clubbing. Astronomers are like a bunch of frat boys on spring break. But look, the door's unlocked. Shall we?'

Roger's cheerful demeanor was perfectly open and non-threatening, but it suddenly occurred to me that entering a deserted tower with a man I didn't know wasn't the brightest idea. On the other hand, could it be much worse than going into the Luxembourg at night to meet a tree spirit? Or into the Forest of Fontainebleau to meet Hellequin?

'Okay then,' I said, 'to the light!'

Roger grinned at me. 'Absolutely. There'll be plenty of light on top. But we'd better use this on the way up.' He retrieved a flashlight from his bag and flicked it on. 'We've got one hundred and forty-seven steps to go in the dark.'

The view from the top of the Medici Column turned out to be well worth the climb. The Gothic façade of Saint-Eustache towered to the north, and the Seine and Notre Dame were plainly visible to the south. The lights of Paris glittered all around us. Roger took a blanket out of his bag and spread out a picnic of champagne, cheese, bread, and strawberries. It was windy on top of the tower – the only shelter being a wrought-iron cupola – but the night was warm enough that I didn't mind. In fact, after a second glass of champagne I found I didn't mind much of anything.

'This reminds me of climbing up to my roof when I was a teenager,' I told Roger. 'It's funny how being physically high up can make you feel above all your problems.'

Roger nodded. 'I like to think that's why Cosimo Ruggieri had this tower built. Of course, ostensibly, it was because he needed it to conduct his astrological studies, but I imagine that he needed somewhere to get away from the politics of Catherine de Médicis's court.'

'Cosimo Ruggieri? That's the name of the guy who used this tower?'

'You've heard of him?' Roger asked with a look of pure delight on his face. 'You *are* a fellow nerd, aren't you?'

I laughed. 'I haven't just *heard* of him. Remember the watch I showed you? Look.' I held up the watch pendant I'd made only a few days ago. 'It's inspired by one I saw at the Musée des Arts et Métiers that was supposedly owned by Cosimo Ruggieri.'

'Really?' Roger bent over the watch, examining the front and back carefully, tracing the etched stars and planets with his fingertips. He looked positively reverent. 'What an amazing coincidence . . . and an amazing watch.'

'I'll make you one. It's the least I can do for you show-ing me this tower. Tell me more about Ruggieri. You say Catherine de Médicis was his patron?'

'Off and on. In 1570 she built the palace that once stood attached to this tower because of a prediction Ruggieri had made, but then in 1572 she accused Ruggieri of plotting against her and practicing necromancy. He fled Paris. But then Catherine just as suddenly and mysteriously pardoned him and assigned him the revenue from an abbey in Brittany.'

'And what did he use this tower for?' I asked, looking up at the metal structure above us.

'No one really knows, but for years after Ruggieri died there were local legends that during thunderstorms a figure dressed all in black could be glimpsed standing on the tower. But that could have been because of the circumstances surrounding his death.'

'And what were those?'

'He lived into advanced old age – some thought he was using his sorcery to prolong his life – but eventually it was rumored around town that he was finally dying. Priests were sent to his rooms to hear his last confession, but Ruggieri roused himself and threw them out, screaming that they were mad and that there were no other demons than the enemies who torment us in this world. The priests were so offended at this treatment that they denied Ruggieri a Christian burial. When he died, the people dragged him through the streets of Paris and left his remains in the gutter. Some, though, claimed that he didn't die at all, that he crawled into the catacombs beneath the streets of Paris and there, maimed and dying, found a way to restore his life, and that the figure in black that appears on top of the tower during thunderstorms is Ruggieri, seeking the energy from the lightning to rejuvenate himself. There is one legend that claims that Ruggieri finally found immortality, but with one catch. He must grow old repeatedly and experience the same wrenching pains of death that he experienced being dragged through the streets of Paris, and only *then* can he be reborn each time as a young man. But with each lifetime, he ages faster. Imagine knowing that you had that pain to look forward to at the end of each lifetime, and that you would experience it again and again.'

'That would be a curse,' I said, looking down at my watch. How strange that he had made a watch that showed the progress of time across the years. Maybe he'd had a presentiment of the way he would die – and the rumors that would be spread about him after his death. 'Better to die once and for all.'

'I suppose . . . Are you cold?' Roger asked, moving closer to me. 'Here . . .' He took off his jacket and draped it over my shoulders. It felt warm from the heat of his body. He left his arm around my shoulders and I didn't move it away. With his other hand Roger pointed at the sky. Perhaps to take my mind off the gory story he had told me.

'Look, there's an unusual alignment tonight. The moon's with Jupiter and just past full. You can't see the rest of the alignment, between Jupiter, Neptune, and the wise centaur, Chiron, with the naked eye, but they're all there tonight, present and accounted for, at twenty-six degrees of the Water Pourer, shining with the moon.'

Roger pointed out stars and we talked about inconsequential matters until the sun came up. As we watched the sun come up over Paris, turning gray, shadowy buildings rose and gold, I reflected that unless Will was successful in his quest, this was something I'd never get to do with him.

a Voice like Leaves

Will arose just after dawn, thick with sleep, and walked to Marguerite's lodgings. He knocked on the door for a while, until a bonneted woman in the house adjacent raised her second-floor window and shouted down, '*Still* that clamor, boy, or I'm comin' at ye with a hammer.' Will desisted, though with a final knock that might have split the door in two had the side of his hand been sharper. His exasperation was understandable. If anyone was inside, they had stayed stock-still since his pounding started; he had not detected a sliver of movement. His intuition and darkening hopes told him no one was there. Marguerite had fled, and to where and for how long he could not guess. Maybe forever, a time span *she* could encompass!

But he had to know for certain she was gone.

Will circled the house three times, like a wolf scouting out hunting territory. But he still saw no flicker of movement and, at first, no means of access. On the fourth and most forlorn survey, he saw something he hadn't seen before. A second-floor window overlooking the fenced backyard was now half open, and a propped wooden ladder invited ascent. Will trembled with emotion and irrational hope at the sight. He didn't ponder much who had opened the window or set up the ladder. Perhaps a workman, resting in the yard with his ladder during Will's earlier circuits, was beginning his workday now.

Will, pumped with adrenaline, then performed a maneuver he couldn't have dreamed himself capable of. After a running start he leaped, grasped the top of the fence with two hands, and twirled himself over into the yard with a pinwheel motion. As if he already belonged to the fey, he reflected. He mounted the ladder and entered the house, announcing himself to no reply.

A half hour later Will sat exhausted on the first floor, back against the front door, legs stretched out wearily. He stared dazedly at the blank wall opposite. He'd been around the interior of the house three times and found no one and nothing, indeed no sign that anyone had ever lived in the house. And no workman. Been through every closet, every nook and cranny, stared hard up the chimney, scoured the ancient, stone-damp cellar. Nothing. Clearly she had gone from here, probably from London, perhaps from England. She could be anywhere now. Or nowhere.

As he got up to leave, dead with despair, he caught sight of a fragment of parchment in a corner of the foyer, its color so closely matching the paint's that he had previously missed it. He went over, saw two torn sheets of parchment, and suddenly fevered over with fresh anticipation. A light was in his eyes. Will picked up the parchments.

The first sheet had the letters *te* and *ve* on top of it, with smudges of black ink between the letters, as if more writing had been rubbed away. The second sheet had a detailed ink sketch of a church. It meant nothing to Will in the instant he beheld it, but in the pregnant seconds that followed, he stumbled over the sketch's mate in his memory, in a French history book he had pored over with his tutor. It seemed more plausible with each passing second that this was a sketch of Saint-Julien-le-Pauvre, the oldest church in Paris.

This realization had a mate in his thoughts, too, just like the sketch: Marguerite loved him! Why else would she be signing him with this church? She must be beckoning him to meet her at the church, circumspectly. The demonic attack suffered by these sheets of parchment, their tears and smear, showed she had plenty to be fearful of. Will had no doubt the sketch was a summons, any more than he doubted the message *Love, Marguerite* had been smeared to . . . *ve* . . . *te*.

Demon-mangling. Tears and smears. That was the second message of these parchments. He suspected John Dee, but couldn't fathom a motive, as Will needed to see Marguerite for Dee to obtain the box and the ring. That horrid Lightning Hands was another candidate. But Will realized it didn't matter how these sheets had gotten defaced, nor why the vandalizing was incomplete. He was sure that this was a summons, and that its meaning was that Marguerite loved him.

Will decided to leave for the church right away, to get to Dover on horseback and board the first boat to Calais, then take a coach to Paris. He could purchase a new set of worldly goods there, humble as they would be. All that mattered now was Marguerite. Carefully folding and putting the sheets of parchment in his pocket, he left the house and started running toward his horse's stable, to begin the journey that would bring Marguerite back into his arms.

Two days later, Will dismounted from the Calais-to-Paris carriage, about two blocks west of Saint-Julien-le-Pauvre. He wanted a chance, however brief, to gather his thoughts. Lodgings, clothes, provisions, could wait. He would think while walking to the church. And he walked, with a lilt in his step unlike any he'd felt since his days of strolling toward a rendezvous with Marguerite in London.

Dawn bouqueted the cobblestone streets with rose and lavender light, and Will breathed the sweet summer air of a neighborhood distant from the knock and murk of Paris commerce. He wasn't 100 percent certain he would find Marguerite in the church upon his arrival, but he was sure they would be meeting soon. He couldn't fathom any other reason for her leaving the sketch behind but to direct him to a rendezvous. Just as Will thought he might jump out of his skin with excitement, he rounded a corner and there was the church, and the park adjacent to it.

Will calmed himself down with an effort; he needed to compose himself. Marguerite could be waiting for him in a church pew! He pictured her in a rose dress with a gold veil – the colors of the Paris dawn – her loveliness illimitable, veiled in awe before the god of love. The pagan god of love that was, Will conceded to himself with a blush, for their love was not of the bodiless and self-sacrificial kind revered in churches. His wasn't, that was for sure.

The front doors of the church were made of heavy oak. They faced southwest and were in the shadows of stone arches, the brilliant splash of dawn outlining the church spire above them. To their left was a grove of elm and maple trees; in between the grove and a church rampart was a grassy area encircled by a wooden fence, containing a sapling about five feet high. A stone bench sat right outside the fence.

On a maple branch extending over the enclosure, a distinctive-looking pigeon perched. Will had not seen the likes of it in England, with its exceptionally long neck and brown feathers. The bird seemed to have a peculiar intelligence in its eyes, and its gaze held Will's for a lingering moment. As Will stared, the bird gestured with its beak at the church doors twice, then winked. Accidental motions, perhaps, but when Will pointed at the doors in a questioning manner, the pigeon nodded vigorously. Will was so fascinated by the bird's apparent intelligence that he set off toward it now instead of the doors, wishing to get a closer look, wondering if it had any more messages for him, but it responded by flying off. Then Will, his eyes bright enough to burn a hole through the church's stone walls, walked calmly to the front door and slipped inside the dim, shadowy interior.

The church was smaller than he'd anticipated, maybe ten or so pews in all, and right now no one was in it. This zero registered without even having to cross his consciousness. He took a sharp breath, the damp and chill air feeling like a dagger in his chest. Just then a priest strolled out from behind the altar, beginning to light candles. Will could think of nothing but finding an obscure place among the pews, anonymous enough that he could recover his equilibrium after this disappointment. After all, nothing was lost. It might have been unreasonable to expect

Marguerite at dawn. He did not know how long it had been since she'd left the sketch for him. She could not spend all her waking hours here! Patience! Let him give it a day, *at least*, before feeling any disappointment.

Will sat at the end of a pew a few rows from the rear. There he could swivel his head and see the entrance behind him, yet he was not an obtrusive presence to the priest. And he need not turn his head constantly. The rustle of a garment, exhalation of a breath, creak of the door, would announce a newcomer. He tried to relax, gaze affixed near an altar buried in shadows. The first glimmer of sunlight was coming through mottled-glass windows but hadn't reached the main body of the church yet. Will sat in a half world of drowse and love, trying to recover from his disappointment, soon in a reverie of prospective reunion with Marguerite, of her removing her veil to proclaim him her 'god of love.'

A rustle came from the doorway. A slight head motion told him four women were arriving together, the first of the morning's congregants. None of them Marguerite. Such disappointing rustles repeated themselves right up to the 8:00 a.m. mass. When Will was sure that Margeurite wasn't coming to attend the morning service, he exited the church, preferring to soothe his disappointment in the fresh air and sunlight. He sat on the stone bench facing the sapling, which also had a view of the entrance. But Marguerite did not come to Saint-Julien-le-Pauvre, not that sunwashed August day or during its pink-veined evening, nor on the subsequent day, on which a wan sky mirrored his declining mood. Nor during the thunderstorms *that* evening, when he refused to shelter even briefly lest he lose sight of the entrance. Logic said Marguerite would search the grounds for him if she came and did not find him in the church, but logic held no sway. Will sat rain-soaked and grim in the storm for an hour, the very atoms in the lightning bolts visible to him like incandescent pinpricks. Marguerite never came.

Had she left the sketch to taunt him? Was she urging him to seek *Christian* immortality, as she was never going to give him any other sort? Or was something more awful lurking behind her absence – some mortal fate that had waylaid her on the way from London to Paris? Or had the insidious Mr Dee, whom Will now thought he should never have confided in, decided to cut Will out of the situation and pursue box and ring on his own? Being immortal might not prevent Marguerite from being locked in a tower somewhere, until she gave up box and ring, or prevent her from being tortured for them. As far as Will knew, there was nothing unusual about her physical strength.

Or maybe she'd gone back to the poet?

Or maybe she just didn't care?

The church locked its doors every evening at eleven. Just once, on the night before this gloomy storm, Will had stayed on afterward anyway, sitting on the bench for a prolonged dark while until at last slumping over into sleep. The rising sun had awoken him, a caress so fine on his eyelids that at first he thought the rays were Marguerite's fingertips, until he opened his eyes onto an empty bench.

Tonight, even as rain relented and a warm breeze picked up from the south, he knew he couldn't maintain another vigil. Hot as he might want his hopes to be, the storm had washed away fire to reveal ice. As high as his spirits had soared on recognizing the sketch, so low did they plummet now. Chilled, even trembling, with rain as he was, Will closed his eyes with fatigue and felt as if he had dived into a black pool, an anti-pool to the one he and Marguerite had lingered by. The swans from that pool were circling him now, but he could only see the black one, and him vaguely, a faint outline in murk. His white mate was invisible. Marguerite was gone.

As soon as the 11:00 p.m. priest padlocked the doors, Will trudged back to his lodgings.

In the next two weeks Will visited the church twice daily, at 10:00 a.m. and 10:00 p.m., but his vigils were over. He might stay a few minutes at 10:00 a.m. or an hour or two, mostly the latter, depending on his mood, but he never stayed past the early afternoon. At night he would be there only until the closing. In the early visit the pain of Marguerite's nonappearance would soon become unbearable, searing like a physical wound, an excruciating sadness. In the second, he often arrived numbed by daylight activities, especially drinking, but the pain would reach him nonetheless. He'd gone beyond casting about for explanations, as if his wound were congealing, but that didn't help with the pain.

Hope of her coming had receded, yet he *was* determined to wait until the end of his life! He might be only nineteen, but there was no life for him beyond Marguerite.

Eventually, at the end of one of the meandering walks that often filled his afternoons, he stumbled on a street that brought life into this dreadful time, something to anticipate each day besides disappointment. The rue Quincampoix was little more than an alley threading its way through the commercial center, but the alley contained bustle and clamor, hands raised with shouts, animated conversations while printed flyers were flung about. Will's French was mediocre, yet he recognized that the din in the alley was not French, nor any language he was familiar with, but was a number-laced jargon sequenced to fingers held aloft in various configurations. This number world reached him in the same creative place that had arranged his thoughts into metrical poetry. Soon he realized that this was the phenomenon Guy Liverpool had spoken of, Paris's primitive stock market, more confined and more boisterous than London's Exchange Alley. 'The future of Europe,' Liverpool had called it.

Will made Quincampoix part of his postchurch walking routine, luxuriating in mania and cacophony, feeling at home as if Guy Liverpool had been prescient on his future. It was a strange place to be soothed, but it was also the opposite of the dark, cold solitude at the church. The rue Quincampoix was rambunctious with raw emotions, even if they were mostly greed, anger, and envy. At least they weren't the emptiness of his beloved's absence. By the fourth or fifth visit, talking to no one and not knowing a word of this tongue, he had figured out what was going on. The flying hands, shouts, and whirled papers were bids to buy or sell stock certificates, which were percentages of ownership in companies.

His figuring out inspired, one afternoon, historical thoughts. Street markets must have been gathering momentum for a while now, in a citied world well beyond the grassy hills of Somerset in which he'd come of age. Despite their brief past, such markets could have a long future. London and Paris were not the simple castles and manors of medieval times. They were gigantic entities, growing and growing. Indeed rue Q's mayhem, boom and sink of ask and bid, was like a pulse in the street, maybe the tiny, incipient heart of an endless city to be, a world capital.

Of course, still, Marguerite was all that mattered. The thought of her drove him back to his lodgings, so he could rest and dine before returning to Saint-Julien-le-Pauvre. He *must* not miss his 10:00 p.m. appointment, ever. It was still his main reason for living.

The next afternoon, having eaten too heavy a lunch and drunk one too many glasses of ale, he thought for an instant he glimpsed, halfway down rue Quincampoix, Guy Liverpool. He was conversing with two men, one a tall African man in rainbow robes who resembled the Moorish doorman at the poet's London residence, the other leaving a resemblance to Lightning Hands. Will was so startled that he turned and walked in the other direction without observing further. He did not want to make his presence in Paris known to a past assailant, or an intermediary with Dee, or anyone either man knew. But while walking away, he reflected that if he again spotted Guy or the Moor or Lightning Hands, he might find it diverting enough to approach them.

The next morning Will as usual visited the church, did not find Marguerite, and went to his bench to wait another hour or two. If he hadn't been in the throes of despair the fine weather might have cheered him ... might even have inspired him to write a poem ... Instead the warm sunshine on his face coaxed him into sleep.

When he awoke, the sunshine was hot on him, then suddenly blocked by a round face, as if a man had arrived before him out of nowhere. Will blinked, attributing this effect to sun dazzle but not *sure* that was the cause and reared back to get a better perspective on the man standing over him. He was one of the oddest-looking men he'd ever seen, with a huge, bald head like a gargantuan eggshell, square and compressed facial features, nervous eyes, and a rotund body not quite as small as a midget's. He wore a gardener's mud-streaked work clothes and held pruning shears in one hand.

The man looked as astonished to see Will as Will was to see him.

After a silence, Will asked, as affably as his nervousness allowed for, 'Where did you come here from?'

The man glanced lovingly at the sapling, then spoke to Will in a peculiar voice. The timbre was that of leaves speaking, a fluttering with a faint rasp of bark in the background, and with a tint of wind, a tone of green that seemed to hue and ripple his words as Will heard them. Nobody could have resembled a tree less, but Will had the uncanny sense that he was listening to leaves.

'That's hard to say,' his voice floated. 'I don't know . . . I dozed off a few hours ago in my workshed and . . . where do *you* think I came from?' The man shook his head dazedly, as if the contemplation of such a question made him feel faint.

Will had a vision of a cluster of twigs in the shape of a hand, of veinlets in leaves carrying human blood. 'Let's start with who you are,' Will suggested. 'That might tell me where you came from.'

'Oh, that's simple. I'm His Majesty Henry IV's botanist, Jean Robin. Gardener extraordinaire.'

Will restrained himself from laughing; he did not want this poor soul to feel humiliated. No doubt his bizarre appearance had made him an outcast, and that could be where his apparent interest in insinuating himself into the society of trees originated. As if to corroborate the thought, the brown pigeon swooped down and perched on Jean Robin's left shoulder. Then Jean Robin provided a few more details about himself. 'I am the discoverer of the tree *Robinia pseudoacacia fabacées* this sapling will become. And a poet has told me that my head is the green globe around which Paris orbits.'

Will nodded. 'I am most impressed by your résumé, Monsieur Robin.' He paused, pondering what the leaflike quality in Jean Robin's voice could be. Whatever it was, Will felt he had gained an insight from hearing leaves speak. Just as atoms made matter not quite what it appeared to be, maybe distinctions between lifeforms weren't quite what they seemed to be either. He wondered if Jean Robin could be a sort of bulb that had originally sprouted up from a tree root. The man's voice wafted from him like green-veined wind from treetops. *I am speaking to leaves*, Will thought. *To leaves*. Will shared this insight with the gardener.

'Likely you did come here from your shed. Or from the garden you have created. That's not surprising. You are of the leaves, Monsieur Robin. I can hear it in your voice. The very wind could have blown you here!'

Will thought Jean Robin was blushing, a faint gleam of green streaking his otherwise pinkish skin. He was certainly smiling. 'You are much too kind, sir. My weight forbids such transport. Let's just leave my mode of travel to the mysteries. Life without mysteries wouldn't be much, would it? But please accept my gratitude nonetheless, sir. You must be a poet, to have conjured up ideas such as leaves talking. What sort of poems do you write?'

Jean Robin cocked his head to one side and eyed Will as if the species of a poet could be determined in the same way as a flower's, with careful observation and knowledge.

'Sonnets,' Will replied emphatically. He felt suddenly that this conversation was his most joyous moment in Paris since arriving, though he knew that wasn't saying much. He leaned back, exhaled a deep breath. The fresh, blue midday sky inspired him. For the briefest of instants he felt free of his burdens. He sat upright again on the bench with relief.

'Write me a poem then, sonneteer,' Jean Robin requested. 'A poem that tells me where I came from.'

Will found himself reciting a sonnet he'd neither written nor read. To his regret, he did not write it down, for afterward he could only recall fragments of it. The recitation itself was exhilarating. The poem seemed to come from a deep, quiet place, deeper than earth, quieter than light:

I see, one day, you'll live within a tree,
your skin turned bark, your fingers slender leaves,
your arms thick roots and branches. Wind believes,

Will continued, as crowns shimmered in a quickening breeze,

that you and woods, already now, are one. I do not flee
from such a merge of leaf and skin, a mystery
like why the moon is smaller than the sun,
or what was here the day the earth began,
or love that brings one immortality.
Jean Robin, you're well-blown here now by wind –
a deeper sort than that caressing night –
from leaf-fringed dreams, and great my pleasure to
meet you, become a sturdy lifelong friend;
I do not know just when my vigil ends,
but Marguerite is nigh! Your sign is true!

Will's mouth hung open after the last two lines because he had no idea what their logic was – how Jean Robin could be a sign of Marguerite's nearness – and expressing such optimism unnerved him; nothing was surer to jinx any hope for her than prematurely celebrating her return. But then Jean Robin's applause for the poem raised his spirits, and Will saw nearby branches were moving up and down in approbation, too, leaves quivering, maybe even the sun exhaling some extra light.

His pain over Marguerite was hardly forgotten, but for an instant peace was in his heart.

Jean Robin began to laugh while clapping, to appearances with joy and not mockery, a sound with a flute of music added to its leafery. The most singular laugh Will had ever heard.

'I too have my "love that brings one immortality,"' Jean Robin said when he'd quieted down. He gazed with fondness again at the sapling, and for a moment Will saw tears glistening in his eyes. 'All of my flowers, shrubs, and trees are precious to me, this one most of all. *Robinia* and its descendants, and *their* descendants, will live on far longer than I can. But I, their seeder, will live on through them.' He fell silent, as if his store of eloquence were spent, and Will saw the wind pick up in the trees, as if that were where Jean Robin's breath had gone.

Will had to agree with him. 'You are *so* right, sir, about living on that way, though it's not the sort of immortality I seek. And I don't seek mine for immortality's sake, but only because I have had the odd fortune to fall in love with an immortal and want to always be by her side. But you are of the trees and their everlastingness. That is why your words flutter to me like leaves. That is why your head reminds me of the bulb of a flower,' he added hesitantly, worried Jean Robin could be offended. But Jean Robin grinned as if pleased with Will's metaphor. 'You have the spirit of the trees in you. And no doubt they have your spirit in them as well!'

'As, no doubt, does the woman of whom you spoke in your sonnet have your spirit in her! Might it be that your Marguerite . . . no, I shouldn't ask. It would be too intrusive of me . . .'

'No, go ahead. Ask!'

'Well . . . ahem . . . I happen to have a few acquaintances here in Paris who . . . ahem . . . enjoy the benefits of immortality. They are of the genus *fée*, what you English call fairies. Is your Marguerite one of them?'

'Yes!' Will exclaimed, astounded. Perhaps this strange little man was an emissary sent to lead him to Marguerite. 'Yes, she is. You say you know others? Perhaps my Marguerite will be with them. Could you direct me to them?'

Jean Robin nodded his bulbous head while plucking a

broken branch off the ground. 'I have a dear friend, a scholar of the marine life, who should be able to direct you better. She lives in the *faubourg* Vauvert, a mile south of here, just beyond the Carthusian monastery. Her name is Madame La Pieuvre. If anyone in Paris can tell you where your beloved is, it's she. Madame La Pieuvre has her . . . ahem . . . hand in every pot.' Jean Robin chuckled as if he'd made a brilliant joke. Will didn't quite get it, but he happily wrote down Madame La Pieuvre's name and address and promised he'd seek her out immediately.

'Good luck on your quest for immortality, young man,' Jean Robin said as he bid him farewell, waving the branch in the air.

'And on yours!' Will called, glancing back at the little man. Another trick of sunlight eclipsed Jean Robin's figure for a moment, and all Will saw were swaying branches as if Jean Robin had already merged with his beloved *Robinia pseudoacacia* and thus found his own leafy immortality ahead of Will's.

He took a final glance at the steps of the church as he walked off and spied a scrap of paper there, conspicuous and unmoving despite a brisk breeze. Will could not resist a sudden urge to retrieve it.

His eyes came aglow, and he beamed more profoundly than he had when receiving Madame La Pieuvre's name and address from Jean Robin. Remarkably, this apparently random scrap of paper also had her name and address on it. Even more remarkable was the clearly recognizable handwriting the name and address were written in, one that brought elation to Will's features.

Marguerite's.

19

The Vestiges

I went straight from the Medici Column to the Gare Montparnesse, glad I'd thought to bring the Poland Spring bottle with me. As soon as I settled into my seat, I fell fast asleep. When I awoke, the train was hurtling past fields of yellow sunflowers. A turreted château flashed by, and the silver gleam of a river. Swans? One black and one white like in my dream? I couldn't tell for sure; the train was moving too fast. We passed more fields, some green, some tawny gold, limned by dark green rows of poplars. Old stone farmhouses, a lone tower on a hill that reminded me of something, then more buildings clotting together like beads of mercury until the countryside became outskirts and we were pulling into Poitiers.

I roused myself recalling that I only had nine minutes to switch trains. Plunging out into the chill morning air (the digital clock on the platform flashed 7:39 . . . then 7:40), I scanned the station signs for the train to Lusignan, didn't see it, recalled that I had to look for the final destination on the line, which was written on a slip of paper some-where in my bag, found it while the clock changed to 7:42, and then scanned the signs for La Rochelle Ville and saw that the train was boarding on Track 3 – the other side of the station – and would be leaving in six minutes.

I raced up a flight of stairs and down another, colliding with morning commuters, a nun, and an entire troop of mud-speckled French Boy Scouts. I jumped onto a waiting train, asked breathlessly if this was the train to Lusignan, was told no, and was directed to the train on the opposite side of the platform. As I darted across the platform toward an already closing door, the strap of my backpack snagged on a metal railing, wrenching my shoulder backward and catching the watch chain around my neck. I heard the snap of metal and felt the chain slide from my neck. *Stop!* I screamed as the watch fell. For one long moment the chaos of the platform seemed to freeze: Boy Scouts arrested in the middle of hauling duffel bags to their shoulders, a nun caught mid-sneeze, the sweat from a train conductor's brow suspended in the air as he leaned out the window of the front car, and, directly in front of me, a figure in long black coat and wide-brimmed hat, his face in deep shadow, his hand in mid-air, reaching for the falling watch, then *touching* it. Alone of all the occupants on the platform the man in black could move, albeit slowly. His gloved hand seemed to be moving through molasses as it reached the time piece, and his fingers splayed across its complicated gears . . .

'Grab it!' a voice inside my head cried.

I reached out and snatched my watch out of the man's hands, my hand moving far more quickly than his. *I could move faster!* For a moment his head rose and I felt the force of his gaze on me even though I still couldn't make out his eyes. The watch, now firmly in my hand, seemed to pulse, as if the fabric of time itself was a living thing, and the watch was its beating heart. Then I unsnagged my backpack from the railing and darted past the frozen businessman, the sneezing nun, and the Boy Scouts in their soiled uniforms, and dashed through the gap in the train doors. As soon as I did, the doors slid closed behind me, and the motion inside and outside the train recommenced. A whistle blew, a voice announced the departure of the train for La Rochelle Ville, and we were moving. I looked out the glass doors to see the man in the black coat slowly turning to watch the train pull out of the station, his head swiveling to face me.

Recalling the leap he'd made over the Luxembourg gate, I kept my eyes on him until the train had cleared the platform and he was only a black smudge in the distance. Then I sat down, clutching my watch, staring at the hands placidly ticking off the time. Had it been the watch that made time stop on the platform? But how? I'd made the watch myself and I wasn't aware of endowing it with any supernatural time-stopping abilities. Still, I was glad the watch hadn't broken. I spent the rest of the trip fixing its chain with the pair of needle-nose pliers on my Swiss army knife, my mind engaged with another problem. Why had the man in the black coat followed me to Poitiers? How had he been able to move when no one else (but me) could? And was he even now following me to Lusignan?

I stared out the window uneasily at the green countryside. We'd entered a verdant valley with a river flashing below – the Vonne, I recalled from my guidebook – trees encroaching so close to the track that the car filled with a green watery light. I waited until the conductor announced Lusignan, then leaped up and out the train doors as if I were in an espionage movie trying to evade Russian spies. But no one got out with me. The platform was deserted and remained so after the train pulled out. The station – a two-story, cream stucco house with green shutters and geraniums in the window boxes – was locked and shuttered. I stood for a moment watching the train to La Rochelle Ville disappear in the distance, feeling as if I'd somehow slipped off the map of France.

All the time I was in Paris I'd listened to American tourists complain about the crowds. They should come here, I thought, starting off down a cobblestone street that ran narrowly between high stone walls. I didn't see a single person on the walk into the center of town. If people were stirring in the houses I passed, they did so silently behind thick stone walls and heavy wooden shutters. Or maybe they were all on their *grandes vacances* in Brittany or the Midi. Even the town square was deserted.

Beside the ancient church I did see a sign for the rue de la fée Melusine and, following that, a bar named for her. I followed signs for 'the Vestiges' of the Château into an open square where a few workmen in green coveralls were strewing gravel on empty paths. There was a small Office de Tourisme, but its sign told me it wasn't open until 10:00 a.m. I climbed a hill, lured by café umbrellas and plastic flags, but found only an empty park with a double allée of pollarded trees, colored lights strung in between them, and stone, lichen-covered benches. I sat down on one of the benches and looked out over the Vonne valley, feeling sadness seep into me with the chill of the old stone.

In the story my mother had read to me the Château of Lusignan was a great castle with flags flying from its many towers. Melusine had built it for her husband, Raymond, and their descendants ruled there for over four hundred years. Now there was nothing, not even a plaque to commemorate where it had once stood. There wasn't enough left perhaps to even attract a few tourists. It felt as if Melusine and the dynasty she had founded had evaporated as surely as she had dissolved into water. What was left to return her to? What would she make of her once grand home?

I wandered back down the hill and past the closed tourist office, noticing now a small wooden sign pointing again to LES VESTIGES DU CHÂTEAU. I followed the arrow down a steep, narrow dirt path that clung to the hillside below the park. As I descended, I heard the rush of water and glimpsed flashes of silver between the trees – the Vonne running below in the valley. I came across a stone wall, a bit of toppled tower covered with grass and moss, like something from a Piranesi etching. I followed the stone wall through a narrow passageway into a round clearing full of wildflowers and dragonflies. Looking up, I saw the railing of the park and understood that the park was laid out on the foundations of the old château and these were its crumbling battlements. The vestiges, upon which the village held its fêtes. I imagined dances at night, children running in and out between the trees, old men sitting on the benches that once held up the walls of the Château of Lusignan.

I thought at last that Melusine would have been happy to see the château she raised tumbled down into rocks and moss. In the cracks of one of the walls I found a thin stream of water burbling up from some underground stream, even now seeming to erode the rock foundation further. I took out the Poland Spring bottle, uncapped it, and held it over the spring.

'You can go home now,' I said, pouring the water into the spring.

The water from the bottle joined the stream, then pooled for a moment in the cupping rock. A faint mist rose from the pool and spiraled upward. Everything was perfectly still in the grove; even the dragonflies paused in their flicker and dart. I felt the way I had on the platform in Poitiers, that time had stopped, that I was *outside* time. The mist wreathed itself into a sinuous shape – a woman with serpent tail and batlike wings. She turned to me and I saw the same green eyes I'd seen staring up at me from a pile of goo on Governors Island, only these eyes were full of joy.

'Thank you, Marguerite, my sister, for bringing me home at last.'

'It's Garet,' I said, recalling that Melusine had called me *Marguerite* and *sister* on Governors Island just before she'd dissolved. 'Do you remember . . . ?'

'I remember *everything*,' she said with a shudder that made the mist ripple into shards of rainbows. 'Did you find the box?'

'Yes, but then Will Hughes took it. He's taking it to the Summer Country to summon the creature that made Marguerite mortal—'

'You must sssssstop him!' Melusine hissed, water droplets spraying my face. 'She becomes stronger each time she's summoned, feeding on the need of those who call her. If she gets loose . . .' The water molecules that made up

Melusine wavered in the air with her agitation. I was afraid she was about to break up again, but then she steadied herself and went on, 'She'll destroy everything if she escapes the lake.'

'Why?' What I really wanted to ask was, if I stopped Will from summoning the creature in the lake, then how could he become mortal? And if he didn't become mortal, how could we ever be together? But those questions all seemed a bit self-centered in the face of global annihilation. 'Why does she hate humanity so much?'

Melusine rippled in the air, her molecules refracting rainbows. 'It'ssss a long sssstory,' she sighed.

I sat down on a rock beside her. 'Go ahead. I have hours before my train.'

'In the beginning the Summer Country and the human world ran side by side like two streams running to the sea.' Melusine's voice trilled like church bells in the still air, her lisp gone. I felt that she'd told this story to herself and others – perhaps heard it from others – many times, and like a stutterer who only stutters on her own words but not set pieces, she was able to recite it flawlessly. 'At first fey and humans lived peaceably side by side but with little interaction as we were too different. We fey were . . . *ethereal*.' A pulse of air and water demonstrated what she meant. 'But the longer we interacted, some of us became more . . . *corporeal*.' The droplets in the air became heavier and grayer, like the sky before rain. 'Most of us then only wanted to *play* with the humans, but some of us became so enamored of them they wanted to *be* human. We took shapes that combined their features with the animals they loved. We appeared as winged men and fish-tailed women' – she swished her own tail – 'as centaurs and unicorns and dragons. We learned what it was like to feel the sun on our faces and the rush of water over our skin. We learned what hunger and thirst felt like, and desire and love . . . and pain.' The heavy droplets began to fall. I was afraid she'd disappear entirely, but she collected herself in time and reassembled her molecules. She looked thinner, though, and fainter, and I wondered if she would have enough time to finish her story.

'The pain drove some of us further into our own world, which made our world *deeper* and began to separate the worlds. But others of us had become addicted to the sensations, the pain as well as the joy – I think maybe there were some who actually came to like the pain best of all because it made them feel most *alive*. Some say those were the ones who began taunting humans to hurt them, but others say it was the humans who, frightened by the strange shapes we took, tortured some of us. Whoever initiated the cycle of pain, once set in motion, no one could stop it. Our leaders believed it would be best for all – humans and fey – to dwell separately. The two streams of being were diverted, the worlds divided. Only some of us refused to go back to the Summer Country, especially the ones who had become addicted to pain, both the giving and receiving of it. They became what you would call *demons* and grew so awful that our leaders saw they could not leave the humans alone to deal with them. They set four guardians to watch over the human race and patrol the demons, one for each element. But the presence of the Watchtowers enraged the demons. There was a war and for the first time fey killed fey. One of the Watchtowers, the bravest warrior, my sister Maeve, was killed.'

Oberon had told me that one of the Watchtowers had been killed in a war, but he hadn't said which – and I hadn't realized that Melusine was her sister.

'Wait, does that mean you were a Watchtower?'

'Yessss,' she moaned, her lisp back in force. 'I loved mankind as your ancestor Marguerite loved it. But when our sister Maeve was killed, our fourth sister was so stricken she turned against mankind. She would have destroyed every last human, so Marguerite and I, aided by the leaders of the fey, trapped her in a lake that lay between the two worlds.'

'That's the creature in the lake?' I demanded. 'She's your sister? And Marguerite's sister, too? Which makes her . . .'

'Your great-aunt. Yessss.'

'So if I went to her and asked as a special favor for her grandniece to give Will Hughes his mortality back . . .'

A sudden chill fell over the grove. Melusine, her molecules now sharp as pinpoints, coiled in the air, her scales bristling. She lashed out so fast I thought she was going to strike me, but she stopped inches from my nose, her wings beating the air above our heads.

'Do you think she'll obey the call of kin when she cared nothing for me, her ssssisssster? She has dwelt in the lake for millennia, her heart growing colder with each passing year. Her only joy is feeding off the hearts of those who come to ask her favors. They say she only grants a wish if she's sure it will bring the supplicant grief. I told

Marguerite that when she asked to be made mortal, and look what happened – as soon as she was mortal, her lover betrayed her and became a monster—'

'And yet she didn't stop loving him. Nor have her descendants. Oberon told me that Marguerites have fallen in love with Will life after life – that he's spent an eternity trying to keep them apart.'

'Exsssactly,' Melusine hissed, spraying water in my face. 'What worse punishment than to know each descendant will be plagued by love for that . . . *man*. Even worse than what I have had to suffer. Loving a mortal man only ever leads to pain and heartache. You'd be best advised to leave Will Hughes to his own fate, which, if I know my sister, will be to be eaten alive.'

I was going to tell her that not all men were worthless. I might not be able to make any definitive claims for Will Hughes, but I knew some really decent men – such as my father, my friend Jay, and Becky's new boyfriend, Joe Kiernan – but before I could launch into a defense of the male gender, I saw another spiral of mist rising from the spring. Following my gaze, Melusine turned to watch just as the mist formed itself into a man in medieval armor.

'I cannot blame you,' a voice rang out like a deeper bass bell to Melusine's crystalline tinkles, 'for so hating my sex after how I treated you, Wife. I have bided all these long years, among the vestiges of our home, for a chance to tell you I am sorry for ever doubting you.'

Melusine quivered, each droplet swelling like dusky grapes. I could feel her hesitation, heavy as coming rain. All the centuries of wounded pride hung in the air between them. Would a simple apology suffice?

It did. I saw it first in her eyes – recognition, forgiveness . . . and then a love so startling in its clarity that the whole grove filled with light. She embraced him, water swirling into water, two streams once divided racing to join one another again. As they merged, I felt my own face grow wet, but then as they began to sink, a fountain in reverse, I collected myself.

'Wait! You haven't told me where I'm supposed to go next.'

'I should think it would be obvious,' Melusine's voice rilled in the air, its timbre already merging with the rush of the Vonne far below us. 'The place where my sister Morgane dwells is protected by an enchanted forest which you have to pass through first. Val sans Retour, they call it. The Valley of No Return.'

20

Effigy in Stone

Of all the ways I'd imagined embarking for the Summer Country, speeding down the E50 at 140 kilometers per hour in a Peugeot had not been one of them. But there I was, strapped into the passenger seat, trying not to squeal every time Octavia La Pieuvre used one of her hands to peel a hard-boiled egg or reach in the backseat for the map. She still had two hands on the wheel, after all, and seemed to be an expert driver.

'I drove an ambulance in both World Wars,' she said when I complimented her. 'Nothing like dodging exploding artillery shells to hone one's reflexes. This' – she gestured at the straight highway running between flat fields – 'is child's play. I want to get to the hotel in Paimpont before dark so we can both get a good night's sleep. We'll need it tomorrow.'

When I'd related to her that Melusine had said we had to go to the Val sans Retour, her pearly skin had turned ashen gray, but she wouldn't tell me why the place frightened her. I'd looked it up on the Internet and found out that the Val sans Retour in the forest of Brocéliande, the modern forest of Paimpont, was mentioned in Arthurian legend as the place where the enchantress

Morgan le Fay had trapped her faithless lovers. Was it just a coincidence, I wondered, that Melusine had said her sister's name was Morgane?

'This creature below the lake, Mor—'

All of Octavia's hands flew up in the air and the car swerved momentarily into the next lane. 'We don't speak of the Watchtower who betrayed humanity.'

I clucked my tongue impatiently. 'We're on our way to see her and ask her favors. I should think saying her name was the least of our problems.'

Octavia's hands resettled back on the steering wheel, but she still looked inky.

'And besides,' I added. 'It's not like I've never heard the name before. Morgan le Fay, half sister of Arthur, sorceress, is pretty famous. Is this woman under the lake the same person?'

Octavia sighed, but didn't answer. She tilted the rearview mirror with one hand and tisked at the inky flush on her face. Only when she had withdrawn a seashell-shaped compact from her purse, administered powder to her face, and clicked shut the compact with a decisive snap did she answer my question.

'Morgan le Fay,' she declaimed loudly, as if inviting the universe to smite her, 'Morrigan, Modron, Muirgen . . . her names are legion. She is the oldest of the four Watchtowers and the most . . . elusive. She is the gentle queen who escorts Arthur to Avalon, but also the enchantress who ensnares men in the Valley of No Return. She is Morrigan, the crow queen of war and destruction, and Modron, goddess of fertility and the harvest. She ruled over death and birth and could grant immortality to humans and mortality to the fey. They say she loved humanity best of all, but when her sister Maeve was betrayed and killed by a man, she determined to destroy the whole race. Her sisters Marguerite and Melusine tricked her into the pool at the center of the forest of Brocéliande and trapped her there using her own snares and spells.'

'The forest of Brocéliande? Okay, here's something I don't get. If you already knew that Morgane was trapped in a lake in the forest of Brocéliande, and you know that Brocéliande is the modern-day Paimpont, then why couldn't you just go to Paimpont, find the lake, and ask Morgane to make you mortal? Why did you need me? And why did I have to sit in a church in Paris for a week and then go to Fontainebleau and Lusignan?'

'The mythical forest of Brocéliande is not a place of this world. It can't be found on a map of France. You can't reach it on the E50' – she gestured with several hands to the blur of highway outside the car windows – 'or take a TGV from Montparnesse and expect to find the door open to Brocéliande. You could wander for days – for months, *years* even – in the forest of modern-day Paimpont and never find the pool where Morgane dwells. When Melusine and Marguerite imprisoned her there, they set spells to guard the approach so only a very few – those vetted by the fey – could find the pool. Even though you have gone through the steps and been sent on by Jean Robin, Sylvianne, Hellequin, and Melusine, you still have no guarantee that you'll find your way to the pool. The final test will be in the Val sans Retour . . . and it won't be an easy one. And, as the name implies, there won't be any second chances. Either we'll find the pool tomorrow or we'll remain in the Valley of No Return forever.'

After that dire pronouncement there didn't seem to be much more to say. We both lapsed into silence, Octavia intent on driving fast while I stared out the window at flat fields and turreted towns in the distance. I got the best sense of where we were from the large decorative billboards of each town – a cathedral for Chartres, a portrait of Proust complete with tea and madeleines for Illiers-Combray, bicyclists for Tours. Eventually I drifted off to sleep. When I awoke, we'd left the highway and were on a narrow country road bordered by towering trees. We passed rough stone cottages with brightly painted red or blue doors and delicate lace curtains in the windows.

I yawned and looked over at Octavia. 'Are we there?'

For answer she pointed to a sign painted on the side of a gas station. A lascivious, doe-eyed fairy in skimpy dress sat on a toadstool beneath the words BIENVENU À LE PAYS DE LA FÉE MORGANE. I'd been surprised by the lack of tourism surrounding Melusine's old home, but there didn't appear to be any lack here in Morgane's old stomping ground. We passed a camping ground decorated with tin cutouts of fairies, dragons, and wizards. The campers themselves were wearing long dresses and floppy shirts. It looked like a Woodstock reunion. A sign advertising a FÊTE MÉDIÉVALE explained the archaic dress. This must be a French version of the Renaissance Faires popular in America. When we pulled up to the Relais de Brocéliande, a half-timbered lodge sitting above a walled town, abbey, and lake, the parking lot was full of painted minivans and VW Beetles circa 1968.

'Is there something going on here this weekend?' I asked.

Octavia shrugged as she pulled a cloak over her shoulders. 'There's always some sort of festival or fair going on here. The young people are quite enamored of fairies and Arthurian legend. I often wonder what Arthur and Guinevere would make of it all.'

Before I could ask if she'd actually known Arthur and Guinevere, Octavia was out of the car and striding briskly up the ramp to the hotel, pulling a Louis Vuitton valise behind her. By the time I had wrestled my battered duffel out of the trunk, she was already at the front desk signing us in. As she handed her credit card to the clerk, I noticed how tired she looked – and how *dry*. Of course, I realized, she hadn't had a chance to hydrate since we'd left Paris. My guess was confirmed when I heard her ask if there was a tub in her room.

'I'll need to . . . rest for a while if we're to attempt the forest tomorrow,' she said as we followed the bellboy up to our separate rooms. 'Do you mind if I leave you on your own for the rest of the evening?'

'Not at all, Octavia. Is there anything I can get for you? Some . . . bottled water?'

'Yes, that's a good idea. If you wouldn't mind having room service send up two dozen oysters and three liters of Perrier and telling them just to leave the tray in the room. Thank you, my dear.' She touched my hand and I was alarmed to feel how dry and papery her skin felt.

'I'll do that,' I said. 'Would you like me to stay with you?'

'No, dear. It's best that I'm alone. I need to focus all my reserves.'

I had the restaurant send up the oysters and water and waited outside the room to make sure the waiter left the tray without disturbing Octavia in her bath. I could hear the splash of water from behind the closed door and could only hope that she was all right.

Seeing those oysters made me hungry myself, so after a quick stop in my room I went down to the hotel restaurant, which was on a terrace overlooking the old abbey and lake. Quite a few seafood offerings were on the menu even though we were miles from the sea. I supposed that even in the landlocked section of Brittany the sea wasn't so very far. Even here, something in the soft lambent light, shading toward evening, the lush wild roses on the side of the road, and the rough stone cottages spoke of the sea.

I ordered a bottle of the local Breton apple cider and the Moules Frites Mariniers, which arrived in a bath of bright saffron yellow broth, and ate them, scooping the flesh out with one of the pointed shells, looking out on the lake – the Étang de Paimpont, as the guidebook called it, the pool of Paimpont. The water was pink where the setting sun was reflected, but dark closer to the shore where dense forest cast its shadow. Perhaps it was the effect of my second tankard of the deceptively strong cider, but as the sun sank behind the tops of the trees across the lake and their shadows lengthened, I had an impression that the woods on the opposite shore were creeping toward me. Consulting the local map on the place mat, I saw that the Val sans Retour was part of those woods. So this lake might well be the pool where Morgane was trapped – or at least its earthly equivalent. I wasn't entirely sure I understood what Octavia meant about the forest and the pool not being *of this world*, but as the water darkened from pink to red to violet, I could almost imagine that the thin membrane that separated the worlds was stretched taut over the surface of the lake and that it might at any moment break . . .

Then a loud group of British soccer players descended on the restaurant, a radio from the nearby campground drifted across the water, and with a mingled sensation of relief and regret, I was very much in *this* world again.

I paid my bill and then, because my nerves felt too on edge to go back to my empty and unfamiliar hotel room, walked across the street toward the abbey. The path was quiet, most of the tourists only now having dinner. I had the abbey to myself save for a lone worshipper sitting in the back of the church, who muttered her prayers, with bowed and deeply shawled head. I walked up the center of the nave, hoping the sound of my footsteps wouldn't disturb his or her meditation. The space was so vast and bare that my footsteps echoed as if from the bottom of a well. Looking up, though, I thought I was at the bottom of the sea. From the thirteenth-century Romanesque style of the church I was expecting a plain stone, rounded vault, but what I found instead was a wooden roof lined with thin, interlocking strips of wood springing out from a center seam so that it looked like the hull of a boat. It *was* the hull of a boat, I realized after staring at it for several minutes, the overturned hull of a massive, ancient ship.

'Let the dove, or the fish, or the vessel flying before the wind be our signets.'

Startled at the voice, I jerked my head down so quickly that I made myself dizzy. The long, narrow, dark shape before me spun like an arrow on a compass and then settled into the figure of a black-robed priest, with a grizzled but kindly face and an Irish accent.

'I noticed you were surprised by our ceiling. Our founding fathers often used ships to represent the church, but only a few went so far as to craft their church *from* a ship. Local legend has it that this was the original ship that brought the seven founder saints from Wales to these shores, but,' he said, winking, 'some of my more unorthodox and fanciful parishioners believe that this is one of the ships that sailed from Ys when that benighted island was drowned.'

'And what do you believe?' I asked before considering what a rude question that was to ask a man of God.

But the priest only laughed. 'I believe the people who built this church were grateful for safe harbor in a storm and built it to give thanks to God – whatever name they gave their God.' He smiled and lifted pale blue eyes to the curved hull of the ceiling. 'And I have always thanked God for the shelter of his ship and prayed to be steered on my way by a beneficent wind.'

'That's a good prayer,' I agreed, returning the priest's smile and thinking of those ominous shadows stealing across the lake outside. 'I'll remember it.'

The old priest bowed his head and made the sign of the cross in the air between us. Then he turned and made his way back down the long nave, his own footsteps curiously quiet on the stone floor. Perhaps he went barefoot, I thought, as he turned in the single ray of evening light coming through the stained-glass window at the back of the church. For a moment his face shone red-gold – the same color as the Breton cider I'd drunk earlier. Then, as he turned away, his black cloak merged with the shadows and he vanished.

I took a step forward, a cry rising in my throat, but stopped when I felt a breeze waft against my face. What had the priest prayed for? To be steered by a beneficent wind? I turned in the direction of the breeze until I was facing a side chapel. The small niche was dominated by a raised sarcophagus upon which lay an effigy carved out of black stone. Moving closer, I saw that the figure was of a medieval knight laid out in all his armor. I'd seen dozens like it at the Cloisters – armored knights sleeping for eternity equipped with sword and mace, often at their feet a loyal dog or crouching lion. The feet of this knight, though, lay on the bent neck and broken wing of a dying swan. Dying because an arrow had been shot through her heart. I let my eye travel upward from the swan's long neck to the knight's face. There, carved in blackest stone some seven hundred years ago, lay the familiar face of Will Hughes.

21

Love in the Woods

Madame La Pieuvre had proven to be a spectacularly different sort of person, Will reflected with some bitterness, a few days after his interview with her. But the results of her guidance had been exactly the same as with all the other 'signs' he had tried to follow to Marguerite.

He was sitting on a boulder in the dense woods adjacent to the gardens at Fontainebleau and felt as bleak as he had in his most discouraged moments in Paris. Madame La Pieuvre had been part octopus and had numerous arms to prove it, she was as witty and charming as anyone he'd ever met, and she had a flotilla of servants in her enormous mansion to serve him an exceptional dinner and a variety of gorgeously colored drinks, all of which he'd never heard of or tasted before. Madame La Pieuvre had freely told him that she had heard from Marguerite recently, that Marguerite was in Fontainebleau, and that she would love for a man named Will Hughes to come there and see her; hopefully Madame might run across Will in Paris and tell him! All Madame asked in return for this priceless information was a bit of advice from Will on investing, upon learning of his own interest in the nascent stock markets of England and France.

But, having scoured Fontainebleau from end to end now, from the château's most beautiful corner to the forest's thickest bramble, from the most intricate walk in the garden to the finest gleam on the château's sloping roof, from the most obscure window to the noon-splashed depths of the pond in the woods, he'd found no sign of Marguerite. And he was prepared to admit to himself that Jean Robin, church steps' note, and all else notwithstanding he might be no closer to Marguerite now than he was in their most painful days of separation back in London.

Will could not gain entrance through any of the château's heavily guarded doors, for this was one of Henry IV's most zealously secured residences. Will could have been impaled for giving a guard the wrong look. But he'd managed, climbing thick-foliaged trees that afforded concealment on a moonlit night, to look fruitlessly into quite a number of the château's rooms. No one.

Marguerite must have known, when she chose to summon Will here through Madame La Pieuvre, of the obstacles to entry. She'd had ample opportunities to leave him a new sign and had left him none. If she had *seriously* summoned him here . . . for his most excruciating thought now was that she hadn't summoned in any benign way, that she merely toyed with him like wind with a leaf, a dark wind of lingering anger over their last fight, a wind that she lashed out at him with. Marguerite's inaccessibility, her invisibility, her absence, seemed to suggest one thing: as in Paris, the purpose of offering hope was to torment him. Will was being tortured to death by his own love!

On the second day he purchased a spyglass in a nearby

town and concealed himself in a bramble in the woods to avoid the suspicion of capital espionage. Then he relentlessly scanned all the château's windows day and night, hoping for the merest glimpse of that ineffable face, her glide past a window in profile or shadow. A look directly at him was by now his wildest ambition. Indeed he would have settled for the sight of her in rapt conversation with an attentive courtier – with a prince – settled for their rapturous kiss! – rather than this void. He could not settle for what he did get out of all his desperate scrutiny: nothing.

On this third day at Fontainebleau, Will was sitting on a rock he had come to regard as his friend, on the edge of tears, staring into a stand of poplar trees across a rough path on a gray, windsplit afternoon. It hadn't taken much for Will to convince himself that the rock was his friend. Wasn't it composed of atoms just as he was? They had that in common. People used the term *flesh and blood* to refer to their family members. But atoms were an even more intimate bond, as they *made up* flesh and blood. Look at the lifestyle and mentality of his friend the rock. Much to admire there. He/she was self-sufficient, no disastrous entanglements for the heart and mind, even if it had such organs. It certainly didn't travel wildly from place to place in pursuit of disingenuous and possibly malevolent signs; it didn't travel at all. The rock was a soul mate. Will would sit here right now and soak up the gray air, and the breeze with its hint of rain, alongside the rock. The rock was quiet, but at least now Will needn't feel so all alone.

Then Will suddenly noticed, amidst the poplars, that one tree seemed different. He knew it could be his imagination, and a desperate imagination at that, but the tree seemed to have a slender, angular face near the top of its branches. Almond-shaped, sap-glistening eyes were staring directly at him. Other trees were bending away from him in the recurring gusts, but this tree leaned consistently toward him, peering at him to get a closer look. Will gasped in amazement as the tree stepped fully out of its grove and took a gigantic stride across the path toward him.

A face was clearly visible near the top of its crown, but the trunk, several feet below the face, shrouded in underbrush, turned out to be not quite a trunk. It forked midway down into two bark-sheathed legs . . .

Will was tempted to flee, but decided to maintain his ground. He wasn't going to get far anyway against the giant strides this creature could take. So far she – something in the way the tree moved made Will think of her as female – hadn't displayed anything in the way of teeth, her apparent mouth an irregular pink gash in the silver, speckled bark of her highest branch. Her fingers and hands were glossed over with benign-looking leaves; her feet were shaggy roots like slippers. No cutting edges.

Tree woman, if that's what she was, continued to gaze down at him from a few feet away, at last shaking her slanted head as if in disapproval. Long branches coming out of her scalp that seemed to be her hair but resembled a myriad of bark-covered snakes rippled with her motion. All the branches were greened with poplar leaves, except for one of bright gold.

'What are you doing here, Sad Boy?' the creature asked him in a rasping voice, as if her vocal cords were pieces of broken wood, roughing up against one another as she spoke. 'You've been haunting these woods recently, with some sorrow of yours. I'm watching you and wearying of it. These are *my* woods, except when that horror of horrors comes around. So fess up! Now!'

'I fess up, as you put it, to few. Actually, right now, to none.' Will appreciated her interest, but saw no reason to confide in this ungainly stranger. 'I can't fit you in as a confidant after such a brief introduction.' He glanced upward, as if to emphasize how little room there was to fit her in anywhere.

Then he felt twigged fingers grasping his right shoulder from above, an arm shadowing his face against the gray light, leaves that dangled against his neck not altogether displeasing in their silken touch. The hand began to draw him toward her, and Will felt the undeniable strength of this creature, and he felt a bit fearful. He tried to surge out of her grip. After a stalemate he felt her let go, with the snapping of a few twigs; whether that happened from his tugging or hers, he couldn't tell. The let-go was sharp, and he fell and sprawled flat on the rough ground, his hands bracing his fall at the last instant. To add to this ignominy he heard a high-pitched, brittle crackling high above him. Laughter! The witch – or whatever she was – was laughing at him.

The nerve!

Will leaped up and drew himself up to a rather flamboyant full height. He was angry, but under sufficient control that he took a few precautionary, further steps back once standing. He was surprised to see the creature, branch-arms, twig-fingers, and all, drooping, as if she was disappointed in his retreat. Will saw a new glistening in her eyes, as if resin had dripped there all of a sudden.

Tears?

'Why can't you confide in me, Sad Boy?' the creature asked in a softer tone. 'I live in a world of silent trees, rocks, and dirt. Am I cursed to never hear meaningful speech again?' She extended her right arm toward him, slowly, as if she shyly sought an embrace.

Despite his wounded pride over falling, Will felt sympathy for her. He stepped forward and took one of the leaved twigs on her right hand between his thumb and forefinger, gently. 'What's your name? I can't confide in someone without knowing' – he hesitated over gender again, but, after glancing up at the lengthy branches that were her hair, went on – 'her name!'

'I am Sylvianne the Dryad.' After a moment's hesitation she added, shocking Will, 'And the truth is, I love you.'

'You what?!' Will was tempted to respond sarcastically, but he caught himself and instead replied, 'Why how very magnificent of you to say that, my dear.' Given her tree-someness, he didn't see much risk of this entanglement going further. Isolated and despondent as he was, was he supposed to turn away an unexpected admirer completely?

Her lips – faint pink lines in bark – barely fluttered, but Will guessed this was a smile. 'Does "magnificent" mean hope?' she asked in a plaintive tone.

Will let go of her twig finger and grasped her entire right hand firmly in his. 'It might under nearly all circum-stances, my dear, but common decency now makes me warn you that there is another.'

'Another?! Is that whom you're looking through your

Galileo cylinder for? But you don't even seem to know where she is!'

Will wondered if her sharpness was jealousy. Sylvianne appeared mercurial in her moods.

'You queried me on my sadness, madame. Do you want illumination on this point or not?'

'Unburden yourself in a wordspill, Sad Boy!'

Despite wondering at her peculiar language – perhaps English was not her native tongue – Will unburdened himself. Sylvianne listened impassively for the most part, though at one point crossing her leafy arms and shrugging in a way that seemed to make the entire forest tremble. When Will finally got to Marguerite's immortality, his burning need to attain it, and his current frustration, Sylvianne bristled.

'*Stop!* You insolent human!' she shrieked at Will, who felt her voice as if he were wood and it a saw. He retreated a half dozen steps from her.

'How dare you speak of immortality to me as something inaccessible, impossible, that only this lady of the night' – Will bristled in turn at *this* reference – 'Marguerite or whatever her name is, can grant you. *I* am one of the grandest immortal creatures in the universe. And *I* can grant immortality to whomever *I* choose. Insulting me, Sad Boy, is not the way to gain my favor. By imputing my powers to another, no less. Believe me, it just isn't.'

An angry tear dripped down gleaming from Sylvianne's almond eye.

'I am so sorry, madame,' Will said humbly. 'I did not mean to give offense.'

Something like a sly look settled then over Sylvianne's

features. 'And why should I grant you immortality anyway, Sad Boy? So that – that – slut' – she coughed in disgust, and spit a clump of resin on the ground – 'can perpetually enjoy your charms?'

Two contradictory emotions boiled up in Will, one blinding him with rage, the other exalting him with hope. Even as he recoiled from this monstrous mischaracterization of his beloved, it crossed his consciousness that Sylvianne could make him and Marguerite whole through eternity if he engaged in just the right bit of flattery, if he massaged her delusion, if he seduced her into thinking . . .

'Can you really grant immortality?'

She looked at him shrewdly. 'Not to just anyone. It could only be given to a . . . loved one. And I don't exactly grant it. But I can take you there, Sad Boy. Let's put it that way. I can take you there.'

'You can?' Will looked Sylvianne up and down as lasciviously as anyone could, a gaze she appeared to bask in.

Then she gathered herself together again, more coldly. 'And what of it?' she barked at Will.

'You do have a certain elegant beauty,' he mused aloud. His eyes met hers for a lingering gaze. 'In fact, I hear my poet's voice speak within when I gaze at you:

You are more elegant than any swan,
or monarch, star: you make all numbers one.
Alluring as sunlight in winter's storm,
you turn eternity so bright and warm!

Sylvianne began to blink rapidly, and then her eyes were glistening once again.

'Note that I've simply said before that there was another,' Will went on provocatively. 'I didn't say she was an insurmountable obstacle.'

'You've painted her as the center of your world,' Sylvianne complained.

'Ah, but women love a romantic,' Will explained. 'So why shouldn't I try to appeal to you? I am a poet. Poets exaggerate because they do not really live in this world.'

'Are you saying there is a chance for me?' With an impetuous rustling of leaves, she took a few strides toward him.

'As an immortal, I would revisit all the decisions in my life,' Will said coyly.

'That's not a lover speaking, that's not even a poet,' Sylvianne said harshly. 'That's a clerk.' She flung her right hand at him, and it came dangerously close to slapping his face.

Will knew a decisive moment had arrived. A dryad was a supernatural creature, so he could not question Sylvianne's knowledge of immortality, but he doubted she would make him an immortal in exchange for mere words. 'As an immortal, I know I would be strongly drawn to you.'

'You're not now?!' With a gigantic rippling in her leaves, she began to stalk off. Will gasped with disappointment; his one hope was leaving!

But then he had a positively luminescent intuition. Maybe Sylvianne herself *was* the purpose of Marguerite's directing him, through Madame La Pieuvre's agency, to Fontainebleau. That seemed to contradict Marguerite's love for him, but, maybe this was all the help she could render him.

Will raced toward a wild embrace of Sylvianne. He flung himself at her as if she were Marguerite, utterly persuaded that Sylvianne was the gateway to his true love. And indeed the dryad's leaves about him quickly became silken and sweet. He could hear her moaning softly, well above, almost in the sky. Her greenery wrapped around him as if in a whirlwind, and he felt as if he were in a merge of inner vision and outer ecstasy, at other moments making love to a voluptuous, black-haired woman whom his senses told him was Marguerite – but he couldn't see her face – at still other times feeling as if he were a tree, sap in his veins on fire, woods whirling around him, a returned sun dazzling with summer heat, Sylvianne kissing the back of his neck while whispering, 'I love you.' It was all confusing and fragmented, yet ecstatic and sun-bright.

At the end Will found himself lying across the same rock where his adventure had begun, gasping and spent. He didn't *feel* any more immortal than he had an hour before, shaking his arms and legs to make sure. No. Not that he had any idea what immortality felt like. But he didn't feel anything but the spent afterglow of love.

Sylvianne had gone back across the road where he had first seen her, staring down at him somewhat critically. 'Do you love me now?'

Will smiled as sweetly as he could. 'Yes. As I have always loved you. As I will always love you. You are mine, Sylvianne. *You are mine!*'

Sylvianne's look changed to lascivious. Her eyes took Will in greedily; she made him feel uncomfortable, and cheap, and disloyal to Marguerite. But the main thing was, now he was either immortal or about to become that –

hadn't Sylvianne promised? He gave her a penetrating gaze. 'I don't *feel* any different.'

'Yes, you do. You feel the exhilaration of having loved me!'

'Yes, that, of course. But I don't quite feel . . . immortal. I thought I would know it when I felt it. I don't.'

Sylvianne cluck-clucked sympathetically, as if to a child. 'Come here, Sad Boy.'

With a sigh, Will got up, crossed the road, and tentatively approached Sylvianne. He felt none of the erotic rush of before, but he did feel a serene, pleasing sensation at coming so closely into her presence. The next thing he knew, it was as if he were swinging in a hammock, supported by two of Sylvianne's lower limbs rocking him, and she was planting a sap-rich kiss on his forehead. She reached up to her scalp, snapped off a branch, and laid it in Will's lap. It was gold, and glimmered in the renewed afternoon sunshine as if a piece of the sun had fallen there.

'Will, you take this gold branch with you to the pool at Paimpont and stand on its western bank at sunset. Hold the branch up so that it can summon the sun's rays to it like a magnet. That is the key to entering the Summer Country, where immortality is the rule. Morgane will see the glittering key and take you across, and you can return here as you please as Will Hughes, immortal. I will be waiting for you, darling. We can marry, for you are the grandest mortal I have ever beheld. As an immortal, you may well be my equal!' Sylvianne swooped down with a whoosh and planted another gummy kiss on Will's forehead. Then her voice turned to ice.

'But if I find out that you have tricked me, Will Hughes,

and gotten me to give you this immortal key because of your obsession with that scarlet trash, I and my multitudinous legions will track you down to whatever corner of the earth you hide in and impale you on one of the earth's cracked bones. *There* you can hang for all eternity, instead of being held safely in my arms, an object lesson for the winds and birds, for humanity, to see. And even at that your fate will be a much too kind one.'

Will, disappointed to learn he wasn't already immortal, found himself shivering at the scale of her threat. It almost made him reconsider even his love for Marguerite. But Sylvianne was simply overwrought at the depth of her love for him, he reassured himself. That could change. She might encounter someone else she really loved. He'd just have to take his chances.

Will grasped the gold branch firmly in his right hand and struggled down from her hammocklike embrace. As he stood again, he was surprised to find himself directly facing Sylvianne's features; at a glance down he saw that her trunk legs were splayed out at right angles beneath her. She was kneeling to be on the same level as him!

'Thank you for this gift,' he told her, 'which I pledge to use to ensure our union.'

Sylvianne smiled, and her eyes teared up once more.

Will suspected that she still didn't trust him, but she did seem prepared to let him go now, at least for a trip to Paimpont and back. None of her moods, good or bad, seemed to last long anyway. He should take advantage of this one. He hugged her trunk and kissed her lips, which flooded his mind with memories of the fantastical interlude they had shared and flooded his mind even more with recollections of his black-haired vision-lover. Then he left, striding briskly down the path toward the town, where he could book passage on the stagecoach to Paimpont.

All Will heard from behind was a sigh. Perhaps a lament.

All he saw in front of him was Marguerite, her beautiful face in his memory. She blotted out the woods, the gardens, the château, even the wind-caressed sun.

Because she was the sun.

22

The Reeds

I didn't sleep well that night. The room was musty, but when I opened the windows to let in fresh air, loud voices and music wafted up from the restaurant. Whenever I closed my eyes, I saw Will's face carved in stone. His ancestor's, I'd gathered from the inscription on the sarcophagus base: Guillem de Hughes – but still, seeing his features like that made him, my present Will Hughes, seem dead.

As well he might be. Octavia had told me what Morgane did to some of her supplicants. If Will had made his way here months ago and been successful in gaining his mortality back, wouldn't he have come to find me by now? Or had Morgane granted him his mortality only to take his life away in his first mortal breath in four hundred years?

By the time I went downstairs to meet Octavia at breakfast, I felt as though I were made of stone. She, however, looked fresh and plump as the just-shucked oysters she'd consumed last night.

'Oh my,' she exclaimed through a mouthful of brioche, 'have some coffee. We have a hard day ahead of us.'

She was dressed as if for a safari through the Kalahari Desert, in khaki shorts that showed off her shapely legs and a safari jacket that hid her many arms. As I had my café au lait and croissant, she showed me the contents of our matching rucksacks: water canteen, chocolate bars, bread and cheese, flashlight, first-aid kit, compass, rope, waterproof matches, a Swiss army knife, and a cotton Liberty-print scarf that matched the one tied jauntily around Octavia's slim neck.

'This looks like we're going on a weeklong expedition.'

Octavia's forehead creased with worry. 'Just a week? You're right; we should bring more food.' She went back up to the buffet and, after making sure we were alone in the dining room, used all her hands to gather up pre-packaged cheeses, packets of Nutella, rolls, fruit, and hard-boiled eggs. When she got back to the table, she divided the supplies between our two packs.

'There's no telling how long it might take to find our way into the Summer Country or whether we'll be able to stay together. The Valley of No Return is set with snares for the faithless lover – and to Morgane a faithless lover is one who loses faith for even a moment. Once lost there, we could wander for centuries with no sense of direction and no sense of time. There is no direction there, nor time as we know it.' Octavia surveyed the heavily loaded packs, her forehead undulating with concern. I'd once seen a YouTube video of an octopus squeezing through the neck of a Coca-Cola bottle. Octavia looked as though she were considering diving into my backpack and concealing herself wetly in the water canteen. 'But this will just have to do. If we get lost up there, starving will be the least of our problems.'

* * *

The trailhead to the Val sans Retour was a half hour's drive away, in the village of Tréhorenteuc. There was a car park, a souvenir shop, and a café advertising Galettes de Bretagne and local cider. The trail was carefully marked along with a list of popular sites: the Mirror of the Fairies, the Rock of False Lovers, and the Tomb of Morgane. We passed half a dozen hikers in the first mile: a family with toddlers in tow, teenagers in flimsy footwear giggling and mooning over the Miroir des Fées, and a man outfitted in olive-green cargo pants, anorak, wide-brimmed hat, and wraparound, gogglelike sunglasses who looked as if he were kitted out for a hike up Mt Everest. We passed a young British couple standing in front of the sign explaining the legend of the valley, the woman teasing her husband that if he got lost, she'd know it was because he 'fancied that slag down the pub.' The atmosphere was so carefree and ordinary that it was hard to imagine we were embarking on a quest to find a monster.

'Isn't it dangerous for these people to be here?' I asked Octavia when she paused to take a sip from her canteen. 'Why don't they stray into the Summer Country?'

'They haven't followed the path you've tread,' she answered, wiping her mouth, 'and they're not trying to get to the Summer Country. But' – she paused, glancing into the deep woods – 'some *do* stray into the Summer Country. Every year we hear of disappearances in these woods. Some come back disoriented, dehydrated, confused about what has happened to them, and some' – she took another long swallow of water – 'some never come back.'

She screwed the top back on her canteen and set off

again at an even faster pace. I followed, glancing left and right into the woods on either side of the path. It was pretty here, much more wild than Fontainebleau. These trees had never been pollarded or arranged in allées. I recognized oak and beech among the occasional slim limbs of poplars, which reminded me uneasily of Sylvianne. Ferns and wildflowers grew beneath the trees. It was hard to imagine anything malevolent in these woods, but still I quickened my pace to keep up with Octavia, which became easier as the trail became steeper and she slowed down, losing some of her original steam. As the trail climbed out of the hardwood forest of beech and oak and into scrub pine and gorse, the sun fell heavier on our heads and she also stopped more frequently for drinks of water.

'Are you okay?' I asked when I found her sitting on a rock fanning herself with all her hands at once.

'It's just so exposed up here,' she replied, gesturing toward a field of tall grass and purple gorse. 'I'd forgotten. I came here once with . . . *une amie* . . . before I knew Adele, you understand. We were on a sketching tour of Brittany . . . she was an artist, a student at the École des Beaux-Arts before she met Paul Gauguin and that crowd and came to work at Pont-Aven along the coast not far from here.' Octavia smiled wanly. Her skin, I noticed, was turning a pale blue, like skimmed milk. I untied her scarf from around her neck, soaked it in water from my own canteen, and pressed it against her forehead. I could feel the heat of her skin through the damp cloth.

'I think we should get you in the shade,' I said, scanning the hilltop for a cool spot. A sign pointed farther down the path toward the HÔTEL DE VIVIANNE, which I gathered from the guidebook was a Neolithic stone circle. But the sign said it was still a kilometer away. The trees here were all too stunted and prickly to offer shade under the noonday sun. Across the field of grass I spied a broad rock protruding from the ground like the spine of some ancient reptile. Perhaps on the other side of it there would be some shade.

'Come on,' I said, 'I think I see a good spot.'

Octavia shook her head. 'I just need to rest a moment. You go on . . .' She raised her large, liquid eyes to mine. They seemed to swim in her pale face like swollen raisins bobbing in vanilla pudding.

'I'll just go see if there's shade over there,' I said, alarmed at her appearance. The last time I'd seen someone look this bad was Melusine when she melted into a pile of goo. 'I'll be right back.'

'Be careful not to get lost,' she said, her eyes drooping. 'Use your compass.'

'Okay.' I took the compass out of my backpack. I didn't really need it, of course. I had the compass stone embedded in my hand, but I thought it would reassure her to see me pointing it at the rock and reading off coordinates. 'Fifteen degrees northwest,' I said aloud, slipping the chain of the compass over my head for good measure, where it bumped against my watch chain. When I looked down, though, I saw that Octavia had already closed her eyes and slumped down to the ground with her back against the rock. Her eyes twitched beneath her eyelids as though she had fallen asleep and was dreaming . . . of whom? I wondered. Adele? Or the *amie* she'd come here with in the late-nineteenth century? As I followed a narrow path across the waist-high grass, I wondered if thinking about her old lover would qualify Octavia as a 'faithless lover.' Could she be trapped in this valley for such a small indiscretion? It didn't seem fair, especially for an immortal creature who had lived for centuries. How could she help but have loved others before she met Adele – maybe dozens of others? How many women might Will have loved over the centuries? He'd told me when we first met that he'd loved the original Marguerite, but that he'd avoided her descendants. That last part hadn't turned out to be true.

In a vision granted me by a brooch I'd found in John Dee's antiques shop, I'd relived the memory of one Marguerite Dufay, who'd had an affair with Will in the eighteenth century. Then I'd watched them dance at Versailles, Will's eyes gleaming behind his masquerade mask. I'd watched Marguerite try to save Will from a gang of street thugs and die in the attempt – her last sight Will's face above her. *She* had certainly loved him. Had he loved her? I found myself hoping so even though the thought gave me a pang of jealousy. If he hadn't, it might mean he was a terribly shallow man – as vain and shallow a young man as he had conceded himself to be when he'd fallen for the first Marguerite.

I'd reached the large rock outcropping now and saw that it formed a ridge above a gorse-filled glen. The wind was cool here and smelled sweet from the purple gorse, but there was no shade. Below in the glen, though, was a circle of standing stones – dolmens and menhirs that had once been the site of some sort of prehistoric worship. Perhaps it was the Tomb of Morgane advertised in the guidebook and the path through the grass was a shortcut. It looked as if it could be a tomb. Two stones leaned together to form an arch in front of a shadowy passage into a raised mound. I couldn't tell from here how far the passage went into the mound – and the thought of entering a Neolithic tomb made me shiver – but at least the archway would give Octavia a respite from the sun.

I turned around to cross the field, but I couldn't find the path I'd taken. The wind had picked up, whipping the tall grass into a choppy sea. That was why I couldn't see the path, but it didn't really matter, I knew that the rock where I'd left Octavia was fifteen degrees southeast from where I stood. I didn't need to look at the compass because I had one embedded in my hand. I could *feel* the right way to go. Besides it was only a ten-minute walk away.

It wasn't so easy to stay on course, though. The grass thrashed against me, pushing me left, then right. I'd strayed into an area where it was taller – above my head in places – and thicker. It was no longer grass, really, but some bamboolike reeds that were hollow and whistled as the wind blew through them. The sound was hypnotic – a flutey whispering that took on the shape of words.

Do you love him? the reeds sang. *Does he love you? Do you love him? Does he love you?*

I do love him, I answered angrily, pushing my way through the reeds. *And he loves me.*

The reeds chuckled, their dry stalks tickling my ankles and elbows as if trying to get me to join in on the joke.

Does anyone ever really love anyone else? they asked.

Stupid question. My father and mother had loved each other—

Had they? Wasn't your mother planning to leave your father when he died? Hadn't your father betrayed her by gambling and losing all their money – your college fund included?

It's complicated, I answered, thinking back on all I had recently learned about that last year of my mother's life. She *had* been planning to leave us when her car crashed on our way back from a college visit to the Rhode Island School of Design, but that was because she knew John Dee had found her and would try to hurt my father and me unless she drew him away from us. She was trying to protect us because she loved us. My father's misguided business ventures had come out of the same well-intentioned instincts to keep us safe.

Or to make himself feel important. He gambled your college fund away not for your sake, but for his. Your mother wanted to leave for years but was only waiting for an excuse. That's what false lovers do – they find excuses for their selfish behavior. But all they're ever doing is looking out for themselves. You think Will took the box because he wanted to make himself mortal to be with you?

For the answer to their own question, the reeds snickered.

If that's why he took it, where is he? Where is he? Where is he?

With that last question echoing in my ears I stumbled out of the field into a clearing. The rock in front of me looked like the rock where I had left Octavia, but she wasn't there. I looked down the hill in the direction we'd come from, but it was hard to make out the path. Had it been this overgrown when we'd come up it? I looked in the opposite direction where I'd seen the sign pointing to the Tomb of Morgane, but the sign was gone. Was it the wrong rock? I circled it, looking for some sign that Octavia had been there, but found nothing. All I had to do, though, was look at the compass and check that the rock I'd just come from was fifteen degrees northwest from this rock. I held up the compass and waited for the needle to stop spinning.

And waited.

The needle kept spinning. I sat down on the rock, my legs suddenly wobbly, and looked around. The spot looked as I recalled it: pine forest, rocks, patches of purple gorse, grass, large rock across the field . . . but it wasn't *quite* the same. The pine forest was denser, the shadows darker, the purple gorse lusher and more vibrant, the grass taller and greener . . .

. . . and still snickering.

He doesn't love you. You don't love him.

Octavia had said that the Valley of No Return was set with snares for the faithless lover. Once proved unfaithful, you could wander forever directionless in a place where no compass could show you the way. I had come to that place. I had doubted Will's love for me, and now my love for him, and had lost my *direction*. Literally. I looked down at the spinning compass gripped so tightly that my hand throbbed.

No, that wasn't why my hand throbbed. I dropped the compass and stared at my hand. A dark red spot like a blood blister pulsed in the center of my palm. The compass stone. It was vibrating as if it were trying to jump out of my skin. And it hurt like hell.

I unwound the cotton Liberty-print scarf from my neck and tied it around my hand, binding it tight to ease the pain. It helped a little, but I still felt that insistent tug pointing me toward the rock across the reeds.

I wasn't going back in those reeds. No way. No how.

I drank a little water and ate half a chocolate bar. I'd wait here. Octavia would be back for me. I slid down onto the ground, leaning my back against the rock, which felt wonderfully cool. At least the sun wasn't so hot anymore. It must be getting late.

I reached for my watch pendant, and looked at it. The hands were spinning around, the little suns and planets racing through their midnight-blue sky, the tiny tree in the window shedding and growing leaves as in a speeded-up nature film. It made me dizzy to look at it, so I tucked the watch under my shirt. Then I looked up into a sky so hazy that I couldn't tell which direction the sun was coming from. It felt somehow as if the light were coming from everywhere and nowhere at the same time. A lambent, diffuse light that was rather ... pleasant. This spot was actually quite nice. The wind had abated and now blew only gently through the reeds, more a lullaby than a recrimination. The reeds no longer chanted that Will didn't love me and I didn't love him. Instead they gently whispered, *What does it matter? What does it matter?* If not for the annoying ache in my hand, I would have been perfectly comfortable.

I dug in my pack for the first-aid kit and found a small tin of acetaminophen. I swallowed two and then, for good measure, two more. The pain soon faded to a pang, like a half-forgotten heartbreak dulled by the passage of time. As

I closed my eyes, I had a momentary glimpse of Will doing just what I was doing, leaning against a rock, waiting. *Let him wait*, I thought, and then I fell asleep.

23

The Most
Scientific Medicine

Will caught the next coach for Paimpont as it was leaving, and as the sky started to purple, and as the wind began to rise as if a storm were in the distance. The other passenger in the cabin greeted Will in a peculiar French, one that had traces of both German and English accents to it. 'Valentine Russwurin the Second, Doctor of Physic *and* Surgery,' he introduced himself.

'Will Hughes, poet and stock trader.'

Perhaps Russwurin found Will's French unusual as well, for he then asked him where he was from.

'England. Lately of London,' Will replied, as the carriage began to roll.

'How serendipitous. That's my hometown as well. Adopted hometown. I am originally born in Schmalkalden, Germany.'

'And I am born in Somerset, England.'

They shook hands on their geographical frankness. Then they rode on in silence for a while, Will eyeing Russwurin furtively. Even though the man was seated, Will could discern that he was exceptionally tall and broad, clad in a thick, black overcoat despite the August heat. His triangular, reddish orange goatee reminded Will a bit of Dee's, but his eyes weren't anything like Dee's: they were a friendly brown that had first engaged, then twinkled. The large black leather satchel on his seat next to him was likely his doctor's bag. Will sensed Russwurin observing him as well, but no matter how suddenly he would glance back at him, he could never catch his eyes directly upon him.

They rode on through countryside that gradually changed from farms to woods. Will felt a chill from the forest's obscurity, barely illumined by a sliver of just risen moon, despite the reassurance that he was on the final leg of his journey to immortality. He was carrying the golden branch in a slender canvas bag he'd purchased in the Fontainebleau market before boarding the coach, one he'd initially placed on the seat next to him. He put it on his lap now though, caressing the top of the bough within the bag. As if it were a talisman that could ward off unseen dangers.

Russwurin followed Will's hand with his eyes and smiled. 'A favorite walking stick? Planning to do some hiking when you arrive?'

'Traveling,' Will replied euphemistically, referring to crossing to the Summer Country.

'But I didn't observe you to be carrying any luggage.'

'I'm hoping to meet a friend in Paimpont, who will provision me. And you?'

Russwurin's expression suddenly and startlingly grew angry. 'I'm a fugitive. Of sorts.'

'Really?'

'The nitpickers of London's medical kingdom have

chased me from their municipality despite that I am a brilliant doctor, despite the lives I have saved and the suffering I have eased.' Russwurin patted his satchel to emphasize his profession. 'Nonsense about licenses and diplomas. The truth is that they are mired in the Galenic rut of antiquity, oblivious to the alchemical brilliance of Paracelsus and others, which will be the future of medicine for as far as the eye can see.' Russwurin winked at Will. 'One example of perhaps particular interest to your generation is the use of mercury to treat the Italian disease.'

'The Italian disease?'

'You may be more familiar with it under its most recent name, of growing popularity in London: syphilis. Galen could not cure what he had never heard of. In any event I am off to Audierne in the far west of Brittany, where the great John Dee has offered me the protection of his scientific reputation, to serve the populace to their benefit and not that of clerks who collect fees the way beetles collect dung.'

Will kept his unease at the mention of Dee's name to himself. A mere coincidence no doubt, facilitated by the man's far-flung fame, yet . . . curiosity got the best of him. 'Do you know Sir Dee?'

'We have corresponded through intermediaries. John Dee supports the cause of the most scientific medicine and alchemy possible, whatever the local prejudices or greed opposing them. He is a general in the war for health and truth. I am but a private, if a particularly distinguished one. Happy to serve.'

Russwurin was looking directly at Will now, with a

glitter in his eyes that Will found unnerving. He glanced away and could suddenly feel the coach slowing down, could hear the driver calling to the horses to halt. They were pulling over on the right side of the road, where the woods were even deeper and thicker than on the other side. A rosy moon was now full over the horizon, showering tinted light as if a fine rain of blood were falling. All coincidence, no doubt, but Will found it downright creepy that they were pulling over unexpectedly and his lone fellow passenger had had recent dealings with, was on a mission certified by, John Dee. The driver, who had silently dismounted, surprised Will and Russwurin at the window facing the woods. He shouted that he was taking a break to relieve himself and moved into the trees with a great crackling of twigs and shunting aside of branches.

Twenty minutes later, the driver had not returned, and Will and Russwurin were both pacing anxiously up and down the road near the carriage. It seemed pointless, Will thought, to suggest going in the woods to look for the driver: he could have gone off in multiple directions, and if someone or something *had* caused him misfortune on his humble errand, there was no reason to think that entity couldn't cause Will and Russwurin misfortune, too. But Will did wonder which of them might be the first to bring up another delicate question: were either of them willing to drive the coach onward now so they could both go forth with their business? Certainly the carriage and its horses could be restored to the owner at some further time and destination, and certainly the driver's troubles might better be a problem for the local authorities by now.

The wind remained brisk, the sky was clouding over,

and Will thought he could hear thunder at a considerable distance. He hoped it wasn't the roar of some far-off and unfathomable beast!

Just then he heard a rustling from the underbrush as if the driver might be returning. Unsure whether he was going to embrace him or reprimand him for his excursion, Will drifted over into the narrow space between carriage and woods, followed by Russwurin. Will was curious at a minimum to see the expression on this insolent man's face. But then he was shocked by the sight of tiny bolts of light zigzagging about twenty feet away from him down a slight slope. It was like a miniature exhibition of slash. And then it all pinwheeled up the slope toward him, and Will was aghast to see Lightning Hands spill up to the crest of the road, wearing a white cape, white trousers, and white shoes, all emblazoned with gold bolts. Lightning Hands came toward Will to greet him as though he were an old friend, right hand extended, but then Will noted an ivory palm pistol in the hand pointed at him. Then he felt something sharp pierce his left shoulder. As he pitched forward after this numbing blow, he could see, just within the field of his left eye, Russwurin holding a giant needle. At the same moment Lightning Hands, grinning, was approaching him and reaching for his golden branch with his left hand. That was all he could remember.

Will came groggily awake in the underbrush at the edge of the road around dawn the next morning. He felt a dull ache in his left shoulder, but otherwise he seemed none the worse for wear as he rolled over, tried out his limbs in order, and got to his feet. The golden branch was gone but, he reassured himself by patting his secret pants pocket, his wad of francs was still with him. The fiends had only been interested in the branch, which after all could be of massive value simply for being solid gold, let alone for being a portal to immortality.

Will breathed a sigh of relief that they hadn't found his bounty in francs, with which he was going to travel to Paimpont. The branch might be gone, he told himself with fierce determination, but Sylvianne had still let the secret out! If he could get to the Paimpont pond at sunset and summon rays with a mirror, or a jewel, or a sword, that might get Morgane's attention just as well. Or even just being in proximity to the pond, day or night, might do the trick. After all, Sylvianne had as much as guaranteed Morgane's solicitousness in the matter. Why, he might as well be in the Summer Country already!

In minutes, Will, waving just a couple of his francs in the air like a banner, flagged down a horse rider, who took him on board for just five francs to the town of Piermont, where he caught the next coach to the walled town of Paimpont. There, he located the pool quickly after his arrival – right after renting a second-floor room in one of the inns that lined the dusty main street – seeing it on his first exploratory walk beyond Paimpont's east wall, and sitting down on a grassy bank to observe it.

The pool was an irregular oval with the stillness of a stone on this windless morning, shimmering green in the sun as if some spirit of the earth lurked within it. Will felt fascinated by it as he gazed and gazed. To his left was the town, across from him the abbey, and to the right deep woods that seemed to grow denser and blacker the more he looked at them. Will swiveled his gaze back to the abbey and fantasized for a moment that he saw Lightning Hands and Dr Russwurin emerging from the chapel into the sunshine. Their heads were down with shame – they were chastened, reformed – they were bringing him the golden branch in apologetic penitence, testing the water with their feet to see if they could walk across it to him. The Summer Country was near! They took a few steps, ankle deep, knee deep, waist deep, and then the vision of them burned off as if the sun itself had gotten tired of it. He went back to staring at the empty pool, and the empty footpath that circled it. Then he heard the faintest of rustling noises, behind him and to his left, up the bank. He turned around with an irrepressible hope, though the sound was likely from a bird that had fluttered to the ground.

Marguerite stood in a silver dress, offering him a tentative smile. The smile lit Will up as if a lightning bolt in liquid form had been poured into his veins. In two strides he was next to her and embracing her, then pulling himself back to more fully take in her beauty: the deep blue pools of her eyes, and the expressive tenderness with which she gazed at him.

Will kissed Marguerite softly on the lips and whispered, 'I thought I would never lay eyes on you again. I have been in such despair as no one might believe. Where have you been?'

Marguerite stepped back from him and glanced away into the pool, and though the water was only a few yards below them, the look in her eyes was further away than any Will had seen there before. Not of this world. Exalted as he felt, it made him tremble.

'What's wrong?' he asked.

Marguerite took Will's hand and together they sat down on the bank. 'I had to go away,' she said, still looking at the water. 'But I did it for us, not just for me. I left you signs because in the world I was in I couldn't communicate with you any other way. I hoped you would follow, and I'm thrilled you have. But I cannot say more of where I've gone, or exactly why. Perhaps someday, but not now. Let's just say that I've been in touch with a part of my past I'd lost connection with, that there I realized how incredibly much I love you, and now I may turn my full attention to you.' She turned her gaze from the pool to Will, though not before casting one lingering glance upon the water. She kissed him and put her arms around him.

Golden branch gone, John Dee's promise again in mind, Will could not help glancing down at her hand, and saw that her ring finger was bare. He winced, but no doubt she had the ring with her personal property, wherever she stayed. He had neither the desire nor a plan to once again directly confront the topic of immortality with her. The risk of bringing it up, given the recent disaster, was too great.

He got up, Marguerite following, and they began to stroll around the pool's circular footpath. Sunlight rippled along overhanging leaves, creating an effect of their being underwater. Flashes of silver beneath the pool's surface seemed to be darting fish, but when he glanced more closely at them, they disappeared. Marguerite's hand in his was as delicate as the yellow flowers that bordered the path, and as finely elegant as the abbey's architecture. His own palpitating blood was as uplifting as the love

Marguerite seemed to have rediscovered for him, to his joy.

They spoke not a word as they circled the pool. But when they returned to the grassy slope where they'd started, the sun mere inches higher in the sky, Will felt as if a whole new cycle in his life had begun. He devoutly hoped, and sensed, that Marguerite might feel the same.

Her humble lodgings were remarkably similar to his; in fact her one window was directly across the street from his. Gold sunlight filled its modest pane when they arrived, and by the time they left again to dine, the glass was a sweet shade of lavender, a star twinkled, and the touch of their hands had a feeling of permanence to it as deep as eternity – even if not quite as long.

24

The Standing Stones

It was twilight when I awoke. Or at least what passed for twilight in this directionless, timeless place. Great swaths of indigo, violet, and chartreuse swirled in giant loops in the sky like the northern lights or van Gogh's *Starry Night* minus the stars. There were no stars and no moon.

For a moment I didn't know where I was.

Then I remembered that I was nowhere.

I laughed at that and something laughed with me. The reeds. Yes, I remembered them. Under the swirly sky they glowed silver and algal green and moved like the sea. I got up, bracing my hand against the rock to help myself, and cried out in pain. My hand was wrapped in a cotton scarf – pretty, that, I wondered who had given it to me – I must have hurt my hand, but I couldn't remember how.

What does it matter? What does it matter? the reeds sang. I trailed my hand along one and the pain eased as if I had dipped it into cool water. They *were* cool. Parting a sheaf I saw that a bluish mist filled the space between each stem. The mist seemed to be pouring out of the hollow reeds through tiny holes – like a sprinkler system. I stepped into the reeds and felt the mist caress my face and hands. It felt lovely, like swimming. I took another step and the reeds clicked behind me like a bamboo curtain closing behind a sexy movie star entering an opium den . . .

I had watched old movies like that with someone once but I couldn't remember who . . .

What does it matter? What does it matter?

It didn't. I waded deeper into the reeds, which clicked behind me and kept clicking even after I had passed through them. It sounded as if someone were following me, but when I turned, all I saw was mist. I turned again and went deeper, moving my arms in a breaststroke . . .

Someone had taught me how to swim once. A woman with a beautiful face . . .

What does it matter? What does it matter? the reeds sang.

It didn't. She had died. She had left me. Everybody left eventually. Everybody died . . .

But there was someone who couldn't die . . .

What does it matter? the reeds sang, *He left, he left, he left* . . .

But the throb in my hand was saying something else. *He's here, he's here, he's here.*

Where? I spun around, agitating the reeds into a miniature cyclone of snapping. Something moved in the mist, a dark shape . . . but then it vanished. My hand throbbed again and I untied the scarf and held it up. A tear-shaped diamond glowed at the center of my palm. I took a step in the direction it pointed and the pain eased. But the reeds thrashed.

I took a step in the opposite direction and the pain flared up, but the reeds swished gently and cooed, *Yes, yes.*

The stone in my hand wanted me to go one way and the reeds another.

I stood still for a long time wondering which I ought to listen to. Stone or reeds? Reeds or stone?

Follow us, follow us, the reeds sang.

He's here, he's here, the stone cried.

Who is he? I wondered. A face appeared, a face carved in black stone. A dead face. Was the stone leading me to his grave?

Yes! the reeds hissed. *To his grave and yours. He will drag you down into his grave.*

Tears stung my eyes like pinpricks. His grave. He was dead then. He had come here to find a way to be alive and he had died. For me. He had come here and risked this place that was no place for me.

No, no, no, the reeds cried, beating against me. *For himself, for himself, for himself . . .*

But I shook them off and stepped in the direction the stone pointed. The reeds threw themselves at me in a frenzy, but I pushed on, holding my arms up to shield my face from their assault. It was like swimming upstream while being attacked by piranhas. The reeds lashed at my arms like machetes and twined themselves around my ankles like snakes. *We are snakes*, a reedy voice whimpered, but the voice was weak. I ignored it and kept going. All I could see was his grave. I wasn't even sure who *he* was, but I knew that he had come here willing to die for me and I couldn't let him lie alone in that grave unmourned.

I fell out of the reeds onto hard, stony ground, my momentum tumbling me down a rocky incline. I rolled in a blur of dirt and rocks, down and down until I crashed into something hard. Then I lay still, every part of my body throbbing with pain.

Every part of my body except my right hand.

I opened my eyes and saw that I was surrounded by tall, looming figures in gray robes. No, not figures – stones – a circle of nine standing stones that I felt I had seen earlier. Even when I'd identified the objects as stones, though, the feeling of being surrounded by interested spectators didn't dissipate. I sat up, keeping a wary eye on the stones, half afraid that they would close in on me if I tried to move out of the circle, but they remained still and impassive . . . only . . . hadn't there been nine of them when I first opened my eyes? I counted them. There were eight. I must have imagined the ninth one. The stones couldn't move. Could they? And if one *had* moved, where would it go? The sky, still mottled purple and blue like a bruise, gave enough light to illuminate the entire valley I'd fallen into, and I was alone in it. The only spot I couldn't see fully was the area under the stone arch – the passage that led into the hill . . . the tomb. Yes, that's what it was. I'd come through the reeds to reach the tomb because I knew he was here – even though I still couldn't quite remember who *he* was. I could see a face carved out of black stone and I knew he was dead and that he had come here for me . . . but the order of those things was confused. I had the distinct impression that he had died before coming here for me, but then maybe that was because time didn't flow straight here. Just as the light seemed to come from nowhere and everywhere, so time flowed here in ripples and eddies with no beginning and no end.

And if that was so, how could he be dead?

I looked into the dark passage. It gaped blackly, like an open mouth waiting to swallow me.

Something here *could* eat me, someone had told me that. I could feel fear flowing out of the black hole like a stream of cold air. I wanted to turn and run back to the reeds to lose myself in them again. I could do that. I would forget everything in the reeds. Eventually I would forget *him*, and wouldn't that be better if he was dead?

I took a step backward, afraid to turn my back on that blackness, and another. The chill wind coming out of the hole dissipated. If I kept moving back, I could get away and eventually I would forget . . .

But I didn't want to forget. I took a step forward and felt the cold streaming out of the hole. The cold of the grave. I took two more steps into that stream and felt the cold envelop me. I was shaking all over by the time I reached the arch; every muscle in my body wanted to flee in the other direction, but I stepped over the threshold into the dark.

I touched one hand to each side of the stone arch. The stone felt icy, but that was better than when, several steps later, my fingers touched nothing. The stone arch opened up into a larger chamber beneath the mound. I could feel the space widening, but I still couldn't see anything. I couldn't do it. I couldn't walk into that blackness . . .

But then I remembered that I didn't have to. I raised my right hand and snapped my fingers. They were shaking so badly it took three tries, but on the third try a flame appeared at the tip of my thumb. I held it up and a high-domed chamber leaped into fitful light. The walls were covered with the painted figures of animals and men, and creatures who were both – horned men and women with tails and wings – the gods of the fey. They were incredibly beautiful and somehow horribly sad.

I looked down and saw four rectangular plinths carved from a pure white stone that glittered in the light of my thumb-flame. Stepping forward I saw that two of the plinths were empty, but carved figures lay on the other two. The first was of a woman dressed in full battle armor, her long hair in a braid that lay over her cuirassed breasts. A fillet lay across her high forehead. A name flickered through my mind. *Maeve*. The sister who was killed. This was Maeve. Her sister Morgane had made this tomb for her. She was so beautiful that I stared at her for many seconds before looking at her companion.

His body and hair were carved out of black stone, but his face was as white as hers and as beautiful . . . and *familiar*. I moved closer and held the flame directly over him. It flickered on his broad brow, wide cheekbones, chiseled nose, and full lips. I touched my hand to those lips, recalling the feel of them on my lips, my face, my throat . . .

His lips parted, sharp teeth flashed in the flickering flame, a rush of black swept over me, extinguishing the flame and knocking me back against cold stone – but not as cold as the body pressed against me and the teeth at my throat.

'Will!' I screamed, the name torn out of me as his teeth pierced my skin. Memory flooded into me with the cold. I remembered the first time he had drawn my blood after I'd been poisoned by the manticore, and the second when I'd called his name on the wind, and the third when we'd made love on Governors Island.

'It will be difficult to stop once I start,' he had said that last time.

He wasn't trying to stop right now. He was sucking my blood with an urgency I hadn't felt those other times. Because he was starving.

'Will!' I cried again. 'It's Garet. We're in the Valley of No Return. I came here to find you.'

He moaned at my name but only drank deeper. I could feel myself becoming weak. Soon I would pass out and Will would keep drinking. He'd been here for months – if time meant anything here – hiding from sunlight in this tomb, starving to death. He might not even remember who I was.

'Will.' My voice was barely a whisper now. 'It's . . . Garet . . . I came . . . to find you. I love . . .'

My throat went numb; the venom the vampire released to anesthetize his victim had frozen my vocal cords. I felt the venom spreading from my throat down my chest into my stomach, seeping into my arms and legs. I was limp in his arms, pinned between him and the wall. All was black and cold here in Maeve's tomb, which would soon be my tomb.

'Garet?'

The voice came as if from far away. I was lying on the ground now, staring up at the blackness, but then a light flickered in the nothingness and swelled into a face. A face etched with terror.

'Garet! I didn't know it was you! I didn't know anything! I'd lost who I was. All that was left was the hunger. Garet, please don't die. Hold on.'

'Cold,' I managed to say, forcing the word out of my frozen throat.

His eyes widened. Then vanished. The light vanished and I was left alone in the dark.

Had he left me? Or had I died? I couldn't tell. All I knew was darkness and cold, and then there was light again – lots of light and noise and heat. A fire was burning in the center of the domed room. I watched Will throw armfuls of sticks on the fire. They burst into flames but burned so quickly he had to keep adding more. He flew in and out of the room so quickly he became a blur – a bat flitting above the hectic flames, always adding more sticks to the crackling fire.

They weren't sticks, though. They were reeds. Will was burning the reeds, and as they burned, they cried out.

He doesn't love you, he doesn't love you, he doesn't—

'Shut up!' I yelled. 'It's pretty obvious he does!'

Will turned in midflight and landed by my side. His face glowed gold in the light of the burning reeds, his lips red – from my blood, I realized.

'You're alive,' I said, then laughed. 'Or as alive as you get.'

'I feel more alive than I have in four hundred years,' he said, grasping my hand. 'When I thought I'd killed you . . . I . . . I wanted to die. Garet, I love you.'

'I know,' I said, touching my finger to his bloody lips. 'And I love you. So what the hell are we doing in this place? We need to leave *now*.'

'But you're too weak.'

'No, I'll be all right. Help me up.'

He scooped me up in his arms, and I let myself lie there

for a moment, cradled against his chest, which still felt warm from the blood he'd drunk. His lips touched mine and my mouth opened. We could stay here tonight, I thought, and make love . . . what was one more night?

One more night, the smoldering reeds moaned. *One more night.*

'I think,' I said, my lips moving against his, 'that there are traps here for faithful lovers as well as faithless ones.'

'I could make love to you here *forever*,' he said, his jaw clenched.

'*Exactly.*'

He sighed and put me down on my feet. 'I think that's what happened to *them*.' He pointed to the far side of the tomb, behind an empty plinth. White bones lay in a mingled heap. Two bodies that had twined themselves together in death. I shivered. Not from the cold but from the sudden urge to lie down beside them with Will and make love together until the flesh fell from our bones.

'Yeah,' Will said, 'we'd better go now. Before it gets light again. I can't tell here how long the night lasts.'

'But if you get stuck in the daylight . . .'

'We'll have to risk it. If we stay here any longer . . .' He stroked my face, let his hand trail down my neck, caressed my breast . . .

'Yeah. Now.' I grabbed his hand before it got any lower and pulled him toward the door, pushed him through. We stumbled out into the circle of standing stones. Eight standing stones.

'Were there only eight stones when you got here?' I asked.

'By the time I got here I wasn't in any shape to count

stones. I was half out of my mind from wandering in the reeds.' He was striding up a hill, pulling me behind him, heading away from the reeds.

'What did they say to you?' I asked, half dreading his answer. What awful things had the reeds said about me to make him doubt his love for me? But it seemed to me that unless we faced what the reeds had said to us, we would forever hear their whisperings. 'They told *me* you couldn't love me or else you'd have already become mortal and come back to get me.'

He stopped on the crest of the hill and turned to face me. 'They told me I didn't deserve you. That if you knew all the evil I had done in my four hundred years as a vampire, you wouldn't love me. That the Will you thought you loved was a mirage. That once you saw the real me, you would realize I was a monster and run screaming.'

I looked up at him. He was above me on the hill so he seemed even taller, a giant looming over me. The violet fluorescent light in the sky made his skin glow like marble and his lips stand out a deathly blue. I felt my heart thud with fear. I touched my hand to my chest . . . and found the watch pendant. I gripped its cold metal in my hand and felt resolve settle in my heart.

'I'm still here, aren't I?' I said.

He grinned. 'God knows why, Garet. But I hope I never give you cause to regret it.' He turned away and I watched him start to climb over the hill, leaving the Valley of No Return. Maybe it was called that because once you crossed it, there was no going back to who you were before. Although I felt resolved to love Will as he was, I knew that he would always torture himself with his past deeds. If only he *could* go back to who he was before he had committed those terrible deeds. If only the last four hundred years could be erased. It seemed the only way he'd ever forgive himself.

But that couldn't be. I let go of the watch and followed Will into our future.

a Poem and a Letter

I've learned that love's perfection isn't time,
or anything that can be measured. No,
it's merge beyond all comprehension, rhyme
between two hearts and minds. A river flows
into another, and they love the sea;
two butterflies, sunkissed, both dart and dance
in ecstasy of nearness. Fleetingly,
they've reached communion, passion's deepest trance.
And even humble atoms, that I sense
within my very flesh, will spin and glow,
attracted to a neighbor, or the sun.
Amazing, Marguerite, what I now know—
as student of our separation's pain—
It's not how long. It's seeing you again!

Will wrote this sonnet late that night, after Marguerite was asleep. He sat in a chair by the window and wrote in the pale light of an amber half-moon, quill-point scratching across parchment as if with a will of its own. He wrote partly to reconcile himself to this new situation in which they were joyously together but he must not wish for anything more, and partly to send a love letter to Marguerite.

But even as he laid down his quill and read his sonnet over with satisfaction unbecoming a working poet, he sensed disquiet deep within him, like a ripple at the bottom of a deep well. He tried to suppress this unease, and the idea accompanying it, that he could *never* reconcile himself to the gulf of time between them, but was unable to.

No, he *must* be with her always, he reversed himself, out on the vast promontory of time on which she lived. Even if fierce winds tried to blow him off continuously. If he wasn't out on that promontory with her, he would die. Not just physically (eventually) but spiritually *right now*! The realization tore across his mood like a cyclone. He tried to suppress it, but it was the truth. Sadly, he folded his reconciliation poem and put it back in his pocket. Maybe at some other moment he'd feel differently, give it to her. But not now.

Then, in the shadowy light of the amber half-moon, he began to noiselessly scan Marguerite's travel chest for where box and ring could be hidden, assuming she had them with her. This time, without success.

The next day, Will and Marguerite dined at 1:00 p.m. at the most elegant establishment in Paimpont, the unassumingly named Goat & Boar. They were sitting at a sumptuously provisioned oak table with a rainbow awning when a slender foot messenger, clad in black, approached Will. He asked him to confirm his identity and, satisfied, gave him a letter in a scarlet envelope, which Will put into his pocket unread.

Marguerite gazed quizzically at him. 'Not interested?'

He smiled awkwardly. He wasn't sure whom it could be

from and didn't want to share such an uncertainty with his beloved. A missive from an old flame in Somerset – Bess, perhaps? – couldn't be ruled out. 'Boring – business – I'm sure,' he muttered. 'Nothing worth disrupting our time together for.' He tried to smile more engagingly. He'd never discussed any sort of business with Marguerite. Their conversations tended toward the ethereal.

The look she returned his with was penetrating, bordering on disbelieving. But she didn't pursue her skepticism, and the letter seemed to vanish as they lapsed into silence, then drifted on to other exchanges. Early on the evening of the same day, as Marguerite napped before supper, Will went to his chair by the window and read the letter, which turned out to be from John Dee.

My good Sir—

I sit in my tower room at Pointe du Raz, at the very ends of the earth. It is the middle of the night and a summer storm is howling, so that my skull might cave in. The surf crashes against the stone foundation of the tower so as to topple it, and the ocean is whipped to a boiling froth that might cleave my skin right off if I fell in. Nonetheless all I have on my mind is you, good boy: why have you not come to see me with those items I requested? Why, when immortality is at your fingertips, when you and I could stand atop this breathless pinnacle together, are you nowhere in my sight?

I know you have been in Paris, my boy, and I know that you have now journeyed to Paimpont. For my

spies are everywhere. Paimpont is not so far from
Pointe du Raz. You can leave immediately on the final
leg of a wonderful journey, should you will it. Come
to me in my tower with those items I've requested,
Will Hughes. Come. Note: you will only be admitted
after the sun has set. *But come!*

Faithfully yours, [signed] John Dee

Will folded the letter back in its envelope and sighed
with an uncertainty his rational mind found startling. For,
even after the previous day's encounter with Russwurin,
who added another connection on top of the Paris alley
sighting between Lightning Hands and Dee, he could still
not rule out dealing with the man. Not if nothing else
worked regarding immortality. Reuniting with Marguerite
had been wonderful and uplifting, but it hadn't solved the
problem. Maybe Dee had nothing to do with the robbery,
and maybe he had planned it – but then discovered the
golden bough to be worthless to him – but in either event,
Will could not continue with Marguerite this way.

As he then turned to look at her in bed, he noticed, even
in the waning light, that a few bricks in the wall near her
head seemed slightly out of line with the others. The
pattern was subtle, but he was looking at it from exactly the
right angle now. It seemed the bricks might have been
placed there more recently than the others, or by a
different set of hands. Curiosity flooded him, but he
couldn't explore the anomaly with Marguerite a few feet
away. The bricks could not likely be removed easily, let
alone silently.

The abbey's bell rang the half hour, Marguerite stirred,

and Will cast aside any absurd second thoughts that he wasn't immediately rushing off to see Dee without the required objects. Awakening suddenly, Marguerite began to struggle up into a sitting position, and Will took her in his arms and kissed her passionately. Soon enough they had dressed and were on their way out to sup at Goat & Boar. Will cast a glance at the errant bricks as they left the room, and something stirred deep within him, something with wings that were akin to hope.

Sometime in the middle of the night, Will was awoken by a thunderclap so loud it was as if he had been sleeping on a nearby cloud. A reddish orange cloud, he imagined, from the strange light that filled the room. He sat straight up in bed, and before he knew his own name observed that Marguerite was not in their bed, nor in the room. He was lacerated by panic for several long seconds, even as he fumbled about for clothes to go outside in, before he had the thought that she could simply be taking a walk. She loved to walk and had slept a lot more yesterday than he had, hence might have arisen because she was unable to sleep.

Will went to the window and saw immediately the source of the strange light: the full moon had a bloodred cast to it. Despite some nearby thunderclouds, it bathed the town in ruby light. Perhaps this was why Marguerite had gone out – to observe the effects of the crimson moonlight on the abbey and the lake. But as he looked about anxiously, he saw no sign of her or anyone else in the street. As he turned back to the room, planning to leave and search for her, he caught another glimpse of the irregular bricks he'd noticed the night before.

He approached them with that same tingling hopefulness, almost breathlessness, he'd felt the previous evening.
Will sat on the side of the bed and with gentle fingertips
established that four of the bricks were loose. Tenderly,
brushing off dust as it fell on his hands, he removed the
bricks and placed them on the bed. Then he extended his
right hand into a dark opening and, feeling around in a
space that seemed to have no rear boundary, brought out
the ring and the shallow silver box that Dee had referred
to, neither of them with any covering or wrapping over
them, and laid them on the bed. Nothing else seemed to
be in the opening. He gazed with sentimental fondness at
the gold-and-black ring. For the first time he noticed a
pattern carved into the stone – a tower with an eye above
it. The eye made him feel doubly like a thief as he slipped
the ring into his pants pocket. He felt so guilty that he took
off his own ring, the silver signet ring with his family
crest of a swan rising, and put it in the compartment as a
token of his commitment to return.

Will glanced next at the box: it was the one Dee had
described, and it also had a fine oval pattern of lines etched
into the cover that seemed to be moving now, rippling as
if it were the image of the ocean in a tidal surge. As if calling him to the ocean.

As if calling him to Pointe du Raz.

Will blinked at the dizzying motion of the lines and
turned away. He tried to collect himself. He might have
stuffed the ring in his pocket, and he might be intrigued by
the box, but he'd made no decision to go to Pointe du Raz.
None! Especially after the coach to Paimpont horror.
Going would also mean leaving Marguerite, for he could

hardly ask her to cooperate in his quest for immortality after they'd had such conflict over it. That Dee had been able to track his whereabouts to Paimpont was almost certainly due to reports from miseries such as Lightning Hands and Russwurin, or worse, and that hardly recommended Dee as a person he wanted to put his fate in the hands of. Theft was theft, and to leave with these items, even if he'd somewhat replaced one of them, was theft from his beloved.

A flash suddenly erupted from the box as if some incendiary material inside it had exploded. The lid flew open and silver flames erupted upward, nearly reaching the ceiling. Will could smell something like gunpowder in the air, with a strongly sulfurous tinge to it. Then he felt himself shoved over backward into a prone position on the bed, as if invisible hands, or a violent wind, had pushed him down.

As he struggled back to a sitting position, Will had the odd sense that he might have blacked out while prone on the bed. He sensed some small acceleration in time, and the sky outside seemed palpably brighter when the flash and flames receded. He had no sense of how long he'd entered the blackness or where it had been located. But he had this odd sense of time lapse as an external change and not an internal blackout, some room he'd entered, almost some nation he'd become a part of. A place far away, and a new Will Hughes emerging from this sojourn in eternal darkness. It was all so irrational, and hazy . . . but *this* Will Hughes, like a man possessed to a new way of thinking, did want to go to Pointe du Raz, over-whelmingly so. He wouldn't hear of doing otherwise. This

Will Hughes *only* wanted to be with Marguerite for eternity. Or else not at all! And he felt no caution about Dee ambushing him as Lightning Hands and Russwurin had done. Will would be extraordinarily cautious and have a weapon on him.

He scribbled a note to her and put it in the wall compartment:

My love, if you're reading this, you know I have borrowed your ring and your box, and my deepest apologies for not being able to notify you first. With any luck and Godspeed I will be returning them (and myself) to you shortly! I know what meager reassurance my own ring, left in the absence of yours, provides. Trust me that I would not have taken such an extraordinary measure as removing your property without the most absolute justification, and that my loyalty to you, I trust, will soon be rewarded by the most perfect harmony between us. In the meantime I am, lovingly, your servant and ever-devoted [signed] Will Hughes.

He cursed Dee for his night-visit requirement; otherwise he might well have been able to next see Marguerite, in the joy of new immortality, this very evening! He gathered up his belongings and concealed the box among them.

He was halfway out the door when another thought occurred to him, a thought that brought hot blood to his face. Although he'd paid in advance for the room, he had not left a gratuity for the maid, a sweet, simple girl who had been tireless in her ministrations to him throughout his stay. It was bad enough he was abandoning Marguerite; it was an outright affront to his conception of himself as a gentleman to stiff the maid. He removed several gold coins from his pocket and, depositing them in a pouch, left them on top of a chest with a quickly scrawled note: *Pour Anne Marie, Merci!* Satisfied that he had behaved like a gentleman even in dire circumstances, he descended to the street and walked briskly to the farrier's on the edge of town, where he retained a horse to ride to Pointe du Raz. The quick storm had cleared, and the sun was rising blood-red behind him as he rode out onto the main road. In his face was a hot wind from the west, rough and dust-streaked, like one that might blow down an alley in hell. In his mind was Marguerite and how, when he returned to her on the morrow, their problems would be gone forever.

26

Blood Moon

As soon as we were over the crest of the hill, the light grew brighter. For a moment I was afraid it was the rising sun, but then I saw that it was only the full moon – a huge, rust-colored moon that hung over the next valley like a glowing jack-o'-lantern. A small village nestled in the crook of the valley a mile or so away was blood-tinged as if it had lately been the scene of a massacre. The lake beside the village reflected back the ruddy face of the moon.

'Is that Paimpont?' I asked. 'It's closer than I thought.'

'It must be. I recognize the abbey, but . . .' Will looked thoughtful. The moonlight gave his skin a menacing cast.

'I saw the tomb of your ancestor there,' I told him. 'Guillem de Hughes.'

'A bloody crusader. When I first came here, I was so excited to discover that it was the ancestral home of the Hugheses, but then the more I learned, the more I found that the whole family history was soaked in blood. From that first selfish bastard who shot his swan bride to keep her from leaving to mercenaries and crusaders to . . . well, to *me*. Over the years I've come to wonder if becoming a vampire wasn't the natural evolution of my lineage.'

'Don't talk like that. John Dee tricked you by

summoning that vampire, just as Morgane tricked Marguerite. Melusine told me that Morgane only ever grants requests that she knows will turn out badly for the supplicant.'

'Did she?' Will asked, his lips curling in an angry smile. 'That sounds about right. And yet, I stole this box from you' – he patted a leather satchel slung across his chest that I hadn't noticed before – 'and we have come all this way so that I could ask her to make me mortal.'

'But that's a reasonable request. You deserve to be mortal. I don't see how that could turn out badly.'

Turning to me, Will caressed my face, traced the line of my jaw, and tilted my chin up so he could see the marks his teeth had made on my throat. 'You have an awful lot of faith in the monster that almost killed you.'

'But you didn't,' I said, clasping his hand in mine. 'You stopped yourself. A monster wouldn't have been able to stop, but you did. So you're not a monster.'

He lifted his hand to my throat and stroked the torn flesh. I trembled at his touch, not from fear but from the sudden overwhelming desire to feel his teeth there again. 'Let's hope for both our sakes you're right,' he said. Then he turned, took my hand, and led me into the blood-lit valley.

As we descended, we walked through deep woods that obscured our view of the village, but when we reached a clearing just above the lake, we could make out the village landmarks: the tower of the abbey across the lake, the gate to the walled town – closed now, and bolted with heavy iron locks – and across from the gate the half-timbered inn looking especially quaint and rustic in the moonlight. I couldn't make out the car park from here or – I realized as we drew closer – any cars on the road at all.

'The village looks like something out of the Middle Ages,' I said to Will. 'Maybe they got rid of the cars for the Renaissance Faire.'

'No,' he said, pulling me under the shadow of a tree. ' "I have a feeling we're not in Kansas anymore." '

'What?' I asked, confused.

'It *is* the Renaissance. This is how Paimpont looked in 1602. See that cottage? I remember getting my horse shod there in 1602.'

The building looked familiar to me, too, only I recalled it housing a gas station and sporting a large sign that welcomed visitors to the Fairy Country. 'Maybe they took down the sign,' I said. 'Just because it looks like sometime in the seventeenth century . . .'

I felt Will's grip tighten on my arm. I turned and saw that his face had gone as rigid as the stone effigy in the abbey. 'Not just any time in the seventeenth century,' he said through gritted teeth. 'It's the night I stayed here with Marguerite. The night she gave up her immortality for me and I, fool that I was, left her to trade my soul for eternal life.'

'How do you know?'

'Because there she is.'

I followed his riveted gaze down to the edge of the pool. At first I saw nothing and hoped that the image of his lost love was only a delusion left over from his long confinement in the Summer Country. Because as distressing as it would be to think that Will had lost his mind, I was pretty sure I preferred that to the idea that we had traveled back in time to the turn of the seventeenth century.

But then I saw her. She was wearing a dark cloak, but when she moved, a flash of white appeared at the hem, a glimpse of the long nightgown she must have worn when sneaking out of bed – the bed she had shared with Will! – and coming down to the lake. Her long black hair hid her face, but when I took a step forward, cracking a branch beneath my foot, she turned and revealed, startlingly clear in the moonlight, her face . . .

My face!

I started to gasp, but Will clamped his hand over my mouth. For a long moment Marguerite stared into the dark woods above her, her brow furrowing with concentration. What would she think if she saw us? To an immortal fey, visitors from the future might not seem impossible. We could warn her that she was about to give up her immortality for nothing, but then she'd never have mortal children. My mother would never be born, nor would I.

After a long moment she turned back to the pool and sat down on a circular stone overhanging the water. She remained still for several moments, then she leaned over the pool, nearly touching her lips to the water, as if whispering something to it.

Will released me and moved forward, his feet gliding silently over the ground. I tried to follow him, but my footsteps crackled like fireworks in the still night. Will was already at the edge of the woods, crouched in the shadow of an overhanging branch. A pang of jealousy, sharp as Will's teeth, tore through me. Of course, it was *her* he'd wanted all along. I was a pale facsimile. When I'd seen Marguerite's face, I'd thought it was identical to mine, but now watching her whispering to the water, I realized how wrong I'd been. She radiated an unearthly serenity I could never hope to assume. No wonder Will was drawn to her. They were alike – two immortals. If Will stopped her now, they could remain immortals together. What would it matter to them if I would never be born?

As if in response to my despair the ground beneath my feet began to shake. An earthquake, I wondered, or was the fabric of time splitting again, this time to spit me out into a limbo of the never-born? But then I realized that the rumbling was coming from the lake. With a Klaxon-like cry, the water split open, disgorging an enormous creature of sinewy muscle that shot straight up into the sky and then hovered there, held up by incongruously delicate wings. The seal creature looked down at Marguerite with cold, impassive eyes. A moment ago I couldn't have imagined anything daunting the self-assured Marguerite, but now I marveled that she didn't bolt and run from the apparent malevolence of this creature.

But she didn't. Instead she engaged the creature in calm discourse, the words of which I couldn't make out, but the tone of which – surprisingly calm and reasoned – was clear. As they talked, I crept quietly down to the perch where Will crouched and listened, confident that the thrash of the water – still disturbed by Morgane's rising – would cover the slight sounds of my approach. Even Will failed to hear me, so engrossed was he in Marguerite and Morgane's conversation. By the time I was close enough to hear, I gathered that Marguerite had already asked her sister to make her mortal. Morgane was laying out the ground rules of the deal – that all Marguerite's descendants would assume the role of Watchtower, 'guarding against usurpers and vipers crossing the boundary from mortal to immortal in either direction. And even guarding humankind, loathsome as it is, along with ourselves, from those malefactors like werewolves, shape-shifters, incubi, or—'

Morgane abruptly fell silent and raised her black eyes to look past Marguerite . . . directly toward Will and me. Had my movement given us away? But it wasn't me she fixed her gaze on – it was Will. I saw Will stiffen. This would be his opportunity to step forward and reveal himself, to tell Marguerite that she needn't make the sacrifice she was planning. But he didn't. Instead he straightened up and stared back at the creature. In the moonlight I saw the flash of teeth as he bared his fangs. Morgane responded by baring her own longer fangs, not in a snarl but in a nasty smile.

'—or *vampires* who would seek to conquer or destroy humankind, or we fey or both. You must especially swear to abhor all vampires.'

That bitch! She knew what Will was – what he would become – and she was deliberately binding Marguerite and her descendants to perpetual enmity with the man Marguerite loved. I had half a mind to stop her myself . . .

But it was already too late. Marguerite was now swearing an oath binding her to the terms of Morgane's deal, and Morgane, with a parting taunt that Marguerite would 'know soon enough' that she was a mortal, disappeared beneath the water.

Marguerite stood up and remained for a moment staring at the water, as if she expected – or perhaps feared – her sister's return. Then she grasped the collar of her cloak and drew something out of the cloth. Silver gleamed in the moonlight, and then, quick as a dragonfly's dart, Marguerite stabbed her index finger with the pin. I couldn't see the blood from where we were, but I saw Will's nostrils quiver and I knew he could smell it. He was still hungry from his long months in Maeve's tomb. Would he give in to his hunger and pounce?

But he held himself in place as Marguerite turned and walked back in the direction of the inn. When she had passed out of sight, I stepped toward him and gingerly touched his arm. When he turned to me, I saw that tears of blood streaked his face. I reached for him, but he shook his head and strode away, down to the shore of the lake.

'Morgane!' he called. 'Show yourself! You have a lot to answer for, you bitch!'

The water swirled and once again disgorged a creature, but this time instead of taking the shape of a monstrous seal, Morgane appeared as a woman – a beautiful woman with long, seaweed hair that only partly veiled her bare breasts. She rose from the lake until the water reached her waist.

'Will Hughes, I presume,' she cooed. 'Is this the man who stole my pathetic sister's heart?'

'It's you who are pathetic. You added that part about protecting humanity from vampires because you couldn't bear to see Marguerite happy. You knew what I had – what I will – become.'

Morgane laughed. 'So you *are* from the future. I guessed as much. And who is this?' She tilted her head to look at me, and I felt a chill as if I'd been plunged into the icy pool. 'She looks enough like my sister to be her spawn. Let me guess, he says he loves you and wants . . .' She tilted her head the other way as if listening to something whispering from the water. 'Oh, it's too rich!' she exclaimed. '*Now* he wants to be mortal so he can be with *you*. Make up your mind, Will Hughes.'

'I have made up my mind, Morgane. I want to share a mortal life with Garet. All I require of you is for you to do for me what you just so easily did for Marguerite. I have the box . . .' He reached into the bag strapped across his chest.

Morgane laughed. 'Do you? I think you'll find your present counterpart has it. You see the box is a constant. It exists outside time and space. When you traveled back in time, it merged with its past incarnation. I believe you'll find your bag is full of rocks.'

Will dug into the bag and came up with a fistful of rocks, which he promptly threw at Morgane. She deftly ducked and laughed.

'Don't despair, my boy. You don't need the box. You only need to follow your past self to his rendezvous with John Dee, and then, when Dee has used the box to summon the vampire who made you, you must get a little of that vampire's blood. Drink his blood and you will be mortal again. Then you and my great-niece can wallow in the dung heap of humanity together.'

'You swear – on your oath as a Watchtower – that this is the truth?'

The sneering smile left Morgane's face. 'What makes you think that I am still bound by that oath?'

'Because as evil as you are, you still would not leave the world without its last Watchtower. And because I know there is one mortal whom you loved. Still love . . .'

'Don't name him!' Morgane shrieked, rising from the water, revealing that below her waist grew a scaly tail. 'Do not pollute his name with your undead lips!'

'Arthur,' Will whispered. 'King Arthur. You loved him. You carried him to the Summer Country when he was dying and granted him immortality.'

'I tried. He refused the gift of immortality. He preferred to share his death with that ninny Guinevere.'

'And you granted him that, didn't you?'

Morgane's face transformed from a mask of rage to something almost tender – for only an instant – then she shrugged. 'They deserved each other.'

'You did it because you loved him. Swear on Arthur's name that you are telling the truth that I can regain my humanity by drinking the blood of the fiend who made me.'

'I swear it,' she said, her face somber. 'On Arthur's name. Now go. Your requests have made me tired.'

'Gladly,' Will said, taking my hand. He pulled me away as Morgane began to sink beneath the water, but before she disappeared, just as her lips were level with the pool, she locked her eyes on mine and spoke her parting words:

'Remember, even when he becomes mortal, the blood of all his kills will still stain his hands.'

27

1602: Primordial Heat

Marguerite had known the blood moon was a sign that the fabric between the worlds was tissue-thin, and that it heralded the best possible moment to gain access to the Summer County. But instead of going outside upon observing it, she returned to bed, unwilling to leave Will just yet.

Marguerite gazed adoringly at Will's sleeping features, brushed an errant lock of hair from his forehead. The crimson light bathed his limbs and hers, uniting them in a baptismal bath of bloodlight. Perhaps, she thought, it was an omen, a sign that she would soon share with Will the blood of a mortal. She felt a profound longing just then, deeper than any she'd experienced in all the centuries she'd lived. And that was to live out her life in a harmonious relationship with Will.

She had missed him terribly while she'd been away from him, missed him so that every drop of her immortal blood, every pore of her unaging skin, felt incomplete. Yet that intense ache was nothing compared to the ecstasy she'd been feeling since their reunion. These emotions combined now to forge a terrible yet thrilling imperative: she *must* make herself mortal, so that she could be with him more fully and more naturally than up until now.

Belonging to different classes of beings was always going to be a barrier between them. It would spark fights that could lead to the end of their relationship. And trying to make Will immortal was too risky. The forces that needed to be unleashed could kill him. Marguerite would be better able to withstand them, transforming in the opposite direction. If they later decided they needed immortality, they could avail themselves of the kind everyone else did: having children. She shivered with pleasure at that thought, in the moonlit darkness of the room. The corners of Will's mouth in sleep seemed to turn up slightly, in a smile, as if he were dreaming her thoughts. Yes, they were soul mates. That was a kind of forever time itself could never match.

Marguerite saw that she had no choice but to turn mortal, saw it with the same clarity those who gazed into the pool at Paimpont without deceit received. She would go to the pool and wrestle with Morgane for the portal reentry Marguerite believed to be her entitlement. Reentry might happen on the shore, or underwater – in the air – it might require a simple plea, or a thousand hours of arguing. But it would happen. She had made up her mind.

Marguerite took one last look at the room in which they had spent so much of their reunion, a room that she could see, even with the moon behind clouds, had taken on a blood-lit glow. As if her decision to become mortal had a life force, one so fierce that it had excited the atoms in the room to primordial red heat. The glow was like a marker, she thought, delineating her long past life from her much shorter, but much more fulfilling, life to come. She kissed Will on the forehead and made her way down to the pool.

The thing that frightened Marguerite the most about summoning her sister from the pool was Morgane's ability to change her shape. She could emerge from the water as a mermaid with a monstrous face, or as a hummingbird, or as a fire-spitting dragon. The one option Marguerite was reasonably certain Morgane would not choose was to appear as herself, the sister she had grown up with in their immemorial past. It would create too much intimacy and connection.

The last time Marguerite had seen her, anguish had serrated Morgane's features upon her learning of their sister Maeve's demise in war. They were the most agonized expressions Marguerite had ever seen on a human, or nearly human, face. She didn't anticipate anything like them now, but she suspected Morgane would not receive her request to leave their family's tradition kindly. Nor the reason for it.

As she prepared to kneel, overlooking the pool, a crackling sound from the woods behind her made her whirl around. She stared into the dark forest that rose steeply from the shore, using all her preternatural senses to detect an intruder, but the sense she got from the forest was ambiguous. She felt some kind of presence – or *presences* – but no threat. She felt as though some benevolent being might be watching over her. Almost as if some sister of the Watchtower had come to aid her in her quest. But that couldn't be. Of her sisters, Maeve lay dead in a tomb in the

Val sans Retour, Melusine haunted a castle hundreds of miles from here, and Morgane lay beneath the pool. And no one would call *her* benevolent. No, it must have been her overwrought imagination.

She tried to relax, body and spirit. It was useless to focus on the enormity of what she was attempting. That would make her do nothing. She relaxed until she could feel her spirit assume wings and begin to glide along the predawn sky directly above, as if looking down at and watching over her. When she could see from that lofty vantage point and gaze calmly into the pond, she felt at peace, whole. She had unified different parts of her being. She could speak to Morgane.

'Beloved sister, it's me, Marguerite,' she whispered to the pool. She knew Morgane's abilities enough to know the volume of her voice didn't matter. Morgane could hear to the ends of the earth, to the pitch-black bottom of the sea. 'Please come up and meet me. I need your help on a matter of vital importance ... vital ...' Marguerite imagined her words radiating in the pool like moonlight, growing dimmer and dimmer, but still audible.

Silence, for several seconds.

Then Marguerite thought she heard a faraway rumble, way down in the water, so deep it was near the center of the earth.

Silence again, for several seconds. Now a less muffled roar, lasting nearly half a minute. She couldn't identify what sort of creature it came from. But the sound did have an undercurrent of agony to it.

Silence, for several more seconds.

Then a bellowing so loud Marguerite had to clasp her palms over her ears. The pool's placid surface became tumult and surge, cauldron and whitecap. Morgane shot up out of the center of the pool, a winged seal about twenty feet in length, hovering as a bird might have, then twisting to face Marguerite. She had no talons, claws, or other weaponry. But she wasn't blubbery, either. She was a trim giant seal, and something in her lean, glistening frame unnerved Marguerite. Her sister was unlikely to attack her, but the language Marguerite read in her musculature was dominance and anger. Marguerite had better watch what she said, she told herself. The fleeting centuries had not made them closer.

'What sort of advice could I possibly give you, worldly sister?' Morgane asked her condescendingly. 'I, who seclude myself in such a different world?' The voice was human and showed no influence from her shape.

But Marguerite would answer prudently. 'My question arises regarding the boundary between our worlds. You are the only person in either world fit to answer it,' she flattered, although her statement was also accurate. 'What is of greater value, immortality or love?'

'Neither is worth anything. You know that, dear sister. Why do you ask?'

Marguerite asked because she hoped to fool Morgane into a theoretical statement that could lead to an agreement. 'If immortality is worthless as you say, it might reasonably be bargained for something trite, no? Something as trite as, even, let's say, love?'

Morgane growled before replying, more a bear than a seal. And more a creature than human. This put

Marguerite's nerves on edge and signaled to her that Morgane did not have endless time for talk.

'If our family had no sense of honor left, yes, by all means trade immortality for love! But fortunately that is not the case. Come, my dear. You obviously have some dreary circumstance on your mind. What is it?'

Marguerite took a deep breath. 'I have fallen in love with a mortal and want to relinquish my immortality so we can have a life together. I understand that if I am allowed this transformation, I may have to take on some new worldly responsibility to uphold the family honor. I am willing to do that.'

'What is the name of the dung heap?'

Marguerite chose not to object to her sister's coarseness. It would have been futile; the only way to get her agreement was to cooperate with her. 'Will Hughes,' Marguerite said in a soft voice. 'The now estranged firstborn of Lord Hughes of Somerset. He's an angel.'

'I do not know him,' Morgane replied clinically, as if she were a naturalist referring to a species of reptile. 'Nor, needless to say, do I have any inclination to. But is this pathetic turn of fate what you want for yourself, Sister?' Morgane's seal eyes opened wide and quizzically.

'I do not need to live forever. And I cannot live without my beloved. I must become a mortal.'

'Then you can be one,' Morgane said swiftly, surprising and delighting Marguerite with her unexpected assent. 'And, yes, the part of me that is analytical says, "Let her spend her mortal life rolling around with slime. It is a typical human decision."'

But then Morgane spun in a full circle in the air,

twitching with rage, and by the time she glared down at Marguerite again, her eyes were dark pools with red, vertical pupils. Sudden-grown fangs reached out toward Marguerite.

'The part of me that is royal, however, that supervises the tradition of the D'Arques nobility, damns your blasphemous decision and is tempted to refuse it. But I overrule my indignation as it is simply too sweet, dear sister, to contemplate you with that filth until you perish!' Her fangs seemed to gleam with relish. 'So I accede to your wishes, with the conditions being that all of your descendants will be mortal, and the first female born in each generation will continue your appointed role of Watchtower, guarding against usurpers and vipers crossing the boundary from mortal to immortal in either direction. And even guarding humankind, loathsome as it is, along with ourselves, from those malefactors like werewolves, shape-shifters, incubi, or—'

Morgane looked over Marguerite's shoulder as if contemplating the eons through which Marguerite's descendants would struggle. The view seemed to amuse her. Her mouth curled back over her fangs in a cruel snarl.

'—or vampires who would seek to conquer or destroy humankind, or we fey or both. You must especially swear to abhor all vampires.'

Marguerite nodded and uttered the words required to seal the oath, with a sense of relief despite Morgane's insults. The obligation required as compensation could have been far more onerous. Or so, at least, she wanted to think.

'Go then, wretch. May you never besmirch my presence

with your foulness again. And that will go for your descendants as well.'

'Nothing horrible you say makes you any less my sister. No matter how much you hate the thought of it. I still love you.'

'You are no sister to me. Nor are you fey any longer, except in name and your one obligation on pain of annihilation. Never again in spirit, or blood. Go, thing! Of two worlds that together are none! Go!'

Marguerite hesitated. 'Is that it? Nothing else happens? How do I know that I have been . . . changed?'

Morgane sneered. 'You will know soon enough.' She dived back into the pool, ripples from her plunge visible in the first blush of dawn.

Marguerite stood and watched the ripples in the water dissipate. It was fine for Morgane to say that she would 'know' that she had become mortal, but she required proof. She stuck her cloak pin, shaped like a small dagger, into her index finger. She gasped at the pain and then stared in fascination at the drop of blood that welled up, beaded, and spilled down her finger. She regarded this proof of mortality somberly. An appropriate mood, she reassured herself. What kind of person would she be if she weren't somber at a moment as portentous as this?

Marguerite turned to walk back to their room and awaken Will to her glorious news. She went up the grassy slope, pausing for a moment to listen to some stirring in the woods, but she no longer possessed the preternatural senses to detect what nocturnal creature might be moving there. And an unaccustomed sensation pricked her bosom as sharply as the pin had her finger. Fear of the unseen.

How do mortals do it, she wondered as she passed through Paimpont's main gate, how did they live with such blindness and uncertainty? Then came a second sensation she'd never before felt – fatigue. The physical part of the sensation wasn't new; even as an immortal she'd felt weariness and a need to sleep. But this feeling was more . . . it was fatigue with an edge. In her blood as well as in her mind – in all of her the deep tiredness of a body that has learned for the first time that it is going to die. Mortal fatigue.

Passing under the granite arch that welcomed visitors to Paimpont, she shed a single tear of regret. Instantly, the thought of Will waiting for her warmed it gone.

28

The Brooch

We watched Marguerite go into the inn from the shadowy archway of the town gate. Five minutes later she reappeared, her face gleaming wet in the moonlight. She looked frantically from side to side as if unsure what direction to go in. It was painful to watch the self-assured immortal creature of half an hour ago suffer such mortal uncertainty, but even more painful to see Will witness it.

'I always wondered how she reacted to my theft and desertion,' he whispered. 'I'd always hoped it was with anger.'

'I think she's in the denial stage,' I remarked clinically. 'But I bet anger will be next.'

'*You* sound angry. Have I done something to offend you?'

'You wanted to stop her, didn't you? If you'd stopped Morgane from making Marguerite mortal, the two of you could have stayed together as you are right now.'

'That's not my wish, Garet. Why—?'

I silenced him by grabbing his arm and directing his attention back to Marguerite, who'd finally made up her mind and was running toward the small cottage Will had pointed out to me earlier as the local farrier's.

'We need to get into her – my – our room,' Will said, stumbling over his pronouns. I couldn't blame him. Encountering your past self with your old love while trying to explain your feelings to her descendant and your present lover would flummox most men. I didn't need to make it any harder by throwing a jealous snit.

'Let's go then.'

We snuck up the back stairs to the second floor. The inn bore little resemblance to the modern Relais I'd booked into with Octavia La Pieuvre (where *was* Octavia, I spared a moment to wonder, had she ever gotten out of the Val sans Retour?), but I did recognize the view when we reached the room. It was the same view I'd had from my modern-day room. I stood at the window telling myself that I was keeping a lookout for Marguerite, but really I was trying to avoid looking at the rumpled bedclothes and the intimate story they told. When I turned around, I caught Will staring at the bed, fingering the hem of the linen sheet.

'What are we doing here?' I asked. 'Shouldn't we be following Will – I mean past-Will?'

'We can't follow him on foot. It'll be dawn soon; I'll need cover. We'll have to hire a coach and for that we'll need money. Here . . .'

He lifted a small leather sack from a chest beside the bed. 'It's not much but it should pay for a coach. It's a shame. Leaving a tip for the maid was the one selfless act I performed in this whole fiasco and now it's . . . *undone.*' He placed a queer emphasis on the word, as if it had suggested to him other things that might also be *undone*. 'But we need it.' He opened the chest and pulled out a long dress of sprigged muslin. 'Here, you'll need this, too. It's Marguerite's. She must have been too upset to take it. It'll fit you, of course . . .' He started to hand it to me, but then pressed the cloth against his face. 'Lavender and rose. I'd forgotten her scent . . .' Then, catching my glare, he collected himself. 'But I much prefer yours, of course.'

I snorted as I pulled the dress over my tank top and shucked my jeans off.

'And then what will happen?' I asked while Will laced up my dress. 'How are we going to get this vampire's blood?'

'Right after the creature changed me, I attacked it and threw it out the tower window. When it lands on the rocks below, I'll be there waiting to drink its blood. If Morgane's telling the truth, I'll become mortal.' He pulled the laces tight, tugging me toward him. I felt the length of his body pressed against my back. He gathered my hair into a knot and pressed his lips to the nape of my neck. 'Are you sure you won't miss . . . *this*.' His teeth dragged across my skin and a quiver moved down my spine directly into the place where his hips spooned against mine. As I felt him harden, I wondered if we could spare a little time . . . but the thought of making love in the bed where he and Marguerite had made love – albeit over four hundred years ago – chilled my ardor. I took a step away and turned to face him.

'I suppose there are things we'll both miss,' I said, trying to be honest, 'but it's your choice whether you want to live as a mortal or as how you are now. You chose to become immortal four centuries ago. Are you really sure you're ready to choose differently now?'

My question seemed to take him by surprise. Before he

could answer, a piercing musical trill filled the room. 'A lark,' Will said, 'warning us of the dawn's approach. We'd better go.'

He brushed his lips lightly against mine and hurried from the room. As I followed him, something sharp stabbed through the thin slippers I'd put on with Marguerite's dress. I knelt and pulled a pin out of my foot. It was the brooch that Marguerite had used to stab her finger. It must have fallen from her cloak in her hurry. The pin, which was long and rather lethal-looking, still bore the stain of her blood. I quickly pinned it inside the bodice of my dress, where Will wouldn't see it and be reminded of Marguerite by it, but where it would be handy if I had need of something sharp.

29

The Swimmer

Will reached Pointe du Raz about an hour before sundown. On one speedy horse, his journey from Paimpont,
which had begun at 4:30 a.m., might have taken only five
or six hours, which would have meant a wait through a long
afternoon before seeing Dee, perhaps wandering around
the nearby village, or seaside cliffs. But the day was
extraordinarily hot and humid, and Will's tired horse had
thrown a shoe in Pontivy, and it had taken hours before a
farrier had been found to reshoe it. At Audierne he had
stopped to water his horse and was told that the south cliff
road had been damaged in the last storm and he should
take the northern, and longer, route. So Will, weary from
weather and waiting, found himself with only an hour or so
to prepare for his session with Dee.

Walking around Pointe du Raz, Will easily recognized
the tower Dee had referred to. Rising from a stone abbey,
it was about five stories high, of black stone, and seemed
medieval in origin, broad slits for archers to aim through
rather than windows.

A huge seaside cliff jutted out into the ocean near the
tower, and Will climbed a footpath hewn into its granite
face. He wanted to get a better view of the tower, and to

take his mind off the enormity of what was coming. The path was narrow and had many twists, turns, and reversals, high grass on the land side and a plummet to jagged rocks on the sea side. Will had to discipline himself not to look down lest he experience vertigo. But the late-day salt air was brisk, refreshing him, and the view out to sea compelling. When he encountered an embankment of grass-tufted red earth to rest on, he took the opportunity.

He gazed at the tower from this perspective and observed that the archers' apertures were only one to a floor, each facing seaward. He wondered at the single-mindedness of builders in the long-ago past, who worried only about enemies from the sea, none from land. But the tower had survived – perhaps for several centuries – so the builders might well have known what they were doing. If only he were so confident right now . . . but he *was* certain about his decision, he reprimanded himself, when eternity with his beloved awaited this portentous encounter. People worshipped on Sundays in the less than certain hope of such an outcome, and here he had it at his fingertips! He shivered with anticipation. As if to mimic him, a gull flying above the tower shimmied in a gust of wind, then coasted down to smoother air.

Will cast a sweeping glance to the west, taking in the off-shore island of Île de Sein, its fishing boats returning for the evening. The sun was low in the sky, descending toward a dark stone tower at the center of the island. As it set, brilliant light spilled across the sea, cleaving the dark water, laying a rubied path between the island and the shore. Perhaps it was an omen of his coming immortality?

As Will went back down the wind-washed path toward

the tower, he kept a careful eye on the sun's sinking disk, its orb first split by the island tower, then its upper arc of flame bisected by the horizon, then dipping beneath it. Another shudder of anticipation went through him. He saw a twinkling light go on in the island tower and then, as if in response, one go on in the top room of the tower just below him. Startled, Will nearly took one step too many over the crumbling edge of the path. He pulled back just in time. All he could see in the room was a candle's twinkle. But he speeded up his pace as if he'd seen Marguerite herself.

Approaching the tower, Will observed that the entrance to it was actually through the abbey, which had been built right up against the tower's stone façade. High tide had come into an inlet in front of the abbey to a distance of fifty feet or so from the front door. Will amused himself in the lingering heat by walking ankle depth through the water's foamy surge, scooping up a few palmfuls of water and splashing them over his sweat-streaked face, as if baptizing his upcoming transformation in some ritual. The last rays of the setting sun dyed the water red. As he cupped the water, it felt to him as if he were anointing himself with handfuls of blood. A fitting baptism, he thought, for birth into immortality.

A friar so deeply cowled that Will could not make out his face led Will silently to the door of the tower, then motioned for him to continue on his own.

The way up the tower was a serpentine iron stairs lit by torches on each landing that faced the one door on each floor. Will tread with caution up the stairs, their gloomy half-light between floors interrupted by moths and shadows. He felt tension over his destiny above and at the ominous darker shadows; his knees would tremble, or he might pause to take several deep breaths. But he made it up to the top floor, drew himself up to his fullest height, clutched the all-important satchel possessively to his side, reassured himself by feeling Marguerite's ring in his pocket, and knocked on John Dee's door.

'Who is it?'

Will recognized the deep voice. 'Will Hughes at your service. Per your request. I have brought the essentials.'

The grin splitting Dee's triangular-bearded face as he opened the door was as wide as the ocean. But no expression could have been colder. His amber, glittery gaze transfixed Will's. It suggested inner depth, but also had the opaqueness of a lizard's scales. Had Will grasped the affect more fully, he might have fled down the airless stairs and left immortality for another day.

Dee extended his right hand as if to shake Will's, but then swung it farther and tried to grab the satchel. Will blocked the maneuver by swiveling away at the last instant. Dee, like a good sport, patted Will amiably on the shoulder. 'A pleasure to meet you again, young man. Perhaps you are right to approach me cautiously. I am not offended that you do not trust me with your bag. For what is of greater value than immortality? Indeed, let us have a frank discussion before our exchange is completed. Come, sit on my *suffah*, please. It has a stirring view of the sea.'

Will obliged him by sitting on the elegant bench upholstered in oriental fabric Dee had referred to as a *suffah*, and looking out at the ocean through an archer's slit across from him that seemed to have widened. From the cliff this opening had looked no more than four to five inches across, but now it was something like a two-foot square in shape, a small window. Will kept a viselike grip on his satchel, wrapping it to his chest with crossed arms, and wondered how his impression from the cliff could have been so wrong. Then he looked farther out to sea, a view that was indeed majestic. The tower on the island off the coast was silhouetted against a violet sky. The ocean had turned a deep purple, reminding Will of a line the poet had once quoted from the Greeks: *the wine-dark sea*. Will then turned his attention to Dee, who was staring with a bemused expression at the satchel and Will's fierce grip on it.

'I understand your covetousness,' Dee said. 'The box is rare and potent. Not to mention such a beautiful ring, concealed somewhere on you now, on your person or in the satchel. But you might want to relax your grip a little. After all, it is *I* who will need box and ring to effect your transformation – you do have the ring with you, don't you?'

Will nodded.

'I will need it to summon a creature who can make you immortal. *I* will do that. So, alas, you will have to release box and ring into my possession before my end of the bargain can be concluded. In other words, good man, the news is that you *will* have to trust me. Otherwise we are fiddling away our time over nothing. There is no other way.'

Will saw the logic of what Dee was saying, but he didn't like it.

Then he was startled by a brisk wind that entered the

room, undulating tapestries that hung on the walls, strewing papers from Dee's desk to the floor, even rippling the strands of Dee's thinning hair. It was chilly and dense with surf and salt. Will glanced out the window and saw fresh-blown waves cresting up the beach close to the tower. A line of dark thunderclouds was amassing in the west behind the tower on the small island. He had the strange impression that the tower was standing between the storm and the mainland, as if guarding the shore from some barbarian invasion.

Will affixed Dee with the most intimidating stare he could muster. 'Who is this amazing being you will summon, who will bring me immortality?'

Dee ignored Will's forbidding expression, smiled benignly back. 'We are dealing with forces of great potency here, my lad. You can hardly expect beings associated with such forces to be sweet and cuddly. That is the only perspective I can offer. Suffice it to say that if you cannot deal with the fearsome, you should not be here. Otherwise, the sooner you hand over box and ring, the sooner we can proceed.' Dee's soft look transformed to one of impatience.

Again Will saw Dee's logic, but his heart told him to hesitate. He had not thought through this meeting enough in advance. He hadn't realized this sort of vulnerability could occur.

'Sir Dee, can you provide me with proof – or at least evidence – that this process is going to be successful before I hand over these objects to you, however temporarily? They're not my property. I need to return them to my beloved.'

'Ah, the beatific Marguerite,' Dee said, as if he'd forgotten about her. 'I'm sure she will be overjoyed to have her possessions returned. Your solicitousness about them, and her, is to be admired. But, no, if you want to make a point of it, you can't have "evidence" or "proof." The transaction belongs to a realm in which such concepts don't exist. On one side of your decision is the great John Dee with his impeccable intellect and moral grandeur, and the ecstasy that will be yours spending eternity with Marguerite. On the other side is a sniveling coward's surrender to weakness. I cannot make the choice for you, Hughes. I can say which choice I think you're going to make, given your sound judgment, your physical beauty that suggests a moral one as well, in fact your magnetic presence sitting here before me now.'

A glitter came into Dee's gaze that made Will uncomfortable. 'I could be wrong about your choice. In that case please withdraw from me before I cast your pestilence into the sea. But I hope I am right. It is up to you. I await your judgment.' The glitter in Dee's eyes subsided into something else more subdued, more remote. A less acute longing? Will couldn't tell.

Still uncertain, he relaxed his possessiveness about the satchel enough to lay it on a cushion to his side. Dee remained several paces away at the opposite wall. Will then took the ring out of his pocket and held it up before him in the dim candlelight, looking at it as if the duration of his gaze could ensure its power. At one angle the stone appeared blank, but then tilted to another angle the design appeared. A tower. Perhaps this tower. Perhaps Marguerite's ring had been leading him to this very tower . . . to this fate. Surely that was a sign.

He looked up from the ring and was startled to find Dee's face only inches from his own, his amber eyes riveted on the ring. Dee's hand was stretched out, his long, yellowish fingernails nearly touching it. Will shrank back from the avarice in Dee's eyes and the man's clawlike hand, clutching after the ring in Will's fist. But then why had he come if not to relinquish the ring and the box into the wizard's hands? He was unwilling to return to Marguerite still a mortal. He would have to trust Dee.

He handed the box over to him first, then the ring. Dee touched a pattern of concentric circles on the box with one of his long fingernails. In the flickering candlelight the lines seemed to move . . . they *were* moving. They began to revolve in circles like a model of Ptolemy's universe that Will's science tutor used to bore him with. Faster and faster, like a whirlpool, so fast that looking at them began to make Will dizzy. He wrenched his eyes away and saw that the whirlpool effect was not limited to the lid of the box. The air above the box was moving in the same circular motion, the disturbance expanding outward in a reverse conical shape that picked up the papers on Dee's desk and tossed them into the wind like autumn leaves before a storm . . .

A storm that had spread to the sea. The water outside was now thrashing, as if in response to the maelstrom raging here in the tower room. Dee carefully placed the box on the windowsill, lifted the lid, and lowered the ring into the box. He chanted a string of Latin words out of which Will, never the best Latin scholar, caught only *vita* and *perpetua*. Perpetual life. Yes, that's what he had come for, he reassured himself, even as he began to feel an oppressive, stifling sense of being crushed in the room, a sort of airless panic. Perhaps the storm was sucking air out into its vortex. This claustrophobic breathlessness tempted Will to flee room and tower immediately, without box and ring. But a moment's glance outside dissuaded him.

A flash of silver light leaped from the box, streaked across the water, and struck the tower on the island off the coast. In response, a silver beam emanated from the tower, lighting a path back across the ocean. In the unearthly light, Will could see that the ocean was boiling like an evil witch's potion. A long, low moan issued from the depths of the ocean.

'He has awoken,' Dee said, a ghastly smile on his face. Then, pointing his crooked and yellowed nail out the window: 'He is coming!'

'*What* is coming? The creature that will make me immortal? It's coming from the sea? What exactly is it?' Will asked the questions in quick succession while backing away from the window, realizing only now that he should have asked these questions sooner. But it was too late. Dee was right. It *was* coming. Something was swimming through the water at an impossible rate, heading straight toward the tower.

Out of the corner of his eye, he could see Dee chuckling at him. Dee pushed himself back from his desk, leaned against the wall in his chair, and laughed even more enthusiastically when he saw how tormented Will was. His jovial relaxation said to Will, *You're* mine, *now*. All *mine*. Will suddenly knew that he had made a terrible mistake. He had to get out of here before the monster Dee had summoned reached the tower. He sprang for the door . . .

and found his way blocked by the tall, cowled friar who had opened the abbey door for him before. A flash of lightning lit his face, and Will gasped in horror. It was Charles Roget – Lightning Hands himself!

'You! You scoundrel!' Will cried, backing away. 'You followed me here!'

In answer Roget lifted his hands, rubbed his fingertips together, and flung a ball of lightning at Will. The missile hit Will square in the chest and sent him flying across the room, crashing into the wall. He slid to the floor and lay stunned, staring up at Dee and Roget.

'Why should I follow you here when this is my abbey? My dear friend Sir John Dee and I have been waiting for you. Waiting for you and for our honored guest.'

Roget pointed at the window above Will's head. Looking up, Will saw that the honored guest had arrived.

The creature appeared to be an amalgamation of all the nightmares of the deep. Needle fangs curved down several inches below his chin, dripping with blood, perhaps from gulls encountered crossing the beach and going up the tower walls. His crimson-irised eyes seemed hot with hate, and their flame-pupils seemed drawn toward Will's tender lips. This monster coming through the window had the beak of a squid, the scales of a sea serpent, and thousands of trailing locks that were actually, on closer scrutiny, writhing eels festering on its head. Each of the eels had sharp, tiny fangs that seemed to incline toward Will as fermenting stench might be drawn toward perfume.

At the points of the thing's ears, red snake heads had teeth.

The thing was on him, its webbed hands closing around Will's throat. Its stocky body weighed enough that the impact when it landed on Will was crushing, nearly asphyxiating him as it almost merged him into the wooden floor. Before he could blink, the venomous fangs were in arteries in his neck, drawing blood out and replacing it with supernatural filth, sending shivers of excruciating pain down through his capillaries and nerve endings. Gasping, Will survived near suffocation, but then he nearly blacked out with revulsion at the thing's closeness, and his realization that fangs were in him.

He saved consciousness only with a steely determination to kill the swimmer. As to the vilest of blood exchanges, Will had no idea how long it went on, for time seemed both compressed and yet somehow elongated in this hell cell of a room. He could definitely sense that the new blood was ugly and stained. As the writhing eels began to chew at his face, he grew even more enraged. The swimmer was trying to mutilate his features in a way that would match them up with his obscene blood and might also make him hate himself the way the swimmer hated him. Worse, Will saw that the swimmer's features were becoming more human as he fed – not only more human, but more like Will's own features! The swimmer was trying to *steal* his beauty from him along with his humanity!

With this realization, Will suddenly found within himself a vast new strength, one he worried had something to do with the diabolical assault on him, but one he was going to make use of regardless. If it was too late to save his soul, it wasn't too late to save his appearance. Which, he realized, he might be living with for a long time now. Forever.

Will thrust the half-human, half-reptile vampire upward as if it were made of papier-mâché, red-ribboned saliva dripping from its mouth onto his face as he did so. He gripped it by torso and neck in his newly steely arms and shook it violently back and forth in an effort to break its neck. He could hear by its breath, corrugated as if rough metal rubbed against rust in its throat, that he hadn't yet. So he bent it over the windowsill and tore its head back until he *could* hear, with a sound like a log being snapped in two, that he had broken its neck. He flung the carcass out the window. It fell onto the rocks below with an impact that seemed to make the tower shudder. Thunder had stopped and rain was slowing, and any liquid trace of the monster's existence would dry into extinction by dawn, Will thought with grim satisfaction.

With burgeoning confidence, he turned back to Dee and Roget and began walking slowly toward them. As he approached, though, Dee showed no sign of fear. 'This is your immortality, son of the devil Will Hughes,' he cackled, a grin smearing his features. 'A vampire's! Courtesy of one of the most special vampires in the world, Marduk, an esteemed creature whom you've seen fit to treat so shabbily. And after the favor he did for you! Shame on you, Hughes. Marduk will be missed – if he is really gone,' Dee added, turning to Roget. 'Perhaps you ought to check, *mon cher abbé*, and see to the horses as well.'

Will thought about trying to stop him, but let him go. His energy should be focused on this other fiend, Dee.

Dee continued lecturing Will. 'You'll live forever of course, as long as you feed on blood at night and avoid the sun at all costs, for sunlight will burn you alive. Now I have a box and ring that will make me ruler of this mortal world, in addition to my occult kingdom.'

Dee must have had a trapdoor of some sort behind the desk, for without another word he snatched the box and the ring and disappeared downward from Will's sight.

A vampire! Will knew something had gone terribly wrong but . . . a vampire! In those first shocked instants he failed to think about how limited the places Dee could have escaped to were and let him get away. If Will had dared to think that he himself might have the power to fly, or to glide through the air for distances, he might have exited by the window and caught his tormentor. But he had not even dreamed about such powers yet. He simply wanted his stolen life back – Marguerite as his lover, her property to return to her – for he knew he had been betrayed by Dee in the most insidious way, which included being tricked into betraying her.

He raced, torn and breathless, bleeding from various wounds, incisors already growing, down the pitch-black, airless stairs. The storm, or Dee in flight, had snuffed out the torchlights. Then Will wandered around the base of the tower, confused, eyes scanning the horizon fruitlessly in every direction. He heard the sound of horses and saw, on the promontory above the beach, the silhouette of a coach racing up the north coast road. Dee had escaped him.

Will felt a tingling in the roots of his incisors and touched those teeth cautiously with his fingertips. He recognized what was happening. 'My Lord, I'm a night-sucking freak,' he exclaimed, sinking to his knees in the sand. He raised his face to the sky and let loose an anguished scream, rending his shirt to pieces in his distress. Yet, even at this worst moment of his existence – a wretched existence that would now spin out for centuries – the gift of poetry that his mentor had bequeathed him did not fail him. He felt the words rising up in his throat as if they leaped into being along with his new fangs.

'My day now night, and night now day,
eternity's my enemy!
Instead of solace, treachery.
Instead of love, blood has its way!

I am transformed to fanged grotesque,
to stalker manic for new blood
to savor, drink, at any risk,
the thrill of veins my only mood.'

When he had finished, he dropped his head . . . and saw a glint of gold in the sand. Could it be? Will reached down quickly for the metal object, grasping it in a handful of sand as if it alone might save him. Yes, it was! In his flight, Dee had dropped Marguerite's ring! At least he had the ring back. With this he could try to approach her again! Perhaps she would know of some way to reverse this terrible curse. Or at least her companionship would make his existence bearable.

30

Signal

The trip to Pointe du Raz was fairly uneventful. We managed to hire a driver to take us when I balked at Will's suggestion that I drive the coach. We told the driver that Will was indisposed and needed complete darkness for the duration of the trip. Will gave him the directions he'd written out and impressed upon him the importance of sticking to the route, 'even if you're told the south cliff road is out,' Will insisted. Once we were inside the coach and Will had made sure that the curtains were securely tied over the windows, he retreated to a corner and, drawing his hood low over his face, fell into a sleep that so externally resembled death I had to resist the urge to shake him awake.

He could be woken, he told me, but I should only do so in an emergency since he would need all his resources when we reached Pointe du Raz. Since being bored out of my mind in a dark box with a nearly dead man for twelve hours wasn't an emergency (I tried to read the Brittany guidebook or sketch in my notebook, which were in my backpack, but it was too dark), I let him sleep, but the moment the coach stopped and I smelled ocean, I sprang from its confines as if escaping my own tomb . . .

. . . and nearly killed myself by falling over a cliff into the sea. The coach was stopped on a narrow track clinging to the side of a rock cliff.

'Why did you stop here?' I asked in my fractured, modern-day French.

The driver said something completely incomprehensible and jabbed a finger ahead of us. Peering around the front of the coach, I saw what the problem was. A large chunk of the road ahead had crumbled into the sea. Its remnant wasn't wide enough for the carriage to pass. We'd have to continue on foot – I could see our tower destination below the road, not far off – only Will couldn't do that until the sun had set.

Shading my eyes, I looked out to sea where a fiery orange sun hung just above an island a few miles offshore. It would set in a half hour or so. We'd just have to wait.

I conveyed this to the surly driver in a combination of hand signs and fractured French that made him sniff with the same disdain I'd encountered in a dozen waiters in Paris. Some things never change, I thought, sitting down on a rock to watch the sun set. As it descended toward the island, it seemed to settle for a moment at the top of a tower that stood at its center. The sight reminded me of something . . . after a moment I realized what. The ring Will wore – the one he had taken from Marguerite – was engraved with a tower topped by an eye surrounded by rays. I had learned last year that it was the symbol of the Watchtower. Was it a coincidence that the tower on the island looked so much like it?

I took my Brittany guidebook out of my backpack and looked up the Pointe du Raz. The island, I saw right away, was the Île de Sein, which local legend claimed was the last remnant of the mythic island of Ys.

Monsieur Lutin had told me that the *fées de la mer* – the boat people – came from Ys. Could the tower on the Île de Sein be the original Watchtower?

What happened next suggested to me that it was.

The sun dropped below the peak of the tower, filling its top chamber with orange light. A ray of light, like a flaming arrow, shot out of the tower and headed toward the mainland where I stood – almost directly at me, but not quite. The beam of light reached the next promontory to the north, where another tower stood, and turned the glass on top of that tower a fiery red, so bright I had to close my eyes against the glare.

Behind my closed eyes I still saw the island tower, only the red light in my vision came from a fire burning from its battlements. Out of the fire shot a blazing arrow. I tracked its passage across the sea, across an impossible distance, its progress reflected in the black ocean, until it landed in the tower at Pointe du Raz. Immediately a fire burst into flame from the top of the second tower. Seconds later an arrow was shot from that tower, arcing south toward another promontory. Suddenly I was watching the scene from far above, my vision granting me a bird's-eye view of the whole peninsula, and I could see the arrow reach a third tower and set ablaze there a third bonfire. I watched as the entire southern coast of Brittany was dotted with blazing signal fires, and then – as my view expanded – I watched the line of fires extend across France, stretching toward Paris. This, I understood, was an ancient alarm system created by the sisterhood of the Watchtower to warn humanity of some coming danger. But what was the danger? What was coming?

I opened my eyes, alert to the threat, but the scene in front of me was utterly peaceful. The ocean had gone eerily still. The last streaks of red were fading into the calm water. A lone figure below on the beach waded through the crimson-flecked waves scooping up handfuls of water like a playful child.

'What an idiot,' a voice behind me pronounced.

I turned and found Will, his face absorbing the last purple vestige of dusk. He was looking down at the figure on the beach with utter disdain. I looked from figure to figure and realized they were the same man.

'I thought that the red light on the water was a sign of my ultimate ascension to immortality. Little did I know what evil was about to come across on that bloody, watery path.'

'The vampire? It came across the sea?'

Will nodded, lifting his eyes from his past self on the beach, who now left the water and began walking toward the tower.

'Marduk.' He pronounced the name in a hoarse whisper that startled me. I'd never seen Will look so afraid of anything before. 'A bloodsucking demon from the maws of hell. He terrorized Europe during the Dark Ages, leaving a trail of devastation wherever he went. Eventually the Watchtowers captured him and trapped him beneath their strongest tower – the tower of the Île de Sein. He could only be summoned with the box and the Watchtower's ring, which I foolishly gave to Dee.'

Will turned and watched his past self enter the tower. 'I

hesitated at the last minute. I almost didn't give them to him. If I followed him up into that tower now, I could stop him . . . me . . . and I would never become *this*.'

'But then you and I would never have met,' I said.

He wrenched his eyes away from the tower and looked at me with a bittersweet tenderness. 'Would you regret that so very much, Garet? Have I brought you anything but grief and danger since we met?'

'You saved my life from the manticore,' I said, shuddering at the memory of the stone statue that Dee had brought to life. 'And later you saved me from Oberon's spell of paralysis.'

'But if Dee had never gotten possession of the box, he would never have needed you to open it in 2008. You would never have been dragged into this world.'

'If we start messing around with the past, who knows what effect our actions might have. I might never have been born.'

Will touched my face and sighed. 'You're right. We can't risk making any changes. It's just . . . I wish I could erase the evil I've done over the last four hundred years. I wish I could come to you cleansed of my sins. As innocent as that man who's climbing the stairs to the top of the tower right now.'

'The one you just called an idiot?' I asked, moving closer to him. He wrapped his arms around me and I nestled against his chest. He felt as cold as marble. He hadn't fed since last night in Maeve's tomb, and he'd need his strength to battle the vampire Dee was summoning.

Just then we heard snores from the direction of the seated driver and glanced up at him, to see that he seemed to have fallen sound asleep. We smiled at each other, and then I curled my hand around the back of Will's neck and brought his lips down to mine. He kissed me – but guardedly. His whole body was rigid. When I tried to guide his lips to my neck, he pulled back.

'No, Garet, it's too soon after I fed from you last. You'll need your strength, too . . . and besides . . . we're out of time. Dee has set the box in the window. Look.'

Will turned me around by the shoulders and pointed me toward the tower. At first I saw nothing but its dark, monolithic shape rising above us. All light had gone out of the sky, but then the moon appeared over the top of the tower, spilling a wash of silver that glinted at the highest window. A ray of silver light burst forth from the window and streaked across the sky toward the Île de Sein. Far off at sea an answering beacon flared, a mirror image of the fiery arrow I'd seen in my vision, only this signal was deathly cold. The flash of light was followed by a long, low moan, like a foghorn . . . or some ancient leviathan bellowing from the deep.

'The signal from the box has awoken him. He's coming.'

I stared at the sky, expecting a winged shape, but saw nothing except inky storm clouds massing in the west beyond the lit tower on the Île de Sein. To the east the sky was clear. The moon had now risen high enough to light a silver path across the sea. The ocean, calm a few moments ago, churned. The swath illuminated by the moonlight looked like river rapids.

Then I realized that it was only this part of the ocean that was disturbed. Something was moving through the water. Something either very big or very strong. Or both.

'He's here.' Will pulled me away from the edge of the cliff and toward the coach. 'It's better if you wait inside the coach. I don't want you anywhere near that *thing*.'

But my eyes were glued to the churning surf. Surely nothing in reality could be worse than what my imagination was conjuring from beneath those waves.

I was wrong.

The thing that crawled out of the surf was far worse than anything I could have imagined. The moonlight caught its thousand scales, edging them with razors. When it stood up on webbed feet, seaweed streamed from its limbs like a torn funeral shroud. Only when it began its lumbering slither across the beach did I see that the streamers of seaweed were actually long eels that sprouted from its head. Sharp fangs curled out of its open mouth.

'That creature attacked you and made you a vampire?' I asked as Will pushed me into the coach.

'You thought all vampires looked like the ones in movies?' Will asked, his face set and grim. 'That's the monster that spawned me. It lay beneath the ocean for a thousand years, feeding off the creatures of the deep, its teeth and appetite growing. As he fed from me, he started to look more human – and God knows if I hadn't killed him, he might have grown human-looking enough to pass among humans again. The thought of drinking that creature's blood . . .' A look of revulsion passed across Will's face. 'I don't want you to see me do it,' he said, looking into my eyes. 'Promise me you'll stay here.'

'But what if you need help—'

He barked a short, mirthless laugh. 'With *that* thing? Please, Garet, just promise me to stay here.'

'Okay, if you promise not to take any unnecessary chances. I want you back.'

He looked at me as if he wasn't quite sure he believed me, but then he gave my hand a sharp squeeze. 'That's what we both want.' Then he disappeared into the night.

Will had told me to stay in the coach, but he hadn't told me not to watch out the window. When I drew back the curtains, I could make out Will's figure on the edge of the cliff, his face white in the moonlight and his eyes riveted to the tower window. I couldn't see the tower, but I didn't have to. I could read the horror going on in there from the expression on Will's face. How badly he must have wanted to stop it! That was himself – his younger, more innocent self – up there, making the biggest mistake of his life. Given the chance, who wouldn't take back his worst mistake?

A cry of pain rent the night and I guessed that hideous creature had attacked young Will. I saw my Will take a step forward to the edge of the cliff, his arms tensed against the wind, poised to leap up to the tower. But then he let his arms fall. A long, despairing moan from the tower rode the wind, a cry so anguished the gulls in their cliff aeries tried to drown it out. Even the waves on the beach seemed to crash in answer to that cry, the ocean coiling back in outrage at the young man's pain. My Will bowed his head. His face, white a moment ago, was black with tears of blood.

He dashed them away angrily and tensed again. Another cry came from the tower, this one infuriated. This was young Will attacking the creature who had made him. Then a bellow like the one that had come from the sea before . . . cut short as Will and Marduk appeared at the window struggling, Will's hands wrapped around Marduk's throat . . .

Then *my* Will was gone. One moment he was poised on the edge of the cliff, the next moment he had vanished. Just as quickly I was out of the coach, running down the footpath to the beach. I'd listened helplessly to young Will cry out in pain; I couldn't sit by while *my* Will battled this demon.

I reached the beach just as Marduk hit the rocks beneath the tower. The impact shook the ground so hard I stumbled on the sand. When I got up, my Will was standing over the beast. I ran to him, unable to stop myself. I had to see if the creature was really dead. I reached Will and looked at where he was staring.

For a moment I thought there had been some awful mistake. That Marduk had won the battle and thrown young Will to the ground where he lay now broken on the rocks, instead of the reverse. Somehow, some little thing Will and I had done had changed the course of events, and *this* time the creature had destroyed young Will. Any moment now *my* Will would vanish into the vortex of time, dissolved into grains no more substantial than the sands beneath our feet. And what would happen to me? Where would I be if I'd never met Will Hughes?

But after a moment when neither of us vanished into the vortex of time, Will spoke. 'He was stealing my face. Look . . .'

I glanced down and saw that although the broken figure below us had Will's face, he still had the webbed fingers and reptilian skin of Marduk. Will laughed. 'I thought he was stealing my beauty. *That's* what finally made me angry enough to fight back. That's how vain I was. But he wasn't just stealing my *looks*, he was stealing my *identity*. *See?*'

Will knelt beside the creature and lifted a limp webbed hand. Patches of human skin had grown over the scales. One of the fingers was beginning to detach from the webbing. On it was a ring. The silver ring with the swan insignia, identical to the one I was wearing.

'I wasn't even wearing this ring in 1602, but somehow it knew the ring was part of who I was. What kind of demon is it that can suck a man's essence out along with his blood?'

I shivered. 'I don't know, but I know it's a good thing it's dead. Look, it's beginning to decay.' I pointed to a webbed foot. Scales were flaking off and blowing away in the wind. 'We don't have much time. You have to . . .'

I couldn't even say it. The thought of drinking from that . . . *thing* turned my stomach. What if Morgane had been lying? What if drinking from Marduk didn't make Will human, but made him like *Marduk*? I reached for Will to stop him, but he had already bared his fangs and bent his head to Marduk's neck. An instant before Will's teeth sank into the creature's neck, Marduk's eyes opened.

I screamed.

But it was too late. Marduk's fangs sank into Will's neck instead, his half-human, half-webbed fingers clamped over Will's skull. Will flailed, unable to free himself. I kicked the creature but it was like kicking a slimy concrete wall. I looked around desperately for a weapon, but nothing was on the beach but flimsy driftwood and nothing on my person but a flouncy dress . . .

. . . pinned with Marguerite's brooch. I tore it off. The pin was long and sharp, but it would feel like a mosquito bite to Marduk. But maybe if I stuck it someplace vulnerable . . .

I gripped the brooch in my right hand with the pin sticking out between my index and middle fingers, the way my mother had taught me to do with my house keys when I was walking home alone on city streets, and drove it into Marduk's right eye.

He loosened his bite on Will's neck enough to scream, giving Will just enough leverage to get out of his grip and bash his hand hard up against his nose. Cartilage splintered like a lobster's claw in a nutcracker. Will grabbed the creature's shoulders and slammed its head back against the rock. Another chitinous crack – but the creature still had its claws in Will. It used them to flip Will over his own head. Will's body hit the stone base of the tower and slid down limply to the ground.

I tore my eyes off Will and looked back at the creature. He was standing, listing to one side on one webbed flipper and one human foot. Human flesh rippled over reptilian scales like Saran wrap stretched over garbage. His face was a wreckage of scale and flesh out of which Will's eyes – one whole, one bloody – stared at me. A human mouth stretched over razorsharp fangs. It was smiling.

'Well met, Watchtower,' it rasped. 'I'd stay to get better acquainted, but I'm not at my *best*. I promise, though, that we'll meet again.'

He bowed stiffly at the waist, tattered seaweed and eel-skin dangling from his ragged hair, then he half limped, half slithered toward the north side of the tower, where he was pulled into a waiting coach by someone inside. Lamplight flared at the coach window, revealing a coat of arms painted on the door – three rearing wolves across the top and two on the bottom flanking diagonal lines with crosses – and in the window, a pair of yellow eyes. I recognized the coat of arms and the eyes as belonging to John Dee, but that wasn't all I recognized. A third man was in a friar's robe, his hood pushed back to reveal a face lit up by the lamplight. Oddly enough he was much older than when I had last seen him, but I still recognized Roger Elden from the Hôtel des Grandes Écoles.

31

The Beast

Before I could do anything to stop them, the coach with Dee, Marduk, and the friar with the striking similarity to Roger Elden pulled away. Should I try to follow? But there was no way I could catch up to them on foot. The coach was racing up the hill toward the north coast road. Even if I could get back to our coach in time, it would be unable to get across the beach on the damaged south coast road. Besides, there was my Will to attend to – if he was still alive.

He lay in the shadow of the tower as still and cold as the stones looming above him. I crouched beside him, unable to see his face well in the dusk. I tried listening for breath or heartbeat before remembering that a vampire had neither. I stroked his hair back from his brow and my hand came back sticky. Even his blood was cold.

I wept then, leaning against the tower wall, my Will's head cradled in my lap. He'd risked everything to become mortal by drinking Marduk's blood and died in the attempt. All my fears that he loved Marguerite more than me were gone. He had chosen mortality – and me – and died for his trouble.

While I sat there, someone came out of the tower and

stumbled in the sand – a figure so familiar I thought it was the ghost of the man who lay dead in my lap until I remembered it was *young* Will, inexperienced Will as he had been in 1602.

A seething, all consuming, completely irrational hatred for young Will seized me. It was his *fault* all of this had happened – *his* self-absorbed quest for immortality on the pretext of being in love that had led us here. The least he could have done was kill Marduk thoroughly enough that his future self wouldn't get killed by him! In the next few minutes my hatred turned to contempt as young Will fell to his knees on the sand, tore his shirt open, raised his face to the moon, and howled. Perhaps he thought he'd become a werewolf, I thought snarkily.

> *My day now night, and night now day,*
> *eternity's my enemy!*
> *Instead of solace, treachery.*
> *Instead of love, blood has its way!'*

A poem? Was he really composing a poem?

'You were right,' I said to *my* Will. 'You *were* an idiot. How did you ever become the man I love?'

'Four hundred years of living the consequences of my mistakes,' he answered hoarsely.

I peered hard into the shadowy face below me. 'Will? Are you . . . ?'

'Still dead,' he answered, struggling to sit up, and rubbing his head. I touched the back of his head gingerly and felt the skull solid where a moment ago it had been broken. In return he touched my face and brushed my tears away. 'I failed. And I let loose that monster . . . Marduk. What happened to him?'

'He left with Dee in a coach. There was someone else with them. An old man I think I recognized.'

'The abbot, no doubt, that rogue Charles Roget. Which way did they go?'

'They took the north road.' I could wait to tell him that his abbot looked like a man I'd met in twenty-first-century Paris.

'We have to get back in our coach and try to overtake them on the south road at Quimper. We have to destroy . . . *that thing.*'

'What about . . . ?' I gestured toward young Will, who was still ranting in verse, too caught up in his own drama to notice us.

Will sighed. 'He's almost done. He'll spend the day cowering in a cave. At nightfall he'll walk to Audierne, buy a horse, and then ride to Paris to find Marguerite. He still thinks they have a future. There . . . he's found her ring.'

The moonlight caught a glint of gold in the sand. Young Will crouched down and kissed it.

'He thinks that now at least he has the ring to give back to Marguerite, but she'll refuse it . . .'

Will's voice trailed off, his head drooping. I shook him, alarmed that he'd lost consciousness again. It had been too long since he'd fed. I still had Marguerite's brooch, its sharp pin stained with Marduk's blood. The thought of that tainted blood mingling with my own was the only reason I hesitated before drawing the little dagger across my wrist. Will stirred when he smelled my blood and this time he was too weak to turn it down.

*　*　*

Once he'd revived, we returned to the coach, woke the still-snoring driver, and set out after Dee and his colleagues. On the road to Quimper I told Will about recognizing Roger Elden.

'Roger Elden?' he repeated the name thoughtfully. 'The man I knew in 1602 went by the name Charles Roget – more commonly known as Lightning Hands for his ability to wield lightning.'

'Wait, Roger Elden told me about a man named Cosimo Ruggieri who conducted experiments with lightning. He took me to the tower that Catherine de Médicis had built for him.'

'Really?' Will asked, one eyebrow raised. 'I didn't know you had that much time for sightseeing when you were in Paris.'

I let out an exasperated sigh. 'I was waiting for you for over a week! And is that really the point you want to bring up right now? That I spent a night up on a sixteenth-century tower with a man, or that the man might have actually been a four-hundred-year-old evil sorcerer?'

'The whole night . . . ?' Will began, but then seeing my expression, changed tack. 'Okay, I agree. The important thing is whether the man with Dee and Marduk now is Cosimo Ruggieri. Tell me everything this Roger person told you.'

Ignoring the disdain he had interjected into Roger's name, I recounted the stories Roger Elden had told me about Cosimo Ruggieri. How Ruggieri had been banished and then forgiven by Catherine de Médicis and then assigned the revenues of an abbey in Brittany.

'So he could have been the abbot there,' Will said. 'I remember thinking at the time that he didn't look like your average friar.'

'No, I suppose not. Especially considering that he refused the last rites on his deathbed.' I told him the story of how Ruggieri was dragged through the streets of Paris. Then I told him the rumors that Roger had relayed, about him dragging himself into the catacombs and finding an eternal life that condemned him to aging and suffering over and over again.

'That sounds worse even than the immortality I chose,' Will replied, yawning. It was almost dawn. He'd need to sleep soon. His eyes snapped open though when he spied a coach on the north road approaching the intersection. 'That's them,' he said. 'Whoever the third party is, we need to follow Marduk and find out where he hides. We must destroy him before he grows any stronger.'

Before I could ask how we would do that, Will passed out. Unable to endure another day closed in the coffinlike interior of the coach, I climbed up next to the driver and told him to follow the other coach. When it was clear I was going to stay outside with him, he sniffed his disapproval and whipped the horses into a jerky trot that nearly sent me toppling from my seat. I caught my companion smirking as I righted myself. He smirked, too, when it started to rain and asked in mock politeness if 'Mademoiselle' wouldn't rather go inside and seek shelter with 'Monsieur.' I supposed I could have risked opening the coach door in the murky gray light, but I didn't trust the driver to stay on the other coach's trail. Twice when we lost sight of it, he assured me that there was nowhere for it to go. There was only one major road and it led to Rennes.

Despite his assurances I urged him to go faster, but the horses were clearly tiring and we had to stop in Josselin to let them rest. I paced up and down the cobblestoned street in the rain, impatient to go, and unwilling to let the carriage out of sight. I considered rousing Will and making him switch carriages, but I was afraid that in his weakened state even minutes in this gray daylight would harm him. The driver, dry and cozy in the window seat of a pub with a pint of ale and a pipe, observed my anxiety with amusement. I could see him pointing me out to his new pubmates, who laughed heartily at whatever story he was telling about me.

Although there was no reason to continue riding on the outside, a perverse urge made me stick to my perch beside the driver all the way to Rennes. We reached the coach inn there a little after dark.

'Voilà,' my tormenter pronounced, pointing at the black coach bearing Dee's coat of arms. 'What did I tell Mademoiselle? Your quarry has gone to ground here.'

As soon as Will was awake, we made inquiries at the inn, but we discovered that the three gentlemen who had arrived in the previous coach had hired another one immediately and had left.

'Did they say where they were going?' Will asked.

The innkeeper squinted at Will. 'One of the men looked much like you, monsieur. A profligate brother, perhaps?'

Will flinched, but then he nodded stiffly and through gritted teeth told the innkeeper a story about a 'simple-minded' younger brother who had fallen into bad company, from which Will was endeavoring to rescue him.

The innkeeper clucked his tongue sympathetically and told us that the 'evil-looking, yellow-eyed man' had named Paris as their destination. Then he told us where we could hire a coach to take us to Paris. Before we left, he shook his head and tapped his nose. 'You can't fool me, though. That man is not your younger brother. He looked ten years older than you. He's absconded with the family money, hasn't he?'

Will grunted noncommittally, but I saw that the news alarmed him. When we were seated in our new coach, he told me why.

'Marduk shouldn't be aging – vampires don't age. It must mean he's unable to maintain the shape he's stolen, which means he'll either die before he reaches Paris – or be forced to assume another shape, which will make it harder for us to track him down.'

'Why do you think they're making for Paris?' I asked.

'I'm not sure, but I imagine Dee has his reasons. He knew what creature he was summoning. He must have some plan for Marduk . . . no doubt one that requires Ruggieri's help . . . and whatever that plan is' – Will shuddered, which I'd never seen him do before – 'we have to stop it.'

Will shuddered again and I realized he was actually shivering. 'What's wrong?' I asked. 'You look like you've caught a cold, but you can't . . . . can you?'

'I need more blood,' he hissed. 'But not from you. You've already given me too much. We'll have to stop.'

Will told the driver to pull over on the outskirts of a small village, saying he needed to stretch his legs. He strode away toward the huddle of stone buildings, disappearing in the fog. I tried not to think about where he was finding his blood while I waited. The driver – this one more polite than our last, but also more taciturn – observed a stony silence as we waited for Monsieur.

We waited so long I was afraid that Will had been caught in the act. I was beginning to picture villagers with pitchforks storming the coach when Will appeared suddenly out of the fog and, with a terse command to the driver to go quickly, swept into the coach beside me. His cloak was soaked through. His face was white and drawn, his skin as icy as when he had left.

'What happened?' I asked.

'The whole village was on alert. There'd been an attack earlier tonight. A young boy had been garroted, hung up by his feet and drained of blood.'

'Ugh! Do you think it was Marduk?'

'A vampire wouldn't bother with the garroting or wait for the blood to drain out. Possibly Dee and Ruggieri are collecting blood for Marduk because he's too weak.' Will lapsed into a thoughtful silence – a chilly silence. The fog seeped into the coach, clinging to our damp clothes. Soon I was shivering almost as much as Will.

Will tried to hunt again at the next town but found all its occupants sheltering behind locked doors and shuttered windows. The few villagers not in their homes huddled together in the pub, whispering of monsters of the night that drank blood. Each town we passed through was similarly shuttered and barred, as if news of the bloodletting had traveled as quickly as wildfire. Or perhaps these villages were always on guard against such monsters.

Will thought we should find out. In a small village near

Chartres, he sent me into an inn to ask for food and drink and see what I could find out, my too basic French notwithstanding. At first the innkeeper was not going to let me in, but then seeing a lone woman he relented and unbarred the door.

'Mademoiselle must not be alone on the road tonight,' he said, his eyes nearly bulging out of his head. 'There is something very bad afoot.' He lowered his voice. 'Some say *la bête* has come back to these parts.'

I thanked him for his advice and assured him that I'd stay in my coach until I reached Paris. He was so rattled that he didn't seem to notice my French was modern, accented, and error riddled. When I rejoined Will, I told him what the innkeeper had said. 'He called it *la bête*. I know that means "beast," but he said it like it was a *particular* beast.'

'La Bête du Gévaudan,' Will said through chattering teeth. 'A creature that terrorized the mountains of the Haute-Loire for one hundred and one days. The beast killed over a hundred people by tearing their throats out. Only the beast of Gévaudan wouldn't hang a victim up to drain his blood. *And* the Beast of Gévaudan was abroad in the eighteenth century. Perhaps Marduk terrorized the countryside before then and the legends of strange beasts can all be traced back to him. At any rate, I'll have to wait till Paris to feed. The hunting's always easy there.'

It was a sign of how far gone Will was that he'd say something so unguarded to me. I tried not to dwell on the many, many years of preying on innocent victims the remark revealed. Will looked too pathetic to blame for anything right now. His cheeks were sunken, his eyes glassy, and his limbs trembled like an epileptic's. I had hoped that when dawn came he would fall into an easier rest, but he continued to shake and now called out in his sleep. He called my name, but also Marguerite's and even someone named Bess. Through my own chattering teeth I muttered, 'One more woman's name, mister, and I'm pushing you out into the sunlight.'

But he'd already sunk from articulate syllables into moans and sharp cries. I drifted into sleep myself eventually, a broken, restless sleep, punctuated by feverish dreams.

I was running down a wide, flat allée, Hellequin's hunt hard on my heels. They'd been pursuing all along, through Brittany and into the past, and now they were almost upon me. I looked back over my shoulder and there was Hellequin, a vicious grin below his bloodred/night-black mask, his tattered cloak billowing behind him. I saw Octavia La Pieuvre's face surrounded by her fluttering tentacles, and Monsieur Lutin's, and Melusine's, her wings flapping dryly in the wind, her eyes green flakes of lichen.

'All your friends are here,' Hellequin said, grinning. 'Come join them.'

Something about his voice was different. It wasn't the voice I remembered from Fontainebleau, but one I'd heard somewhere else . . . recently . . .

'Even your darling Will is here.' He held his cloak out and I saw Will's face, desiccated as an autumn leaf, his mouth frozen in a scream of pain. I looked up into Hellequin's eyes – but they weren't Hellequin's eyes, they were the yellow eyes of John Dee.

I turned to run but was blocked by a dark figure. I

looked up into Will's face. Relief flooded through me, but then he lifted a clawed hand to his brow and tore his skin away revealing Marduk's face – only he now had the face of a wolf. This was the beast Hellequin pursued. The famous Bête du Gévaudan.

I startled awake in the coach. I must have slept through the whole day because Will was awake also, staring at me as if a monster's face were hidden beneath *my* flesh. Perhaps he'd had his own nightmares.

'We're here' is all he said.

'Here?'

'Paris.'

He drew the curtains open. We were crossing a bridge lit by torches. Looming above us was the dark mass of Notre Dame, gargoyles silhouetted against the violet dusk.

'How will we find Dee, Ruggieri, and Marduk?'

'We'll follow the trail of blood they leave behind them,' he answered glumly. 'But now, my dear, I have to . . . go out.' He said it as if he were going to a play. 'I'll instruct the driver to take you to a house where you'll be welcome and safe. I'll come there before dawn . . . unless . . .'

He didn't have to finish his sentence. If he found Marduk and won, he would drink his blood and come back to me a mortal. But if he found Marduk and lost, he wouldn't be coming back to me at all.

32

The Watchtower

Young Will spent his first day as a vampire cowering in a seaside cave, hidden from the sun, watching a family of crabs burrow in the sand. Was this his fate, he wondered, to spend eternity with the lowliest creatures of the earth?

At dusk he walked to Audierne and rented a horse to ride to Paris. He thought it would take him days, but soon the horse was moving at a supernatural speed, as if he had transmuted his own frantic energy into the horse. The horse now had the ability to jump substantial obstacles in their path, like a stream thirty feet across. When he looked back at it, Will suspected that this ride marked the beginning of his ability to transmigrate his own atoms over distances. In this case, he was actually transmigrating the horse.

By midnight he was within twenty miles of Paris and it was there that he experienced the second phenomenon of his enhanced powers. He 'saw' Marguerite. Not in the flesh, but in a sort of vision. He saw her sitting by the Seine in the shadow of Notre Dame. For an instant, he was elated. Then she turned her head and Will could see the wan, almost tearful expression on her features, and his spirits sank. Perhaps she was simply missing him. But as a fellow immortal, he asked himself, shouldn't she at least have been able to *sense* his arrival in her world? Shouldn't the stunning news of his immortal transformation – wretched as its circumstances had been – have reached her somehow and outweighed his absence? It startled Will how, absent fangs, he could take a favorable view of the nightmare at Pointe du Raz. But he *so* needed this reunion with Marguerite to be harmonious.

On the contrary, Marguerite looked so weary at the moment, it were as if disappointment over his absence had turned her blood to that of a mortal's. Atomsight had given him the ability to look into veins; his own bubbled with vigor since Dee's tower, with a diamond-blue sheen brimful with the depths of time. However cruel his new life might be, to himself and others, he recognized how immortal his new blood was. But Marguerite's blood, as she sat by the Seine, had no such quality. He shuddered icily. No doubt it was the psychological effect of his absence, but the aura about her now, or the lack of one, made her look . . . mortal . . . and, worse, made him long for her blood.

In a panic as bad as any he'd experienced in Dee's tower, he urged his horse faster toward Marguerite now, not to attack her but to learn her situation before it was too late. He hoped for every inch of the ride that a reversal of their natures had not happened. Or that, if he was sensing one all too accurately, the reversal could in turn be reversed. For otherwise his world was about to come crashing down, and in the worst irony of all, forever.

Will tied up his horse a block south of Notre Dame, as he

wanted to come to Marguerite as unobtrusively as possible. The moon was higher now, and he observed its rubied sphere reflected in the Seine's black mirror as he walked to the top of the riverbank. He slowed with the beautiful sight, then thought about a dark similarity between this walk and his earlier one in Paris, the dawn walk on which he'd first approached Julien-le-Pauvre. That walk had brought, for the longest of intervals, futility. And he was afraid now that this one would be bringing him ruin, a most bitter ending. He paused, almost at the edge of collapse despite his physical powers. But he gathered himself together and went on. Better to know his fate now than to postpone it. And her fate as well.

Marguerite had moved halfway down the bank in the time since he'd dismounted, as if gathering up the courage to dive in. Maybe she could sense his approach, he surmised, though why so morbidly he couldn't fathom and was terrified to ponder. He started down the bank and called softly, 'Marguerite.'

She turned without getting up, and though she smiled, she looked so depleted he felt crushed. He sat down next to her, taking her left hand gently in his right. She brought his hand to her lips and kissed it. They sat holding hands for the longest while, in a strange immobility, gazing at the moon in the Seine as if it were an oracle and they were waiting for an answer.

A breeze tore the gleam into a thousand shards, red knives, and they both sighed. Finally Will spoke. 'I'm sorry I had to take off so suddenly. I had business.'

She turned to him, cupped his chin in her palms, and kissed him. 'I had business, too.' She shrugged, gazed up and down the river. 'But all's well that ends well. Now we are together.' She put her left arm around Will. 'My comrade. My soul. My mate.'

Will was thrilled by her words and unnerved by her listless tone. Why was she so subdued? Was it because he hadn't returned box and ring, which she hadn't even mentioned yet? And why hadn't she made reference to immortality, that great gulf between them that had now been bridged?

'Together at last,' he whispered back. 'But tell me, my dear. Do I seem different to you in any way?'

Marguerite replied in a livelier, almost jovial tone. 'Why Will Hughes, I do believe you have that magical glow about you again tonight. The one that has so enchanted me many times, though not so much in recent weeks, when you've had that unfortunate preoccupation. Which, I have the grace to tell you, is vanished now.'

'Preoccupation . . . it's what?'

'Vanished! The chasm between us is no more. For I am mortal, too.'

Shocked at having his worst intuition confirmed, Will nonetheless had the aplomb to respond, 'How on earth did that come about?'

Her look went far away. 'Those details are better left for another time. Let me just say that a family member rendered the necessary assistance.'

For the second time this night, Will felt the tingling of bloodlust. He could smell Marguerite's mortal blood now – it hadn't been his imagination – and it smelled *delicious*.

'Family member?' he asked through clenched lips.

She nodded. 'My sister. But let's not go into that. Let's

just enjoy this moment of being back together. "Forever," as mortals say. Which for them – for us – simply means the length of their lives. Which is more than enough for me, so long as I am with you.' She rubbed Will's cheek affectionately. Her spirits seemed to be improving, which baffled Will. Perhaps she had no sense of what had happened to him, and her earlier listlessness had simply been from the lesser vigor of mortality, and sadness over his absence.

Once Marguerite took her hand from his cheek, Will could feel the tips of his growing incisors brush against the interior of his mouth, below. In seconds he'd have to maneuver them beyond his lips, to avoid excruciating pain, and their moonlit enamel would give him away. He might as well make his confession now.

'I have a terrible truth to tell.' He reached across to caress her.

She grasped his hand and pressed it closely to her. 'Terrible? How can that be? This is the most glorious moment of our lives!'

'It may still be, if either one of us can reverse what has happened to us in the past forty-eight hours.' He extended both hands out toward the moon-jeweled river, palms up, in a gesture that combined resignation with small hope. 'Can you reverse what happened to you?'

Marguerite got up and swept around in front of Will as though she were a wind, half standing, half crouching, gazing at him as if she wasn't sure if he was angel or demon. She might be mortal now, Will reflected, but the light in her eyes came from another world. 'What has happened to *you*, my love?' she asked in a wild voice.

'The venomous John Dee has tricked me,' Will said as matter-of-factly as he could. 'I have not been honest with you about the use I made of your box and ring, which you may observe I do not have with me – or at least not the box.' He glanced at her hand and for the first time noticed she wore his silver ring. It gave him courage to go on. 'At the depth of my despair over our separation, I was crazy enough to seek counsel from Dee. He offered me the bargain of immortality in exchange for the use of your box and ring. He kept one part of his bargain, though he omitted major details about what immortality meant to him, but he did not return your box. The ring I have. Sadly Dee – and his cohort Charles Roget – has escaped, but I will find him and justice will be done.'

'What details did he omit?' Marguerite asked in a stunned voice. 'Oh, Will, how could you deal with that man – that thing – he's the soul of Satan himself!'

Will began to weep, for he had no answer for her. He heard Marguerite gasp. She touched his face and brought back a bloodred hand, as if touching him had wounded her.

As long as he would live, a portentous thought now, he would never forget the expression in Marguerite's eyes: they loathed him, they recoiled from him, they hated . . . him! Or not so much him as what he had become. But was there a difference? He knew in the instant he asked this bleak question that there wasn't. And that was when his world fell apart. His lover had become his hater. He had bargained away his Christian soul for that of a night thing, a crawler and bloodsucker. Marguerite was right to loathe him. The Will Hughes she had loved had destroyed himself.

Slowly, Marguerite seemed to regain control of herself.

She had been staggering a little down the riverbank away from him, but now she stopped moving. The expression in her eyes calmed from loathing to uncertainty. She might be conquering her revulsion with thoughts of their past love, Will reflected hopefully. Which emboldened him to speak.

'I may be a creature of the night, but I still love you. Tell me, sweet love, is there really no hope for us? Can't you walk back across the bridge you went to the mortal side over? Would your family member not help you out, seeing as circumstances have . . . changed?' His beseeching gaze was desperate, but he could tell from her expression what her answer was going to be.

'Alas, Will, it's not possible. My family member hates humans with a vengeance, and I would be coming to her as a human. She would not recognize me as kin, and she would never honor a human request. What's worse, I have made a pact with her to guard the mortal world against supernatural creatures like yourself, whom she hates even more than humans, vampires in particular.

'You're benign enough at this moment, but who knows what sort of monster you may turn into in the future, with all the desolate years ahead of you, always needing to feed on your own kind, or what used to be your own kind. Eventually you won't be able to feed without developing a hatred for your prey. No animal can. And your prey is a class of beings that I now belong to.'

Will had to admit to himself that, teeth full in, he was starting to feel hunger pangs. In one unwilling moment he beheld the tenderness of Marguerite's neck, pale flesh just to the left of . . . ugh! – he caught himself. But the damage to his esteem was done. He was not the same Will Hughes anymore. And would never be again.

'And you can't make the journey the other way,' Marguerite went on. 'The only person who knows how to make *that* happen, except for Dee with my box and ring, is my sister, and she would sooner die than make me happy. Let alone you. If Dee hangs on to my box, he could do it, but he'd prefer to die also. Believe me.'

Will could see a tear on Marguerite's cheek, and her lower lip quivered. Moonlight made the tear look like a drop of blood. He felt a sliver of lust for it, then shuddered with despair.

She wiped it away. 'I shall not weep in front of you, Will Hughes. Though I shall weep many hours, indeed many years, once you are gone. Now it is my official duty, as Watchtower between the worlds, to order you begone! To cast you from my presence! To bid, indeed command, that you return to the nether regions to which you belong! I suggest you seek the catacombs – that is where creatures of your sort generally go.'

Will had an unbidden thought of the cliff cave at Pointe du Raz where he had spent the day. Compared to this Parisian locale of horror, it was home.

'May I protest against this bitter exile you order? Exile from you and thus from life itself? I know of no Watchtower, no such authority, no such guardianship. I reject the Watchtower. But not you my love. Never you.' He took a step toward her.

'You know the Watchtower now,' Marguerite told him in an authoritarian tone, snapping her fingers. Flames burst from her fingertips. Will felt the heat lick at his skin and knew she had the power to destroy him. 'You know what you need to know.'

She fled from him along the river with an alacrity, an evanescence, that suggested she might still have one foot in another world. Will blinked, and she was gone.

Immortality, like memory, was not so easy to shrug off, he thought. For Marguerite, it would never really be in the past.

Yet Will knew this couldn't be entirely true, for that antagonistic look in her eyes, a totally human look, had been all too real. He also knew better than to follow her, for there lay the worst heartbreak of all, trying to rule fate when fate ruled him. Numb with grief, and trembling with a nightstalker's fear of being uncovered, Will ignored the latter to sit for a while. He stared into the blood moon of the Seine, an implacable face of this new world to which he'd been admitted, and waited for a breeze to break up its otherworldly shimmer and release him from its grip.

One came along. It shattered the moon into a thousand fragments of rosy ice. Will retreated up the bank, intending to mount his horse and ride back to Pointe du Raz to search for Dee and demand he return him to his mortal state. Despite his hunger and thirst. But halfway to his horse, he caught sight of a distraught young woman just emerged from a tavern, weeping while meandering drunkenly near an alley. A quick survey of the street told him no one else was about. The pale skin of her neck was as alluring as Marguerite's had been. And why shouldn't it be? For his nocturnal needs, one young woman compelled him as another did: theirs seemed the sweetest blood of all to salve his thirst and fill his hunger, an intuition that would prove valid over the centuries.

In a single stride five times the length of his normal one, he was at her back, pushing her headlong into the alley, one hand over her mouth to stifle her cry, the other bracing her fall – his humanity lingered – as his mouth opened and his tongue tasted teeth-drawn juice of her neck. As she fell prone, only his incredible arm strength kept her above the ground, her face never quite touching the rough and soiled pavement of the alley.

When his swallows ceased at last, he lowered her gently to the ground. He caressed her neck gently, feeling for her pulse to assure himself that she was still . . .

'Alive? Yes, she's still alive.'

Will looked up and found to his horror that he was not alone in the alley. A hooded figure was standing in the shadows.

'But not all your victims will be so lucky,' the man said in an angry snarl.

'Who . . . ?' The man's voice was familiar and – more amazing still – he seemed to know his thoughts, as if he somehow shared his mind. 'How . . . ?'

'Is this where you want to spend eternity? In the shadows hiding from your beloved, or . . .' The man stepped out of the shadows and lowered his hood. Will gasped at the sight of the man's face. He'd thought discovering that Marguerite was mortal was the worst surprise of the night, but this . . . *this* got even further under his skin.

'Or would you like me to show you another way?'

33

Château Hell

The coach took me across the Seine to the Left Bank and went south down a long, straight street. Although much looked different from the Paris I'd left a few days ago, this street looked familiar. I recognized the imposing edifice of the Sorbonne and a number of other academic buildings. Although they weren't wearing jeans and backpacks, the scholars in robes walking the streets in rowdy groups laughed as loudly and drunkenly as their twenty-first-century counterparts.

As we drove farther south, though, the city looked less and less familiar. Where I'd have expected the Luxembourg Gardens we passed instead a monastery. We drove through a gate in a stone wall and into a rural area, then pulled up to an elegant château, its limestone façade distinguished by a tall, octagonal tower.

Which looked familiar.

As I got out of the coach, I turned around in a slow circle, trying to get my bearings, but without the Eiffel Tower flickering in the distance or the light of the observatory tower . . .

'Monsieur,' I asked the driver, 'what sort of monastery did we just pass?'

'It belongs to the Carthusians.' Then, crossing himself, he added, 'But this ground was once the site of Château Vauvert, which many say was the home of the devil himself. It is not a good place, mademoiselle, but it is where Monsieur told me to take you.'

'It's okay,' I told the driver. 'I think I know who lives here.'

As soon as I'd given him permission, he whipped the horses into a gallop and sped away. As I walked to the door, I recalled that the Château Vauvert had taken up the ground that was occupied in twenty-first-century Paris by the Luxembourg Gardens and the Paris Observatory. I also remembered that the expression *go to Vauvert* was synonymous in French with *go to hell* because of the reputation of the château, from which strange screams and cries were often heard. It *was* a lonely place, I reflected, staring up at the enormous doorway of the later château that had taken its place. This château was decorated as if it guarded an entrance to the underworld. Caryatids framed the doorway, voluptuous women whose lush bodies resolved into scaly tails. Sea creatures swarmed across the arch above the door. I lifted the heavy iron doorknocker – carved in the shape of a seahorse – and knocked twice. The sound echoed in the still night. When the door opened, I was only half surprised to find Madame La Pieuvre, her silver hair piled high on top of her head, wearing a low-cut brocade dress with a wide lace collar from which hung a long train.

'Octavia,' I said with a relieved sigh. 'I've never been so happy to see anyone in all my life!'

A smile dimpled her plump, white cheeks, but she

looked confused. 'Do I know you, my dear?'

'You will,' I said with a more tired sigh. 'It's a long story. I know it's a lot to take on faith, but . . .'

'I'm sure I've taken a lot more on faith,' she said with a sympathetic pat on my shoulder. 'Come on in, *ma chère*, and you'll tell me your long story over dinner.'

Madame La Pieuvre took me to the top room of the château's octagonal tower, which was lit by cleverly designed lanterns and fitted out with a telescope and a number of other astronomical devices I wouldn't have thought had yet been invented.

'I have some observations to make later,' she said, waving me toward a silk-upholstered chair. 'I'll ring for our supper to be brought here.'

Supper was a delicious fish stew seasoned with Provençal herbs. 'Bouillabaisse, my favorite!' I exclaimed.

'*Bouillabaisse*? What a lovely word for it. I'll have to remember that.'

When I'd slaked the worst of my hunger and drunk two glasses of a delicious sparkling white wine that she was amused to hear me call champagne, I told Madame La Pieuvre my story. I told her all of it, from my first glimpse of the silver box in New York City, about which she had heard rumors, to our trip to the Val sans Retour. I thought she'd stop me there, but she continued to listen with the same grave attention, her gray eyes as placid as a morning fog rolling over the sea, to my entire marvelous tale. The only sign she made that this part of the story had affected her was that she poured us each a glass of green liqueur, which she told me the local Carthusian monks had made.

'They call it Chartreuse,' she told me. 'I love it for its color.'

I sipped the surprisingly potent liqueur and continued with my story. When I finished, she asked me one question.

'May I see that timepiece you crafted?'

I slipped its chain over my head and handed it to her, surprised that this was the detail that most interested her. She examined the front of the watch, opened it, watched its gears moving, then turned it over. Her eyes widened when she saw the design of the Watchtower on the back.

'This wasn't on the original watch you saw,' she said.

'No, I added it.'

'Do you know why?'

I shook my head. 'It just seemed to belong there.'

She closed the watch and handed it back to me. 'I imagine Cosimo Ruggieri strived for years to find the correct symbols to make his time machine work, but only a descendant of the Watchtower would know what symbol to add.' She rose to her feet and crossed to the north window, where her telescope was set up. Her arms, released from her train, plucked instruments from shelves as she went.

'Cosimo has been endeavoring to trick time all his life,' she said, adjusting the telescope. 'Here, come take a look.'

I put my eye to the telescope. It was not trained on the heavens, but on the low skyline of Paris to the north. The view of dark, huddled buildings brought home to me the reality that I was not in my time. Paris had not yet become the City of Light. But by the glow of the nearly full moon I could make out the twin, square towers of Notre

Dame, the three towers of Saint-Germain, the Tour Saint-Jacques, and the slim spire of Sainte-Chapelle. Brightest of all, though, northwest of Notre Dame, was a glowing orb. As I watched, a thread of lightning descended from the sky and struck the orb, illuminating a skeletal framework of interconnecting circles and ellipses. It looked like one of the astronomical contraptions I'd spied in the Musée des Arts et Métiers.

'What is that?' I asked, my eye still glued to the telescope.

'Cosimo Ruggieri's tower,' Madame La Pieuvre replied. 'It's been drawing lightning for the last seven nights. I've been watching it, waiting for Ruggieri to return from his abbey in Brittany where my Bretagne friends have been keeping an eye on him, wondering what he was bringing with him that required so much power. Last night I received word that he and Dee had awoken *la bête*.'

'You mean Marduk?' I asked, glancing away from the telescope. Madame La Pieuvre's face, lit by flickering lantern light, was round and pale.

'Yes, *Marduk*. The name is a perversion of the name he took many centuries ago. He called himself Duc du Mar – Duke of the Sea. I am ashamed to say that he was originally one of the *fées de la mer*. He arrived here in Paris on the boats that brought us after the fall of Ys. The aristocracy of Ys was a proud group. They enjoyed the way that humans worshipped them. Some genuinely fell in love with humans . . .' She looked away from me, her face wistful. I recalled that Monsieur Lutin had told me that more than any of the other fairies, the sea fairies had thrived off their contact with humans.

'But others abused their power over their human consorts,' Madame La Pieuvre continued darkly. 'The worst offender was the Duc du Mar. He surrounded himself with human slaves whom he ravished and then disposed of when they no longer pleased him. His appetite was insatiable. Soon he was no longer content with mere physical abuse. He wanted to literally *devour* them. In his attempt to possess his humans wholly, he began to drink their blood. Some say he even ate their flesh.'

'Ugh. How could the rest of you – the other sea fairies – allow that?'

'We weren't sure at first what he was doing. We realized it only when his victims began rising from the dead as vampires. He made hundreds of them. They swept over Paris terrorizing the populace. The *fées de la mer* met and decreed that Marduk – as he then began calling himself – must be stopped, but by then it was too late. Marduk had gained the power to take on the appearance of his victims. Thus he slipped from our grasp and escaped Paris. He went on a rampage across the countryside, leaving a path of drained bodies and vampires in his wake. Eventually we hounded him into the Pyrénées. There, without enough human victims to sustain him, he began feasting on beasts of the wild – boars, wolves, and bears. He took on traits of all the animals he had devoured and became a monstrous beast with an insatiable appetite for human flesh.'

'Like the Beast of Gévaudan,' I said, recalling what Will had told me. I described the legend of Gévaudan to Madame La Pieuvre.

'Yes, that sounds like Marduk – or perhaps one of the creatures he spawned. I'm afraid that the forests of Europe have never entirely been free of such creatures since Marduk went on his rampage. At last we hunted him down to his lair high in the Pyrénées. I was among the hunting party. We captured him, but only after he had taken many lives . . . including that of someone very dear to me.'

Her eyes filled with tears. 'We brought him back to the Île de Sein – to the last vestige of the city of Ys – and imprisoned him in a cave deep beneath the sea. Watchers were set guard in the tower on the Île de Sein – and in the towers on the mainland – to make sure he never escaped, but over the centuries the watchers have grown lax and susceptible to corruption and bribery. Many of the towers fell into ruins – or into evil hands. The tower on the Pointe du Raz, for instance, became the property of Cosimo Ruggieri, a gift from his late patroness Catherine de Médicis. We feared then that Ruggieri was up to no good, but we never suspected that he had the power to call forth Marduk from the sea. But then we didn't know that the English sorcerer John Dee was working with him, or that he'd found, through Will Hughes, a way to gain the silver box and the Watchtower ring from Marguerite.'

'It's not Will's fault. He had no idea what Dee was planning, and he tried to kill Marduk. He *did* kill him, I think, but when *my* – I mean Will from the future – tried to drink his blood, Marduk revived and attacked him.'

'And you say Morgane told you Marduk's blood would make Will human again?'

'Yes. Do you think she was telling the truth?'

Madame La Pieuvre shrugged with typical Gallic resignation. 'Maybe yes, maybe no. One never knows with Morgane. But one thing is clear. We must hunt down

Marduk and destroy him. *Your* Will is free to do what he likes with him when we find him.'

'But how will we find him? We don't know where he is.'

'I think we do. Look again at Ruggieri's column.'

I looked through the telescope. For a moment I thought I was back in twenty-first-century Paris where the Eiffel Tower lit up the skyline with pyrotechnic displays, but the flashing lights came from the Medici Column, which looked now like a Roman candle setting off sparks. At the center of the blaze, the metal cage was glowing and revolving, shooting fireworks into the Paris sky.

'I believe Ruggieri has been preparing the column for Marduk's arrival, and therefore Marduk, Dee, and Ruggieri will be in the Hôtel de la Reine. I only hope they haven't gone ahead with their experiment tonight.'

'They haven't.'

The voice came from the doorway. Will stood beside a flustered maid, his face less pale than when I'd seen him last, but no less grim.

'I tracked Marduk down to the Hôtel de la Reine and spied Dee and Ruggieri feeding him the blood of victims they must have previously slain in anticipation of Marduk's arrival. I overheard them say that they must let the beast rest today before "transforming" him tonight.'

'Were you able to get his blood?' I asked, taking a step toward Will. His cheeks had the flush of blood in them, but he shook his head.

'I couldn't risk it while Marduk was conscious. He's grown too powerful. But during the day while he rests . . .'

'I can draw his blood,' I said. 'If I can get into the Hôtel de la Reine.'

Will looked toward Madame La Pieuvre. They exchanged a look I couldn't decipher. For the first time I wondered how Will had thought to send me to her. How *did* they know each other?

'I can get us into the Hotel,' she said. 'I knew Catherine de Médicis well. She showed me the secret passages she had built. Like any Medici she was an inveterate intriguer – for good reason.'

'Will you go with Garet, Octavia?' Will asked. 'And make sure she comes to no harm?'

'Of course, *mon cher*. When we have Marduk's blood, we will go to Ruggieri's tower. I believe that with the watch Garet has made, the two of you will be able to travel forward to your own time.' One of her arms drifted toward Will's face. At a warning look from him she let it flutter back down. The Medicis weren't the only intriguers, I suspected.

Madame La Pieuvre led us to a room with heavy drawn shutters. 'You will be safe from the light here,' she told Will. She offered to show me to my room, but I said I'd stay with Will until dawn.

'As you please, my dear, only remember that you will need your rest, too. We must be on our guard when we go into the Hôtel de la Reine.'

When she had gone, Will drew me down onto the bed and tried to kiss me, but I turned my face away. 'You two seem very friendly. Was Madame La Pieuvre also one of your conquests?'

Will grasped my jaw firmly in his hand and turned my face so I had to look at him. 'No. I did her a favor. When did you become so jealous? I wouldn't have thought you were the type.'

'I suppose since I've had to take a seventeenth-century tour of your exes,' I replied, hating the bitter tone of my voice but unable to get rid of it. 'You mentioned quite a few in your sleep yesterday. Who is Bess?'

The corner of Will's mouth twitched. 'I called out Bess's name? How extraordinary! I haven't thought of her in centuries. How strange to think she's still alive in these times!'

'Perhaps you'd like to go pay her a visit,' I said, getting to my feet. 'As long as you're in the same century.'

Will was on his feet blocking my way to the door before I'd even seen him move, his hands gripping my shoulders, his face centimeters from mine.

'Is it really these trifles that concern you, Garet? Do you really care about the women I took to my bed over the centuries more than the men and women I took to their graves?'

I started to answer that I shouldn't have to choose, but then I saw the anguish in his blood-rimmed eyes. 'You couldn't help taking blood. It's what Dee made you.'

'But I could have helped killing. I started out believing I could drink without draining my victims, but I soon learned that the blood was too much of an addiction. The first deaths may have been accidents, but then I stopped caring whether I stopped in time or not. All I cared about was the blood. For centuries I was a monster no better than the creature who made me.'

'But then you stopped killing?'

'Yes, about a hundred years ago I learned to control my

thirst enough to leave my victims alive. It only becomes dangerous when I feed from the same source over and over.' He caressed my neck and I felt his touch thrum through my body. I'd been holding myself tight with anger, but his touch made me vibrate like a plucked violin string. 'As I've warned you.'

I sighed and felt the tightness in my muscles melt further. The release brought me an inch closer to him. I could feel the heat of the blood he'd drunk moving through his flesh. Suddenly it didn't matter to me where he'd gotten the blood – or what other women he'd loved in the past. What did the past matter? I had warped time with the timepiece I'd made – couldn't I wipe our pasts clean?

'After tomorrow you'll be free of this curse and free of your past. You can start over. . . . *We* can start over.' I closed the centimeter gap between us and pressed myself against the heat of him. I lay my head on his chest, tilting my head so my throat was bared to his lips. I felt him hesitate.

'Perhaps there is a way to start over,' he murmured as if to himself. Then he lowered his head to my neck. As his lips grazed my skin he whispered in my ear, 'But tonight I want to be with you one last time . . . like *this*.'

As his teeth sank into my neck, every muscle in my body turned to liquid. I would have fallen straight to the floor if he hadn't caught me. I might, I found myself thinking, fall straight into hell in his arms, but it no longer mattered to me. I'd go to hell to be with him. But I didn't fall. Once he had hold of me, I felt the blood in my veins catch fire as if they were filled with that green liqueur Madame La

Pieuvre had fed me earlier. I wrapped my legs around his waist and pressed my mouth against his, tasting my blood on his lips. I could taste, too, the venom his fangs released. It made my mouth tingle and sent a ripple of electricity through my veins. I undid his pants as he carried me to the bed. He was inside me before we hit the bed. I felt his urgency and matched it.

34

The hotel of Crocodiles

I watched death come upon Will at dawn. It wasn't just sleep, I realized, it was as if he died at every dawn. I couldn't bear the thought of his dying one more day. I had to find Marduk.

I closed my eyes, meaning to rest a few moments beside him, but when Madame La Pieuvre woke me, she told me that it was past six in the evening. 'I let you sleep, *ma chère*, so you could be rested for what we have to do, but we must find Marduk before the sun sets.'

When we walked outside the château, the late-afternoon sky was so overcast I was afraid the sun had already set. Black storm clouds hung in the western sky. Madame La Pieuvre looked at them worriedly.

'Another storm. More lightning to feed Ruggieri's machinery. We must hurry.'

'I'm sorry if doing this puts you in any danger,' I told her when we were settled in her carriage.

She shrugged. 'You, being from the future as you are, are a descendant of the Watchtower. It is my duty to help you. Besides, it sounds as if you did me a favor in your time by taking me to the Summer Country.'

'I'm not sure how much of a favor that was. I'm

afraid you might have gotten lost in the Val sans Retour.'

'And yet I was willing to risk the journey. I must have loved – *will* love – this woman Adele very much.'

'Yes, I think you did – I mean, will.' I described Adele Weiss to her and told her what I knew about how they had met during a war. Then, taking my notebook from my pocket, I drew a picture of her.

'She is lovely,' Madame La Pieuvre said, smiling at the drawing. 'I'm glad that I will love someone enough to want to give up my immortality. It gives me something to look forward to.' She gazed out the coach window, her gray eyes as serene as the overcast sky. Four hundred years seemed a long time to wait, but perhaps to a creature who had already lived for millennia it wasn't.

'We're here,' she said as the coach came to a stop. We were in a narrow side street bordered by a high, window-less stone wall.

'This is Catherine de Médicis's palace?' I asked skeptically as we stepped out into a lightly falling rain.

'The southwest corner of it. You didn't think we were going in the front door, did you?'

'No, but . . .' I couldn't see any door at all, just a shallow niche decorated with a large bronze bas-relief panel depicting Venus rising from the sea. Above the wall I could see the Medici Column, and beyond that I saw the spires of Saint-Eustache. I turned around in a circle, recalling the visit I'd made with Roger Elden.

'We're standing right at the entrance to the metro,' I said. 'Or where the metro will be in four hundred years.'

'And what is the metro?' Madame La Pieuvre asked.

'An underground' – I was about to say *train*, but

remembered that she wouldn't know what a train was – 'passage,' I said instead, 'that people use for transportation.'

'That's just what's here now,' she said, bending down before the carved plaque of Venus. She looked as though she were paying homage to the goddess – I supposed that Venus might be one of her gods – but then her fingers found some hidden catch in the grooves of the shell Venus rose from, and the bronze sculpture swung wide-open. A cool, briny gust of air rose from the dark passage behind the plaque as if it truly led to Venus's ocean grotto. I followed Madame La Pieuvre into the dark passage, which became even darker when she swung the door shut behind us. The blackness closed in on me like a hand at my throat – then I snapped my fingers. The tiny flame that sprang out of my thumb lit up a flight of stone steps descending into a pit of darkness that my puny light couldn't penetrate. Madame La Pieuvre's moon-shaped face bobbed beside me. She smiled – a trifle condescendingly, I thought – at my thumb-light and then uncoiled her arms from her cloak. At a flick of her many wrists blue-glowing lights appeared up and down her arms. They cast a blue-green light that lit up the staircase down to the bottom, where it ended in a pool of water.

'Come,' she said, 'these passages flood when it rains. We must be quick.'

I followed her, keeping an eye on her glowing limbs, which floated around her like seaweed. With the salt smell and the sound of water lapping against stone, I felt as though I were sinking in a bathysphere to the ocean floor, but the water at the bottom of the stairs turned out to be only a few inches deep. We had to hold our cloaks and dresses up, which meant I had to extinguish my thumb-light, but I didn't need it anymore. Madame La Pieuvre's bioluminescence, reflected in the shallow water, lit up a level tunnel in a turquoise blaze of light, illumining a lovely mosaic pattern of shells and sea creatures on the walls and ceilings.

'This is pretty,' I said. 'What did Catherine de Médicis use the underground chambers for?'

'A means of escape should her palace be besieged by enemies, a secret entranceway for the sorcerers and witches she employed, and when someone displeased her—'

A scream cut her off. She stopped so suddenly I bumped into her; she wrapped two arms around me to keep me from falling. 'And for torture,' Madame La Pieuvre whispered. 'Only I had thought those days were over.'

A second scream punctuated her sentence. In the hollow confines of the underground chamber I couldn't tell how close the sound was, or when the scream ended and its echoes began. The echoes seemed to surround us like the voices of all who had ever suffered in this dark, dank place.

A third scream rang out – and was abruptly cut off in a strangled gurgle that was even more awful and seemed to be echoed in the moving water at our feet. Tucking all her glow-ing arms but two in her cloak and pressing one finger to her lips, she pulled me forward. Her footsteps made no sound in the water, but mine sloshed and slapped. When we reached a flight of steps that brought us up onto a dry landing, I was grateful . . . until I saw what lay beyond the landing.

The vaulted room was lit by torches set in iron sconces. Long, pendulous shapes hung from iron hooks in the ceiling. They looked like huge caterpillar cocoons hanging from a tree branch after a rain, water dripping off them into buckets set beneath them ... I blinked, refocused, and opened my mouth to scream. A wet tentacle slapped over my mouth before any sound could come out. I stared at Madame La Pieuvre, whose face had gone inky black, her eyes wide with horror and rage, and then I looked back into the torture room.

The 'cocoons' were human beings hanging upside down from the ceiling, some of them with blood dripping from cut throats into tin pails. Two men first wrangled one of the bodies onto a hook. When the body had been suspended, one of the men took a long knife from a scabbard at his waist and, while his companion held the body still, drew it across the neck.

Only when the blood gushed out did I realize that the body had been alive and I understood that we'd just stood helplessly by while a man was murdered. I moaned beneath Madame La Pieuvre's hand and she pulled me back away from the door and against the wall.

'What was that sound?' a man's voice asked in guttural French.

'A rat,' his comrade answered. 'Or one of the queen's crocodiles. Did you know the queen kept crocodiles down here to discourage her prisoners from escaping? Why don't you go have a look, Gaston?' The man laughed cruelly.

I hoped that Gaston would be dissuaded from looking by his comrade's mockery – or by the threat of crocodiles. Did every city in every time period have that urban legend? I wondered. The sound of footsteps approaching put an end to that line of thought. Madame La Pieuvre shoved me behind her and, with one more warning finger to her lips, turned to face the door. A man appeared on the landing holding a torch at and above the steps leading back down to the water. I saw Madame La Pieuvre unfastening the clasp of her cloak, and then, in less time than it took the cloak to fall to the floor, she surged forward, all eight arms writhing in the air. The man turned at the breeze her movement must have caused and I had time to see the look of horror on his face before she was upon him. One suckered hand wrapped over his mouth and nose, stifling his scream, while the others wrapped around him, keeping him from falling. It looked as if she were gently rocking him to sleep, only I could see his face turning dark in the reflected light of Madame La Pieuvre's bio-luminescence, his eyes bulging, then rolling back and freezing in death. She lowered him gently to the ground and then turned around.

I barely recognized the refined woman I knew. Her face was puffed and mottled, her arms had grown suckers that pulsed like open mouths hungry for more prey . . . which had just appeared in the doorway. The second torturer stood gaping at this creature that was beyond any fictive nightmares he might have dreamed up to frighten his comrade. A small sound came out of him – like air escaping from a punctured tire – and then she was upon him. This time there was no gentle squeezing to death. Madame La Pieuvre tore him limb from limb, tossing pieces of him into the air. When she was done, she shoved the remains down the steps into the water.

'There,' she said, wiping blood from her mouth. 'Let the crocodiles he was laughing about feast on his remains.'

I would have asked her then if those crocodiles really existed, but she had already swept past me into the torture room. She went from body to body, tenderly touching each one with the suckered fingers she'd only recently used to tear a man apart. 'Some of these poor souls have been dead for several days and' – she knelt at the ground and sniffed at the rank stone floor – 'blood has been spilled before that. How long have they been collecting blood and *why*?'

'For Marduk. They must have needed it to make him strong enough.'

'Marduk's never needed any help getting his own blood. Dee and Ruggieri must have some reason to collect this much blood. Something special they have planned.'

I shivered at the thought of any plan that required such wholesale bloodletting – a shivering that wouldn't stop as I followed Madame La Pieuvre further, keeping within the circle of her glow in case we ran into any of those crocodiles. We went through passages lined with bones and skulls piled high above our heads and curio cabinets full of strange instruments and stuffed exotic animals.

'Catherine was quite the collector,' Madame La Pieuvre remarked when she saw me staring at a stuffed aardvark. 'And an amateur sorcerer. She dabbled in the black arts and poisoning, collecting whatever she thought might come in useful to protect her children and further her own dynastic ambitions . . . and yet when she died, she had outlived eight of her ten children, and of the two survivors, Henri the third died seven months after her, leaving only her daughter Margot, whom she had disowned during her life. A sad life. I'm not surprised that Dee and Ruggieri have chosen her abandoned palace for their evil purposes.'

She shook her head sadly and then continued on, leaving me staring at the cabinet full of strange instruments. They reminded me of something, but I couldn't recall what. Only when Madame La Pieuvre's glow had faded and I couldn't see the instruments in the case anymore did I hurry to catch up with her.

She had come to a stop at the end of a hallway. She held an arm out to keep me back . . . and I saw why. Hers wasn't the only source of light anymore. A glow was coming from around the corner. She motioned for me to stay put and then cautiously crept around the corner. After another moment she waved for me to follow her.

The scene in this room was not as blatantly horrific as the one in the dungeon. It was even peaceful. The room was hung with rich tapestries and lit by banks of candles. A body was laid out on a raised dais like a corpse laid out for viewing at a funeral, except that above the head of the 'corpse' was suspended a leather bladder connected to the body by a long, supple reed. Walking closer, I revised my impression from funeral parlor to hospital ER. Liquid was dripping from the bladder, down through the reed, and into a metal shunt fitted into the crook of the man's arm. Amazed, I looked at the face of the man on the table – and was even more amazed to find Will's face.

'It's not Will, you understand,' Madame La Pieuvre whispered as she came up beside me. 'It's Marduk.'

'I know . . . only when I saw him last, he had only partly taken on Will's features. You could still see the monster below the skin, but now . . .'

'He looks like an angel. This is why Dee and Ruggieri are draining their victims. If Marduk fed directly from his victims, he'd take on their features, but feeding like this, he continues to look like Will.'

'But why? Why do they want him to look like Will?'

Madame La Pieuvre shrugged. 'Why *not* choose a beautiful face for your monster? With this face he'll be able to mingle with aristocracy and lure unsuspecting victims to their doom. He's fooled you, hasn't he?'

I tore my eyes away from Will – from Marduk – looked into Madame La Pieuvre's keen eyes, and I knew I'd been looking at the monster with love. 'He looks so much like Will. I'm not sure I can destroy him.'

'Leave that to me. You only need to get what you came for.' She withdrew a small, glass, corked vial and a slender Y-shaped metal pipe from inside her cloak. The end of the short arm of the Y was sharpened to a point. She took out the reed from Marduk's arm and showed me how to insert the sharpened pipe into his vein. 'Physicians use this for bloodletting,' she told me as drops of blood spilled from the pipe into the glass vial. I kept my eye on the vial to help keep it steady in my hand. When it was full, Madame La Pieuvre removed the pipe and corked the vial. Then I looked up and found Madame La Pieuvre staring into the monster's open eyes.

'Go!' she hissed, giving me the vial. 'He's not fully awake yet. As long as I maintain eye contact, he won't be able to move.'

'But—'

'Just go. I'll take care of him. It's almost dusk. Go to the tower. If you follow this passage further, you'll come to the courtyard. Climb to the top and wait there for Will. After I've taken care of Marduk, I'll keep Dee and Ruggieri away.'

I tried to think of an argument against this plan. I started to ask why she didn't just kill Marduk now and come with me, but then I realized she didn't want me to see her tearing apart a creature who looked so much like the man I loved. I didn't want to see that either. So I followed her advice. I ran.

35

The Timepiece

And promptly got lost. The palace seemed to have been built like a maze, constructed according to some Machiavellian architect's scheme to confuse one's enemy. I ran through deserted salons occupied only by faded nymphs and fauns who looked embarrassed to be caught cavorting on their painted ceilings. The few remaining pieces of furniture were shrouded in ghostly canvas drop cloths. I nearly had a heart attack rounding a corner and coming face-to-face with a crocodile's open jaws, but saw that it was only a stuffed specimen.

Past the crocodile's tail I spied the courtyard through a large, grimy window. I couldn't get the window open, but a marble urn sitting beside the stuffed crocodile broke it just fine. I squeezed through, only cutting my hand a little on the broken glass.

The courtyard was full of debris – broken furniture, shredded drapes, three more stuffed crocodiles in varying stages of decay . . . what was the fascination with crocodiles? I wondered as I picked my way across the littered ground. Whatever the reason for Catherine de Médicis's fondness for the beasts, I didn't have time to think about it now. Storm clouds still covered much of the sky, but in the west the sun had sunk beneath the clouds and hovered at the edge of the courtyard wall. It lit up the tower so that it seemed to glow against the inky clouds in the east. When I reached the low, arched door at its base, I experienced a moment of vertigo, recalling going through this same door only a few nights ago with Roger Elden. As I touched the handle, I could almost imagine that I was back in twenty-first-century Paris and that if I turned around, I'd find the metro stop. At the thought the watch pendant grew heavy and cold against my chest. I *could* be back, I realized, if I focused hard enough on the future, but I couldn't go *yet*. Not without Will.

I forced myself to focus on the here and now: the grate of the metal door as it opened, the reek of pigeon droppings in the stairwell, the clank of my feet on the metal stairs. I made myself count all 147 steps as I made my way to the top to keep my mind clear of everything but the present moment. When I went through the trapdoor onto the top of the column, I didn't have to battle my associations with the future. The metal structure was much more elaborate than the bare framework that had survived into the twenty-first century. Amid the iron framework were bright copper rings engraved with arcane symbols. Surrounding the perimeter of the column was a narrow metal catwalk. I moved gingerly out onto it and looked toward the west.

The sun was balanced over the rooftops of the city beneath a sky of fierce, roiling clouds. It looked as if the clouds were trying to squash the sun down into the horizon, to stamp out its light forever. A wave of lightning moved through the clouds – a dense network of veins that looked like the metro map of Paris. The clouds were moving closer to the tower, carrying the lightning with them along with colder air that smelled like the sea. I shivered, wondering what would happen to me if lightning struck the tower while I was on top of it – which surely it would. That's what it was built for. The whole thing was an enormous lightning rod.

The wind blew harder out of the west and the copper rings creaked into life, slowly revolving in their interlocking orbits. I was standing outside them on the catwalk; I thought I would need to be inside to make the time travel work. I'd wait on the catwalk until I saw Will.

No one was in the courtyard, unless you counted the stuffed crocodiles, who, in the murky green light of the approaching storm, appeared to be back in their native habitat of primordial swamp. I scanned the windows along the courtyard, walking around the catwalk, but there was no sign of life in any of them. What had happened to Octavia? Had she been able to kill Marduk? Should I have left her alone with him? But then I remembered how efficiently she had torn apart the second guard and figured she was probably able to deal with Marduk herself. It was too late to do anything but wait. The sun was about to disappear beneath the rooftops of Paris. Will would be on his way now. I knew from experience how fast he was.

When I'd summoned him to Governors Island, he'd come in a heartbeat. When I'd been in danger in the tunnels approaching the High Water Tower in Manhattan, he'd saved me. He'd waited months for me in a cave in the Val sans Retour – and we'd come out of the Val sans Retour together, which was only supposed to be possible for faithful lovers. But was he a faithful lover? I wondered, staring into the stygian gloom of the courtyard as the faltering light in the sky started to vanish. After hundreds of years of carousing was he capable of loving one woman?

A flash of lightning lit up the courtyard, bringing the white bits of broken marble statuary and underbellies of the crocodiles to ghoulish life, as ugly as the jealous thoughts that preyed on me. They would devour me, I suddenly saw, and devour whatever chance Will and I had of loving each other. I had to put them aside. I didn't know what the future would bring for Will and me – didn't even know if we'd be able to get back to our own time – but the only chance we had was to trust ourselves to that future and not dwell in the past. Whatever Will had done in the four hundred years that stretched from this time to ours, those things had helped make him the man – or vampire – I'd fallen in love with.

At the next flash I saw him. He was coming through the same broken window I'd come through. He tilted his face up toward the tower, no doubt looking for me. I called his name, but my voice was drowned out by the rumble of thunder, which was followed by the sharp crackle of fresh lightning, this time directly above the courtyard. This flash lit Will midstride, just past one of the leering crocodiles, and at the window, another figure.

'Will!' I screamed, trying to warn him that he was being followed, but of course he couldn't hear me. The lightning was coming every few seconds now, each flash giving me the briefest, most frustrating glimpse of Will and the cloaked figure following him across the long courtyard. It was like watching the action through strobe lighting. I was so intent on the scene that I didn't notice at first that the metal rings behind me had begun to revolve faster, but when the groan of metal drew my attention and I glanced back, I found that not only were the gears of Ruggieri's contraption spinning, they were also glowing. The metal rings were collecting the light and energy of the storm and throwing them off in a great geyser of sparks that shot fifty feet into the air and then drifted down into the courtyard. Looking back down, I saw that the broken furniture and scraps of cloth had caught fire. Will had vanished. He must have reached the door. The other figure was still threading his way through the debris and smoke. *Good*, I thought, *by the time he gets here, Will and I will be gone.*

I stepped tentatively into the metal cage, into the center of the glowing, revolving circles, and opened the timepiece. The watch gears were revolving and glowing just like the rings on the tower. The watch hands were spinning just as they had when I got lost in the Val sans Retour. The timepiece was working – but *how* did it work? How did I get it to take me and Will back to 2009?

The door in the floor opened. I held my breath until I saw it was Will coming up the steps, then threw myself into his arms so hard he stumbled and nearly backed into the revolving wheels.

'I was afraid you wouldn't make it!' I cried.

He looked down at me, his eyes flashing as green in the glow of the sparks as the Chartreuse I'd drunk at Madame La Pieuvre's. 'I was followed,' he said, his voice hoarse. 'We have to move quickly. Do you have the timepiece?'

I held it up for him. Another flash of lightning hit the top of the cage, and a thin filament traveled down and struck the timepiece. I felt a charge go through me that nearly made me drop the watch, but I held on to it with one hand while drawing the vial of Marduk's blood out of my pocket with the other. 'I have this, too. Do you want to drink it now?'

He shook his head. 'We'll wait until we get to the future. We may need my strength right now.'

I was surprised he wanted to wait, but I put the vial away and held up the spinning watch. 'I'm not sure how to make it work.'

'You're the Watchtower. You only have to say where you want to go.'

'Like Dorothy clicking her heels and saying there's no place like home?'

His fine, marble brow creased in confusion. 'Doroth—,' he began, but then the trapdoor slammed open and another figure rose up. His face was covered by the hood of his cloak, shielding himself from the showering sparks, but then he flung the cloak aside when he saw us. It was Will – or at least someone with Will's face.

'It's Marduk,' the man at my side whispered. 'Changed to look like me!'

I looked from face to face; they were identical. But then why hadn't Will gotten my *Wizard of Oz* reference a moment ago when he himself had said, 'We're not in Kansas anymore,' back in Paimpont? I looked down at the hand that grasped my arm – at the ring on his finger. A black swan on silver – my ring – not the one that Will should be wearing.

When I looked back up, I saw that his eyes were truly green – and malevolent. He snarled and, pushing me back, threw himself on *my* Will, who drew a sword and ran it straight through Marduk's heart.

Marduk screamed and clutched at the wound as Will withdrew the blade, the blood splashing Will's shirt. Then, before he could attack again, Will planted his boot on Marduk's chest and shoved him through the metal cage and over the edge of the tower.

I ran to Will, who stood trembling at the edge of the metal cage, looking down at the body of Marduk lying between two crocodiles. 'He'd better be dead this time,' Will said, spitting.

'I think he is,' I said, looking down at the motionless body. 'But we don't have time to check. The storm is passing. We have to go *now*!'

I pulled Will into the center of the cage and held up the timepiece. It was so hot now it was hard to hold. I closed my eyes and pictured twenty-first-century Paris – the round Bourse du Commerce instead of Catherine de Médicis's palace, the metro stop, the Eiffel Tower. I pictured the people I knew in twenty-first-century Paris – Adele Weiss, Sarah, Becca, and Carrie, even the homeless people who sat in the Square Viviani and the accordion player at the Cluny metro stop. Then I threw in everybody I knew and loved in the twenty-first-century – my father, Zack Reese, Becky and Jay, Joe Kiernan, Maia, the receptionist at the gallery . . . and Will. I pictured my Will in the present and mortal, his face in the sunlight . . .

A blinding flash enveloped us as if the sun I'd conjured in my mind had exploded. I felt Will's arms around me, pulling me down to the tower floor as burning sparks showered down upon us. At some point he must have put his cloak over our heads because when I came to, I was muffled below damp, singed wool.

I pushed the cloak aside. Will stirred and moaned. One of the wheels had fallen across him and seared his cheek. I moved the wheel away and the flesh began to heal in the gray light—

Gray light?

I stood up. In the east the sun was just beginning to rise over the rooftops of Paris – old, slate, mansard roofs.

I spun west and saw, etched in black against the gray sky, the Eiffel Tower.

'Thank God, we're back!' I cried. Will stirred. As he started to sit up, a ray of sunlight reached his hand. His flesh sizzled. He cried out and snatched his hand back under his cloak. I rooted in my pocket and found the vial of Marduk's blood, miraculously unbroken.

'Here,' I said, kneeling beside Will. 'Drink this.'

He looked up at me, his silver eyes wary. I didn't blame him. 'Or we could find you shelter until we're sure it will work.'

He snatched the bottle from me. 'I don't want to hide in the shadows away from you. If I can't be with you, I'd rather die.'

He drained the bottle before I could remind him it wasn't an either/or proposition. I'd have stayed with him even if he remained a vampire. But it was too late. Marduk's blood was moving through him. I could see it spidering through his veins, bulging through his skin. It looked as if it were cracking him open, and it must have felt like that because he screamed as if he were being burned alive. I held him, not caring if I burned up with him, until the fire in his veins subsided. I felt his skin cool – but not all the way to the chill temperature of a vampire. The face he lifted to the sun was flushed with human blood. The tears he shed, clear as glass.

'It worked,' I said. 'You're mortal again.'

He looked at me, holding his hand up to shade his eyes from the sun for the first time in over four hundred years. 'All because of you. I'll never take my mortality for granted again.' He pulled me to him and pressed his lips against mine. Human lips, warm and tasting like salt from his tears – and from mine, which I now let fall. 'I can never apologize enough for everything I've done.'

I shook my head and smiled. 'We have to stop that. Both of us. The past is over.' I held up the timepiece. Its gloss had cracked in the transit. 'See? We can't go back again.'

He returned my smile and kissed me again. I could have stayed like that for a long time, but I could already hear the morning traffic. 'Come on,' I said, getting up and pulling him to his feet. 'We'd better get back to the hotel before the streets fill with people and we have to answer for these clothes.'

Will looked down at his tattered, bloodstained shirt. 'I suppose you're right. I would like to wash this foul creature's blood off me. It smells like rotten fish.'

'Ugh! You're right,' I said as we entered the stairwell. The smell was more powerful in the enclosed space. 'Even after he took on your features, he must have retained some of the qualities of the sea creatures he'd fed on over the centuries. What a freakish monster!'

'I shudder to think of that creature wearing my face. I'm

afraid it will taint my enjoyment of my reflection forevermore.'

I glanced behind me to see if Will was joking, but he wasn't smiling.

'That sounds like the old you,' I said, gentle in my rebuke. 'I thought you'd outgrown that vanity . . .' I stopped when I saw the stricken look on Will's face. At first I thought it was due to my criticism, but then I followed his gaze past me and down a few steps where the light from the still-open trapdoor fell on a dark stain.

'What's that?' Will asked. 'It looks like . . .'

I knelt and touched my finger to the dark spot. It came away bloody and smelling like spoiled sardines. 'Marduk's blood,' I said. 'Given its newness and the time that's passed, he must have survived the fall and then climbed up here.' I looked farther down and saw footsteps on the steps below me. 'He almost reached us.'

'But look – there are footsteps coming up, but then he turned around and went *down*! He might still be below us in the tower!' Will drew his sword and pushed past me. 'I'm going to end this once and for all.'

I heard Will's footsteps racing down the stairs. I followed, terrified at every turning of the spiral stairs that I'd find the two of them locked in combat, but hoping that Will's assumption was wrong. Just because Marduk was back in the tower when I used the timepiece didn't mean he traveled forward in time with us. Did it?

I was relieved when I reached the bottom of the tower without encountering Marduk. Will was standing just outside, blinking in the early-morning sun. He was staring down at the ground. As I came up beside him, he pointed at something. Among the cigarette butts was a bloody foot-print . . . and another . . . and another. I followed the trail of them to the entrance of the metro.

'Shit,' I swore, meeting Will's stricken eyes. 'We brought him home with us!'

Will nodded and then turned in a wide circle, taking in the park, the early-morning commuters (who only gave our clothes and Will's sword passing glances, assuming, I realized, that we were gamers), the entrance to the metro, and the Eiffel Tower in the distance.

'Home?' Will asked, shaking his head in confusion when his circle brought him back to me. 'This doesn't look like home to me. Is this the land of the fey you've brought me to, Marguerite?'

I opened my mouth to object to his calling me Marguerite – I hadn't evolved *that* far past my jealousy – but then saw the bigger problem.

'Will,' I asked, 'how long were you a vampire?'

He looked baffled at the question, but answered, 'It felt like an eternity, but I suppose it was only two days.' He took a step toward me. 'I hope you won't hold that short time against me now that you've saved me.' He looked concerned. Probably because I was crying.

'You're not *my* Will,' I said, not caring how the words might wound him. 'I saved the wrong one.'

Garet's extraordinary adventures continue in

The Shape Stealer

coming soon from Bantam Press

Here's a sneak preview of the first chapters . . .

1

The Little Bridge

Paris in the morning. The streets newly washed by rain.
The smells of coffee and fresh baked bread wafting from
cafés. Sunlight a glittering promise of the day on the Seine.
I'd dreamed of walking like this across the Pont St Michel
with Will Hughes some day. How after four hundred years
of night he would see his first daybreak by my side. To win
that dawn we'd traveled back in time, faced a conniving
alchemist, an evil astrologer, an ancient sorceress, a
monster, assorted crocodiles, and Will's own sordid past
. . . and won a cure. We'd come back using the Astrologer's
Tower, and a timepiece I'd fashioned as a time machine,
and I'd handed Will the cure – the blood of the shape shifting creature that had made him a vampire. He had drunk
and become human. Descending the Astrologer's Tower
we'd learned that the creature Marduk had traveled back
with us. But I knew that together we could handle even
that. When Will looked around him, amazed at the new
world at his feet, I thought it was wonder at the new world
of daylight after four hundred years of night, but it wasn't.
He was amazed because he'd never seen twenty-first-
century Paris. The Will I had brought back with me was not
the man I had fallen in love with. It was his earlier self.

Nineteen-year-old Will Hughes, spoiled Lord's son, callow youth from 1602.

'You're not *my* Will,' I had told him. 'I saved the wrong one.'

'Tell me again what he said to you in the alley?'

We were in the Café Le Petit Pont across from Notre Dame. I was on my second café au lait. Will was sipping his, his childish delight at the beverage beginning to grate on my nerves.

'What my dark twin said?'

I sighed with exasperation. 'I've explained. He's not your dark twin. He's you – four hundred years later. We came from the future – *now* – to find a cure for him.'

Will pouted. My sexy, virile vampire *pouted*. I preferred those lips when they snarled back over fangs. 'He said I was his *better self*.'

I snorted. 'He was flattering you, probably because he knew it would work. Then what did he say?'

'He told me he knew a way that I could become human again and regain my true love Marguerite.' He made moon eyes at me again, as he had every time he'd mentioned Marguerite. I slapped the table.

'I told you, I am not your Marguerite. I'm a distant descendant.'

'Well he told me you *were*. He said I'd find you at the top of a tower in Catherine de Medicis's palace. That I'd have to fight my way there, but when I did I'd find you . . . er . . . Marguerite . . . on top with my cure. And I did fight! There were crocodiles!'

'Yes, you were very brave,' I said for the fifth time. 'But

didn't you ask him *why* he was sending you instead of going himself?'

Will's brow creased. 'Why should I question my dark twin's desire to save me?'

I sighed and lowered my head in my hands. 'No, I suppose you wouldn't.'

'But now that you mention it, he did say one other thing.'

'Yes?' I said, picking up my head.

'He said to tell you – well, to tell Marguerite . . .'

I made a circular motion with my hand to urge him to go on.

'Let's see, what were the exact words? He made me memorize them . . . oh yes, that he was sending you his better self because that's what you deserved.'

'Then you're both idiots,' I said, tossing a euro coin onto the table and getting up. I headed east along the Seine, battling the early morning flow of tourists, not caring if he followed me. But of course he did. He caught up with me in front of the Shakespeare & Company bookstore, where a shopkeeper was setting up the outdoor bins of books in the little square in front of the store.

'I don't know why you're angry with me, good lady. I merely followed the instructions of what appeared to be my dark angel.'

'That's why I'm angry with you,' I said wheeling on him. 'You followed orders; you didn't think to question him, did you? If you had, he might have told you that he was you four hundred years later and merely because he'd done some questionable things in those four hundred years he didn't think he was good enough for me. Then you might have asked, Verily, good sir, have you asked the lady what she thinks? And he would have been forced to admit that the *lady* had already told him that she didn't care what he'd done, that she loved *him*, the man he was with all the experiences he'd had, not the silly boy he'd been four hundred years before.'

Will, who had grown nearly as pale as his vampire self under my tirade, fidgeted with the frills of his shirt cuff. 'I am not silly,' he said. 'And neither was my older self an idiot. We both did what we did for love. Can we not be friends, you and I? We both want the same thing. You want your beloved Will back and I want my Marguerite. Can that not be arranged? I am willing to go back in time and change places with my dark . . . er . . . my older self.'

'That's very gallant of you,' I said, 'only as I mentioned earlier, the timepiece we used to travel back in time is broken.' I held up the watch that hung around my neck. Its glass face had cracked and its gears no longer moved.

I sighed and looked away from him, toward the river and the square in front of Notre Dame where tourists were lining up for morning tours. Time was moving on. Irrationally I felt it was moving me even further away from Will – the real Will, stuck in 1602. But then something occurred to me. *Time was moving on*. Will wasn't stuck in the past. Without Marduk's blood he had remained a vampire which meant he would have continued living from then until now. He must exist somewhere in the present . . . but then where was he? The question quickly made my head hurt. I needed to find someone who understood time . . . Of course! Horatio Durant, the watchmaker who had helped me make the timepiece. He hadn't admitted to any supernatural knowledge, but that didn't mean he didn't have any. I would start with him. Relieved to have come up with a plan of sorts I turned to share it with Will . . . but Will had gone. I spun around in a circle, searching for him, but didn't see him anywhere. He'd vanished into the crowds of tourists streaming along the Seine as completely as his older self had vanished into the stream of time.

2

Softly as a Rose

Despondent over Garet's iciness, Will had turned away from her in front of the bookstore named for his long lost mentor and love rival, its presence another unfriendly rebuke to his spirit. His eyes had wandered across the faces in the crowd, searching for a friendlier mien, when suddenly he had spied a familiar façade. Not a person, but of a building. It was the Church of Saint-Julien-le-Pauvre, where he had kept his Paris vigil over Marguerite four centuries earlier – after they had split up in London in a conflict over his desire to join her in immortality. A sign at her previous lodgings in London had directed him to wait for her at this church. She never showed up, but another sign he encountered there eventually guided him toward Paimpont in Brittany, where he had found her. Perhaps even now there would be a sign there that would lead him to her. He'd headed toward it, leaving Garet behind him in the crowd.

A distinctive tree near the church's north wall, which he recalled clearly from 1602, was still there, now with a plaque on its trunk labeling it 'the oldest tree in Paris.' It was, indeed, an ancient looking specimen. Poor thing, it had weathered the centuries poorly. At some point in its long life it had leaned so far to one side that it had been propped up by a metal girder and its trunk had split in two and been filled with stone. Will sank down onto a bench in front of the tree, feeling at this evidence of the centuries that had passed for him and the tree as if he too needed support and that his heart, too, had been filled with stone. He was still staring morosely at the tree when an odd little man approached him. The man was no more than five feet tall and gave the impression of a human egg, waddling about rotundly on two short legs: of a robin's egg in particular, given the pale blue tint of his summer attire, shorts and a tennis shirt. Dispensing with any social niceties, the man approached Will, closely observed him with deepset blue eyes, and told him that he happened to know that Will was in need of a time portal. The man knew where Will might find such a portal, or where rumors among the fey suggested he might find one.

'How on earth do you know my plight?' Will answered, astonished.

The man allowed himself the smallest crease of a grin. 'It's not on earth that I know your plight. It's in earth.'

'How so?'

'I have familiarity with subterranean circles where certain fey wander. Word travels there. I happen to be Paul Robin, descendant of the great royal botanist Jean Robin, who remains somewhat alive below ground in this very locale, amidst and part of the roots of the tree you see before you. Indeed my great great, and so on, grandfather has heard of your arrival here from his sources, and he has sent me to help you.'

'Arrival at the church? Or arrival in 2009?'

Paul smiled. 'Both. Sources tell me that there's a certain bookstore along the banks of the Seine, Kepler & Dee's, where – assuming you were to find it – if you browse along its shelves long enough, a time portal might open. At least, this is an experience some fey have had. It's through a method called transmigration of atoms, though I have no idea what that is . . .'

But Will did. He had learned of it in London this past unforgettable summer in which he'd fallen in love with Marguerite, and he had some brief experience with it too. Hope flared at hearing the term again.

'Unfortunately I do not have the address of Keoler & Dee's,' Paul Robin went on. But I'm sure that if you walk along the Seine long enough, you will find it. I hope so, anyway.'

Paul Robin wheeled around like an egg spinning on its axis and walked swiftly away, without another word. Will was left staring after him, amidst the fading red and gold sunlight, the burgeoning shadows cast by the church and the trees in the park, wondering if he should take him seriously or not. But the man had known his name and his dilemma. It was worth a try. If he found the portal he'd not only solve his dilemma, but he'd prove to Garet James that he was not an idiot, as she had so rudely called him.

But Will had been strolling along the banks of the Seine for nearly two more hours now, and he hadn't found the store. He'd found a few bookstores, but none with a name like Kepler & Dee's, and the one whose name had rung a bell, Shakespeare & Co., rang it in a somewhat in-flammatory way. Nonetheless, he'd been moved to go inside there and ask if the store had previously been named Kepler & Dee's, but the clerk had only said no, and looked at him as if he were drunk. As had the half dozen people he'd stopped along the way to ask, in his best court French, if they knew the establishment.

Some had stared, a few had laughed. But in general, they all seemed a very civilized bunch, nothing like the rough street crowds of Elizabethan London who could jostle you in the interests of pickpocketing, or out of plain meanness. Still he was becoming tired – he'd like another cup of that excellent beverage Garet had procured for him earlier.

That had been kind of her. Even when she was angry – which he could hardly blame her for after so keen a disappointment as she had suffered – she'd bought him breakfast. And she would have taken him back to her lodgings if he hadn't wandered off. In truth, her coldness hadn't been any more dismissive than Marguerite's final walk away from him in Paris had been when he'd revealed to her that he had become immortal, and she'd broken it to him that she had simultaneously had herself turned into a mortal, under the cruel illusion that she and Will could now be together in harmony. How hopeful a situation was that?

The more he walked on, the more Garet came to mind. Maybe it was the irrepressible nature of youth, which needed someone to love close at hand. But a wave of feeling came over him and, poet at the core that he was, he felt the urge to compose a sonnet. It could begin with a recitation of his lover's quandary, but he wanted it to end with a fervent expression of his new feeling. He sat on a bench on the Pont St Michel and wrote feverishly, in a tumult, scarcely noticing the crowds or the waning daylight. When Will was done he stared down at the lines he had written as though startled by them, as if he had learned something about himself and his situation he couldn't have learned otherwise, as if a hand other than his own had written the poem.

Love Garet? – Marguerite? – I'm so confused:
whichever way I turn, I seem to lose.
My true beloved's buried in the past
and yet Time's twin of hers perhaps could last
as my great love, if she would only see
that I can love her deeply, as truly
as sunlight loves a gnarled and ancient tree
as wind's enamored of the clouds that flee
its western tumult, then pursues them for
as long as there is weather, and birds soar.

I pledge that I am yours forevermore,
as fiercely as Othello, jealous Moor,
yet softly as a rose embraces spring.
Please understand my plight! Let love take wing!

After reading the poem over, Will went to the nearby railing and stared down at the Seine as if he pondered his own fate there, inside a mirror of water tinged with the red light of the setting sun. And it was Garet's face he saw in the water, not Marguerite's. They were similar faces but now, for Will, they were so very different. He recited the poem aloud to himself one more time, and then decided it should be entitled 'Softly as a Rose.'

Yes, he could – perchance he already did – love Garet! He'd go find her and show her the poem – but where would he find her? When he'd left her standing in front of the bookstore he hadn't stopped to wonder where they would meet again. Now he rushed back to the store, but of course Garet wasn't there. And he didn't know the name or address of her lodgings. He turned in a circle twice, searching the crowds for her face, but now that night was approaching the cafés and streets were even more packed. These crowds might be more polite than the Elizabethan mobs he was familiar with, but they were larger than any he had ever seen. The wall of people seemed to go on and on . . . forever. He turned around and around again . . . and found himself facing a man who was staring at him curiously.

'Are you the man who has been asking everyone for Kepler and Dee's Bookshop?' the man asked.

'Yes!' Will exclaimed. 'Do you know where it is?'

'I ought to,' the man replied. 'I am Johannes Kepler.'

The 'Dark Swan' series,
featuring shaman-for-hire Eugenie Markham . . .
Richelle Mead

STORM BORN

Eugenie Markham does a brisk trade banishing spirits and
other entities who cross into the mortal world. Mercenary, yes,
but a girl's got to eat. Her most recent case, however, is
enough to ruin her appetite.

THORN QUEEN

Eugenie's now queen of the Thorn Land. That said, with her
kingdom in tatters, her love life in chaos and Eugenie eager to
avoid the prophecy about *her* firstborn destroying mankind, the
job's really not all it's cracked up to be.

IRON CROWNED

Saving two worlds, one from trespassing entities and the
other from a brutal war, is no easy task. Eugenie's only hope is
the Iron Crown, a legendary object even the most powerful
fear . . . But who can she trust when those closest to her
have their own agendas?

SHADOW HEIR

Shaman-for-hire Eugenie Markham strives to keep the mortal
realm safe from trespassing entities. But as the Thorn Land's
prophecy-haunted queen, there's no refuge for her and her
soon-to-be-born children when a mysterious blight begins to
devastate the Otherworld . . .

All available in Bantam paperback and ebook

The Two Pearls Of Wisdom
and
The Necklace Of The Gods

Alison Goodman

UNDER THE HARSH regime of an ambitious master, Eon is training to become a Dragoneye – a powerful Lord able to command wind and water to nurture and protect the land. But Eon also harbours a desperate secret – he is, in fact, a young woman living a dangerous masquerade that, if discovered, will mean certain death.

Brought to the attention of the Emperor himself, Eon is thrust into the heart of a lethal struggle for the Imperial throne. In this treacherous world of hidden identities and uneasy alliances, Eon comes face-to-face with a vicious enemy who covets the young Dragoneye's astounding power, and will stop at nothing to make it his own.

Against a backcloth of dazzling swordplay, ruthless power struggles and exotic, arcane lore, unfurls a thrilling story of a young warrior who must find the courage to tread the razor line between what is true and what is just.

'Vivid, brutal, terrifying and absolutely fantastic'
FANTASY BOOK REVIEW

'Addictive reading . . . the climax is gloriously tantalising'
SFX

'A refreshing change from the generic. This intelligent, vividly written tale grips from the first page'
THE TIMES

Black Swan Rising

Lee Carroll

Jeweller Garet James isn't the same as everyone else.
She just doesn't know it yet . . .

WITH HER FAIR share of problems – money (lack of), an elderly father, a struggling business – Garet should be just like any other young, single New Yorker. If only it were that simple . . .

It began with the old silver box that had been soldered shut. All Garet had to do was open it. A favour for the frail owner of the antiques shop. Who wouldn't help?

But then things start to change. The city begins to reveal a darker, long-hidden side; Garet finds herself drawn to a mysterious a stranger; and whatever escaped from the box has no intention of going back in . . .

'A unique, imaginative and above all enjoyable tale of vampires, alchemists and fairies in New York'
LOVEVAMPIRES.COM